FAMOUS FIVE
MYSTERY COLLECTION

ENID BLYTON

*Hodder
Children's
Books*

a division of Hodder Headline Limited

CONTENTS

FIVE ON A SECRET TRAIL

CONTENTS

CHAPTER ONE

George is rather difficult

'MOTHER! MOTHER, where are you?' shouted George, rushing into the house. 'Mother, quick!'

There was no answer. George's mother was out in the garden at the back of Kirrin Cottage, picking flowers. George yelled again, this time at the top of her very strong voice.

'MOTHER! MOTHER! Where are you? IT'S URGENT.'

A door was flung open nearby and George's father stood there, glaring at her.

'George! What's this row about? Here am I in the middle of some very difficult . . .'

'Oh Father! Timmy's hurt!' said George. 'He went . . .'

Her father looked down at Timmy, standing meekly behind George. He gave a little snort.

'Hurt! He seems all right to me. I suppose he's got a thorn in his paw again – and you think it's the end of the world or something, and come yelling in here and . . .'

'Timmy *is* hurt!' said George, with tears in her voice. 'Look!'

But her father had gone back into his study again, and the door slammed. George glared at it, looking exactly like her hot-tempered father.

'You're unkind!' she shouted, 'and . . . oh there's MOTHER. MOTHER!'

'Dear me, George, whatever *is* the matter?' said her

5

mother, putting down the flowers. 'I heard your father shouting, and then you.'

'Mother – Timmy's hurt!' said George. 'Look!'

She knelt down by the dog, and gently pulled forward one ear. Behind it was a big cut. Timmy whined. Tears came into George's eyes, and she looked up at her mother.

'Now don't be silly, George,' said Mrs Kirrin. 'It's only a cut. How did he do it?'

'He tried to jump over a ditch, and he didn't see some old barbed wire there,' said George. 'And a rusty piece caught his ear, and ripped that awful cut. I can't stop it bleeding.'

Her mother looked at it. It certainly was quite deep.

'Take him to the vet, George,' she said. 'Perhaps it ought to be stitched. It does look rather deep. Poor old Timmy-boy – well, it's a good thing it wasn't his eye, George.'

'I'll take him to the vet at once,' said George, getting up. 'Will he be in, Mother?'

'Oh yes – it's his surgery hour,' said her mother. 'Take him along now.'

So Timmy was hurried along the country lanes to the pretty little house where the vet lived. George, very anxious indeed, was most relieved to see that the vet seemed quite unconcerned.

'A couple of stitches and that cut will heal well,' he said. 'Hold him, will you, while I do the job? He'll hardly feel it. There, old boy – stand still – that's right.'

In five minutes' time George was thanking the vet wholeheartedly. 'Thank you! I *was* worried! Will he be all right now?'

'Good gracious, yes – but you mustn't let him scratch that wound,' said the vet, washing his hands. 'If he does, it may go wrong.'

'Oh. But how can I stop him?' asked George anxiously. 'Look – he's trying to scratch it now.'

'Well, you must make him a big cardboard collar,' said the vet. 'One that sticks out right round his neck, so that his paw can't get near that cut, however much he tries to reach it.'

'But – but Timmy won't like that a bit,' said George. 'Dogs look silly wearing cardboard collars like great ruffs round their necks. I've seen them. He'll hate one.'

'Well, it's the only way of stopping him from scratching that wound,' said the vet. 'Get along now, George – I've more patients waiting.'

George went home with Timmy. He padded along quietly, pleased at the fuss that George was making of him. When he was nearly home, he suddenly sat down and put up his hind leg to scratch his bad ear.

'No, Timmy! NO!' cried George, in alarm. 'You must NOT scratch. You'll get the plaster off in no time, and break the stitches. NO, Timmy!'

Timmy looked up in surprise. Very well. If scratching was suddenly upsetting George, he would wait till he was alone.

But George could read Timmy's thoughts as easily as he could read hers! She frowned.

'Blow! I'll *have* to make him that cardboard collar. Perhaps Mother will help me.'

Her mother was quite willing to help. George was not good at things of that sort, and she watched her mother cutting out a big cardboard collar, fitting it round the surprised Timmy's head, and then lacing the edges together with thread so that he could not get it off. Timmy was most surprised, but he stood very patiently.

As soon as the collar was finished, and safely round his neck, he walked away. Then he raised his hind leg to scratch at his smarting ear – but, of course, he couldn't get it over the collar, and merely scratched the cardboard.

'Never mind, Timmy,' said George. 'It will only be for a few days.'

The study door nearby opened and her father came out. He saw Timmy in his collar and stopped in surprise. Then he roared with laughter.

'Hey, Timmy – you look like Queen Elizabeth the First in a fine big ruff!' he said.

'Don't laugh at him, Father,' said George. 'You know that dogs can't bear being laughed at.'

Timmy certainly looked offended. He turned his back on George's father and stalked off to the kitchen. A little squeal of laughter came from there and then a loud guffaw from someone at the kitchen door – the milkman.

'Oh Timmy – whatever have you got that collar on for?' said the cook's voice. 'You do look peculiar!'

George was angry. She remained angry all that day and made everyone most uncomfortable. How *mean* of people to jeer at poor Timmy! Didn't they realise how terribly uncomfortable a collar like that was – and Timmy had to wear it night and day! He couldn't even lie down comfortably. George mooned about looking so angry and miserable that her mother felt worried.

'George dear, don't be silly about this. You will make your father cross. Timmy will have to wear that collar for at least a week, you know, and he *does* look a bit comical when you first see him. He's getting used to it, he soon won't notice it.'

'Everybody laughs at him,' said George, in an angry voice. 'He went into the garden and a lot of kids hung over the wall and laughed like anything. And the postman told me it was cruel. And Father thinks it's funny. And . . .'

'Oh dear, George, don't get into one of your moods,' said her mother. 'Remember, Anne is coming soon. She won't enjoy things much if you behave like this.'

George bore it for one day more. Then, after two upsets with her father over Timmy, another with a couple of boys who laughed at him, and one with the paper boy, she decided she wouldn't stay at Kirrin Cottage for one day longer!

'We'll take my little tent, and go off by ourselves somewhere,' she told Timmy. 'Some place where nobody can see you till your ear is better and that hateful collar is off. Don't you think that's a good idea, Timmy?'

'Woof,' said Timmy. He thought that any of George's ideas were good, though the collar puzzled him very much.

'You know the *dogs* laugh at you too, Timmy,' said George, earnestly. 'Did you see how that silly little poodle belonging to Mrs Janes up the lane stood and stared at you? He looked *exactly* as if he was laughing. I won't have you laughed at. I know you hate it.'

Timmy certainly didn't like it, but he really was not as upset about the collar as George seemed to be. He followed her as she went up to her bedroom and watched her as she began to put a few things into a small bag.

'We'll go to that lonely little spot on the common,' she said to him. 'We'll pitch our tent near a little stream, and we'll jolly well stay there till your ear's better. We'll go tonight. I'll take my bike, and strap everything on to the back.'

So, in the middle of the night, when Kirrin Cottage was dark and quiet, George stole downstairs with Timmy. She left a note on the dining-room table, and then went to get her bicycle. She strapped her little tent on it, and the bag containing food and other odds and ends.

'Come on!' she whispered to the surprised Timmy. 'We'll go. I'll ride slowly and you can run beside me. Don't bark for goodness' sake!'

They disappeared into the darkness, Timmy running

like a black shadow beside the bicycle. Nobody guessed they were gone. Kirrin Cottage was quiet and undisturbed – except for the creaking of the kitchen door, which George had forgotten to shut.

But in the morning, what a disturbance! Joanna the cook found George's note first and wondered what a letter in George's writing was doing on the dining-room table. She ran straight up to George's room and looked inside.

The bed was empty. There was no George and Timmy's basket was empty. Joanna went to take the note to Mrs Kirrin.

'Oh *dear*! How silly George is!' she said, when she had read it. 'Look, Quentin – such a fuss about Timmy! Now George has gone off with him, goodness knows where!'

Her husband took the note and read it out loud. 'Dear Mother, I'm going off for a few days with Timmy till his ear is better. I've taken my tent and a few things. Don't worry, please. Tell Anne if she wants to join me, to come to the end of Carters Lane on the common and I will show her where I'm camping. Tell her to come at twelve. Love from George.'

'Well, I'm blessed!' said George's father. 'All right, let her stay away if she wants to – I'm tired of her sulky face and Timmy's hang-dog looks. Tell Anne to join George, and maybe I shall have peace for a few days!'

'George should be all right,' said his wife. 'She's quite sensible really – and she's got Timmy. I'll tell Anne to join her when she arrives this morning.'

When Anne arrived at Kirrin Station, and looked out for George and Timmy, they weren't there – only her aunt was there, smiling as usual.

'What's happened?' said Anne. 'Where's George – and Timmy?'

'Oh, George has gone off by herself,' said her Aunt Fanny. 'Come along, and I'll tell you!'

CHAPTER TWO

Anne joins the little camp

AUNT FANNY soon told Anne about Timmy's ear and the big collar of cardboard that had caused all the trouble. Anne couldn't help smiling.

'Oh Aunt Fanny – George is quite crazy about old Tim, isn't she? I'll go and meet her at twelve, and of course I'll camp with her for a day or two. It's lovely weather and I'd like to. I expect Uncle Quentin will be glad to have us out of the house!'

'How are Julian and Dick?' asked her aunt. She was very fond of Anne's two brothers, George's cousins. 'Will they be coming down here at all these holidays?'

'I don't know,' said Anne. 'They're still in France, you know, on a schoolboys' tour. I feel funny without them! George will be cross to hear they probably won't be coming to Kirrin. She'll just have to put up with *me*!'

At twelve o'clock Anne was standing patiently at the end of Carters Lane. It ran to the common and then ended in a small, winding path that led to nowhere in particular. Big gorse bushes grew here and there, and slender birch trees. Anne, her belongings strapped to her back, and a bag in her hand, looked over the common to see if she could spy George coming.

There was no sign of her. 'Blow!' said Anne. 'I suppose she's changed her mind or something. Perhaps her watch has stopped and she doesn't know the time. She ought to, though, by looking at the sun! How long shall I wait?'

She sat down by a big gorse bush, out of the hot sun.
She hadn't been there for more than a minute when she
heard a hissing sound.

'Pssssst!'

Anne sat up at once. The sound came from the other
side of the bush, and she got up and walked round it.
Half-hidden under a prickly branch were George and
Timmy!

'Hallo!' said Anne, surprised. 'Didn't you see me when
I arrived? Hallo, Tim darling! How's your poor old ear?
Oh, doesn't he look a quaint old dear in that collar,
George?'

George scrambled out of the bush. 'I hid here just in
case Father or Mother should come with you and try to
make me come back,' she said. 'I wanted to make quite
sure they weren't waiting somewhere a little way away.
I'm glad you've come, Anne.'

'Of course I've come,' said Anne. 'I wouldn't stay
alone at Kirrin Cottage while you were camping out.
Besides, I understand how you feel about Timmy. The
collar's a jolly good idea, of course – but it does make
him look comical. I think he looks rather a dear in it, I do
really.'

George was almost relieved that Anne had not laughed
at Timmy as most people had. She smiled at her cousin,
and Timmy licked her till Anne really had to push him
away.

'Let's go,' said George, scrambling up. 'I've got a
lovely camping place, Anne. You'll like it. It's near a
little spring too, so there's plenty of water for Timmy to
drink – and us too. Did you bring any more food? I
didn't really bring much.'

'Yes. I've brought heaps,' said Anne. 'Aunt Fanny made me. She's not cross with you, George. I didn't see your father. He was shut up in his study.'

George's spirits suddenly rose. She gave Anne a friendly punch. 'This is going to be fun! Timmy's ear will soon be better, and he loves camping out as much as we do. I've really found a good place – about the loneliest on the common! Nobody near us for miles!'

They set off together, Timmy at their heels, darting off every now and again when he smelt rabbit.

'When are Julian and Dick coming down?' asked George. 'In a few days? Timmy's ear will be all right then and we can go back to Kirrin Cottage to welcome the boys, and have some fun there.'

'They may not be coming down at all these hols,' said Anne, and George's face fell at once. She stopped and stared at Anne in dismay.

'Not coming! But they *always* come in the hols – or we go away somewhere together!' she said. 'They *must* come! I shall be miserable without Ju and Dick.'

'Well – they're still in France, on a tour or something,' said Anne. 'We shall hear if they're staying on there or coming down to Kirrin when we get back to the cottage. Don't look so woebegone, George!'

But George felt woebegone. The holidays stretched before her, suddenly seeming long and dreary. Her two boy cousins were always such fun – they had had such wonderful adventures together. And now – now they weren't coming!

'We shan't have any adventures at all if the boys don't come,' she said, in a small voice.

'I shan't mind that,' said Anne. 'I'm the peaceful one,

not always on the look-out for something to happen, like you and the boys! Perhaps these holidays will be quite unexciting without even the *smell* of an adventure! Oh George – cheer up! *Don't* look so mournful. You'd better send a letter to Julian and Dick if you feel so badly about it.'

'I've a good mind to!' said George. 'I can't *imagine* hols without the boys. Why – we shan't be the Five – the Famous Five – if they don't come!'

'Woof!' said Timmy, quite agreeing. He sat down and tried to scratch his ear, but the big collar prevented him. He didn't seem to mind and ran off after a rabbit quite happily.

'I think *you* are more upset about that collar than Timmy,' said Anne, as they walked along. 'Are we getting near this place of yours, George? It's a jolly long way.'

'We go up this hill in front of us – and then drop down to a little copse,' said George. 'There's a funny old cottage nearby – quite ruined and empty. At first I thought perhaps people lived there, but when I went nearer I saw that it was ruined. There's a big old rose-rambler climbing all over it, even inside. I suppose the people who used to live there planted it.'

They walked up the little hill and down again, following curving rabbit paths. 'Better look out for adders,' said Anne. 'This is just the kind of place for them. My word, it's hot, George. Is there anywhere to bathe near here – a pool or anything?'

'I don't know. We could explore and see,' said George. 'I did bring my swimsuit just in case. Look, you can see part of the old cottage now. My camp is fairly near there.

17

I thought I'd better camp near the spring.'

They were soon at George's rough little camp. Her tent was up, and she had made a bed inside of the springy heather. A mug, a bag of dog biscuits, a few tins, and a loaf of bread were at one end of the tent. It didn't seem to Anne as if George had brought very much, and she felt glad that she had managed to pack such a lot of things.

'Aunt Fanny cut dozens and dozens of sandwiches,' said Anne. 'She said if we kept them in this tin they wouldn't go stale, and would last us a day or two till we went back. I'm hungry. Shall we have some now?'

They sat out in the sun, munching the ham sand-wiches. Anne had brought tomatoes too, and they took a bite at a sandwich and then a bite at a tomato. Timmy had to make do with a handful of dog biscuits and half a sandwich every now and again. After a bit he got up and wandered off.

'Where's he going?' asked Anne. 'To look for a rabbit?'

'No. Probably to get a drink,' said George. 'The spring is in the direction he's gone. I'm thirsty too – let's take the mug and get a drink ourselves.'

They went off with the mug, Anne following George through the thick heather. The little spring was a lovely one. It had evidently been used by the people who had once lived in the old cottage, and was built round with big white stones, so that the spring ran through a little stony channel, as clear as crystal.

'Oooh – it's as cold as ice!' said Anne. 'Simply delicious! I could drink gallons of this!'

They lay on the heather out in the sun, talking, when

they came back from the spring. Timmy wandered off by himself again.

'It's so peaceful here,' said Anne. 'Nobody near us for miles. Just the birds and the rabbits. This is what I like!'

'There's hardly a sound,' said George, yawning.

And then, just as she said that, there came a noise in the distance. A sharp sound, like metal on stone. It came again and again and then stopped.

'What's that, do you suppose?' said George, sitting up.

'I can't imagine,' said Anne. 'Anyway, it's a long way away – everything is so still that sounds carry from quite a distance.'

The sharp noises began again in a little while and then stopped. The girls shut their eyes, and slept. There wasn't a sound now except the pop-pop-pop of gorse pods exploding in the sun and sending out their little black seeds.

George woke up when Timmy came back. He sat down heavily on her feet and she woke up with a jump.

'Timmy! Don't!' she said. 'Get off my feet, you made me jump!' Timmy obligingly removed himself and then picked up something he had dropped, lay down and began gnawing it. George looked to see what it was.

'Timmy! That's a bone! Where did you get it?' she said. 'Anne, did you bring a bone for Tim?'

'What? What did you say?' said Anne, half asleep. 'A bone. No, I didn't. Why?'

'Because Timmy's found one,' said George, 'and it's a bone that has had cooked meat on it, so it's not a rabbit or anything Timmy's caught. Timmy, where did you get it?'

'Woof,' said Timmy, offering the bone to George, thinking that she too might like a gnaw, as she seemed so interested in it.

'Do you suppose anyone else is camping near us?' asked Anne, sitting up and yawning. 'After all, bones don't grow in the heather. That's quite a good meaty one, too. Timmy, have you stolen it from another dog?'

Timmy thumped his tail on the ground and went on with his bone. He looked pleased with himself.

'It's rather an old bone,' said George. 'It's smelly. Go away, Tim – take it further off.'

The sharp metallic noises suddenly began again and George frowned. 'I believe there *is* someone camping near us, Anne. Come on – let's do a bit of exploring and find out. I vote we move our camp if there are other people near. Come on, Timmy – that's right, bury that horrible bone! This way Anne!'

CHAPTER THREE

The old cottage – and a surprise

THE TWO girls, with Timmy at their heels, left their camping place and set off in the hot sun. Anne caught sight of the ruined cottage and stopped.

'Let's have a look at it,' she said. 'It must be awfully old, George.'

They went in at the wide doorway. There was no door left, only the stone archway. Inside was a big room, whose floor had once been paved with slabs of white stone. Now grass and other weeds had grown between the cracks, and had actually lifted up some of the slabs so that the whole floor was uneven.

Here and there parts of the walls had fallen away and the daylight came through. One window was still more or less intact, but the others had fallen out. A small crooked stairway of stone led upwards in one corner.

'To rooms above, I suppose,' said Anne. 'Oh, here's another doorway, leading into a second room – a small one. It's got an old sink in it, look – and this must be the remains of a pump.'

'There's not much to see, really,' said George, looking round. 'The top rooms must be quite ruined, because half the roof is off. Hallo, here's another door – a back door. It's actually a *door* too, not just a doorway.'

She gave a push at the stout wood – and the old door promptly fell off its hinges and crashed outwards into an overgrown yard.

'Goodness!' said George, startled. 'I didn't know it was quite so rotten. It made poor Tim jump almost out of his skin!'

'There are outhouses here – or the remains of them,' said Anne, exploring the back-yard. 'They must have kept pigs and hens and ducks. Here's a dried-up pond, look.'

Everything was falling to pieces. The best preserved corner of the old place was what must have been a small stable. Rusted mangers were still there and the floor was of stone. An old, old piece of harness hung on a big nail.

'It's got quite a nice "*feel*" about it, this old place,' said Anne. 'Sometimes I don't like the feel of places – they give me an uneasy feeling, a feeling that horrid things may have happened there. But this is quite different. I think people have been happy here, and led peaceful lives. I can almost hear hens clucking and ducks quacking, and pigs gr . . .'

'Quack, quack, quack! Quack!'

'*Cuck*-cuk-cuk-cuk-cuk! *Cuck*-cuk-cuk-cuk-cuk!'

Anne clutched George and the two girls look extremely startled to hear the sudden loud noise of quacking and clucking. They stood and listened.

'What was it?' said Anne. 'It *sounded* like hens and ducks – though I'm not quite sure. But there aren't any here, surely. We shall hear a horse whinnying next!'

They didn't hear a whinny – but they heard the snorting of a horse at once. 'Hrrrrr-umph! Hrrrrr-umph!'

Both girls were now quite alarmed. They looked for Timmy. He was nowhere to be seen! Wherever could he have got to?

'*Cuck*-cuk-cuk-cuk-cuk!'

'This is silly,' said George. 'Are we imagining things? Anne, there *must* be hens near. Come round the back of these stables and look. Timmy, where are you? TIMMY!'

She whistled shrilly – and immediately an echo came – or so it seemed!

'Phee-phee-phee-phee-phee!'

'TIMMY!' yelled George, beginning to feel as if she was in a dream.

Timmy appeared, looking rather sheepish. He wagged his tail – and to the girls' enormous amazement, they saw that he had a ribbon tied on it. A ribbon – a bright blue one at that!

'Timmy! Your tail – the ribbon – Timmy, what's all this about?' said George, really startled.

Timmy went to her, still looking sheepish, and George tore the ribbon off his tail. 'Who tied it there?' she demanded. 'Who's here? Timmy, where have you been?'

The two girls searched the old buildings thoroughly, and found nothing and nobody. Not a hen, not a duck, not a pig – and certainly not a horse. Then – what was the explanation? They stared at one another in bewilderment.

'And where did Timmy get that silly ribbon?' said George, exasperated. '*Someone* must have tied it on.'

'Perhaps it was a hiker passing by – perhaps he heard us here and saw Timmy and played a joke,' said Anne. 'But it's strange that Old Tim *let* him tie on the ribbon. I mean – Timmy's not overfriendly with strangers, is he?'

The girls gave up the idea of exploring any further and went back to their little camp. Timmy went with them. He lay down – and then suddenly got up again, making for a thick gorse bush. He tried to squirm underneath.

'*Now* what's he after?' said George. 'Really, I think Timmy's gone mad. Timmy, you *can't* get under there with that great collar on. TIMMY, do you hear me!'

Timmy backed out reluctantly, the collar all crooked. After him came a peculiar little mongrel dog with one blind eye and one exceedingly bright and lively one. He was half-white and half-black, and had a ridiculously long thin tail, which he waved about merrily.

'*Well*!' said George, amazed. 'What's that dog doing there? And how did Timmy get so friendly with him? Timmy, I can't make you out.'

'Woof,' said Timmy, and brought the mongrel dog over to Anne and George. He then proceeded to dig up the smelly bone he had buried, and actually offered it to the little dog, who looked away and took no interest in it at all.

'This is all very peculiar,' said Anne. 'I shall expect to see Timmy bring a cat to us next!'

At once there came a pathetic mewing.

'Mee-ew! Mee-ew-ee-ew-ee-ew!'

Both dogs pricked up their ears, and rushed to the bush. Timmy was once again kept back by his big collar and barked furiously.

George got up and marched to the bush. 'If there's a cat there, it won't have much chance against two dogs,' she called to Anne. 'Come away, Tim. Hey, you little dog, come away, too.'

Timmy backed out, and George pulled out the small dog very firmly indeed. 'Hold him, Anne!' she called. 'He's quite friendly. He won't bite. I'm going to find that cat.'

Anne held on to the small mongrel, who gazed at her

excitedly with his one good eye and wagged his tail violently. He was a most friendly little fellow. George began to crawl into the bare hollow space under the big gorse bush.

She looked into it, not able to see anything at first, because it was dark there after the bright sunlight. Then she got a tremendous shock.

A round, grinning face stared back at her, a face with very bright eyes and tousled hair falling on to the forehead. The mouth was set in a wide smile, showing very white teeth.

'Mee-ew-ee-ew-ee-ew!' said the face.

George scrambled back at top speed, her heart thumping. 'What is it?' called Anne.

'There's somebody hiding there,' said George. 'Not a cat. An idiot of a boy who is doing the mewing.'

'Mew-ee-ew-ee-ew!'

'Come out!' called Anne. 'Come out and let's see you. You must be crazy.'

There was a scrambling noise and a boy came head first from the hollow space under the bush. He was about twelve or thirteen, short, sturdily built, and with the cheekiest face Anne had ever seen.

Timmy rushed at him and licked him lovingly. George stared in amazement.

'How does my dog know you?' she demanded.

'Well, he came growling at me yesterday when I was in my own camp,' said the boy. 'And I offered him a nice meaty bone. Then he saw my little dog Jet – short for jet-propelled, you know – and made friends with him – and with me too.'

'I see,' said George, still not at all friendly. 'Well, I don't like my dog to take food from strangers.'

'Oh, I couldn't agree more,' said the boy. 'But I thought I'd rather he ate the bone than ate *me*. He's a nice dog, yours. He feels a bit of an idiot wearing that collar, doesn't he? You should have heard Jet laugh when he first saw it!'

George frowned. 'I came here to be alone so that Timmy shouldn't be jeered at,' she said. 'He's got a bad ear. I suppose *you* were the fathead who tied a blue ribbon on his tail?'

'Just for a joke,' said the boy. '*You* like frowning and glaring, I can see. Well, *I* like joking and tricking! Your Timmy didn't mind a bit. He took to my dog right away. But everyone likes Jet! I wanted to find out who owned Timmy – because, like you, *I* don't like strangers messing about when I'm camping out. So I came along.'

'I see. And you did all the clucking and quacking and

hrrr-umphing?' said Anne. She liked this idiot of a boy, with his broad friendly grin. 'What are you doing – just camping – or hiking – or botanising?'

'I'm digging,' said the boy. 'My father's an archae-ologist – he loves old buildings more than anything else in the world. I take after him, I suppose. There was once an old Roman camp on this common, you know – and I've found a place where part of it must have been, so I'm digging for anything I can find – pottery, weapons, anything like that. See, I found this yesterday – look at the date on it!'

He suddenly thrust an old coin at them – a strange, uneven one, rather heavy to hold.

'Its date is 292,' he said. 'At least, as far as I can make out. So the camp's pretty old, isn't it?'

'We'll come and see it,' said Anne, excited.

'No, don't,' said the boy. 'I don't like people messing round me when I'm doing something serious. Please don't come. I won't bother you again. I promise.'

'All right. We won't come,' said Anne, quite under-standing. 'But don't you play any more silly tricks on us, see?'

'I promise,' said the boy. 'I tell you, I won't come near you again. I only wanted to see whose dog this was. Well, I'm off. So long!'

And, whistling to Jet, he set off at a furious pace. George turned to Anne.

'What a peculiar boy!' she said. 'Actually – I'd rather *like* to see him again. Wouldn't you?'

CHAPTER FOUR

That night

IT WAS now tea-time, according to Anne's watch and also according to everyone's feelings, including Timmy's. Timmy felt the heat very much and was always wandering off to the little spring to lap the crystal-cold water. Anne wished that she and George had a big jug that they could fill – it was such a nuisance to have to keep running to and fro with just a mug.

They had tea – biscuits, a sandwich each, and a bar of rather soft chocolate. George examined Timmy's ear for the hundredth time that day, and pronounced it very much better.

'Well, don't take off that collar yet,' said Anne. 'He'll only open the wound by scratching if you do.'

'I'm not *going* to take it off!' said George, touchily. 'What shall we do now, Anne? Go for a walk?'

'Yes,' said Anne. 'Listen – you can hear those sharp, metallic noises again – that's the boy at work again, I expect. Funny boy he must be – coming to dig about all on his own with his comical little dog. I wish we could see what he's doing.'

'We promised we wouldn't,' said George. 'So I don't feel that we even ought to go and peep.'

'Of course not!' said Anne. 'Come on – let's go in the opposite direction, George – right away from the boy. I hope we shan't get lost!'

'Not while Timmy's with us, silly!' said George.

'You'd find your way home from the moon, wouldn't you, Tim?'

'Woof,' agreed Timmy.

'He always says yes to whatever you say, George,' said Anne. 'I say – isn't it a lovely evening? I wonder what Julian and Dick are doing?'

George immediately looked downcast. She felt that her two cousins had no right to go rushing across France when she wanted them at Kirrin. Didn't they like Kirrin? Would they be having magnificent adventures abroad, and not want to spend even a week at Kirrin? She looked so lost in miserable thoughts that Anne laughed at her.

'Cheer up! At least *I* am here with you – though I agree that compared with Ju and Dick I'm very poor company, and not at all adventurous!'

They had a lovely walk, and sat down halfway to watch hordes of rabbits playing together. Timmy was very unhappy about this. Why *sit down* to watch silly rabbits? Rabbits were made to *chase*, weren't they? Why did George always put a restraining hand on his collar when she sat down to watch rabbits? He whined continually, as he watched with her.

'Shut up, Timmy, you ass,' said George. 'You'd only spoil the entertainment if you sent them to their holes.'

They watched for a long while and then got up to go back to the camp. When they came near, they heard the sound of low whistling. Someone was about that evening, quite near their camp. Who was it?

They came round a big gorse bush, and almost bumped into a boy. He got out of their way politely, but said nothing.

'Why – it's *you*!' said George, in surprise. 'I don't know

30

your name. What are you doing here? You said you wouldn't come near us.'

The boy stared, looking very surprised. His tousled hair fell right across his forehead, and he brushed it back.

'I said nothing of the sort,' he said.

'Oh, you *did*!' said Anne. 'You know you did. Well, if

31

you break your promise, there's no reason for us to keep ours. We shall come and visit *your* camp.'

'I never made you any promise,' said the boy, looking quite startled. 'You're mad!'

'Don't be an idiot!' said George, getting cross. 'I suppose you'll be saying next that you didn't act like a hen, and a duck, and a horse this afternoon . . .'

'And a cat,' said Anne.

'Barmy!' said the boy, looking at them pityingly. 'Quite barmy.'

'Are you coming here again?' demanded George.

'If I want to,' said the boy. 'The water in this spring is better than the one over by my camp.'

'Then we shall come and explore *your* camp,' said George, firmly. 'If you don't keep your promise, we shan't keep ours.'

'By all means come if you want to,' said the boy. 'You seem quite mad, but I daresay you're harmless. But don't bring your dog. He might eat mine.'

'You know he wouldn't eat Jet!' said Anne. 'They're good friends.'

'I don't know anything of the sort,' said the boy, and went off, brushing his hair out of his eyes again.

'What do you make of *that*?' said George, staring after him. 'Not a bit the same as he was this afternoon. Do you think he really *had* forgotten about his promise and everything?'

'I don't know,' said Anne, puzzled. 'He was so perky and jolly and full of fun before – grinning all the time – but just now he seemed quite serious – not a smile in him!'

'Oh well – perhaps he's a bit crazy,' said George. 'Are

you sleepy, Anne? I am, though I can't think why!'

'Not very – but I'd like to lie down on this springy heather and watch the stars gradually come sparkling into the sky,' said Anne. 'I don't think I'll sleep in the tent, George. You'll want Timmy with you, and honestly there's so little room inside the tent that I'm quite sure Timmy would lie on my legs all night long.'

'I'll sleep in the open air as well,' said George. 'I only slept in the tent last night because it looked a bit like rain. Let's get some more heather and make a kind of mattress of it. We can put a rug on top of it, and lie on that.'

The two of them pulled a lot of heather and carried it to their 'bed'. Soon they had a fine pile, and Timmy went to lie on it.

'Hey – it's not for you!' cried George. 'Get off – you'll flatten it right down. Where's the rug, Anne?'

They laid the rug on the heather pile and then went to the spring to wash and clean their teeth. Timmy immediately got on to the heather bed again, and shut his eyes.

'You old fraud!' said George, lugging him off. 'You're not asleep. Keep off our bed! Look – there's a nice soft patch of grass for you. That's your bed!'

George lay down on the rug, and the heathery bed sank a little beneath her weight. 'Very comfortable!' said George. 'Shall we want a rug over us, Anne?'

'Well, I did bring one,' said Anne. 'But I don't think we'll want it, the night's so hot. Look – there is a star already!'

Soon there were six or seven – and then gradually hundreds more pricked through the evening sky as the twilight deepened. It was a wonderful night.

'Don't the stars look big and bright?' said Anne,

sleepily. 'They make me feel very small, they're such millions of miles away. George, are you asleep?'

There was no answer. George hadn't heard a word. She was fast asleep. Her hand fell down the side of the heather and rested on the ground below. Timmy moved a little nearer and gave it a small lick. Then he too fell asleep, and gave some small doggy snores.

The night darkened. There was no moon but the stars shone out well from the midnight sky. It was very quiet out there on the common, far away from streets and villages and towns. Not even an owl hooted.

Anne didn't quite know why she awoke. At first she had no idea where she was, and she lay gazing up at the stars in astonishment, thinking she must still be asleep.

She suddenly felt very thirsty. She groped about in the nearby tent for the mug, couldn't find it and gave it up.

'I'll drink from my cupped hands,' she thought, and set off for the little spring. Timmy wondered whether to follow her. No – he would stay with George. She wouldn't like it if she awoke and found him gone with Anne. So he settled his head down on his paws again and slept, leaving one ear open for Anne.

Anne found the little spring. Its tinkling gurgling sound guided her as soon as she heard it. She sat down on one of the stones nearby, and held out her cupped hands. How very cold the water was – and how delicious to drink on this hot night! She sipped thirstily, slopping some of the water down her front.

She got up to go back, and walked a few steps in the starlight. Then she stopped. Wait – was she going in the right direction? She wasn't sure.

'I *think* I am!' she decided, and went on, carefully

and quietly. Surely she must be near their little camp now?

Then all at once she stood still, and felt herself stiffen. She had suddenly seen a light. It had flashed and disappeared. Ah – there it was again! Whatever could it be?

Then, as her eyes strained through the starlit darkness, she suddenly saw that she *had* taken the wrong way – she had gone in the direction of the old ruined cottage, and not the camp – and the light had come from there!

She didn't dare go any nearer. She felt glued to the grass she was standing on! Now she could hear sounds – whispering sounds – and the noise of a football on the stone floor of the cottage – and then the flash of a light came again! Yes, it *was* from the old cottage!

Anne began to breathe fast. Who was it in the old cottage? She simply dared not go and see. She must go back to George, and to Timmy's protection. As fast and as silently as she could she found her way back to the spring – and then, almost stumbling now, made her way to where George was still lying peacefully asleep.

'Woof,' said Timmy, sleepily, and tried to lick her hand. Anne climbed on to the heathery bed beside George, her heart still beating fast.

'George!' she whispered. 'George, do wake up. I've something strange to tell you!'

CHAPTER FIVE

That boy again!

GEORGE WOULD not wake up. She grunted when Anne poked her and prodded her, and then she turned over, almost falling off the small heather bed.

'Oh George – *please* do wake!' begged Anne, in a whisper. She was afraid of speaking out loud in case anyone should hear her. Who knew what might happen if she drew attention to their little camp?

George awoke at last and was cross. 'Whatever is it, Anne?' she said, her voice sounding loud in the night.

'Sh!' said Anne. 'Sh!'

'Why? We're all alone here! We can make as much noise as we like!' said George, surprised.

'George, do listen! There's someone in that old cottage!' said Anne, and at last George heard and understood. She sat up at once.

Anne told her the whole story – though it didn't really seem very much of a tale when she related it. George spoke to Timmy.

'Tim!' she said, keeping her voice low. 'We'll go and do a little exploring, shall we? Come on, then – and keep quiet!'

She slid off the rug and stood up. 'You stay here,' she said to Anne. 'Timmy and I will be very quiet and careful, and see what we can find out.'

'Oh no – I couldn't stay here *alone*!' said Anne in alarm, and got up hurriedly. 'I shall have to come too. I don't mind a bit now Timmy's with us. I wonder he didn't bark at the people in the old cottage, whoever they were.'

'He probably thought it was you messing about,' said George, and Anne nodded. Yes, of course, Timmy must have thought that any noises he heard had been made by her.

They took the path that led to the old cottage. George had Timmy well to heel. He knew he must not push forward unless told to. His ears were pricked now, and he was listening hard.

They came cautiously to the cottage. They could see its dark outline in the starlight, but little else. There was no light flashing there. Nor did there seem to be any noises at all.

All three stood still and quiet for about five minutes. Then Timmy moved restlessly. This was boring! Why wouldn't George let him run forward and explore everywhere if she wanted to know if intruders were about?

'I don't think there's a soul here!' whispered George into Anne's ear. 'They must have gone – unless you dreamed it all, Anne!'

'I didn't!' whispered back Anne indignantly. 'Let's go forward a bit and send Timmy into the cottage. He'll soon bark if there's anyone there.'

George gave Timmy a little shove. 'Go on, then!' she said. 'Find, Timmy, find!'

Timmy gladly shot forward into the darkness. He trotted into the cottage, though it was impossible even to see him go to it. The two girls stood and listened, their heartbeats sounding very loud to them! There was not a sound to be heard, except occasionally the rattle of Timmy's strong claws on a stony slab.

'There can't be anyone there,' said George at last, 'else Timmy would have sniffed them out. You're an ass, Anne – you dreamt it all!'

'I did not!' said Anne, indignant again. 'I *know* there was someone there – in fact, more than one person, because I'm sure I heard whispering!'

George raised her voice. 'Timmy!' she called loudly, making Anne jump violently. 'Timmy! Come along. We've sent you on a silly wild goose chase – but now we'll go back to bed!'

Timmy came trotting out of the cottage and went obediently to George. She heard him yawn as he stood beside her, and she laughed.

'Anne had a bad dream, that's all, Timmy,' she said.

Anne felt cross – very cross. She said no more and they left the old cottage and went back to their heather bed. Anne climbed on to her side and turned over with her back to George. All right – let George think it was a dream if she liked!

But when Anne awoke in the morning and remembered the happenings of the night before, she too began to wonder uneasily if she *had* dreamed what she had seen and heard in the old cottage.

'After all – Timmy would certainly have caught anyone who was there,' she thought. 'And he wasn't at all excited, so there can't have *been* anyone in the cottage. And anyway, why would they come? It's just silly!'

So, when George talked about Anne's dreaming in the middle of the night, Anne did not defend herself. She really could *not* be sure that it had really happened. So she stuck out her tongue when George teased her, and said nothing.

'Let's go and see that boy and his camp,' George said when they had eaten a few rather stale sandwiches and some shortbread biscuits. 'I'm beginning to feel bored, aren't you? I wish Timmy's ear would quite heal up. I'd go back home like a shot then.'

They set off in the direction of the camp with Timmy. They heard a chip-chipping noise as they came near, and then something small and hairy shot out from a bush and rushed up, barking a welcome.

'Hallo, Jet!' said Anne. 'Don't you let Timmy have any more of your bones!'

The chipping noise had stopped. The two girls went on and came to a very messy piece of common. It had been well dug over, in some places very deeply. Surely that boy couldn't have done so much excavating by himself?

'Hey! Where are you?' called George. Then she saw the boy below her, examining something in a trench he had dug out. He jumped and looked upwards.

Then he scowled. 'Look – you promised not to come and disturb me!' he shouted. 'You're mean. Just like girls to break a promise.'

'Well! I like *that*!' said George amazed. 'It was *you* who broke yours! Who came messing round *our* camp yesterday evening I'd like to know?'

'Not me!' said the boy at once. 'I always keep my promises. Now go away and keep yours. Girls! Pooh!'

'Well, I can't say we think much of *you*,' said George, disgusted. 'We're going. *We* don't want to see anything of your silly digging. Good-bye!'

'Good-bye and good riddance!' called the boy rudely, and turned back to his work.

'I think he must be *quite* mad,' said Anne. 'First he

makes a promise – then last evening he broke his promise
and even said he hadn't made one – and now today he
says he *did* make a promise and that he'd kept his and
we'd broken ours. Idiotic!'

They went up a little rabbit path, and into a small
copse of birch trees. Someone was sitting there reading.
He looked up as they came.

The two girls stopped in amazement. It was that boy
again! But how had he got here? They had just left him
behind in a trench! Anne looked at the title of the book
he was reading. Goodness – what a learned title – something about Archaeology.

'Another little trick of yours, I suppose?' said George,
sarcastically, stopping in front of him. 'You must be a
jolly good runner, I must say, to have got here so quickly.
Funny boy, aren't you – very very funny!'

'Good gracious – it's those potty girls again,' groaned
the boy. 'Can't you leave me alone? You talked a lot of
rubbish yesterday – and now you're talking it again.'

'How did you get here so quickly,' said Anne, puzzled.

'I didn't get here quickly. I came very slowly, reading
my book as I went,' said the boy.

'Fibber!' said George. 'You must have run at top
speed. Why do you pretend like this? It's only a minute
or so ago that we saw you.'

'Now *you're* the fibber!' said the boy. 'I do think you
two girls are awful. Go away and leave me alone and
never let me see you again!'

Timmy didn't like the tone of the boy's voice and he
growled. The boy scowled at him. 'And just you shut up
too,' he said.

Anne pulled at George's sleeve. 'Come on,' she said,

'it's no good staying here arguing. The boy's crazy – mad – we'll never get any sense out of him!'

The two girls walked off together, Timmy following. The boy took absolutely no notice. His face was turned to his book and he was quite absorbed in it.

'I've never met anyone *quite* so mad before!' said Anne, rather puzzled. 'By the way, George – you don't suppose it could have been that idiotic boy last night in the cottage?'

'No. I tell you I think you dreamed it,' said George, firmly. 'Though that boy is quite idiot enough to explore an old cottage in the middle of the night. He would probably think it a very good time to do so. Oh Anne, look – there's a pool – in that hollow there. Do you think we could bathe in it?'

It certainly shone very temptingly. They went down to have a closer look. 'Yes – we'll have a swim this afternoon,' said George. 'And then I really think, Anne, we ought to go back to Kirrin Cottage and get a few more provisions. The sandwiches we've got left are so dry that we really shan't enjoy eating them – and as Timmy's ear isn't healed, it looks as if we'll have to stay a bit longer.'

'Right!' said Anne, and they went on back to the camp. They changed into their swimsuits in the afternoon and went off to the little pool. It was fairly deep, very warm and quite clean. They spent a lovely hour swimming and basking and swimming again – then they reluctantly dressed and began to think of going off on the long journey to Kirrin Cottage.

George's mother was very surprised to see the two girls and Timmy. She said yes, of course they could have some more food, and sent them to ask Joanna for all she could spare.

'By the way, I've heard from Julian and Dick,' she said. 'They're back from France – and may be here in a day or two! Shall I tell them to join you or will you come back here?'

'Tell them to come and fetch us as soon as they get here!' said George, delighted. Her face shone. Ah – the Five would be together again. How wonderful!

'Leave me directions to give them so that they can find you,' said her mother. 'Then you can all come back – together. The boys can help to carry everything.'

What fun, what fun! Julian and Dick again, now things would be exciting, things would happen, as they always did. What FUN!

CHAPTER SIX

Storm in the night

IT WAS fun to go back to their little camping place again. It was growing dark, as they had stayed to have a good meal at Kirrin Cottage, and Timmy had eaten a most enormous plate of meat, vegetables and gravy. Then he had sat down and sighed as if to say 'That was jolly good! I could do with some more!'

However, nobody took any notice of this, so he trotted off to have a good look round the garden to make sure it was just the same as when he had left it a day or two before. Then it was time to start back to the camping place, and Timmy heard George's whistle.

'Well, nobody laughed at Timmy this evening!' said Anne. 'Not even your father!'

'Oh, I expect Mother had told him not to,' said George. 'Anyway, I *said* I would stay away till Tim's ear is better, and I mean to.'

'Well, I'm quite willing,' said Anne. 'The only thing I'm a bit worried about is – do you suppose there will be anyone snooping about in that old cottage again?'

'You dreamed it all!' said George. 'You admitted you did!'

'Well, yes, I did wonder if I *had* dreamed it,' said Anne, as they walked up the long Carters Lane to the moor. 'But now that it will soon be dark, I'm beginning to think I *didn't* dream it – and it isn't a very nice feeling.'

'Oh, don't be silly!' said George impatiently. 'You

45

can't chop and change about like that. Anyway, we've got Timmy – no one would dare to upset Timmy! Would they, Tim?'

But Timmy was ahead, hoping against hope that he might for once in a while catch a rabbit. There were so many about on the common at this time of the evening, peeping at him here, making fun of him there, and showing their little white bobtails as soon as he moved in their direction.

The two girls got safely back to their camp. The tent was still up, their heather bed out in the open, covered with the old rug. They put down their loads thankfully, and went to the little spring for a drink.

George yawned. 'I'm tired. Let's get to bed at once, shall we? Or wait – perhaps it would be a good idea to have a look in at that cottage to make sure no one is there to disturb us tonight.'

'Oh no – I don't want to look,' said Anne. 'It's getting dark now.'

'All right – I'll go with Timmy,' said George, and off she went. She came back in about five minutes, her little torch shining in front of her, for it was now almost dark.

'Nothing to report,' she said. 'Nothing whatever – except one bat flying round that big room. Timmy nearly went mad when it flew down and almost touched his nose.'

'Oh. That's when he barked, I suppose,' said Anne, who was now curled up on the heather bed. 'I heard him. Come on, George – I'm sleepy.'

'I must just look at Timmy's ear once more,' said George and shone her torch on it.

'Well, buck up, then,' said Anne. 'That's about the thousandth time today you've examined it.'

'It does seem much better,' said George, and she patted Timmy. 'I *shall* be glad when I can take this awful collar off him. I'm sure he hates it.'

'I don't believe he even *notices* it now,' said Anne. 'George, are you coming or not? I really can't keep awake one minute more.'

'I'm coming,' said George. 'No, Tim – you are *not* sleeping on our bed. I told you that last night. There's hardly enough room for Anne and me.'

She climbed carefully on to the heather bed, and lay looking up at the twinkling stars. 'I feel happy tonight,' she said, 'because Julian and Dick are coming. I was down in the dumps when I thought they might not be coming at all these hols. When do you suppose they'll be here, Anne?'

There was no answer. Anne was asleep. George sighed. She would have liked to plan what they were going to do when the boys came. Timmy's ear would surely be all right in a day or two – and the boys could carry everything back from this little camp to Kirrin Cottage – and then long days of swimming and boating and fishing and all kinds of fun could begin – begin – begin – be . . .

And now George was asleep too! She didn't feel a small spider running over her hand, wondering whether or not to spin a web between her finger and thumb. She didn't hear the scramble of a hedgehog not far off – though Timmy did and pricked one ear. It was a very peaceful night indeed.

Next day the girls were very cheerful. They made a good breakfast of some of the food they had brought, and then spent some time getting more heather for their bed, which, under the weight of their two bodies, was now rather flat and uncomfortable.

'Now for a swim!' said George. They put on their swimsuits, threw cardigans over their shoulders and set off to the little pool. On the way they saw Jet, the little mongrel dog, in the distance, and the boy with him. Jet tore up to them and danced round Timmy excitedly.

The boy called to them. 'It's all right, don't worry, I'm not going near your place! I'm still keeping *my* promise! Jet – come here!'

The girls took no notice of the grinning boy, but couldn't resist patting the little one-eyed mongrel. Jet really was like a piece of quicksilver, darting in and out and round about. He shot back to the boy at once.

The girls went on to the pool – and stopped in dismay when they came near. Someone was already there, swimming vigorously!

'Who is it?' said Anne. 'Dear me, this lonely common seems absolutely *crowded* with people!'

George was staring at the swimmer in utmost amazement. 'Anne – it's that boy!' she said. 'Look – tousled hair and everything! But – but . . .'

'But we've just met him going in the opposite direction!' said Anne, also amazed. 'How extraordinary! No, it *can't* be the boy!'

They went a little nearer. Yes – it *was* the boy. He called out to them. 'I'm just going out. I shan't be a minute!'

'How did you get here?' shouted George. 'We never saw you turn back and run.'

'I've been here for about ten minutes,' shouted back the boy.

'Fibber!' yelled back George at once.

'Ah – barmy as usual!' yelled the boy. 'Same as yesterday!'

He got out and walked off, dripping wet, in the direction of the trenches and pits which he was digging. George looked about for Jet, but she couldn't see him. 'Perhaps he's in the pool too,' she said. 'Come on, Anne – let's swim. I must say that that boy is extraordinary! I suppose he thinks it's funny to meet people, then double back and appear again!'

'He was nicer the first time of all that we saw him,' said Anne. 'I liked him then. I just don't understand him now. Ooooh – isn't this water lovely and warm!'

They had a long swim, got out and basked in the sun, lying on the heather, and then swam again. Then they began to feel hungry and went back to their little camping place.

The day passed quickly. They saw no more of the puzzling boy, or of Jet. They occasionally heard the sharp noise of metal on stone, or of chipping, from the place where the boy was presumably still digging in the old Roman camp.

'Or what he *hopes* is an old Roman camp,' said George. 'Personally I think he's so mad that I don't suppose he would know the difference between a Roman camp and a Boy Scouts' camp!'

They settled down on their heather bed that night but saw no stars twinkling above them this time. Instead there were rather heavy clouds, and it was not nearly so warm.

'Gosh – I hope it's not going to rain!' said George. 'Our tent wouldn't be much good against a real downpour! We could squeeze into it all right, but it's not a proper waterproof tent. Do you think it's going to rain, Anne?'

'No,' said Anne, sleepily. 'Anyway, I'm not getting up till I have to! I'm tired.'

She went to sleep, and so did George. Timmy didn't, though. He had heard the far-off growl of thunder, and he was uneasy. Timmy was not afraid of thunderstorms, but he didn't like them. They were things that growled like enormous dogs in the sky, and flashed angrily – but he never could get at them, or frighten them!

He closed both eyes, and put down one ear, leaving the other one up, listening.

Another thunder growl came, and one large and heavy drop of rain fell on Timmy's black nose. Then another fell on his cardboard collar and made a very loud noise indeed, startling him. He sat up, growling.

The rain came closer, and soon large drops, the size of ten-penny pieces, peppered the faces of the two sleeping girls. Then came such a crash of thunder that they both awoke in a fright.

'Blow! It's a thunderstorm!' said George. 'And pouring rain too. We shall be soaked.'

'Better get into the tent,' said Anne, as a flash of lightning forked down the sky and lit up everything with a quick brilliance.

'No good,' said George. 'It's soaked already. There's nothing for it but to get into the cottage, Anne. At least we'll have a roof over our heads or rather, a ceiling, for the roof's gone. Come on.'

Anne didn't in the least want to shelter in the old cottage, but there was absolutely nothing else to do. The girls grabbed their rug and ran through the rain, George flashing her torch to guide them. Timmy ran too, barking.

They came to the doorway of the cottage and went inside. What a relief to get out of the rain! The two girls huddled down into a corner, the rug round them – but soon they were too hot and threw it off.

The storm passed overhead with a few terrific crashes and much lightning. Gradually the rain grew less and soon stopped. One star came out, and then others followed as the thunder-clouds swept away in the wind.

'We can't go back to the tent – we'll have to stay here,' said George. 'I'll go and get our bags for pillows. We can lie on the rug.'

Anne went with her, and carried a bag back too. Soon the girls were lying in a corner of the rug, their heads on the bags, and Timmy close beside them.

'Good night,' said Anne. 'We'll try to go to sleep again! Blow that storm!'

Soon they were both asleep – but Timmy wasn't. Timmy was uneasy. Very uneasy! And quite suddenly he broke into a volley of such loud barks that both girls woke up in a panic.

'Timmy! What's the matter? Oh Tim, what is it?' cried George. She clutched his leather collar and held on to him.

'Don't leave us! Timmy, what's scared you?'

CHAPTER SEVEN

Strange happenings

TIMMY STOPPED barking and tried to get away from
George's hand on his collar. But she would not let
him. George was not easily frightened, but what with
the thunderstorm, the strange old cottage and now
Timmy's sudden excitement, she wanted him near her.

'What is it?' asked Anne, in a scared whisper.

'I don't know. I can't even imagine,' said George, also
in a low voice. 'Perhaps it's nothing – just the thunderstorm that has upset him and made him nervous. We'll
keep awake a bit, and see if we hear anything peculiar.'

They lay quietly in their corner, and George kept a
firm hand on Timmy. He growled once or twice, but did
not bark any more. George began to think it really must
have been the storm that had upset him.

A rumble of thunder came again – the storm was
returning, or else another one was blowing up!

George felt relieved. 'It's all right, Anne. It must have
been the thunder and lightning in the distance that upset
Timmy. You're silly, Timmy – scaring us like that!'

Crash – rumble – crash! Yes, certainly the storm was
gathering force again! Timmy barked angrily.

'Be quiet! You make more noise than the thunder!' said
George, crossly. 'No you can't go out into the rain, Timmy.
It's begun again, as bad as before. You'd only get dripping
wet – and then you'd want to come and sit as close to me as
possible and make me wet too. I know you!'

'No – don't let him go, George,' said Anne. 'I like him here with us. My word – what a storm! I hope it won't strike this cottage.'

'Well, considering that it must have stood here for three or four hundred years, and have seen thousands of storms, I expect it will come safely through one more!' said George. 'Where are you going, Anne?'

'Just to look out of the window,' said Anne. 'Or out of the place where the window used to be! I like to see the countryside suddenly lit up for just one moment in a lightning flash – and then go back to darkness again.'

She went to stand at the window. There came the crash of thunder, not far away, and a brilliant flash of lightning. Anne stared over the countryside, which had suddenly become visible in the flash – and then disappeared like magic in a second!

Anne gave a sudden cry and stumbled back to George. 'George – George . . .'

'Whatever's the matter?' asked George, alarmed.

'There's someone out there – people!' said Anne, clutching George and making her jump. 'I saw them just for an instant, when the lightning flashed.'

'People? What sort of people?' said George, astonished. 'How many?'

'I don't know. It was all so quick. I think there were two – or maybe three. They were standing some way off – quite still, out there in the storm.'

'Anne, those are *trees*!' said George, scornfully. 'There are two or three small trees standing against the sky out there – I noticed them the other day.'

'These weren't trees,' said Anne. 'I know they weren't.

What are people doing out there in this storm? I'm frightened.'

George was absolutely certain that Anne had seen the group of little trees that she knew were there – they would look just like people, in a quick flash of lightning. No sooner did you see something in a storm than it was gone!

She comforted Anne. 'Don't worry, Anne! it's the easiest thing in the world to imagine seeing things in a lightning flash. Timmy would bark if there were people around. He would . . .'

'Well, he *did* bark, didn't he?' said Anne. 'He woke us both up with his barking.'

'Ah yes – but that was just because he heard the storm coming up again,' said George. 'And you know he gets angry when he hears the thunder growling.'

Just at that moment the thunder crashed again – then the lightning flashed its weird and brilliant light.

This time *both* the girls screamed, and Timmy gave an enormous bark, trying his hardest to get away from George.

'There! Did you see *that*?' said Anne, in a shaky voice.

'Yes. Yes, I did. Oh, Anne, you're right! Someone was looking in at the window! And if we saw him, he must have seen *us*! Whatever is he doing here in the middle of the night?'

'Well, I told you I saw two or three people,' said Anne, still shakily. 'I expect it was one of them. Maybe they saw the cottage in one of the lightning flashes, and thought they might shelter here – and sent one of their number to see.'

'Maybe. But what in the world is anyone *doing*, wandering about here at night?' said George. 'They can't possibly be up to any good. Let's go home tomorrow, Anne. I wish the boys were here! They'd know what to do, they would have some good plan!'

'The storm's going off again,' said Anne. 'Timmy has stopped barking too, thank goodness. Don't let him go, George. You never know – those people, whoever they are, might do him harm. Anyway, I feel safer when he's with us!'

'I wouldn't dream of letting him go,' said George. 'You're trembling, Anne! You needn't be as scared as that! Timmy won't let you come to any harm.'

'I know! But it wasn't very nice suddenly seeing some-body looking in at the window like that, outlined in a lightning flash!' said Anne. 'I can't possibly go to sleep again. Let's play some silly game to take our minds off it.'

So they played the Alphabet game with Animals. Each had to think in turn of an animal beginning with A, and a mark went to the one who could keep it up longest! Then they went on to B and to C and to D.

They were doing the Es when they heard a loud and very comforting sound.

'Timmy's snoring,' said George. 'He's fast asleep. What an elephantine snore, Tim!'

'E for elephant,' said Anne, quickly.

'Cheat! That should have been *my* E!' said George. 'All right. E for Eland.'

'E for Egg-Eater,' said Anne, after a pause.

'Not allowed – you made that up!' said George. 'My mark!'

By the time they got to M, Anne was two marks ahead, and the dawn was breaking. It was a great relief to the two girls to see the silvering of the sky in the east and to know that soon the sun would be up. They immediately felt much better. George even stood up and went bravely to the window, where there was nothing to be seen but the quiet countryside outside, with its stretches of heather, gorse bushes and silver birches.

'We were silly to be so scared,' said George. 'I don't think we'll go back home today after all, Anne. I hate running away from anything. The boys would laugh at us.'

'I don't care if they do,' said Anne. 'I'm going back. If the boys were here, I'd stay – but goodness knows when they'll come – it might not be till next week! I'm just NOT staying here another night.'

'All right, all right,' said George. 'Do as you like – but for goodness sake tell the boys it was *you* who wanted to run away, not me!'

'I will,' said Anne. 'Oh dear – now I feel sleepy all over again. I suppose it's because daylight is here and everything seems safe, so I know I can fall asleep.'

George felt the same! They cuddled down together on the rug again and immediately fell asleep. They did not wake till quite late – and even then something woke them, or they might have slept on for hours, tired out with their broken night and the fright they had had.

They were awakened by something scuttling round them, making a very loud noise indeed. Then Timmy barked.

The girls awoke and sat up, rather dazed. 'Oh, it's *Jet*!' said Anne. 'Jet, have you come to see if we're all right, you dear, funny little one-eyed thing!'

'Wuff-wuff!' said Jet and rolled over on his back to be tickled, his long thin tail wagging all the time. Timmy leaped on him and pretended to eat him. Then a loud voice called to them.

They looked up. The boy was standing at the door, grinning widely.

'Hallo, sleepy-heads! I came to see if you were all right after that awful storm. I know I promised I wouldn't come here, but I felt a bit worried about you.'

'Oh. Well, that's nice of you,' said Anne, getting up and brushing the dust from her skirt. 'We're quite all right – but we had rather a peculiar night. We . . .'

She got a hard nudge from George and stopped suddenly. George was warning her not to say anything about the people they had seen – or the person at the window. Did she think they might have anything to do with this boy? Anne said no more and George spoke instead.

'Wasn't it a dreadful storm? How did you get on?'

'All right. I sleep down in a trench, and the rain can't get at me. Well – so long! Come on, Jet!'

The boy and the dog disappeared. 'That was nice of him,' said Anne. He doesn't seem crazy this morning, does he – quite normal! 'He didn't even contradict us. I think I quite like him after all.'

They went to their soaked tent and got a tin of sardines out to eat with bread and butter. Just as they were opening it, they heard someone whistling and looked up.

'Here comes that boy again!' said Anne.

'Good morning. I don't want to butt in – but I just wondered if you were all right after the storm,' said the boy, without even a smile. The girls stared at him in amazement.

'Look – don't start being crazy all over again!' said George. 'You know jolly well we're all right. We've already told you.'

'You haven't. And I *didn't* know!' said the boy. 'Well, I only came out of politeness. Sorry to see you are still barmy!'

And off he went. 'There!' said Anne, vexed. 'Just as we thought he was nice again, and not crazy, he starts all over again. I suppose he thinks it's funny. Silly ass!'

They set their things out to dry in the sun, and it was half past twelve before they were ready to pack and go back to Kirrin Cottage. George was rather cross about going, but Anne was quite firm. She was NOT going to spend another night on the common.

George was just strapping a package on her bicycle, when the two girls heard the sound of voices – and then Timmy went quite mad! He barked wildly, and set off down a path at top speed, his tail wagging nineteen to the dozen!

'Oh! It can't be – surely it can't be Julian and Dick!' shouted George, in sudden delight, and she shot off after Timmy.

It was! It *was* Julian and Dick! There they came, packs on their backs, grinning all over their faces! Hurrah! The Famous Five were all together once more!

CHAPTER EIGHT

All together again!

THERE WAS such excitement at the arrival of the boys that at first nobody could make themselves heard. Timmy barked at the top of his very loud voice and simply would *not* stop! George shouted, and Dick and Julian laughed. Anne hugged them, and felt proud of two such brown, good-looking brothers.

'Ju! We never guessed you'd come so soon!' said the delighted George. 'Gosh, I'm pleased to see you!'

'We got fed up with French food,' said Dick. 'I came out in spots and Julian was sick, and it was SO hot. Phew! Next time I go there I'll go when it's cooler.'

'And we kept on thinking of Kirrin and the bay, and you two girls and Timmy,' said Julian, giving George a friendly punch. 'I think we *really* got a bit homesick. So we packed up before we should, and flew home.'

'Flew?' said George. 'You lucky things! And then did you come straight down here?'

'We spent the night with Mother and Dad at home,' said Julian, 'and then caught the first train here that we possibly could this morning – only to find that you weren't at Kirrin!'

'So we packed camping-out things in smaller bags and came straight along to you!' said Dick. 'I say, George, old thing, do you think you could possibly make Timmy stop barking? I'm going a bit deaf!'

'Shut up, Tim,' ordered George. 'Let other people bark a bit. Do you notice his collar, Julian?'

'Can't help seeing it!' said Julian. 'He looks a scream in it, doesn't he? Ha ha! You're an Elizabethan dog with a ruff, Timmy – that's what Uncle Quentin told us – and that's what you look like, old fellow!'

'He looks most comical, I must say,' said Dick. 'Enough to make a cat laugh, hey, Timmy!'

Anne looked at George. Goodness, what would she say to hear *Julian and Dick* laughing at Timmy and making fun of him! Would she lose her temper at once?

But George only grinned. In fact she gave a little laugh herself. 'Yes – he does look funny, doesn't he? But he doesn't mind a bit!'

'You know, we came here to camp because George couldn't bear people laughing at . . .' began Anne, thinking that she wouldn't let George get away with this! But George gave her such a beseeching look, that she stopped at once. George could never bear to look small in front of Julian and Dick. She prided herself on being just like a boy – and she was suddenly certain that her two cousins would think she was 'just like a *girl*' if they heard the fuss she had made about people laughing at Timmy's collar.

'I say – you two seem to be packing up,' said Julian, looking at the package strapped to the back of George's bicycle. 'What's happened?'

'Well – it got a bit lonely and Anne was . . .' and then in her turn George caught a beseeching look from Anne! She knew what it meant. 'I didn't tell tales on *you* – so don't tell tales on *me* – *don't* say I was scared!'

'Er – Anne was certain that there was something funny going on here,' went on George, who had quite meant to

64

say that Anne was scared and insisted on going home. 'And we didn't feel that we could tackle it ourselves – though if you had been here we wouldn't have *dreamed* of going home, of course.'

'What do you mean – something funny?' asked Dick.

'Well – you see – it began like this,' said George, but Julian interrupted.

'If there's a tale to tell, let's have it over a meal, shall we? We've had nothing to eat since six o'clock this morning, Dick and I – and we're ravenous!'

'Yes. Good idea,' said Dick, and began to undo a big package which he took out of his bag. 'I've a picnic lunch here from your mother, George – a jolly good one, I can tell you. I think she was so relieved to think that she was going to get rid of us that she really surpassed herself! We've got a marvellous piece of boiled ham – look! It'll last us for ages – if we don't give bits to Timmy. Get away, Tim. This is *not* for you! Grrrrrr!'

George suddenly felt so happy that she could hardly speak. It had been fun camping with Anne – but what a difference the boys made! So confident of themselves, so merry, full of jokes, so idiotic, and yet so dependable. She felt that she wanted to sing at the top of her voice!

The sun had been hot again that morning and had dried the common beautifully. It wasn't long before the Five were sitting down in the heather with a very fine feast before them.

'I wouldn't sell anyone my hunger for a hundred pounds,' said Dick. 'Now then – who's going to carve this magnificent piece of gammon?'

There were no plates, so they had to make sandwiches of the ham. Dick had actually brought some mustard, and dabbed it generously over the slices of ham before George put them between pieces of bread. 'Aha, Tim – this is one way of making sure you won't get even a *bite* of these wonderful ham sandwiches!' said Dick. 'You can't bear mustard, can you? Ju, where's the meat we brought for Tim?'

'Here. Pooh – it smells a bit strong,' said Julian. 'Do you mind taking it to a nice secluded corner, Tim?'

Timmy immediately sat down close to Julian. 'Now – don't be so disobedient!' said Julian, and gave Timmy a friendly push.

'He doesn't understand the word "secluded",' said George, with a grin. 'Tim – buzz off a bit!'

Timmy understood that and took his meat a little way away. Everyone took a ripe red tomato, and a little lettuce heart from a damp cloth brought by Julian, and settled down happily to munch sandwiches.

'Lovely!' said Anne, contentedly. 'Goodness gracious
– I can hardly believe we had such a peculiar time last
night!'

'Ah – tell us all about it!' said Dick.

So first Anne, then George related all that had happened. Anne told of the night she had seen a light in the
old cottage and had heard whispers and footfalls inside.

'We did think I might have been dreaming,' she said,
'but now we don't think I was. We think I really did see
and hear those things.'

'What next?' asked Julian, taking his third sandwich.
'This all sounds most interesting. Quite Famous Five-ish,
in fact!'

George told of the storm in the night, and how they
had had to leave their heather bed and go to shelter in the
old cottage – and how, in the flashes of lightning, Anne
had seen two or three people standing outside – and then
how they had *both* seen someone standing silently, looking in at the window.

'Strange,' said Julian, puzzled. 'Yes – something is up.
I wonder what? I mean – there's absolutely nothing on
this lonely bit of common that's at all interesting.'

'Well – there are the remains of an old Roman camp,'
said Anne. 'And a boy there who is examining them to
see if he can find anything old and interesting.'

'A completely *mad* boy,' said George. 'He doesn't
seem to know what he says or doesn't say. Contradicts
himself all the time – or to put it another way, tells the
most idiotic fibs.'

'And he apparently thinks it's awfully funny to meet us
somewhere, and then double round on his tracks and
appear suddenly somewhere else,' said Anne. 'Sometimes

I can't help liking him – other times he's too idiotic for words.'

'He's got a little one-eyed dog called Jet,' said George, and Timmy gave a sudden bark as he heard the name. 'You like Jet, don't you, Tim?'

'This all sounds most interesting,' said Dick. 'Pass me the tomato bag, Ju, before you eat the lot. Thanks. As I said, *most* interesting – a one-eyed dog, a mad boy, Roman remains – and people who come to an old ruined cottage in the dead of night and look into windows!'

'I wonder you two girls didn't pack up and go home,' said Julian. 'You must be braver without us than I thought possible!'

George caught Anne's eye and grinned mischievously, but said nothing. Anne owned up, red in the face.

'Well – I did tell George I was going home this very morning, I was so scared last night. George didn't want to, of course, but she was coming, all the same. But now you've turned up, things are different.'

'Ah – well, do we stay on, or don't we, Ju?' said Dick. 'Are we scared or are we not?'

Everyone laughed. 'Well – if you go back *I* shall stay on alone!' said Anne. 'Just to show you!'

'Good old Anne!' said Dick. 'We all stay, of course. It may be nothing – it may be something – we can't tell. But we'll certainly find out. And the first thing to do is to have a look at the Roman remains and the mad boy. I'm looking forward to meeting him, I must say! After that we'll tackle the ruined cottage!'

Timmy came up to see if he could get any tit-bits. Julian waved him away. 'You smell of too-strong meat, Timmy,' he said. 'Go and get a drink. By the way, *is* there

68

anything to drink here, George?'

'Oh yes,' said George. 'A lovely spring. Not far off, either. Let's take the remains of our meal there, and the mug. We've only got one unfortunately, so it's no good getting water unless we all sit by the spring and take turns at the mug. Come on!'

The boys thought that the spring was a really splendid one. They grouped themselves around it and took turns at filling the mug and drinking from it. They were now eating slabs of Joanna's fruit cake and it was very good.

'Now, you girls unpack again,' said Dick, when they had finished their meal. 'Goodness, I did enjoy that! We'd better unpack too, Julian.'

'Right. Where shall we put our things?' asked Julian, looking around. 'I don't somehow like to leave everything under that little tent, with a mad boy about, and a one-eyed dog. I feel that both of them might like the rest of that ham.'

'Oh, it's too hot to leave ham out in this sun,' said George. 'We'll have to put it into the old cottage, on a shelf. We'll put *everything* there, shall we? Move in properly, in case it rains again at night. It's so tiresome to have to bundle everything indoors in the dark and the rain.'

'I agree,' said Dick. 'Right. We'll move into the ruined cottage. What fun! Come on, everyone!'

They spent the next half-hour taking their things into the cottage and putting them in corners or on shelves. George found a dark corner behind the fireplace where she put the food, for she was half-afraid that Jet, nice little dog though he seemed, might perhaps smell the ham and gobble up most of their food.

'Now!' said Julian. 'Are we ready to go and see the Roman remains and the Mad Boy? Here we go, then – the Famous Five are off again, and who knows what will happen!'

CHAPTER NINE

A little exploration

THE FIVE walked off together, Timmy at the back, delighted to have all his friends with him again. He kept nudging first one person's heels and then another, just to remind them that he was there.

As they came near the old camp, they saw a boy sitting beside a bush, reading.

'There's that boy we told you of!' said George. 'See?'

'He looks fairly ordinary,' said Dick. 'Very absorbed in his book, I must say. Determined to take no notice of us!'

'I'll speak to him,' said George. So, as they drew near, she called to the boy.

'Hallo! Where's Jet?'

The boy looked up, annoyed. 'How do I know?'

'Well, he was with you this morning,' said George.

'He was not,' said the boy. 'He's never with me! Please don't disturb me, I'm reading.'

'There you are!' said George to the others. 'He came to see us this morning with Jet – and now he says the little dog is never with him. Quite, quite mad!'

'Or plain rude,' said Dick. 'Not worth bothering about, anyway. Well, if he's not doing any excavating in his Roman camp, perhaps we can explore it without being ordered off!'

They walked on slowly and came to the camp, and at once heard a cheerful whistling going on, and the sound of someone digging. George looked over the top of the

71

dug-out trench in surprise. She almost toppled in, she was so amazed at what she saw!

The boy was there, digging carefully, whistling as he did so! He brushed his tousled hair from his hot forehead and caught sight of George and the others. He looked rather astonished.

'How on earth did you get down here so quickly?' said George. 'Do you have wings or something?'

'I've been down here all the afternoon,' said the boy. 'For at least an hour, I should think.'

'Fibber!' said George. The boy looked very angry, and shouted back at once.

'I'm tired of you two girls – and now you've brought your friends too, I suppose you think you can come and aggravate me even more!'

'Don't be an idiot,' said Dick, feeling as puzzled about this boy as George and Anne had been. How in the world had he run around them and got down in the trench so quickly? Did he enjoy playing tricks like that? He really didn't *look* mad!

'Is this your property, this old camp?' asked Julian.

'No. Of course not. Don't be daft!' said the boy. 'As if I could own a whole camp like this! It was discovered by my father some time ago, and he gave me permission to work here for the hols. It's pretty exciting, I can tell you. See my finds?'

He pointed to a rough shelf where stood a broken pot, something that looked like an old brooch, a long pinlike thing, and part of a stone head. Julian was at once interested. He leapt down into the trench.

'I say – you've certainly got something there!' he said. 'Any coins too?'

'Yes – three,' said the boy and put his hand in his pocket. 'I found this one first – then these two close together yesterday. They must be hundreds and hundreds of years old.'

By this time all the others were down in the trench too. They looked about with much interest. Evidently the place had been well excavated by experts, and now the boy was working here and there on his own, hoping to find something that had been overlooked.

Dick went out of the trench and began to clamber about over the great stones and rocks. A small animal suddenly caught his eye – a young rabbit.

It stared at him in fright and then disappeared behind a slab of stone. It peeped out at Dick again, and he was amused. He went cautiously over to the slab, and the little rabbit disappeared – but soon two or three whiskers poked out. Dick got down on hands and knees and looked behind the slab. A dark hole was there.

Dick pulled out his torch and flashed it into the hole, wondering if the small rabbit was hiding there, or whether it was the entrance to a burrow.

To his surprise there was a very big hole indeed – a hole that seemed to go down and down and down – his torch could make out no bottom to it.

'It's far too wide for a rabbit hole,' thought Dick. 'I wonder where it leads to. I'll ask that boy.'

He went back to where the boy was still showing his things to Julian, talking eagerly. 'I say,' began Dick, 'there's a most interesting hole behind one of the stone slabs over there – what is it?'

'Oh that – my father says it was explored and that it was only a place for storage – meat in hot weather, or loot, or something like that. Actually nothing whatever was found there – most uninteresting. As a matter of fact it may be nothing to do with the camp at all.'

'I say, look – here's another shelf with things on it,' said George, suddenly spying a little collection of things on a rough shelf in another part of the trench. 'Are these yours too?'

'Those? No,' said the boy. 'Nothing to do with me at all. Don't touch them, please.'

'Whose are they then?' asked George, curiously. The boy took no notice whatever of her question and went on talking to Julian. George took down a beautiful little round pot.

'Hey! I told you NOT to touch those!' yelled the boy, so suddenly and angrily that George almost dropped the pot. 'Put it back – and clear out if you can't do what you're told.'

'Easy, old man, easy!' said Julian. 'No need to yell at her like that. You scared that little dog of yours and made him jump almost out of his skin! We'd better go, I think.'

'Well – I don't like being disturbed too much,' said the boy. 'People always seem to be wandering around. I've turned off quite a lot.'

'People?' said Julian, remembering Anne's story of two or three figures standing outside the cottage the night before, and of someone looking in. 'What kind of people?'

'Oh – nosey ones – wanting to get down and explore – disturbing me – it's surprising how many idiots there are wandering about this lonely place,' said the boy, picking up a tool again and setting to work. He grinned suddenly. 'I don't mean you. You really *know* something about this kind of thing.'

'Was anyone about last night?' asked Julian.

'Well – I rather think so,' said the boy. 'Because Jet here barked like mad. But it might have been the storm that frightened him – not that he's *usually* frightened of storms.'

'What's your name?' asked Dick.

'Guy Lawdler,' said the boy, and Dick whistled.

'My word – is your father the famous explorer, Sir John Lawdler?' he asked. The boy nodded.

'Well, no wonder you're so keen on archaeology!' said Dick. 'Your father's done pretty well in that line, hasn't he?'

'Come on, Dick!' said George. 'Let's go now. We might have time for a swim in the pool. We forgot to tell you about that.'

'Right,' said Dick. 'Come on, Julian. Good-bye, Guy!'

They left the rather desolate old camp and went back to the cottage to get their swimsuits and change. It wasn't long before they were running over the heather to the pool.

'Hallo – Guy's having a swim!' said Dick, in surprise. Sure enough, a boy was there, his hair falling over his forehead as usual.

'Hey, Guy!' shouted George. 'Have a swim with us!'

But the boy was already getting out of the water. Dick shouted. 'Wait a minute – don't go. We'd like to have a swim with you, Guy!'

But the boy turned defiantly. 'Don't be an ass!' he said. 'My name's not Guy!'

And, leaving four astonished people behind him, he ran lightly over the heather and disappeared.

'There you are – he's mad after all!' said Anne. 'Don't

bother about him. Come on in – the water's lovely and warm.'

They lazed about afterwards and began to feel hungry. 'Though how *any* of us could feel hungry after eating about fifty sandwiches between us at lunch-time, I don't know!' said Dick. 'Race you back to the cottage, Ju!'

They changed back into ordinary clothes and then had tea – fruit cake, shortbread biscuits and tinned pineapple on bread. They kept the juice and diluted it with cold spring water – it was simply delicious.

'Now let's explore the cottage,' said Dick.

'We already have, Anne and I,' said George. 'So I don't expect you'll find anything much.'

They went methodically through the old house, and even up the old stone stairway to the two rooms upstairs – though they could hardly be called rooms, for they had very little roof and not much wall!

'Nothing much here, that's certain,' said Dick, clattering down the stone stairway. 'Now let's go to the outbuildings – not that there's much left of them either!'

They examined everything, and came last of all to the old stables. It was dark inside, for the windows were very small, and it was some seconds before anyone could see properly.

'Old mangers,' said Dick, touching them. 'I wonder how long ago it is since they were used – and . . .'

'I say!' said George, suddenly. 'There's something funny here. Anne, look – this bit of floor was undisturbed yesterday, wasn't it?'

Anne looked down at the big white flagstone on which George was standing. It was quite obvious that it had been lifted, for the edges were not as green with moss as the others were, and the stone had been put back a little crookedly.

'Yes – someone's been interested in this stone – or in what is beneath it!' said Dick. 'I bet something is buried underneath!'

'Those men last night – that's what they came about!' said George. 'They went into these stables and lifted this stone. Why?'

'We'll soon find out!' said Julian. 'Come on, everyone, loosen it with your fingers – then we'll heave it up!'

CHAPTER TEN

What can be happening?

FORTY FINGERS and thumbs were very hard at work trying to loosen the heavy stone. At last Julian got hold of a corner which could be held more easily than any other part of the stone. He tried to lift it and it came away a little.

'Help me this side, Dick,' said Julian, and Dick put his strong fingers there too. 'Heave-ho!' he said – and up came the stone.

It went over with a crash and Timmy barked loudly, jumping aside. Everyone peered down – and then looked exceedingly disappointed!

There was nothing there at all. Not even a hole! The black earth, hard as iron, lay underneath, and nothing else.

They all stared down at the dry, hard earth, puzzled. George looked up at Julian.

'Well – that's strange, isn't it? Why should anyone lift up this heavy stone if there is nothing hidden underneath?'

'Well, it's clear that whoever was here didn't find anything – nor did he *hide* anything either,' said Julian. 'Dear me – why should anyone lift up a heavy stone and put it back – just for nothing?'

'He was obviously looking for something that wasn't here,' said Anne. 'The wrong stone, probably!'

'Yes. I think Anne's right,' said Dick. 'It's the wrong

stone! Probably there is something very interesting under the *right* stone! But which one is it?'

They all sat and looked at one another, and Timmy sat too, wondering why all this fuss was made about a flat white stone. Julian thought hard.

'From what you've told me, Anne – about seeing a light in the cottage that first night you were here – and hearing voices – and then seeing those figures outside last night in the storm – it looks as if someone is urgently hunting for something round about here.'

'Yes – something under a stone. Treasure of some sort, do you think?' said George.

Julian shook his head. 'No. I hardly think that much treasure would be hidden anywhere about this old cottage – all the people who lived here must have been fairly poor. The most they would have hidden would have been a few pieces of gold, and that would have been found long ago.'

'Well – someone modern might have hidden something valuable here – even something stolen,' said Anne.

'Yes. We can't tell. It's obviously important and urgent to somebody,' said Dick. 'I wonder if the people that Guy said came bothering him were anything to do with this?'

'They may have been,' said Julian. 'But they have clearly decided that what they are looking for is here now, whatever it is. And they must have been most annoyed to find you and Anne here last night, George. That's why someone came and looked in at the window, I expect – to make sure you were asleep! And you weren't.'

'I don't know whether I want to stay on here or not now,' said Anne, alarmed. 'If they haven't found what they want, they'll probably come again – in the night too.'

'Who cares?' said Dick. 'We've got Timmy, haven't we? I'm not turning out of here because somebody's got a habit of turning up big stones!'

Julian laughed. 'Nor am I. Let's stay on! And I don't see why we shouldn't do a bit of pulling up of stones ourselves! We might come across something very interesting!'

'Right. It's decided that we stay on then, is it?' said Dick. 'What about you, Anne?'

'Oh yes – of course I'll stay,' said Anne, not wanting to in the least, but knowing that she simply could not bear not to be with the others.

The Five walked round and about the cottage for a while, trying to make out where the people that the girls had seen the night before had come from – from what direction did they come and where did they go?

'The figures I saw first in the lightning stood about there,' said Anne, pointing. 'Let's go and see if there are any footprints. It was pouring with rain and the ground must have been very muddy.'

'Good idea,' said Dick, and off they went to where Anne had pointed. But it was a heathery piece of ground, and difficult to tell even if anyone *had* trodden there, for the heather was thick and springy.

'Let's look just outside the window now – the one where Anne saw someone looking in,' said Dick. And there they had a find! Just in front of the window were two quite deeply printed footmarks. One was slightly blurred as if the maker of them had turned his foot sideways as he waited. The other was very clear indeed.

Dick got out a piece of paper. 'I rather think I'll measure these,' he said, 'and make a note of the pattern on the soles. They had rubber soles and heels – look at the markings – crêpe rubber I should think.'

He measured the prints. 'Size eight shoes,' he said. 'Same as yours, Ju.' Then he carefully drew an exact picture of the sole and heel markings.

'You're quite a detective, Dick,' said Anne, admiringly, and he laughed.

'Oh, anyone can copy footprints!' he said. 'The thing is to match them up with the owner!'

'I have a feeling it's getting on for supper-time – if anyone *wants* any supper,' said George. 'It's half-past eight! Would you believe that the time could fly so fast?'

'I don't *really* feel very hungry,' said Dick. 'We've done pretty well today.'

'Well, don't waste our precious food if you don't feel hungry,' said George. 'We shall have to keep going home for more if we eat everything too quickly.'

Nobody felt terribly hungry. They made a cosy corner in the cottage and had a slice of cake and a biscuit each, with a drink of pineapple juice and spring-water. George had had the bright idea of filling the big empty pineapple tin, and they each filled a mug from it in turn, and drank.

'It's getting dark,' said Julian. 'Are we going to sleep inside the cottage or out?'

'In,' said Dick, promptly. 'We'll make things just as difficult for any night prowlers as possible!'

'Right,' said Julian. 'I bet they won't be pleased to find old Timmy here too. Shall we go out and get some heather for beds? I don't fancy sharing a thin rug between the four of us.'

Soon they were all dragging in armfuls of the springy heather. They laid it in the front room, in two corners, for the boys thought they would rather be in the same room as the girls, in case of danger.

'You need an awful lot of heather to make a *soft* bed,' said Dick, trying his. 'My bones seem to go right through the clumps and rub against the floor!'

'We can put our anoraks over our heather,' said Julian. 'That will help. The girls can have the rug. We shan't need any covering, it's so hot.'

By the time they had finished, it was dark. George lay on her heather and yawned. 'I'm going to sleep,' she announced. 'We don't need to keep guard or anything like that, do we? Timmy will bark if anyone comes near.'

'You're right. I really don't think we need take turns at keeping awake,' said Julian. 'Move up, Dick – you've left me no room.'

Julian was the last to go to sleep. He lay awake puzzling over the lifted stone slab. It was clear that someone had expected to find something under it. How did they know it was that particular slab? Had they a map? If so, it must have shown the wrong stone – or perhaps the searchers read the map wrong?

Before he could work it out any further, he was asleep. Timmy was asleep too, happy because all the others were under his care. He had one ear open as usual, but not *very* much open!

It was enough to let him hear a small mouse of some kind run across the floor. It was even enough for him to hear a beetle scraping its way up the wall. After a while his ear dropped down and he didn't even hear a hedgehog outside.

But something caused his ear to listen again and it pricked up. A noise crept inside the cottage – a noise that got louder and louder – a weird and puzzling noise!

Timmy woke up and listened. He pawed at George, not knowing whether to bark or not. He knew he should not bark at owls, but this was not an owl. Perhaps George would know.

'Don't, Timmy,' said George sleepily, but Timmy went on pawing her. Then she too heard the noise and sat up in a hurry.

What a truly horrible sound! It was a whining and a wailing, rising and falling through the night. A sound of misery and woe, that went on and on.

WHAT CAN BE HAPPENING?

'Julian! Dick! Wake up!' called George, her heart beating wildly. 'Something's happening.'

The boys awoke at once and so did Anne. They sat and listened to the weird noise. What in the world could it be? There it went again – wailing high in the air, and then dying away with a moan, only to begin again a few seconds later.

Dick felt the roots of his hair pricking. He leapt off the heather bed and ran to the window. 'Quick! Come and look at this!' he cried. 'What is it?'

They all crowded to the window, Timmy barking now as loudly as he could. In silence the others gazed at a very strange sight.

Blue and green lights were shining here and there, sometimes dimly, sometimes brightly. A curious round white light was travelling slowly in the air, and Anne clutched George, breathing fast.

'It won't come here,' she said. 'It won't, will it? I don't like it. What is happening, Julian?'

'I wish that awful wailing, whining noise would stop,' said Dick. 'It gets right inside my head. Do you make anything of all this, Julian?'

'Something very strange is going on,' said Julian. 'I'll go out with Timmy and see what I can find.' And before anyone could stop him, out he went, Timmy barking beside him.

'Oh Julian – come back!' called Anne, listening as his footsteps became distant. They all waited tensely at the window – and then suddenly the wailing noise stopped and the strange lights gradually began to fade.

Then they heard Julian's footsteps coming back firmly in the darkness.

WHAT CAN BE HAPPENING?

'Ju! What was it?' called Dick, as his brother came in at the doorway.

'I don't know, Dick,' said Julian, sounding very puzzled. 'I simply – don't – know! Perhaps we can find out in the morning.'

CHAPTER ELEVEN

Interesting discoveries – and a plan

THE FOUR sat in the dark and talked over the horrible noises and the weird blue and green and white lights. Anne sat close to Julian. She really was frightened.

'I want to go back to Kirrin,' she said. 'Let's go tomorrow. I don't like this.'

'I didn't see a thing just now,' said Julian, puzzled, his arm close round Anne. 'I seemed to go quite close to those wailing sounds – and then they stopped as soon as I got fairly near. But although Timmy barked and ran around, there didn't seem to be anyone there.'

'Did you get near the lights?' asked Dick.

'Yes, fairly near. But the odd thing was that they seemed high up when I got near them – not near the ground as I expected. And *again* Timmy couldn't find anyone. You would have thought if there was anyone about, playing the fool, that Timmy would have found them. But he didn't.'

'Woof,' said Timmy, dolefully. He didn't like this funny business at all!

'Well, if *nobody's* making the noises and lights, it makes it even worse,' said Anne. 'Do let's go home, Julian. Tomorrow.'

'All right,' said Julian. 'I don't feel particularly thrilled about all this myself. But there is *one* idea I've got in my mind which I'd like to sort out tomorrow.'

'What's that?' said Dick.

'Well – it may quite well be that somebody very badly wants us out of here for some reason,' said Julian. 'And that somebody may want to come and lift other stones and have a thorough search all over the place – which he can't do with us around. So he's trying to frighten us out!'

'Yes, I believe you are right, Julian,' said Dick. 'Those noises – and lights – they would be enough to scare anyone out of a place. Too eerie for words! Well, let's have a good snoop round in the daylight, to see if we can find any trace of a trickster!'

'We will – but it's extremely odd that *Timmy* didn't find him,' said Julian. 'Timmy can smell anyone out of any hiding place! Yes – we'll have a very very good hunt round tomorrow.'

'And if you find nothing and nobody, we'll go home?' asked Anne.

'Yes, we will. I promise you,' said Julian, hugging Anne. 'Don't worry. You shan't have to stay here one night longer, unless you want to! Now, let's try and go to sleep again!'

It took the four a long time to go to sleep after all this excitement in the middle of the night. Anne kept listening for the wailing noises again, but none came. She kept her eyes shut tightly in case she should happen to see any more of the strange lights outside the window.

George and the boys lay awake too, puzzling out the problems of lights and noises which were not apparently caused by anyone! Julian especially was puzzled.

Only Timmy was unconcerned. He went to sleep before anyone else, though he kept one ear *wide* open – and up went the other one when George moved, or Dick whispered to Julian.

The excitement of the night made them all sleep late. Julian awoke first, and stared at the low ceiling in surprise. Now – where was he? In France? No. Ah, of course he was in the old ruined cottage!

He woke Dick, who yawned and stretched. 'Remember those strange lights and noises last night?' asked Dick. 'What a fright they gave us! It seems silly to think we were all so puzzled and scared, now that the sun is shining in at the window, and we can see the countryside around for miles!'

'I'm pretty certain someone is trying to scare us away,' said Julian. 'We are in their way here – they want to do some thorough explorations and they can't, because of us! I've a good mind to take the girls home, Dick, and come back here with you.'

'Anne might go, but George wouldn't,' said Dick. 'You know what old George is – she doesn't like to miss out. Let's not decide anything till we have had a look round this morning. I don't really believe there's anything spooky about this at all – I agree with you that it's just a few tricks to frighten us away.'

'Right,' said Julian. 'Let's wake the girls. Hey, George! Anne! Sleepyheads! Get up and get us breakfast!'

George sat up, looking furious, as Julian intended. 'You jolly well get your own b . . .' she began, and then laughed as she saw Julian's amused face.

'I was only just striking a little match to set you alight!' said Julian. 'Come on – let's all go for a swim in the pool!'

They set off together happily in the warm sunshine, Timmy padding along, his tail waving vigorously. As soon as they got to the pool, they saw the boy there, floating lazily on his back.

'There's Guy!' said Anne.

'I wonder if he will admit to his name or not this morning!' said George. 'Remember how he told us his name was Guy – and then said it wasn't a little while after? Silly ass! I can't make out if he's quite mad, or just thinks it's funny to keep playing the fool!'

They came to the pool. The boy waved to them, grinning. 'Come on in – it's fine!'

'Is your name Guy this morning or not?' called George.

The boy looked surprised. 'Of course it's Guy!' he said. 'Don't be idiotic! Come on in and have a game.'

They had a fine swim and a mad one. Guy was like an eel, swimming under the water, catching their legs, splashing, swimming away fast, doubling round and going underwater just as they got up to him!

At last they all sat panting on the edge of the pond, the sun shining down warmly on them.

'I say, Guy – did you hear anything strange last night?' asked Dick. 'Or see anything?'

'I didn't *see* anything strange – but I thought I heard somebody wailing and crying in the distance,' said Guy. 'Just now and again when the wind brought the sound this way. Jet didn't like it at all – did you, Jet? He went and hid under my legs!'

'We heard it too – quite near us,' said Julian. 'And saw strange lights.'

They discussed the matter for some time, but Guy could not really help them, because he had not been near enough to the noises to hear them as clearly as the others had.

'I'm getting hungry,' said George, at last. 'I keep

thinking of ham and tomatoes and cheese. Let's go back to the cottage.'

'Right,' said Julian. 'Good-bye, Guy – see you some-time soon. Good-bye, Jet, you mad little thing.'

They went off together, their swimsuits almost dry already in the sun.

'Well, Guy was perfectly sensible this morning,' said Anne. 'Funny! I wonder why he's so silly sometimes.'

'See – isn't that him – running down the path there – to the right, look!' said George, suddenly. 'Now how did he get there so quickly? We left him by the pool!'

It certainly looked like Guy! They called to him, but he didn't even look round or wave, though he must have heard them. They went on, puzzled. How could one person be so different each time – and why? What was the point?

They had a good breakfast and then went out to look round and see if they could find anything to explain the strange happenings of the night before.

'The noises seemed to come from about here, when I came out last night,' said Julian, stopping near the little group of trees. 'And the lights seemed to start about here too – but not near the ground – they were high up, above my head.'

'Above your head?' said Dick, puzzled. 'That seems odd.'

'It doesn't!' said Anne. 'Not a *bit* odd! What about those trees there? Couldn't somebody climb up them and do the wailing and whining there, with some strange instrument – and set off the weird lights?'

Julian stared up at the trees and then round at Anne. He grinned suddenly.

'Anne's got it! Clever girl! Of course someone was up there – or maybe two people – one doing the noises with some weird instrument and the other playing about with fireworks of some kind. Not the noisy kind – just coloured fire or balloons lit up from inside.'

'Yes! *That's* why the lights seemed to be so high up, when you came out!' said Dick. 'They were sent out by someone up in a tree!'

'And floated away to scare us,' said Anne. 'Golly – I *do* feel glad that it was silly tricks like that that frightened us so. They wouldn't frighten me *again*!'

'It explains something else too,' said George. 'It explains why Timmy didn't find anyone! They were safely up trees! I bet they hardly breathed when they knew Tim was down below.'

'Yes. Of course! That puzzled me too,' said Julian. 'It

93

was too spooky for words when even old Tim couldn't find anyone real about – just noises and lights!'

'Here's something, look – a wrinkled little rubber-skin – pale green!' said Dick, picking something up from the ground. 'That's what those lights were – balloons lit up from inside in some way and sent floating away in the air.'

'Most ingenious,' said Julian. 'I expect they had quite a lot of funny tricks at their disposal last night. Yes – they certainly mean to scare us away!'

'Well, they won't,' said Anne, unexpectedly. '*I'm* not going, for one. I won't be scared away by stupid tricks!'

'Good old Anne!' said Julian, and clapped her on the back. 'Right – we'll all stay – but I've got an idea.'

'What?' asked everyone.

'We'll *pretend* to go!' said Julian. 'We'll pack up everything – remove our things from here – and go and camp somewhere else. But Dick and I will *hide* somewhere here tonight – and watch to see if anyone comes, and where they look for whatever it is they're hunting for, and why!'

'That's a fantastic plan,' said Dick, pleased. 'We'll do it! Roll on, tonight! Adventure is about – and we'll be ready for it!'

CHAPTER TWELVE

A good hiding place

THE FIVE spent quite a pleasant day, but when late afternoon came, they decided that it was time to carry out their plan and pack as if they were leaving.

'I imagine someone is spying on our doings,' said Dick. 'And won't he be pleased to see us apparently on the point of leaving!'

'How can anyone be spying?' asked Anne, looking all round as if she expected to see someone behind a bush. 'Timmy would be sure to sniff out anyone in hiding.'

'Oh, he won't be near enough for Timmy to smell out,' said Dick. 'He'll be a long way off.'

'Then how can he possibly see us – or know that we're leaving?' asked Anne.

'Anne – I don't know if you've heard of field-glasses,' began Dick, solemnly. 'Well, they're things that can spot anything half a mile away . . .'

Anne went red and gave Dick a punch. 'Don't be an ass! Of course – that's it! Field-glasses used by someone on a hillside somewhere – trained on the old cottage.'

'Actually I think I know where the someone is,' said Dick. 'I've caught sight of a little flash every now and again on the hill over there – the kind of flash that is made by the sun on glass – and I somehow think that our spy is sitting near the top of the hill, watching us carefully.'

Anne turned to look at the hill, but Julian at once

spoke sharply. 'No – don't stand and stare up there, anyone. We don't want the watcher to know that *we* know we are being watched.'

They went on with their packing, and soon began to stagger out with their bundles. George was told to strap her things on her bicycle, and stand well out in the open as she did so, so that the watcher on the hill would be able to observe all her doings.

Julian was in the midst of carefully folding up his things to go into his knapsack, when Anne gave a sudden exclamation.

'Someone's coming!'

Everyone looked round, imagining that they would see a sinister-looking foreigner, or someone peculiar in some way.

But all they saw was a countrywoman hurrying along, a shawl over her head, and a basket under her arm. She wore glasses, had no make-up on, and her hair was pulled straight back under the shawl. She stopped when she saw the Five.

'Good afternoon,' said Julian, politely. 'Isn't it glorious weather!'

'Beautiful,' said the woman. 'Are you camping out – you've certainly chosen a very good time!'

'No – actually we're packing,' said Julian. 'We've been sleeping in the old cottage, but we've decided to move out. Is it very, very old?'

'Oh yes – and it's supposed to have strange things happening in it at nights,' said the woman.

'We know that!' said Julian. 'My word – we were pretty scared last night, I can tell you – weird noises and horrible, ghostly lights. We decided not to stay there any longer.'

'That's right,' said the woman. 'Don't you stay! You get as far from this place as you can! I can tell you, *I* wouldn't come by it at night. Where are you going?'

'Well, our home is at Kirrin,' said Julian, evading the question. 'You know – on Kirrin Bay.'

'Ah yes – a fine place,' said the woman. 'Well, don't you stay another night! Good-bye!'

She hurried off, and was soon lost to sight.

'Go on packing,' said Julian to the others.

'The watcher is still up in the hills. I caught sight of a flash again just then.'

'Julian, why did you tell all that to the woman?' asked Anne. 'You don't usually say so much when we are in the middle of something funny!'

'My dear, unsuspecting Anne – do you mean to say that you thought that woman was really what she pretended to be – a woman from a nearby farm?' said Julian.

'Well – wasn't she?' said Anne, surprised. 'She looked like one – no make-up – and that old shawl – and she knew all about the old cottage!'

'Anne – farm women don't have gold fillings in their teeth,' said Julian. 'Didn't you notice them when she smiled?'

'And her hair was dyed,' said George. 'I noticed it was blonde at the roots and black above.'

'*And* what about her hands?' said Dick. 'A farmer's wife does a great deal of hard, rough work, and her hands are never white and smooth – they are rough and brown. This woman's hands were as white as a princess's!'

'Well yes, I did notice them,' said Anne. 'And I did notice too that she sometimes spoke with an accent and sometimes without.'

'Well, there you are!' said Julian. 'She's one of the unpleasant gang that tried to scare us last night – and when the watcher on the hill reported that we appeared to be packing up and going, she was told to go and make sure. So she pretended to be a country-woman and came by – but unfortunately we weren't quite so stupid as she thought we would be!'

'You certainly fooled her!' said Dick, with a grin. 'The gang will be down here tonight, digging up all the big stones they can find. You and I will have a marvellous time, snooping round them.'

'You'll be careful they don't see you, won't you?' said Anne. 'Where will you hide?'

'We haven't planned that yet,' said Dick. 'Now come on and we'll make a new camp somewhere that won't be easily seen. You and George and Timmy can sleep there tonight, and Ju and I will come and watch here.'

'I want to come too,' said George at once. 'Anne will be all right with Timmy.'

'You aren't joining us this time, George,' said Ju. 'The fewer people watching the better. Sorry, old thing – but you'll have to stay with Anne.'

George scowled and looked sulky at once. Julian laughed and slapped her on the shoulder. 'What a *lovely* scowl! One of your best! I haven't seen it for quite a long time. Keep it up, George – go on, scowl a bit harder, it suits you!'

George grinned unwillingly, and pulled herself together. She hated being left out of anything, but she did see that it was no use having a crowd of people watching that night. All right, she would stay with Anne and keep her company.

It seemed as if the watcher on the hills must have gone, because there were no more sudden flashes such as came when he lifted his field-glasses to watch the Five.

'That disguised countrywoman has convinced the watcher that we're going! Any ideas, anyone, where we can go? Not too far away – but somewhere where the watcher can't follow us with his glasses, if he's still up there.'

'I know a place,' said George. 'There's a simply colossal gorse bush on the other side of the spring. And underneath it is all hollow and dry. It's almost like a kind of gorse cave.'

'Sounds all right,' said Julian. 'Let's go and find it.'

George led the way, trying to remember exactly where it was. Timmy followed, still in his enormous cardboard collar, which was now rather the worse for wear. George stopped when they had gone a little way past the spring.

'It was somewhere here,' she said. 'I know I could still hear the sound of the spring when I found the hollow under the bush. Ah – there it is!'

It certainly was a great bush, green and spiky outside, with a few yellow blooms on it still. Under it was a big hollow place, where the ground was soft and fine, scattered with dry old prickles.

The main trunk – for it was almost a trunk that supported the big bush – was not quite in the middle, so there was a good bit of room. Julian caught hold of the branches that hid the hollow, using a folded sheet of paper to hold them by, for the bush was very prickly.

'This is fine,' he said. 'Plenty of room for you two girls – and Timmy. My word, he'll have difficulty with his collar though, won't he – squeezing in and out!'

'Take it off!' said Dick. 'His ear really is practically healed now. Even if he scratches it, he can't do much damage. Dear old Timmy, we simply shan't *know* you without your collar.'

'Right,' said George. She took a quick look at the ear. It was still covered by a piece of elastoplast, but it was quite obvious that the ear was healthy. She cut the thread that bound the two ends of the circular collar and then bent it so that it came off.

They all stared at Timmy, who looked most surprised. He wagged his tail gently as if to say 'Well – so you've taken that thing off – I wonder why?'

'Oh Tim – you look sort of *undressed* without that collar now!' said Anne. 'It *is* nice to see you without it, though. Good old Tim! You'll guard me and George tonight, won't you? *You* know that we're in the Middle of Something again, don't you?'

'Woof,' said Timmy, wagging his tail violently. 'Woof!' Yes – he knew all right!

CHAPTER THIRTEEN

On watch in the cottage

IT WAS getting dark – and under the gorse bush it was very dark indeed! All the Five had managed to squeeze in there, and Timmy too. One torch only was allowed to be used at a time, to save the batteries of the others.

The Five were having supper. The ham was now practically finished, but there were still a few tomatoes and plenty of cake.

Julian opened the last tin of sardines, and made some sandwiches for himself and Dick to take with them. He also wrapped up two enormous chunks of cake and pocketed two slabs of chocolate each.

'We shall need something to while away the time when we're on the watch tonight!' he said, with a grin. 'I don't know if the Weepies and Wailies and Floating Lights will be along to give us a show – but I fear not. They would be wasted on an empty cottage!'

'I do hope you'll be careful,' said Anne.

'Anne – that's the seventh time you've said that,' said Dick. 'Don't be an ass. Don't you understand that Ju and I are going to *enjoy* ourselves? You'll be the one that has to be careful.'

'How?' asked Anne, surprised.

'Well – you'll have to be careful of that big black beetle squatting over there,' said Dick. 'And mind that a hedgehog doesn't sit down on your bare legs. And be careful in case a snake wants to share this nice safe warm place with you . . .'

'Now *you're* being an ass!' said Anne, giving him a punch. 'When will you be back?'

'We shall be back at exactly the moment you hear us squeezing under here,' said Julian. 'Now Dick – what about it? I think we might be going, don't you?'

'Right,' said Dick, and began to squeeze out carefully so as not to be pricked more than he could help. 'Oh – why are gorse bushes so horribly spiteful! Jab jab – anyone would think the bush was *trying* to prick me!'

The two girls sat quite still when the boys had gone from the bush. They tried to hear their footsteps, but they couldn't. Dick and Julian trod too softly on the wiry grass.

'I do so hope they'll be . . .' began Anne, and George groaned.

'If you say that again I shall slap you, Anne! Honestly I shall.'

'I *wasn't* saying it,' said Anne, 'I was only going to say that I hope they'll be *successful* tonight. I'd like to get back to Kirrin and have some fun bathing and boating, wouldn't you?'

'Yes. And some of Joanna's marvellous cooking,' said George. 'Sausages and mash – and tomatoes with it.'

'Yes. And fried plaice fresh from the sea with Joanna's best chipped potatoes,' said Anne. 'I can almost smell it.'

'Woof,' said Timmy, sniffing hard.

'There! He thought I meant it!' said Anne. 'Isn't Timmy clever?'

They had a pleasant talk about how very very clever Timmy was, and Timmy listened and wagged his tail so hard that he made it quite dusty in the gorse hollow.

'Let's go to sleep,' said Anne. 'We can't talk all night – and keeping awake won't help the boys!'

They curled up on the rug they had brought and cuddled together – not so much for warmth, because it was a hot night, but because there was so little room! Anne put out her torch, and the little place immediately became black and dark. Timmy put his head on George's tummy. She groaned.

'Oh Tim – be careful, please! I had rather a lot of supper!'

Anne giggled and pulled Timmy's head close to her. It was comforting to have old Timmy there. She agreed with George that he was the best dog in the whole world.

'I wonder what the boys are doing now,' she said, after a while. 'Do you suppose they are in the middle of something exciting? Perhaps they are!'

But they weren't! Julian and Dick were feeling extremely bored at that minute. They had gone cautiously to the cottage when they had left the girls, not using their torches at all, for fear of giving anyone warning that they were about. They had debated beforehand where would be the best place to hide, and had decided that it would be a good idea to climb up the little stone stair and hide in the roofless rooms above.

'There's no roof there – and hardly any walls,' said Dick. 'We can peep over any side to watch – and no one would guess that anyone was above them, spying down! It's a good thing it's such a starry night – once we get used to the dim light, we shall be able to see fairly well. Pity there's no moon.'

They had approached the cottage very cautiously indeed, stopping at every step and listening with bated breath for any sound. But there was none.

'Not even the light of somebody's torch, either,' said Dick in Julian's ear. 'I don't think anyone is here yet. Let's get into the cottage and up those stairs as soon as we can.'

They tiptoed into the cottage, not daring to put on their torches. They fumbled across to the little stone stairway, and climbed it with as little sound as they could. Holding their breath made their hearts thump loudly.

'Can you hear my heart thumping?' Dick whispered to Julian, as they at last stood on the floor of the roofless rooms above.

'No. Mine's just the same, thumping away! Well, we're safely here. Let's just shuffle to and fro and see if there are any loose stones we might fall over, and so give ourselves away!'

They cleared away a few loose stones, and then sat

down silently on the low broken wall of the two ruined rooms. The wind blew gently but warmly. Everything was still except the rose-rambler climbing over the old house. It moved a little in the wind and made a faint scraping noise. Dick caught his hand on a thorn, and sucked his finger. The rambler was everywhere, across the floor, and over the walls and even up what was left of the little chimney.

The boys had been there for about three-quarters of an hour when Julian gave Dick a slight nudge.

'Here they come!' he whispered. 'See – over there!'

Dick looked round and about and then caught sight of a small, moving light, just a prick in the darkness. It cast a faint glow before it.

'A torch!' he whispered. 'And another – and another! Quite a procession! A slow one, too.'

The procession made very little noise. It made its way to the cottage, and then split up,

'Having a look to see if we really *are* gone,' whispered Julian. 'Hope they won't think of coming up here.'

'Let's get behind the chimney, in case,' whispered back Dick. So very quietly they rose and made their way to where the remains of the chimney stood, a dark shadow in the starry night. The chimney was quite big, though rather crumbly. The two boys crouched close to it, on the side farthest from where the stone stairway came up in the corner.

'Someone *is* coming up!' whispered Dick, his sharp ears catching the sound of someone's feet on the stone stairs. 'I hope he gets caught by the rambler – there's a big spray near the top!'

'Sh!' said Julian.

Someone came right up the stairway, and gave a sharp exclamation of annoyance near the top. 'Good!' thought Dick. 'He *has* got caught by the rambler!'

A torch shone out over the ruined rooms, the crumbling walls and the remains of the chimney. The boys held their breath, and stood like statues. The light of the torch played over the place for one second and then a voice called down the stairs.

'No one here. The kids have gone. We can get on with the job!'

The boys let out a long breath. Good – they were safe – for the time being at any rate! The visitors down below were no longer cautious – they spoke in ordinary voices and torches flashed all over the place. Then someone lit two lanterns, and the little cottage shone quite brightly.

'Where do we start?' said a voice. 'Here, Jess – where's that plan?'

'I've got it. I'll spread it on the floor,' said a voice that the boys recognised at once. It was the voice of the 'countrywoman' who had spoken to them that day! 'Not that it's much use. Paul's no good at drawing!'

Evidently the searchers were now leaning over the plan. Voices came up the stone stairway.

'All we know for certain is that we have to find that white stone slab – and we know the size. But we don't know the place, except that we think it *must* be here. After all – we've searched the old Roman camp, and there are no slabs there that size!'

Julian nudged Dick. So some of the visitors that Guy had complained of must have been these searchers! Whatever was it they were looking for, hidden behind a slab of stone?

He knew a minute later! A drawling voice said: 'If we have to get up every great slab in this neighbourhood, we will. I'm going to find that secret way if it's the last thing I do! If we don't find that, we don't find those blueprints – and if we don't find *them*, we might as well go into the poorhouse for the rest of our lives.'

'Or prison!' said someone.

'Not prison,' said the drawling voice. 'It'll be Paul who goes to prison. *He* managed to steal them, we didn't!'

'Can't you get Paul to draw a better plan than this?' said the voice of the 'countrywoman'. 'I can't understand half that's written here.'

'He's ill – almost off his head, too,' said someone. 'No good asking him. He had such a time escaping with those prints, he nearly died. No good asking him, I say.'

'I can't make out this word here,' said the woman. ' "W-A-D-E-R" – whatever does it mean?'

'I don't know – wait, though, I do! It might be W-A-T-E-R – water. T not D in the middle. Where's the well? Anywhere in this kitchen? That's it, that's it. *Water!* I bet there's a slab over the well. That's the way to the secret hiding place!'

Julian clutched Dick. He was as excited as the man down below. They listened eagerly, straining their ears.

'Here's the old sink – and this must be the remains of the pump. The well's underneath this slab – and see the stone is just about the right size. Get busy! Buck up, get busy!'

CHAPTER FOURTEEN

An exciting night – and a surprising morning

SOON THERE came the sound of loud breathing and grunts, as the searchers tried to prise up the stone by the pump. It was obviously very heavy, and very difficult to move, for it had become almost part of the floor itself, through the centuries!

'Drat the thing! It's tearing my hands to pieces!' said a voice. 'Lend me that jemmy, Tom – you don't seem to be doing much good with it!'

After a lot more struggling and panting the stone was loosened. 'Up she comes!' said a voice, and up came the stone so suddenly that it sounded as if most of those pulling at it had sat down very hard on the floor!

The two hidden boys were beside themselves with interest and excitement. How they wished they could go and watch! But it was impossible. They must just listen and try to make out what was happening from what the men said below them.

'Is it a well down there? Yes, it is! My, the water's pretty far down – and black as pitch too.'

There was a silence as the well was examined in the light of torches. Then an exasperated voice, the one with the drawl, said: '*This* is no secret way! Who's going to get through that water! It's just an ordinary small well, and nothing else. That word *can't* have meant Water.'

'All right, boss. What *does* it mean then?' said the woman. '*I* don't know. This isn't a plan, it's a riddle!

110

Why couldn't Paul have made it clear where the stone
slab is – he just goes and does a lot of scribble round it –
and all we can make out is that it's on this common,
somewhere near here – and the secret way is behind the
slab!'

'And all we have to do is to go and look behind dozens
of heavy slabs!' said someone else. 'I'm fed up. We've
lifted slabs in that wretched camp – we've lifted some
here – and we still don't know if we're anywhere near the
right one.'

'Shut up,' said the voice of the drawler but now the
voice was sharp and angry. 'If we have to pull this
cottage down, if we have to lift every slab there is, if
we have to take over that camp, I'll do it! I tell you, this
makes all the difference between wealth and poverty!
Anyone who wants to back out can do so – but he'd
better be careful!'

'Now boss, now boss, don't you fly off the handle!'
said the woman. 'We're all in this! We'll do all you say.
Look, let's start by lifting a few more slabs. There are not
so very many that are the size that Paul figured on this
plan.'

Then began a boring time for the two hidden boys, as
slab after slab was lifted and put back. Nothing was
found under any of them, apparently.

The men went to the outbuildings too, leaving the
woman in the cottage. The boys thought she had gone as
well, and Julian moved a little, feeling rather cramped
after being still for so long. The woman's ears must have
been sharp for she called out at once.

'Who's there? Is it you, Tom?'

The boys stiffened and stood like statues. The woman

said no more. It was not long before the men came back, talking among themselves. It sounded as if there were three of them.

'No go,' said the drawler. 'I think we'll have to search that camp really well again.'

'That's going to be difficult with someone already there,' said the woman.

'We'll deal with him,' said a voice, grimly. Julian frowned. Did that mean that Guy was in danger? He had better warn him!

'I'm fed up with this place,' said the woman. 'Let's go. I don't think the slab is anywhere here! We're wasting our time!'

To the boys' great relief, the four searchers left the cottage and went off together. Julian and Dick leaned over the crumbling wall of the room they stood in, and watched the lights of the torches and lanterns getting dimmer and dimmer over the common. Good! Now they could go back to the girls!

'I'm stiff!' said Dick, stretching himself.

'Well, Ju – we know a lot more now, don't we? It's clear that someone called Paul had stolen some valuable blueprints of something – maybe a new plane, or battle-ship perhaps – and has hidden them in some secret place he knew of about here – and to get to it you have to lift a slab of stone of a certain size.'

'Yes. And we know the size because we've already seen the one they lifted in the old stables,' said Julian. 'I vote we go there and measure it – or measure the one by the sink. I should think that the right slab will be somewhere in the old camp. We'd better tell Guy and let him into the secret. He'll help us to search!'

'What a peculiar business this is to find ourselves mixed up in,' said Dick. 'All because George didn't like people laughing at old Timmy with a cardboard collar round his neck! Timmy's the cause of this!'

The boys went down the stone stairs, and, of course, Dick quite forgot about the rambler, which caught him neatly round the ankle and almost tripped him headlong down the stairs!

'Blow!' he said, clutching Julian and nearly making him topple too. 'Sorry. It was that rambler again. It's ripped my ankle all round. Put on the torch for goodness sake.'

They carefully measured the stone slab by the sink and then made their way out of the cottage and up towards the spring, hoping that they would find the great gorse bush in the dark. They tried to get under the wrong one at first, but at last found the right one. They heard a small welcome bark from Timmy.

'Oh! Julian! Dick! Is it you?' said Anne's voice, as the boys squeezed through into the hollow middle. 'Oh, what AGES you've been! We haven't slept a wink. Keep still, Timmy, do – this place is too small for you to rampage about in!'

The boys settled down and torches were put on. Julian related the curious happenings to the two interested girls. George was thrilled.

'Oh I *say*! Fancy all this springing up out of the blue so suddenly! What are you going to do?'

'Warn Guy first thing in the morning – and then get in touch with the police, I think,' said Julian. 'We ourselves can't stop the men searching the camp, and as soon as they *do* find the slab they're looking for, they can easily get what they want and go off with it!'

'Well, it's really thrilling,' said George. 'I wish I'd been with you. 'I'll never go to sleep tonight!'

But they did manage to drop off to sleep, for they were all very tired. After a few hours, just as dawn was breaking, Timmy lifted his head and growled. George awoke at once.

'What is it, Tim? I can't hear anything.'

But Timmy could, that was certain. George woke Julian, and made him listen to Timmy's continuous growling.

'What do you think he's growling at?' she asked. 'He keeps on and on. I can't hear a thing, can you?'

'No,' said Julian, listening. 'Well, it's no use my creeping out and going searching in the dark for whatever Timmy's growling at. It might be something silly like a weasel or a hedgehog or a stoat. Shut up, Tim. That's enough.'

Although it was as dark as night under the thick old gorse bush, outside it was just getting light. What *was* Timmy growling at? Were there people about again? Or was it just one of the hedgehogs he so heartily disliked?

He stopped growling at last and put his head down on his paws, closing his eyes. George patted him.

'Well, whatever it was, it's gone. Are you comfy, Julian? It's very cramped in here – and hot too, isn't it?'

'Yes. We'll get up fairly early and go to warn Guy – then we'll have a swim,' said Julian, yawning. He switched off his torch and went to sleep again.

It was late when they awoke. Dick was the first, and he looked at his watch. He gave an exclamation.

'Gosh! It's half past eight! Hey, Ju – Anne – George wake up, it's almost afternoon!'

Everyone felt stiff and cramped, and they went off to have a swim and to warn Guy. As they came near the camp, they stopped in amazement.

Someone was howling down in the trench, howling so miserably and so broken-heartedly that the Five felt quite panic-stricken. Whatever in the world could have happened? They ran to the edge of the excavations and looked down into the trench.

The boy was there, lying on his face, sobbing. He kept lifting his head and howling, then putting it down again.

'Guy! GUY! Whatever's happened?' shouted Julian. He leapt down beside the boy. 'Are you hurt? Is Jet hurt? What's the matter?'

'It's Guy! He's gone! They've taken him,' howled the boy. 'And I was so awful to him. Now he's gone. He'll never come back, I know he won't!'

'Guy's gone? But – but *you're* Guy!' said Julian in astonishment. 'What do you mean?'

He felt sure that the boy really *was* mad now – quite mad – talking about himself like that. He patted him on the shoulder. 'Look, you're ill. You come along with us. You need a doctor.'

The boy sprang to his feet, his face swollen and stained. 'I'm not ill! I tell you Guy's gone. I'm *not* Guy. He's my twin. There are two of us.'

Everyone gasped. It took half a minute to think about this and get everything straight – and then, of course many things were clear! There was not one mad boy, there were two ordinary boys – but they were twins! There wasn't, as they had thought, just *one* boy who contradicted himself all the time, who seemed continually to appear suddenly and unexpectedly, and who was sometimes nice and sometimes not.

'Twins! Why on earth didn't we think of that before?' said Julian. 'We thought there was only one of you. You were never together.'

'No. We quarrelled – quarrelled bitterly,' said the boy, tears in his eyes again. 'And when twins quarrel, *really* quarrel, it's worse than any quarrel there is! We hated one another then – we really did! We wouldn't be with one another, we wouldn't eat together, or dig together, or sleep together. We've often quarrelled before, but not like this – not like this! I just pretended that he didn't exist – and he did the same with me!'

'What a to-do!' said Julian, astonished and worried.

'Well now, what's happened to make you so upset? Tell me!'

'Guy wanted to be friends with me again last night,' said the boy. 'And I wouldn't. I hit him and walked away. Then this morning I was sorry and went to find him and be friends – and – and . . .'

He stopped and howled again. Everyone felt very sad and uncomfortable. 'Go on, tell us,' said Julian, gently.

'I was just in time to see him fighting two men, and screaming at them, and kicking – then they hustled him away somewhere!' said the boy. 'I fell down in the trench and hurt my leg – and by the time I dragged myself up, Guy had gone – and so had everyone else!'

He turned away and wept again. 'I'll never forgive myself, never! If I'd made friends last night I could have helped him – and I didn't!'

CHAPTER FIFTEEN

Well done, George!

IT WAS Anne who comforted the boy. She went to him and pulled him down on a stone beside her. 'Let me look at your leg,' she said. 'It's pretty bad, isn't it? Look, I'll bind it up for you. Don't be so upset – we'll help you. I think we know what's happened, don't we Julian?'

The boy looked at Anne gratefully, and sniffed hard. When she offered him her handkerchief, he took it and wiped his face. Dick gave Anne his big hanky to bind up the boy's cut and bruised leg. He must have fallen right into the trench in his fright at seeing his brother fighting and being taken away.

'How do *you* know what's happened?' he said to Julian. 'Can you get Guy back? Do say you can! I'll never forgive myself for this. My twin brother – and I wasn't there to fight by his side when he needed me!'

'Now don't soak my hanky all over again!' said Anne. He gave her a forlorn little smile and turned to Julian again.

'My name's Harry Lawdler, and Guy and I are mad on old camps and buildings and things. We spend almost all our holidays together, digging and finding all kinds of things, like these.' He nodded his head towards the little shelf of relics that the four had seen before.

'Yes, Guy told us,' said Dick. 'But he never said a word about you. We were often very puzzled – we thought you and he were one boy – not two, you see

119

– and we couldn't understand a lot of things you both said. You're so very, very alike.'

'Well, I tell you, we each pretended that the other didn't even exist,' said Harry. 'We're like that. We love each other best in the world, and we hate each other worst – when we quarrel. We're simply *horrible* then!'

'Can you tell us a bit about the people that Guy was fighting?' asked Dick.

'Yes. They were some that came before, wanting Guy to clear out while they had a look round,' said Harry, wiping his face again. 'Guy was pretty rude to them. In fact I heard him say that if they messed about his camp he would throw stones at them – he's like that, you know, very fierce, when he's roused.'

'And you think these were the same people?' said Dick. 'Which way did they go with Guy?'

'That way,' said Harry, pointing. 'I've hunted the whole camp round, but they're gone – disappeared into thin air! It's extraordinary!'

'Let's have a hunt round,' said Julian. 'We might find something. But I imagine that the searchers have taken Guy off with them because he knew too much – perhaps they found here what they were looking for, and saw Guy watching.'

'Oh! Then we're too late!' said George, in deep disappointment. 'They've got what they want – and they'll disappear now and never be caught. I expect by now they are speeding away in a fast car – and have taken Guy with them to make sure he doesn't talk before they're safely in another country!'

'Oh no!' cried Harry. 'He's not kidnapped, is he? Don't say that!'

'Come on – let's have a hunt,' said Julian, and they all made their way among the various trenches and pits, looking for they hardly knew what.

They gave it up after a while. There were too many slabs and stones of all sizes! Besides, what good would it be even if they found the right one? The birds had flown – presumably with what they had come for! In fact, if Guy hadn't come along and seen the searchers, nobody would even have known that they had been in the camp and made a successful search!

'It's no good,' said Julian, at last. 'This is too big a place to know where to look for anything that might help us. Let's go back to the gorse bush and collect our things, return to Kirrin and go to the police. It's the only sensible thing left to do!'

'Come along, Harry,' said Anne, to the miserable twin. He was so full of remorse that her handkerchief was now soaked for the third time! 'You'd better come with us and tell all you know.'

'I'll come,' said Harry. 'I'll do anything to get Guy back. I'll never quarrel with him again. Never. To think that . . .'

'Now don't go all through that again,' said Anne. 'Look, you're upsetting Timmy so much that his tail is down all the time!'

Harry gave another forlorn little smile. They all left the camp and made their way back to the gorse bush. It was only when they got there, and began pulling out the tins of food, as well as the rug and other things, that they realised how extremely hungry they were!

'We've had no breakfast. We've been up for ages, and it's very late. I'm simply starving!' said George.

'Well, if we finish up all the food, we shan't have to carry the tins!' said Dick. 'Let's have a meal. Ten minutes more here can't make much difference.'

They were thankful not to have to sit under the gorse bush again. They sat outside in the sun, and discussed everything.

'I believe when Timmy began to growl and growl about six o'clock this morning, it was because he could hear those people coming quietly by to go to search the camp,' said George.

'I think you're right,' said Julian. 'I bet they searched the camp well – till Guy woke and came on the scene and fought like fury. It's a pity I didn't squeeze out from under the bush and follow them, when Timmy growled.'

'Anyone want a drink?' said George. 'I'll go and fetch some water from the spring. Where's the pineapple tin?'

Anne passed it to her. George got up and took the little rabbit path that led to the spring. She could hear it gurgling and bubbling as she came near – a very pleasant noise.

'Water always sounds nice,' said George to herself. 'I love the sound of water.'

Water! Now why did that ring a bell in her mind just then? Who had been talking about water? Oh – Dick and Julian, of course, when they had come back from the old cottage last night. They had told Anne and herself about the word on the plan – the word that might have been WATER, not WADER.

'I wonder which it was,' said George to herself as she idly held the pineapple tin to the gurling water. She gazed at the beautiful little spring, jutting up from the stony slabs – and then another bell rang loudly in the mind.

'Stone slabs! Water! Why – I wonder – I just wonder –
if one of *these* slabs is the one! This one just here is about
the right size!'

She stared at it. It was set firmly in a high little bank at
the back of the place where the spring gurgled up and
then ran into the clean stony channel. *Did* it hide anything behind it?

George suddenly dropped the tin and ran back to the
others at full speed. 'Julian! Julian! I believe I've found
the slab! It's been staring us in the face the whole time!'

Julian was very startled. So were the others. They
stared up at George in astonishment.

'What do you mean, George?' said Julian, jumping to
his feet. 'Show me!'

Followed by everyone, George ran back to the spring.
She pointed to the white slab behind the water. 'There!'
she said. 'That's the right size, isn't it? And it's beside
WATER – just as it said in the plan you told us about –
only the people thought it was WADER.'

'Gosh, I wonder if you're right, George,' said Julian,
excited. 'You might be – you never know. Sometimes
springs come from underground passages – secret hidden
ways into the earth.'

'Let's try and move it,' said Dick, his face red with
sudden excitement. 'It looks pretty hefty to me.'

They began to struggle with the stone, getting extremely
wet as they splashed about in the spring. But nobody
minded that. This was too exciting for words. Harry helped
too, heaving and tugging. He was very strong indeed.

The stone slab moved a little. It slid to one side and
stuck. More tugging. More pulling. More panting and
puffing!

'I believe we'll have to get help,' said Julian at last. 'It really is too heavy and well-embedded.'

'I'll go and get some of my tools,' said Harry. 'I'm used to heaving stones about with them. We can easily move it if we have the right tools.'

He flew off at top speed. The others sat down and mopped their streaming foreheads.

'Phew!' said Julian. 'What a job this is for a hot day! I'm glad Harry remembered his tools. Just what we want!'

'How funny that he and Guy are twins!' said George. 'I never even thought of such a thing!'

'Well, they behaved so idiotically,' said Julian. 'Always pretending there was just one of them, and neither of them even mentioning the other. I wonder where Guy has been taken to. I don't think he'll come to much harm – but it will be worrying for his family.'

'Here comes Harry,' said Anne, after a pause. 'One of us ought to have gone with him to help him. He's brought dozens of tools!'

The things he had fetched proved very useful indeed, especially a big jemmy-like tool. The stone soon began to move when this was applied by Julian and Harry!

'It's slipping – it's coming away – look out, it will fall right down into the spring!' cried Dick. 'Look out, you girls!'

The stone was prised right out, and fell into the stony channel where the water ran. The five children stared at the opening it left.

Julian leaned forward and looked into it. 'Yes – there's a big hole behind,' he said. 'Let me shine my torch in.'

In great excitement he flashed his torch into the opening. He turned round, his face glowing.

'Yes! I think we've got it! There's a tunnel behind, going down and down. It widens out behind this hole!'

Everyone was too thrilled for words. George gave Dick a punch, and Anne patted Timmy so hard that he whined. Harry beamed round, all his woes forgotten.

'Do we go down now?' asked Dick. 'We'll have to make the opening a bit wider. Earth and roots have narrowed it very much. Let's make it bigger.'

'Then we'll explore it!' said George, her eyes shining. 'A secret tunnel only known to us! Quick – let's explore it!'

CHAPTER SIXTEEN

The secret way

ALL THE children were so excited that they got into each other's way. Julian pushed them back.

'Let's be sensible! We can't *all* make the opening wider – let Harry and me get at it with the tools – and we'll soon make it bigger!'

It took only a minute to hack away at the sides of the hole to make it big enough for even Julian to climb through. He stood there panting, smiling broadly.

'There – it's done! I'll get in first. Everyone got torches? We shall need them! It's going to be dark in there!'

He clambered up and into the hole. He had to crawl on hands and knees for a little way, and then the hole suddenly went downwards and became considerably bigger. Julian could walk in it, if he bent down, for at that point the tunnel was about three feet high.

He called back to the others. 'Follow me! Take hold of each other's shirts or jerseys and hang on. It's pitch black in here!'

George followed after Julian, then Anne, then Dick, then Harry. Timmy went with George, of course, pushing and shoving like all the rest. Everyone was excited, and nobody could talk in a normal voice. They all shouted!

'I'll give you a hand! One good shove and you're in!'

'I say – isn't it dark!'

'What a crawl! I feel like a fox going into its den!'

'Timmy, don't butt me from behind like that! I can't crawl any faster!'

'Ah – thank goodness I can stand up now! What size of rabbit do you think made *this* burrow!'

'It was made by water at some time perhaps. Don't *shove*, Timmy!'

'Water doesn't run uphill, ass! Hang on to my jersey, Harry. Don't get left behind.'

Julian, bent almost double at times, walked carefully along the narrow tunnel, which went steadily downwards. Soon it widened and became higher, and then it was easier to walk in comfort.

'Do you suppose this is the right secret way?' called George, after a time. 'We don't seem to be getting anywhere.'

'I can't tell. In fact we shan't know till we find something hidden somewhere – if we ever do!'

A sudden scuttering noise in front of him made Julian stop suddenly. Immediately everyone bumped into the one in front, and there were shouts at once.

'What's up, Ju?'

Julian's torch shone on to two pairs of bright, frightened eyes. He gave a laugh.

'It's all right – just a couple of rabbits using our burrow! There are small holes running out of the tunnel which, I imagine, are rabbit burrows. I bet we're giving the bunnies a shock!'

The tunnel wound about a good deal, and then suddenly the rather soft ground they were treading on turned to rock. The passage was now not so high, and the children had to bend down again. It was most uncomfortable.

Julian stopped once more. He had heard another sound. What was it?

'Water!' he said. 'There must be an underground stream here! How thrilling! Everyone all right?'

'Yes!' shouted those behind him. 'Get on, Julian – let's see the water!'

The tunnel suddenly ended, and Julian found himself in a big cave with a fairly high roof. Almost in the middle of it ran a stream – not a very big one, and not a very fast one. It gurgled along in a small channel of rock, which it had carved out for itself through hundreds of years.

Julian shone his torch on it. The water looked very black and glittered in the light of the torch. The others came one by one out of the tunnel and stared at the underground stream. It looked rather mysterious, slipping through the cave, gurgling quietly as it disappeared through a hole at one end.

'Strange,' said Dick.

'It's not unusual, this,' began Harry. 'In some parts of the country round about here, the ground below our feet is honeycombed with many little streams. Some come up as springs, of course, some join other streams when they come out into the open, others just run away goodness knows where!'

Julian was looking up round the cave. 'Does our tunnel end here?' he wondered. 'Is this where we have to look for whatever is hidden?'

'We'll have a look round the cave and see if there are any exits,' said Dick. Using their torches the five separated, Timmy keeping close to George, not seeming in the least surprised at this underground adventure.

'I've found another tunnel over here, leading out of the

cave!' called Dick. No sooner had he said that than Anne called out too.

'There's one here as well!'

'Now – which do we take?' said Julian. 'How annoying that there should be two!'

'Would the fellow – what's his name – Paul – have marked the correct underground way on his plan?' said George. 'I mean – I don't see how he could possibly expect either himself or anyone else to find what he had hidden, if there are numbers of passages to choose from down here!'

'You're right!' said Julian. 'Let's look about and see if we can find anything to help us.'

It wasn't long before Dick gave another shout. 'It's all right! This is the passage to take, over here – the one I found just now. There's an arrow drawn in white chalk on the wall.'

Everyone crowded over to Dick, stepping across the little stream as they did so. Dick held his torch up and they all saw the white arrow, drawn roughly on the wall.

Julian was pleased. 'Good. That helps a lot! It shows we're going the right way – and that this *is* the secret way that Paul chose. Come on!'

They entered the tunnel, left the little stream behind, and went on again. 'Anyone got any idea in which direction we're going?' called Dick. 'East, west, north, south?'

Harry had a compass. He looked at it. 'I think we're going rather in the direction of the old Roman camp,' he said.

'Ah – that's interesting,' said Julian. 'This tunnel was probably used in olden times.'

'Guy and I have seen the plan of the camp as it probably used to be,' said Harry. 'And there are plenty of tunnels and caves and holes shown on it – just roughed in, not a proper plan of them. Gosh, I never thought I'd be exploring one! My father warned me not to, in case of roof-falls and things like that.'

The tunnel suddenly forked into two. One passage was nice and wide, the other narrow. Julian took the wide one, thinking that the other was really too narrow to get through. But after a minute or two, he stopped, puzzled.

'There's a blank wall of rock here – the tunnel's ended! We'll have to turn back! I suppose we should have taken that very narrow opening.'

They went back, Harry leading the way now. Timmy suddenly took it into his head that *he* would like to lead, too, and made himself a real nuisance, pushing his way between everyone's legs!

They came back to the fork. Harry shone his torch in at the second opening, the very narrow one. There, clearly marked on the right hand wall, was a white arrow in chalk!

'We're idiots,' said Dick. 'We don't even look for the signposts! Lead the way, Julian!'

This tunnel was very narrow indeed, and had rough, jutting rocky sides. There were loud 'aahs!' and 'oohs!' as elbows and ankles were knocked against hard rock.

And then again there came a blank wall of rock in front of Julian, and again he had to stop!

'Can't go this way either!' he said. 'There's a blank wall again – this is a blind alley too!'

There were cries of dismay at once.

'Blow! It can't be!'

131

'What's gone wrong? Look all round, Ju – flash your torch down at your feet and above your head!'

Julian shone his torch over his head, and gave an exclamation.

'There's a hole above my head!'

'Is there a white arrow anywhere?' called Harry.

'Yes! And it's pointing up, instead of forwards!' called back Julian. 'We're still all right – we've got to go upwards now – but how?'

George, who was just behind him, shone her torch on the side walls. 'Look!' she said. 'We can easily get up to the hole. There are rough, natural steps up – made by ledges of rock. Look, Julian!'

'Yes,' said Julian. 'We can manage to get up quite easily, I think. George, you go first – I'll give you a boost up.'

George was delighted to go first. She put her torch between her teeth, and began to climb up the ledges, Julian pushing her as best he could. She came to the hole and immediately saw that it would be quite easy to hoist herself through.

'One more boost and I'll be through!' she called to Julian. And with one last heave George was up, rolling on the floor of a small cave above! She called down in excitement to the others.

'I believe this is the place where those things are hidden! I can see something on a ledge. Oh, do buck up!'

The others followed eagerly. Dick slipped off the rocky ledges in his excitement and almost squashed poor Harry as he fell on him. However, everyone was up at last, even Timmy, who was the most difficult of all to heave through! He seemed to have far too many vigorous legs!

Harry found no difficulty at all. 'I'm used to this kind of thing,' he said. 'Guy and I have explored a whole lot of tunnels and caves in hills and other places.'

George was pointing her torch at a broad ledge of rock. On it was a brown leather bag, and beside it, marked on the rock, was a very large arrow indeed.

Julian was overjoyed. He picked up the bag at once. 'My word – I hope there's something in it!' he said. 'It feels jolly light – as if it's empty!'

'Open it!' cried everyone – but Julian couldn't. It was locked – and alas, there wasn't a key!

CHAPTER SEVENTEEN

Full of surprises

'It's LOCKED – we can't open the bag,' said Julian, and shook it vigorously as if that might make it fly open and spill whatever contents it had!

'We don't know if it's got anything of value in it or not,' said Dick, in deep disappointment. 'I mean – it might be some trick on that fellow Paul's part – he might have taken the blueprints, or whatever they were he hid, for himself, and left the bag just to trick the others.'

'Can we cut it open?' asked George.

'No. I don't think so. It's made of really strong leather. We would need a special knife to cut through it – an ordinary pen-knife wouldn't be any use,' said Julian. 'I think we'll just have to assume that we've got the goods, and hope for the best. If they're not in here, it's just bad luck. Someone else has got them, if so.'

They all looked at the tantalising bag.

Now they would have to wait for ages before they found out whether their efforts had been successful or not!

'Well – what do we do now?' said George, feeling suddenly flat. 'Go back all through that long tunnel once more? I'll be glad to be in the open air again, won't you?'

'You bet!' said Julian. 'Well – I suppose we'd better get down through that hole again.'

'Wait!' said Anne, her sharp eyes catching sight of something. 'Look – what does all this mean?'

She shone her torch on to various signs on the wall. Again there were arrows drawn in white chalk – but very oddly, a line of them ran downwards across the wall of the little rocky room, right to the edge of the hole – and another line of arrows pointing the *other* way, ran horizontally across the wall!

'Well, do you suppose that's just meant to muddle people?' said Dick, puzzled. 'We know jolly well that the way out of this room is down that hole, because that's the way we came into it.'

'Perhaps the other line of arrows means that there's a second way out,' suggested George. They all looked round the little rocky room. There didn't seem any way out at all.

'Where's Timmy?' said Anne, suddenly, flashing her torch round. 'He's not here! Has he fallen down the hole? I never heard him yelp!'

At once there was a great to-do. 'Timmy, Timmy, Timmy! TIMMY! Where are you?'

George whistled shrilly, and the noise echoed round and round the little room. Then, from somewhere, there was a bark. How relieved everyone was.

'Where is he? Where did that bark come from?' said Dick. 'It didn't sound as if it came from below, down that hole!'

There came another welcome bark, and the sound of Timmy's feet. Then to everyone's amazement, he appeared in the little rocky room as if by magic – appearing straight out of the wall, it seemed!

'Timmy! Where were you? Where have you come from?' cried George, and ran to see. She came to a standstill and exclaimed loudly.

'Oh! What idiots we are! Why, just behind this big jutting-out piece of rock, there's another passage!'

So there was! A very, very narrow one, it is true – and completely hidden from the children because of the enormous slab of rock that jutted out from the wall that hid it! They stood and stared at it, shining their torches on the narrow way. The arrows ran round the wall to it.

'We never even looked properly!' said Dick. 'Still – it's a passage that would be extremely difficult to spot – hidden round the corner of that rock – and very narrow at that. Well, I do know one thing for certain about that man called Paul!'

'What?' asked Anne.

'He's thin – thin as a rake!' said Dick. 'No one but a skinny fellow could squeeze through *this* opening! I doubt if *you* can, Julian – you're the biggest of us.'

'Well, what about trying?' said George. 'What does everyone say? This might be an easier, shorter way out – or it might be a harder, longer one.'

'It won't be longer,' said Harry. 'By my reckoning we must be pretty well near the camp now. It's likely that the way leads straight there – though where it comes out I can't imagine. Guy and I have explored the camp pretty thoroughly.'

Dick suddenly thought of something he had noticed at the camp – the big hole behind the slab of stone, where he had seen the baby rabbit a day or two before! What had Guy said about that? He had said there was a great hole underground, which had been explored – but that it was probably just an ancient storage place for food or for loot! He turned eagerly to Harry.

'Harry, would this lead to that enormous hole under-

137

ground – the one that Guy once told me had been explored, but was of no interest – probably just an old store place?'

'Let me see,' said Harry. 'Yes – yes, it *might* lead to that. Most of these underground ways are throughways – ways that led from one place to another. They don't as a rule stop suddenly, but have usually been of use as secret escape routes or something of that kind. I think you may be right, Dick – we're fairly near the camp, I'm sure, and we may quite well find that if we go on, instead of going back, we shall come into the camp itself – probably through that great hole!'

'Then come on,' said Julian. 'It will certainly be a shorter way!'

They tried to squeeze through the narrow opening that led out of the little rocky room. Dick got through all right, and so did the others – but poor Julian found it very very difficult and almost gave up.

'You shouldn't eat so much,' said Dick, unkindly. 'Go on – one more try, Ju – I'll haul on your arm at the same time!'

Julian got through, groaning. 'I'm squashed flat!' he said. 'Now, if anyone makes any more jokes about too much breakfast, I'll pull his nose!'

The passage grew wider immediately, and everyone was thankful. It ran fairly straight, and then went steeply downwards, so that the five slithered about, and Timmy found himself suddenly running. Then it came to a stop – a complete stop! This time it was not a blank wall of rock that faced them – it was something else.

'A roof-fall!' groaned Dick. 'Look at that! Now we're done!'

138

It certainly looked most formidable. Earth, rocks and stones had fallen from the roof and blocked up the whole passageway. There was no use in going on – they would just have to turn and go back!

'Blow it!' said Dick, and kicked at the mass of earth. 'Well, there's no use staying here – we'd better turn back. My torch isn't too good now, and neither is yours, George. We don't want to lose any time – if our torches give out, we shall find things very difficult.'

They turned to go back, feeling very despondent. 'Come on, Timmy!' said George. But Timmy didn't come. He stood beside the roof-fall, looking very puzzled, his ears cocked and his head on one side. Then he suddenly gave a sharp bark.

It made everyone jump almost out of their skins, for the sound echoed round and about in a very strange way.

'Don't, Timmy!' said George, almost angrily. 'Whatever's the matter? Come along!'

But Timmy didn't come. He began to paw at the pile of earth and rocks in front of him, and barked without stopping. Wuff-wuff-wuff-wuff-wuff-WUFF!

'What's up?' said Julian, startled. 'Timmy, what on *earth's* the matter?'

Timmy took absolutely no notice, but went on feverishly scraping at the roof-fall, sending earth and stones flying all over the others.

'There's something he wants to get at – something behind this roof-fall,' said Dick. 'Or perhaps *somebody* – make him stop barking, George, and we'll listen ourselves and see if we can hear anything.'

George silenced Timmy with difficulty, and made him

139

stand quiet and still. Then they all listened intently – and a sound came at once to their ears.

'Yap-yap-wuff-wuff-wuff!'

'It's Jet!' yelled Harry, making everyone jump violently again. 'Jet! Then Guy must be with him. He never leaves Guy! What's Guy doing here? He may be hurt. GUY! GUY! JET!'

Timmy began to bark wildly again and to scrape more furiously than ever. Julian shouted to the others above the barking.

'If we can hear Jet barking, this roof-fall can't be very big. We'd better try and get through it. Two of us can work in turn with Timmy. We can't all work at once, the passage is too narrow.'

Then began some very hard work – but it didn't last as long as Julian feared, because, quite suddenly, the mass of rubble and rock shifted as they worked, and a gap appeared at the top of the heap, between it and the roof.

Dick began to scramble up, but Julian called to him at once. 'Be careful, ass! The roof can't be too good here – it may come down again, and you'll be buried. Go carefully!'

But before Dick could go any further, a little figure appeared on the top of the rubble over their heads, and slid down to them yapping loudly, and waving a long wiry tail!

'Jet! Oh, Jet! Where's Guy?' cried Harry, as the little dog leapt into his arms and licked his face lavishly, barking joyfully in between the licks.

'GUY!' yelled Julian. 'Are you there?'

A weak voice came back. 'Yes! Who's that?' An absolute volley of voices answered him.

'It's us! And Harry! We're coming to you, we shan't be long!'

And it wasn't long, either, before the roof-fall was slowly and carefully climbed by each one – though Timmy, of course, scrambled up, over and down at top speed!

On the other side of the roof-fall was a passage, of course, the continuation of the one the children had come along. Guy was there, sitting down, looking very pale. Jet flung himself on him and licked him as if he hadn't seen him for a month, instead of just a minute or two before!

'Hallo!' said Guy, in a small voice. 'I'm all right. It's just my ankle, that's all. I'm jolly glad to . . .'

But before he could say a word more, Harry was beside him, his arms round him, his voice choking.

'Guy! Oh, Guy! I've been a beast. I wouldn't be friends! What happened to you? Are you really all right? Oh Guy, we *are* friends again, aren't we?'

'Look out Harry, old son,' said Julian gently. 'He's fainted. Now just let's be sensible and everything will come all right. Flap your hanky at him, Dick, and give him a little air. It's only the excitement!'

In half a minute Guy opened his eyes and smiled weakly. 'Sorry!' he said. 'I'm all right now. I only hope this isn't a dream, and that you really *are* here!'

'You bet we are!' said Dick. 'Have a bit of chocolate, then you'll know we're real!'

'Good idea!' said Julian. 'We'll all have some – and I've some biscuits in my pocket too. We'll eat and talk – and we'll make plans at the same time. Catch, Guy – here's a biscuit!'

CHAPTER EIGHTEEN

The way out

GUY SOON told his story. It was much as the others had
imagined.

'I was fast asleep this morning, with Jet curled up to
me,' he said. 'He began to bark and I wondered why, so I
got up to see – and I saw four people in the camp.'

'The four we know!' said Dick, and Julian nodded.
'Go on, Guy.'

'They were looking all over the place,' said Guy,
'prising up rocks, messing about – so I yelled at them.
But they only laughed. Then one of the men, who was
trying to prise up a slab – the slab that covers that great
hole underground, Harry – you remember it? – well, this
man gave a yell and said "I've got it! This is the way in –
down here, behind this slab!"'

Guy stopped, looking very angry. Jet licked him
comfortingly. 'Well,' he went on. 'I set Jet on them,
and they kicked him cruelly – so I went for them.'

'You're a plucky one, aren't you!' said Dick, admiringly. 'Did you knock them all out, by any chance?'

'No. Of course not,' said Guy. 'One of the men pretty
well knocked *me* out though. He hit me on the head and I
went down, dazed. I heard him say "drat this kid – he'll
be fetching help, and we shan't be able to get down and
hunt for the goods.' And then another man said "We'll
take him with us then", and they got hold of me and
dragged me through the opening.'

143

'But how did they get down into that great hole?' said Harry in wonder. 'There is such a steep drop into it. You need a rope.'

'Oh, they had a rope all right,' said Guy, munching his biscuit and chocolate and looking decidedly better. 'One of the men had one tied round and round his waist. They knotted it fast round a rock – that big one we can't move, Harry – and then they swung down on it. All except the woman. She said she'd stay at the top and keep watch. She hid behind a bush some way off.'

'I never saw her when I came along!' said Harry. 'I never thought of looking there! What about you? Did you get down too?'

'Yes. I screamed and shouted and kicked and howled, but it wasn't a bit of good. They made me swing down the rope – and I fell off halfway down and hurt my ankle. I howled at the top of my voice for help, and they hurried me along with them, shaking me like a rat.'

'The beasts!' said Harry, fervently. 'Oh, the beasts!'

'I heard one of them say that there should be a tunnel out of the hole somewhere, it was marked on Paul's plan – whatever that may be – and then I think I must have fainted – the pain of my ankle, you know. And when I came to myself again, we were all here, the three men and I – beside this roof-fall – though I really don't know how we got here. They must have dragged me along with them!'

'And that's all, is it?' asked Julian.

'Not quite. They were furious when they saw the roof-fall, but as soon as they began to scrabble in it a rock rolled down and hit one of the men quite a crack – and after that they were afraid to do anything. They stood and talked for a bit – and then they decided to go and get some tools, and come down again to see if they could remove all this stuff and get through it.'

'Good gracious!' said Julian, startled. 'Then they may be back at any moment!'

'I suppose so. They left me here because they couldn't think of anything else to do with me! They knew I couldn't walk, because of my ankle. I think it's broken. So of course I couldn't possibly find my way out myself! And here I've been waiting for those brutes to come back, and to hack through the rubble to go after whatever it is they want!'

Everyone began to feel rather uncomfortable at the thought that three violent men might be appearing at any moment. 'Is it very far to the opening you came down?' asked Julian. But Guy didn't know. He had fainted, as he had said, and he didn't even know what way they had come.

'It can't be far,' said Harry. 'I think it would be worth while trying to find the opening, see if the men have left the rope there, and get out that way. If Guy's ankle really is broken, he couldn't possibly manage to go back the long way we've come.'

'No. That's true,' said Julian, thoughtfully. 'Well, that's what we'll do then. But we'll go jolly cautiously, without a sound, because it might be just our luck to meet those fellows on their way back here!'

'Shall we start?' said George. 'What about Guy?'

Julian knelt down beside the boy, and gently examined his ankle. 'I've done my first aid training, like everybody else!' he said. 'And I *ought* to know if his ankle is broken or just sprained.'

He examined the swollen ankle carefully. 'It's not broken. I believe I could bandage it tightly with a couple of large hankies. Give me yours, Dick.'

The others watched admiringly as Julian deftly and confidently bandaged Guy's swollen ankle. 'There!' he said. 'You can perhaps hobble on it now, Guy. It may hurt, but I don't think it will damage it. Try. You'll have to go barefoot because your ankle is too swollen for your shoe to go on.'

Very gingerly Guy stood up, helped by Harry. He tried his hurt foot, and it certainly seemed all right to hobble on, though it was very painful. He grinned round at the others' anxious faces.

'It's fine!' he said. 'Come on, let's go! We don't want to bump into those fellows if we can help it. Thank goodness we've got Jet and Timmy.'

They set off down the passage, flashing their torches in front as usual, to show them the way. The tunnel was quite wide and high here, and in a very short time came out into an enormous pit underground.

'Ah – this is the hole I saw down behind the slab where the rabbit went,' said Dick. 'We weren't very far from the camp, as we thought. I'm surprised that when this pit was explored, the underground passages were not discovered, Guy.'

'I expect the men exploring it came to the roof-fall and thought there was nothing beyond,' said Guy. 'Or maybe they were afraid of going further in case of further falls. They can be very dangerous, you know. Many a man has been buried under one and never heard of again.'

They looked round the enormous hole – it was really a huge round pit. Daylight showed in the roof at one place.

'That's the opening into it,' said Guy, eagerly. 'The one I came through, on the rope.'

He limped a few steps forward to look for the rope. Harry held him by the arm, thankful that the ankle was holding up so well. Guy pointed upwards.

'Yes. I can see the rope. The men have left it there, thank goodness. They must have been certain that I couldn't get to it!'

The rope hung down from the little opening high above their heads. Julian looked round at Anne.

'Can you manage to climb up the rope, Anne?' he said, doubtfully.

'Of course!' said Anne, scornfully. 'We do rope-climbing in the gym at school often enough. Don't we, George?'

'Yes, but our gym rope is a bit thicker!' said George.

147

'I'll go up first,' said Harry. 'We've got a much thicker rope, Guy and I, that we use when we want to haul on very heavy stones. I'll find it, and let it down.'

'Well, we can't afford to waste any time, in case those fellows come back,' said Julian. 'I daresay the girls can manage all right. George, you go up first.'

George went up like a monkey, hand over hand, her legs twisted round the rope. She grinned down when she got to the top. .

'Easy!' she said. 'Come on up next, Anne, and show the boys how to do it!'

Before the boys could leap to the rope, Anne was on it, pulling herself up lithely. Julian laughed. He called up to George.

'George! You might have a squint round and see if there's any sign of people about. If they were going to borrow *Guy's* tools, they would have been back long ago, so I think probably they've had to go to Kirrin or some farmhouse to borrow them.'

'They wouldn't get my tools,' said Guy, 'or Harry's. We had them stolen once, and now we always hide them where no one can possibly find them.'

'That settles it then,' said Julian. 'They've had to go a good way, I expect, to get satisfactory tools to tackle that roof-fall. They probably imagine that it's a pretty *big* fall! All the same, keep a watch out, George, till we're all up.'

It was difficult to get Guy up, for he was feeling weak, but they managed it at last. The two dogs had to have the boys' shirts tied round them so that the rope would not cut them when they were hauled up. They didn't seem to mind at all. Timmy was very heavy to pull up because he appeared to think that he had to try and make his legs do a running action all the time – just to help! All that happened was that he began to spin round and round, as he went up!

Everyone was up in the open air at long last, hot and perspiring. Julian had the precious bag safely under his arm. Timmy sat down panting. Then he suddenly stopped panting, and pricked up his ears.

'Woof,' he said warningly, and stood up.

'Quiet, Tim, quiet, Jet,' said Julian, at once aware that somebody must be about. 'Hide, everyone – quickly. It may be those fellows coming back!'

'Wuff,' began Jet, but Guy stopped him immediately. The six children separated and went into hiding at once, each choosing the best place he or she could see. There were plenty of hiding places in the old camp!

They heard voices coming near. Nobody dared to peep out and see who was coming – but Julian and Dick recognised the drawling voice of one of the men!

'What a time we've been!' said the man. 'Just chuck the spades and things down the hole – then we'll all climb down again. Buck up! We've wasted too much time already. Anyone might come on the scene at any moment!'

The spades and jemmies went hurtling down the hole. Then one by one the men went down the rope. The children could not hear the woman's voice. They thought she must have been left behind.

Julian gave a low whistle and all the others popped up their heads. 'We'll spring for it!' said Julian. 'Buck up!'

They all shot out of their hiding places at once and made off – except Julian. He stayed behind for a minute or two. What *could* he be doing?

Julian was doing something very simple indeed! He was hauling up the rope that dangled underground! He slipped it off the rock that held it and tied it round his waist, looking suddenly very bulky.

He grinned a very wide grin and went after the others. How very, very angry those men were going to be!

CHAPTER NINETEEN

Back to Kirrin Cottage

JULIAN RAN AFTER the others. 'What were you doing?' said George. 'Calling rude names down to the men?'

'No. I hope they'll go and dig for hours if they want to!' said Julian. 'They'll soon find that when they've got through it, that roof-fall is nothing much, and they'll go on till they come to the little room – and what they'll say when they find that the bag is gone, I really don't know!'

'I wish I could be there!' said Dick.

'What are we going to do about Guy?' asked Harry. 'He really can't walk *very* far on that bad foot.'

'If he can walk as far as the gorse bush where we've left our things, I've got a bike there,' said George. 'He could pedal with one foot, I should think.'

'Oh yes, I could easily do that,' said Guy, pleased. He had dreaded the thought of having to walk all the way to Kirrin – but neither did he want to be left behind!

He limped along, helped by Harry, who couldn't do enough for him. Jet ran along beside them, excited and happy at being with so many people. Timmy sometimes wuffed a little bark to him, which made Jet as proud as Punch. He thought the big Timmy was wonderful!

They came to the gorse bush, and found their things all safe. The bicycle was there, with its packages strapped to it. George unstrapped them, meaning to carry them herself, so that Guy would not have too heavy a weight to pedal with his one foot. They all started off together, Guy riding ahead on the bicycle.

'We will go to Kirrin, dump our things at the cottage, and get Aunt Fanny to ring the police and ask them if they'll come along and collect this bag from us,' said Julian. 'I don't want to leave it at the police station – I want to see it opened in front of us!'

'I do hope it won't be empty,' said Anne. 'It does feel terribly light!'

'Yes. It does,' said Julian, swinging it to and fro. 'I can't help fearing that Paul, who drew the plan that the men found so difficult to understand, may have double-crossed his friends – drawn a deliberately difficult plan – and then left the bag quite empty in the place he marked on the plan! It would be the kind of hoax that a trickster loves to play – and would give him time to get away in safety.'

'But they said he was ill,' said Dick. 'Still – perhaps he might have been pretending that too! It's a mystery!'

'How are you getting on, Guy?' called George, as they overtook the boy. He kept riding on by himself for a little way, and then resting, waiting for them to catch up with him before he pedalled on again with his one good foot.

'Very well indeed, thank you,' said Guy. 'This bike was a very good idea of yours. What a blessing you had it with you!'

'Your foot doesn't seem any more swollen,' said Anne. 'I expect you'll be able to walk on it properly in a day or two. Oh, dear – it does make me laugh when I think how puzzled we all were when we thought there was just one of you, not twins!'

'We met first one of you, then the other, and thought

you were the same boy,' said George, with a chuckle. 'We were absolutely wild with you sometimes, you seemed so mad and contradictory!'

'Don't remind us of it,' said Harry. 'I can't bear thinking that if I'd only been with Guy, all this trouble of his would never have happened.'

'Oh well – it's an ill wind that blows nobody any good! said George. 'The bad and the good have fitted together very well this time, and made a most exciting adventure!'

'Here's Carters Lane at last,' said Anne. 'What a long walk it seemed over the common. It will be much easier for you to ride that bike when you're on a proper road, Guy. It won't go bumping over heather clumps now.'

They went down the long lane and came into Kirrin at last, realising that they were all very hungry indeed. 'It must be well past lunch-time,' said George, looking at her watch. 'Good gracious – it's a quarter to two! Would you believe it! I hope there's some lunch left over for us – Mother doesn't know we're coming.'

'We'll raid Joanna's larder!' said Dick. 'She never minds so long as she's there to grumble at us while we do it!'

They went in at the gate of Kirrin Cottage and up to the front door, which was open. George shouted.

'Mother! Where are you? We've come back!'

Nobody answered. George yelled again. 'Mother! We've come home!'

The door of the study opened and her father looked out, red in the face and frowning.

'George! How many times am I to tell you not to shout when I'm working? Oh, my goodness me, who are all these?'

'Hallo, Father!' said George, mildly. 'Surely you know Anne and Julian and Dick! *Don't* say you've forgotten them already!'

'Of course not! But who are these?' and George's father pointed to the startled twins. 'They're as like as peas. Where did *they* come from? I haven't seen them before, have I?'

'No, father. They're just friends of ours,' said George. 'Where's Mother? We've just had an adventure and we want to tell her. Oh, and we want to ring the police – and I think we ought to get a doctor to see to Guy's foot – and Father, look, Timmy's ear is healed!'

'Bless us all! There's never any peace when you are about, George,' said her father, groaning. 'Your mother's at the bottom of the garden, picking raspberries – or it might have been strawberries.'

155

'Oh no, Father – it's August, not June!' said George. 'You always . . .'

Julian thought he had better get his uncle safely back in his study before a row blew up between him and George. Uncle Quentin did *not* like being disturbed in his complicated work!

'Let's go and find Aunt Fanny,' he said, 'we can tell her everything out in the garden. Come on!'

'Wuff-wuff!' said Jet.

'Good gracious – that's not *another* dog, is it?' said George's father, scowling. 'How many times have I said that . . .'

'We won't disturb you any more, Uncle,' said Julian, hurriedly, seeing Guy's scared face. 'We'll go and find Aunt Fanny.'

They all went thankfully out in the garden, hearing the house echo to the slam of Uncle Quentin's study door. George shouted.

'Mother! Where are you?'

'Shut up, George – we don't want to make your father leap out of the window after us!' said Dick. 'Ah – there's Aunt Fanny!'

His aunt was very surprised to see him and the others advancing on her. She went to greet them, a basket of raspberries on her arm.

'Well! I thought you wanted to stay away for longer than this!'

'We did – but an adventure descended on us!' said Dick. 'We'll tell you all about it in detail later on, Aunt Fanny.'

'But just now we want two things – can we ring the police – or will *you* – and ask them to come here?' said

Julian, very grown-up all of a sudden. 'There's something that might be very important for them to know. And also do you think we should let a doctor see Guy's foot – he's sprained his ankle, I think?'

'Oh dear!' said Aunt Fanny, distressed to see the boy's swollen foot. 'Yes, he ought to have that seen to properly. Who is he? Dear me – there's another of them! Aren't they alike?'

'Twins,' said George. 'I don't know how I shall be able to tell one from t'other when Guy's bad foot is better.'

'I'm going to ring the police,' said Julian, seeing that his aunt could now only think of Guy's swollen foot. He went off indoors, and they heard him speaking on the telephone. He put it down and came out again.

'The inspector himself is coming,' said Julian. 'Shall I ring the doctor now, Aunt Fanny?'

'Oh yes. His number is 042,' said his aunt. 'How *did* you get such an ankle, Guy?'

'Mother, you don't seem at all interested in our adventure,' complained George.

'Oh, I am, dear,' said her mother. 'But you do have such a lot, you know. What have you been up to this time?'

But before George could do more than begin, a black police car drew up at the front gate, and the inspector of police got out and marched up to the front door. He knocked extremely loudly on the knocker.

Which, of course, had the immediate result of bringing George's father hotfoot out of his study in another rage! He flung open the front door.

'Hammering at the door like that! What's the matter? I've a good mind to report you to the police! Oh – er –

h'm – good afternoon, Inspector. Do come in. Are we expecting you?'

Smiling broadly, the inspector came in. By this time Julian had come back in the house again and greeted him. His uncle went back into his study, rather red in the face, and actually closed the door quietly!

'You wanted me to come along at once, because of something important?' said the inspector. 'What is it?'

The others came into the room now, with Julian's aunt behind them. Julian nodded round at them. 'They're all in this – except my aunt, of course. We've brought something we think may be important. Quite a lot of people were looking for it – but we managed to get hold of it first!'

He put the brown bag on the table. The inspector's eyes went to it at once. 'What is it? What's inside? Stolen goods?'

'Yes – blueprints of some kind, I think. But I don't know what of, of course.'

'Open the bag, my boy! I'll examine them,' said the inspector.

'I can't open it,' said Julian. 'It's locked – and there's no key!'

'Well – we'll soon manage *that*!' said the inspector, and took out a small, strong-looking tool. He forced the lock, and the bag opened. Everyone leaned forward eagerly, even Timmy. What was in the bag?

There was nothing there! Absolutely nothing! Julian groaned in bitter disappointment.

'No wonder it felt so light. It's empty after all. Would you believe it!'

CHAPTER TWENTY

The adventure ends – as it began!

It was a moment of great disappointment for all the children. Although they had talked about the possibility of the bag being empty, everyone had secretly felt certain that something exciting would be inside.

The inspector was astonished. He looked round sharply. 'Where did you get this bag? What made you think it had stolen goods inside – and what kind of blueprints were they?'

'Well – it's rather a long story,' said Julian.

'I'm afraid you'll have to tell it to me,' said the inspector, taking out his notebook. 'Now – how did this all begin?'

'Well – it really began with Timmy hurting his ear and having to wear a cardboard collar,' said George.

The inspector looked most surprised. He turned to Julian. '*You'd* better tell it,' he said. 'I don't want to waste time on cardboard collars!'

George went red and put on a scowl. Julian grinned at her, and began the story, making it as clear and short as he could.

The inspector became more and more interested. He laughed when Julian came to the weird noises and lights.

'They certainly wanted to get rid of you,' he said. 'You were plucky to stay on. Go on – there's something behind all this, that's certain!'

He jotted down the names 'Paul', 'Tom' and 'Jess', the

159

name of the woman. He noted that one man had a drawl. 'Any other clues to them?' he asked.

'Only this,' said Julian and handed his drawing of the crêpe-soled shoe to the inspector. This was carefully folded and put into the notebook too. 'Might be of use. Might not,' said the inspector. 'You never know!'

He listened intently to the tale of the underground passages, and picked up the bag again.

'I can't understand why it's empty,' he said. 'It isn't really like a crook deliberately to mislead his friends when they know quite well where he is and can get at him whenever they like.' He shook the bag hard. Then he began to examine it very very carefully.

Finally he took out a sharp knife and gently slit the lining at the bottom of the bag. He turned it back.

Something was there – under the lining! Something blue, folded very carefully. Something covered with thousands of minute figures, thousands of lines, thousands of strange little designs!

'Wheeeeeew!' whistled the inspector. 'So the bag's *not* empty, after all! Now what is this? It's a blueprint of some project – but what?'

'My father would know!' said George, at once. 'He's a scientist, you know, Inspector – one of the cleverest in the world. Shall I get him?'

'Yes,' said the inspector, laying out the blueprint on the table. 'Get him at once.'

George flew off and returned with her father, who didn't look very pleased.

'Good afternoon, once more. Sorry to disturb you,' said the inspector. 'But do you happen to know whether this document is of any importance?'

George's father took it up. He ran his eyes over it, and then gave a loud exclamation.

'Why – why – no, it's IMPOSSIBLE! Good heavens, it's – no, no, it can't be! Am I dreaming?'

Everyone gazed at him, surprised and anxious. What did he mean? What could it be, this blueprint?

'Er – it's important then?' said the inspector.

'Important? IMPORTANT? My dear fellow, there are only two of these prints in existence – and at the moment I have the second one, which I am checking very carefully indeed. Where did this come from? Why – I simply can't believe it! Sir James Lawton-Harrison has the other. There isn't a third!'

'But – but – there must be if you have one here and Sir James has the other!' said the inspector. 'It's obvious there is a third!'

'You're wrong. It isn't obvious!' shouted George's father. 'What *is* obvious is that Sir James hasn't got his! I'll ring him up – this very minute. Astounding! Most disturbing! Bless us all, what will happen next?'

The children did not dare say a word. They were full of astonishment. To think that the blueprint was so important – and that George's father actually had the pair to this one. What was its importance?

They heard George's father shouting into the telephone, evidently angry and disturbed. He slammed it down and came back.

'Yes. Sir James's copy has been stolen – but it's been kept very hush-hush because of its importance. Good heavens – they never even let *me* know! And to think I spilt a bottle of ink over mine yesterday – gross carelessness. Stolen! A thing like that – stolen out of his safe under his very nose. Now there's only my one copy left!'

'Two,' said the inspector, tapping the copy on the table. 'You're so upset to hear that Sir James's copy has gone that you've forgotten we have it here!'

'Bless us all! Thank goodness! Yes, I *had* forgotten for the moment!' said Uncle Quentin. 'My word, I even

162

forgot to tell Sir James it was here.' He leapt up to go to the telephone again, but the inspector caught his arm.

'No. Don't telephone again. I think we should keep this as quiet as possible.'

'Father – what *is* this a blueprint of?' said George, voicing the thoughts of everyone there, the inspector included.

'This blueprint? I'm certainly not going to tell you!' said her father. 'It's too big a thing even to speak of to you children – or the inspector either for that matter. It's one of the biggest secrets we have. Here, give it to me.'

The inspector placed his big hand on it at once. 'No. I think I must take it with me, and send a secret messenger to Sir James with it. It wouldn't do to have the only two copies in one place. Why, your house might catch fire and both prints might go up in flames!'

'Take it, then, take it! We can't possibly risk such a thing!' said George's father. He glared round at the children. 'I still don't understand how *you* came to possess it!' he said, looking suddenly amazed.

'Sit down, won't you, and listen to their tale,' said the inspector. 'They've done very well. They haven't finished their story.'

Julian went on with it. The inspector sat up straight when he heard where the three men were – down in the great pit below the Roman camp.

'You saw them go down into that pit?' he said. 'Watched them swing down on the rope? They may be there now!' He glanced at his watch. 'No, they won't. They'll be gone.'

He groaned loudly. 'And to think we might easily have

caught three clever rogues. They've slipped through our hands again!'

'They haven't!' said Julian, his voice rising exultantly. 'They're still there!'

'How do you know?' said the inspector.

'Because I pulled up their rope and took it away – look, I've got it round me!' said Julian. 'They can't get out without a rope – and they won't know how to escape any other way. They're still there – waiting for you, Inspector!'

The inspector slapped the table so hard that everyone jumped and the two dogs barked.

'Good work!' he boomed. 'Magnificent! I must go at once and send some men out there. I'll let you know what happens!'

And out he went at a run, the precious blueprint buttoned safely in his pocket. He leapt into the driving seat and the police car roared away at top speed down the lane.

'Whew!' said Julian, flopping back into his chair. 'It's too exciting for words!'

Everyone felt the same, and began to talk at the tops of their voices. Poor Aunt Fanny couldn't make herself heard. But when Joanna came in and asked if anyone wanted anything to eat, they heard her at once!

The doctor came to see Guy's foot, and rebandaged it. 'Rest it for a day or two,' he said. 'It will soon be all right.'

'Well, you'll have to stay here with George and the others, Guy,' said George's mother. 'You can't go excavating in that camp of yours again yet. Harry can stay too. So can Jet.'

The twins beamed. They liked this jolly family, and the adventurous life they seemed to lead. It would be fun to stay with them for a while. They thought it would be even *more* fun, when Joanna arrived with a truly wonderful meal!

'Home-made veal-and-ham-pie! Stuffed tomatoes! And what a salad – what's in it, Joanna? Radishes, cucumber, carrot, beetroot, hard-boiled eggs, tomatoes, peas – Joanna, you're a marvel! What is the pudding?' George asked.

Soon they were all sitting down enjoying themselves, and talking over their adventure. Just as they were finishing, the telephone bell rang. Julian went to answer it. He came back looking thrilled.

'That was the inspector. They've got all three men! When they got to the pit, one of the men called up for help – said some idiot of a boy or some hoaxer must have taken their rope away. So the police – all in plain-clothes, so that of course the three men suspected nothing – the police let down a rope, and up came the men one by one . . .'

'And were arrested as soon as they popped out of the hole, I suppose!' said George, delighted. 'Oh, I wish I'd been there! What a joke!'

'The inspector's awfully pleased with us,' said Julian. 'And so is Sir James Lawton-Harrison too, apparently. We're to get a reward – very hush-hush, though. We mustn't say anything about it. There's to be something for each of us.'

'And for Timmy too?' said George at once.

Julian looked round at Timmy. 'Well, I can see what old Timmy ought to ask for,' he said. 'A new cardboard collar. He's scratching his ear to bits!'

George screamed and rushed to bend over Timmy. She lifted a woebegone face. 'Yes! He's scratched so hard he's made his ear bad again. Oh Timmy! You really are a stupid dog! Mother! Mother! Timmy's messed up his ear again!'

Her mother looked into the room. 'Oh George, what a pity! I *told* you not to take off that collar till his ear was absolutely healed!'

'It's maddening!' said George. 'Now everyone will laugh at him again.'

'Oh no they won't,' said Julian, and he smiled at George's scowling face. 'Cheer up – it's a very peculiar thing, George – this adventure *began* with Timmy and a cardboard collar – and bless me if it hasn't *ended* with Timmy and a cardboard collar. Three cheers for old Timmy!'

Yes – three cheers for old Timmy! Get your ear well before the next adventure, Tim – you really *can't* wear a cardboard collar again!

FIVE GO TO DEMON'S ROCKS

CONTENTS

CHAPTER ONE

Three visitors arrive

'FANNY!' SHOUTED Uncle Quentin, running up the stairs with a letter in his hand. 'FANNY! Where are you?'

'Here, dear, here, helping Joanna with the dusting,' said Aunt Fanny, appearing out of a bedroom. 'Don't shout like that. I'm not deaf, you know. What's the matter?'

'I've a letter here from that old friend of mine, Professor Hayling,' said Uncle Quentin. 'You remember him, don't you?'

'Do you mean the man who came here to stay a few years ago, and kept forgetting to come in for meals?' said Aunt Fanny, flicking some dust off her husband's coat.

'Fanny, don't flick at me like that,' said Uncle Quentin crossly. 'Anyone would think I was covered in dust. Listen – he's coming to stay *today* for a week – instead of next week.'

Aunt Fanny stared at her husband in horror. 'But he *can't* do that!' she said. 'George is coming home today – and her three cousins with her, to stay. You know that!'

'Oh – I'd forgotten,' said Uncle Quentin. 'Well, ring up and tell George to stay where she is – we can't have them while Professor Hayling is here. I shall want to be quite undisturbed – he and I have to confer about some new invention of his. Don't look like that, my dear – this may be very, very important.'

'Well, it's important to the Five that *their* plans

171

shouldn't be spoilt,' said Aunt Fanny. 'After all, George only went to stay with Dick, Julian and Anne because you had some urgent papers to write, and you didn't want to be disturbed – and you *knew* today was the day they were due home. Quentin, you must ring up your professor friend and say he can't come.'

'Very well, my dear, very well,' said Uncle Quentin. 'But he won't like it. He won't like it at all!' He went off to his study to use the telephone, and Aunt Fanny hurried up the stairs to get ready the rooms for the four cousins.

'Anne can sleep with George as usual,' she said to Joanna. 'And the two boys can sleep in the guest room.'

'It will be nice to have all the Five back again,' said Joanna, pushing the vacuum cleaner up and down the landing. 'I miss them – and you should see the cakes I made yesterday – two whole tins full!'

'You're too good to those children, Joanna,' said Aunt Fanny. 'No wonder they're so fond of you. Now, we'll – oh dear – there's my husband calling me again. All right, dear, I'm coming, I'm coming!'

She ran downstairs to the hall, and into the study. Uncle Quentin was standing there, holding the telephone receiver. 'What shall I do?' he almost shouted. 'Professor Hayling has left and is already on his way here. I can't stop him coming. And he's bringing his son with him, so there are two of them.'

'His *son*! Well, really!' said Aunt Fanny. 'There isn't room for them here, with the four cousins as well, Quentin. You know that.'

'Well, ring up George and tell *her* not to come back for a week, but to stay with her cousins,' said Uncle Quentin, crossly. 'There's no reason why they should ALL come here.'

'But, Quentin, you *know* perfectly well that George's aunt and uncle are shutting up the house today, and going on a cruise somewhere,' said Aunt Fanny. 'Oh dear, oh dear! Well, I'll ring up George, and try to stop them all coming!'

So once more the telephone was used, and Aunt Fanny tried anxiously to get in touch with George. For a long time nobody answered, and then at last a voice came. 'Hallo – who's there?'

'Mrs Kirrin here – may I speak to George, please?'

'Oh – I'm sorry – they've already left, on their bicycles,' said the voice. 'And the house is empty except for me. I'm a neighbour come in to lock everything up. I'm so sorry I can't get George for you.'

'Oh – thank you. Never mind!' said Aunt Fanny, and put back the receiver. She gave a heavy sigh. NOW what was to be done? Professor Hayling and his son were on their way to Kirrin Cottage – and so were the Five – and none of them could be stopped. What a household it would be!

'Quentin,' she said, going into the study where her husband was tidying up enormous piles of papers. 'Quentin, listen – George and all the others are on their way here. And HOW I am going to put everyone up, I do not know. It looks as if somebody will have to sleep in Timmy's kennel, and I've a good mind to make a bed up for *you* in the coal-house!'

'I'm busy,' said Uncle Quentin, hardly listening. 'I've all these papers to get in order before Professor Hayling comes. And by the way, my dear, will you PLEASE tell the

173

children to be quiet while the professor is here – he's rather short-tempered, and . . .'

'Quentin, *I'm* beginning to feel rather short-tempered too,' said Aunt Fanny. 'And if . . .' She stopped very suddenly and gazed through the study window in horror. Then she pointed her finger at it. 'Look! What's that at the window?'

Her husband turned and stared in amazement. 'It looks like a *monkey*!' he said. 'Where on earth did it come from?'

A voice called down the stairs. It was Joanna. 'There's a car at the door – I think it's your visitors – a man and a boy!'

Aunt Fanny was still staring in astonishment at the monkey, who was now scratching at the window-pane, chattering in a funny little prattle. He pressed his nose to the glass, just like a child.

'DON'T tell me that your friend owns a monkey – and has brought *him* to stay too!' groaned poor Aunt Fanny. She jumped as a loud bang came from the front door, and went to open it.

Yes – there stood Professor Hayling, the man who had so often forgotten to come in for meals when he had stayed at Kirrin Cottage years before. And by him was a boy of about nine, with a face a little like that of the monkey now on his shoulder!

The professor strode in, calling to the taxi driver behind. 'Bring the luggage in please. Hallo, Mrs Kirrin – nice to see you again. Where's your husband? My word, I've some interesting news to tell him. Ah, Quentin, there you are! Got your papers all ready for me?'

'My dear old friend!' said Uncle Quentin, shaking hands warmly. 'Fine to see you! So glad you could come.'

'This is Tinker, my son,' said Professor Hayling, clapping the boy on the back, and almost knocking him over. 'I always forget what his real name is – we call him Tinker because he's always tinkering with cars – mad on them, you know! Shake hands, Tinker. Where's Mischief?'

Poor Aunt Fanny hadn't been able to get in a word. The professor was now in the hall, still talking. The monkey leapt off the boy's shoulder, and was on the hallstand, swinging on a hat-peg.

Really, it's like a circus! thought poor Aunt Fanny. And the rooms not prepared yet – and what about lunch? Oh my goodness – and all the cousins coming as well. What *is* that monkey doing now? Making faces at himself in the hall mirror!

Somehow or other the visitors were pushed into the
living room, and they sat down. Uncle Quentin was so
anxious to discuss some mighty problems with the professor that he actually fetched a great sheaf of papers and
immediately spread them over the table.

'*Not* in here, dear – in your study please,' said Aunt
Fanny, firmly. 'Joanna! Will you help me take the bags
up to the guest room? And we can make up a bed there
on the couch for the little boy. There won't be room
anywhere else.'

'What about the monkey!' asked Joanna, eyeing it
warily. 'Is he to have a bed too?'

'He sleeps with me,' said Tinker, in an astonishingly
loud voice, and suddenly leapt up the stairs, making a
most extraordinary purring noise as he went. Mrs Kirrin
stared after him in amazement.

'Is he in pain, or something?' she said.

'No, no – he's just being a car,' said his father. 'I told
you he was mad about cars. He can't help pretending to
be one now and again.'

'I'm a car, a Jaguar car!' yelled Tinker, from the top of
the stairs. 'Can't you hear my engine! R-R-R-R-R-R-R! Hey,
Mischief come and have a ride!'

The little monkey scampered up the stairs and leapt on
to the boy's shoulder, chattering in its funny little voice.
The Jaguar car then apparently made a tour of all the
bedrooms, occasionally giving a very loud honk.

'Does your boy always behave like that?' asked Uncle
Quentin, amazed. 'How do you manage to do any work?'

'Oh, I have a soundproof workroom in my garden,'
said the professor. 'I hope your workroom is soundproof, too?'

'No, it isn't,' said poor Uncle Quentin, still hearing the 'car' upstairs. What a boy! How could anyone bear him for more than two minutes? And to think he had come to STAY!

He shut the study door after the professor – but no door could shut out the sound of the small boy honking upstairs!

Poor Aunt Fanny was eyeing all the luggage brought in. Why hadn't the professor gone to a hotel? What was life going to be like, with the Five here, and the professor, and a small boy who apparently thought he was some kind of car all the time. To say nothing of a monkey called Mischief! And WHERE were they all going to sleep?

CHAPTER TWO

A little excitement

GEORGE AND her three cousins were already on their way back to Kirrin. They cycled along the lanes with Timmy, George's dog, loping easily beside them.

'Won't it be fun to be at Kirrin Cottage again!' said Anne. 'It's so lovely to look out of a window and see Kirrin Bay, blue as the sky! I vote we go over to the Island for a picnic!'

'You'll like to have your own kennel again, won't you, Timmy?' said George, and Timmy gave her ankle a quick lick, and barked.

'It's always so peaceful at Kirrin Cottage,' said Dick. 'And your mother's so kind and jolly, George. I hope we shan't upset Uncle Quentin with our talk and fun.'

'I don't *think* Father has any very important work on hand,' said George. 'Anyway, he'll only have you for a week – it's a pity that professor friend of his is coming in a week's time, or you could have stayed longer.'

'Well, a week is quite a nice long time,' said Julian. 'Hallo – there's our first glimpse of Kirrin Bay, look – as blue as ever!'

They were all glad to see the little blue bay, and to catch sight of Kirrin Island lying there peacefully in the sun. 'You're lucky, George, to have an island all of your own,' said Anne. 'One that is really and truly yours!'

'Yes, I *am* lucky!' said George. 'I was never so pleased in all my life as the day Mother gave it to me. It's belonged to our family for years, of course – and now it's mine! We'll go over there tomorrow!'

At last they came to the end of their journey. 'I can see the chimneys of Kirrin Cottage!' said Julian, standing up on the pedals of his bicycle. 'And the kitchen fire is going – I can see smoke. I hope dinner's cooking!'

'I can smell it!' said Dick, sniffing. 'I think it's sausages.'

'Idiot!' said the other three together, and laughed. They rode up to the back gate, and leapt off their bicycles. They put them into the shed, and George gave a shout!

'Mother! We're *home*! Where are you?'

She had hardly finished yelling when Anne suddenly clutched her arm.

'George – what's that? Look! Peeping out of the window there!'

They all looked – and George shouted in astonishment: 'It's a monkey! A MONKEY! No, Timmy. No – come back! TIMMY!'

But Timmy too had seen the quaint little face peering out of the window, and had shot off to investigate. Was it a small dog? Or a strange sort of cat? Anyway, whatever it was, he was going to chase it away! He barked at the top of his voice as he galloped indoors, and almost knocked over a small boy there. The monkey, terrified, at once leapt on to the picture-rail than ran round the room.

'You leave my monkey alone, you big bully you!' cried a furious voice; and through the open door George saw a small boy give Timmy a sharp smack. She raced indoors, and gave the small boy a smack as sharp as the one he had given Timmy! Then she glared at him angrily.

'What are you doing here? How DARE you hit my dog? It's a good thing he didn't eat you up. And what's that creature doing up there?'

The little monkey was terrified. It sat clinging to the

picture-rail, trembling, making a piteous chattering noise. Julian came in just as Joanna arrived from up-stairs.

'What's all this?' she said. 'You'll have your father racing out of his study in a minute, George. Stop barking at the little monkey, Timmy, for goodness' sake! And stop crying, Tinker, and take your monkey away before Timmy eats him.'

'I'm NOT crying,' said Tinker fiercely, rubbing his eyes. 'Come here, Mischief. I won't let that dog hurt you! I'll – I'll . . .'

'You take your monkey away,' said Julian gently, thinking that the small boy was very brave to imagine he could fight old Timmy. 'Run along.'

Tinker made a clicking sound and the monkey dropped at once on to his shoulder, and nuzzled there. It put its tiny arms round the boy's neck, and made a little choking noise.

'Oh – poor little mite – it's crying!' said Anne. 'I didn't know monkeys could cry. Timmy, don't frighten it again, please don't. You mustn't bully tiny things.'

'Timmy never bullies anything!' said George at once, frowning at Anne. 'But after all, what do you expect him to do when he comes home and finds a strange boy *and* a monkey here. Who are you, boy?'

'I shan't tell you,' said Tinker, and marched out of the room, the monkey still whimpering into his neck.

'Joanna – who on earth is he?' asked Dick. 'And what is he doing here?'

'I thought you wouldn't like it,' said Joanna. 'It's that professor friend of your father's, George – the one who was coming to stay next week. He telephoned this morning to say he was coming *this* week instead – and bringing his boy as well! He didn't say anything about a monkey, though!'

'Are they *staying* here?' said George, in horror. 'How *can* Mother let them – she *knew* we were all coming today! How *mean* of her, how . . .'

'Be quiet, George,' said Julian. 'Let Joanna go on.'

'Well, they arrived before anything could be done to stop them,' said Joanna. 'And now your father is shut up in his study with Professor Hayling – the boy's father – and your mother and I are at our wits' end to know where to put you all. The boy and his father – and I suppose the monkey too – are sharing the guest room.'

'But that's where Julian and Dick were going to sleep!' said George, losing her temper again. 'I'll go and tell Mother that boy can't stay, I'll . . .'

'Don't be silly, George,' said Julian. 'We'll manage somehow. We can't go back home because our house will be all shut up now.'

'You could sleep up in the loft,' said Joanna, sounding rather doubtful. 'But it's very dusty and terribly draughty. I could put a couple of mattresses up there for you.'

'All right,' said Julian. 'We'll make do up in the loft. Thanks, Joanna. Where's Aunt Fanny? Does she mind all this?'

'Well – she's a bit rushed,' said Joanna. 'But you know what your aunt is – always so kind, never thinks of herself. That Professor Hayling! Just walked into the house as if he owned it, bringing luggage and that most peculiar little boy – and a *monkey*! Though the monkey seems a nice enough little thing. It came and watched me wash up, and bless me if it didn't try to dry the plates for me!'

The kitchen door swung open and George's mother came in. 'Hallo, dears!' she said smiling. 'I thought I heard Timmy barking. Dear Timmy – wait till you see the monkey!'

'He's seen him already,' said George, scowling. 'Mother, how *could* you take people in when you knew we were coming home today?'

'That's enough, George,' said Julian, who saw how worried his aunt looked. 'Aunt Fanny, we won't be ANY trouble! We'll keep out of the house as much as we can, we'll do the shopping for you, we'll go across to Kirrin Island and keep out of your way, we'll . . .'

'You're kind, Julian,' said his aunt, and smiled at him. 'Things *will* be rather difficult – especially as Professor Hayling never can remember to come to meals on time, and you know what your uncle is! He could forget breakfast, dinner and supper for a whole year, and then wonder why he felt hungry!'

That made everyone laugh. Julian slipped his arm round his aunt and gave her a hug. 'We'll sleep in the loft,' he said, 'and enjoy it, too. We will help with the housework and we'll do any odd jobs too. You've no idea how fine I look with an apron round my waist, and a broom in my hand!'

Even George smiled at the idea of Julian wearing an apron. Then Timmy went suddenly to the half-open door and barked. He could smell that monkey again. He heard a high chattering noise, and pushed the door open at once. What! Was that monkey calling him rude names?

He saw the little creature sitting on the top of the rail at the foot of the stairs. It saw Timmy, and danced up and down, sounding as if it were laughing. Timmy raced to the rail and leapt up, barking fiercely.

The study door flew open and out marched not one angry professor, but two!

'WHAT'S ALL THIS NOISE? CAN'T WE HAVE A MOMENT'S PEACE?'

'Oh *dear*!' said Aunt Fanny, foreseeing this kind of thing happening twenty times a day, now that Timmy and the others were here. She shushed the two angry men.

'Now, now – Timmy just isn't used to the monkey yet. Go back, please, and shut the door. I'll see you aren't disturbed again!'

'WOOF-WOOF!' shouted Timmy, using his very loudest bark, and Professor Hayling shot back into the study at top speed!

'Any more rudeness from Timmy and I'll have him sent away!' roared Uncle Quentin, and he too disappeared.

'WELL!' said George, her face red with anger. 'What does he mean by *that*, Mother? If Timmy goes, I go too! Oh, *look* at that monkey – he's sitting on top of the grandfather clock now! *He* ought to be sent away, horrid little mischievous thing – not old Timmy!'

CHAPTER THREE

Mischief, Tinker – and Timmy!

JULIAN AND Dick set to work to take a couple of old mattresses up to the loft, and some rugs and a couple of cushions for pillows. It *was* rather draughty! But what else was to be done? It was still too cold to sleep outside in a tent.

George was very sulky. 'That scowl will *grow* on your face, George, if you aren't careful,' said Dick. 'Cheer up, for goodness' sake. It's worse for your mother than it is for any of us. She's going to be very busy this week.'

She certainly was! Meals for nine people, five of them very hungry children, were not easy to provide. Joanna did an enormous amount of cooking, the four children helped with the housework and cycled off to Kirrin village in the mornings to do the shopping.

'Why can't that boy Tinker help?' demanded George, on the second day they were at home. 'What on earth does he think he's doing now? Look at him out in the garden rushing all round, making a frightful noise. Tinker, shut up! You'll disturb your father and mine.'

'You shut up yourself!' called back Tinker, rudely. 'Can't you see I'm a Mercedes car, with a very powerful engine? And see how well it stops when I put on the brakes – no jerk at all! And hear the horn – marvellous!'

He gave a remarkably good imitation of a powerful car horn. At once the study window shot up and two very angry men shouted together:

185

'TINKER! What do you think you're doing, making that noise? You've been told to be QUIET!'

Tinker began to explain about the Mercedes, but as this didn't seem to satisfy either of the angry men, he offered to be a little Mini. 'You see, it goes like this,' said Tinker, beginning to move off, making a low purring noise, 'and it . . .'

But the window was slammed shut, so the little Mini drove itself into the kitchen, and said it was very hungry, could it have a bun?

'I don't feed cars,' said Joanna. 'I have no petrol. Go away.'

The Mini purred out of the kitchen on its two legs, and went to look for passengers. Mischief the monkey scampered up, and ran up Tinker's body to his shoulder.

'You're my passenger,' said Tinker, and Mischief held on to his hair as he drove all round the garden at top speed, honking every now and again, but very quietly indeed.

'He's a funny child,' said Joanna to Mrs Kirrin, when she came into the kitchen. 'Not bad really – him and his cars! I've never seen a child so mad on them in my life! One of these days he'll turn into one!'

It began to rain next day and Tinker couldn't go out. He nearly drove everyone mad, rushing about all over the house hooting, and purring like a car engine.

'Now look,' Joanna said to him, when, for the twentieth time, he drove himself all round her kitchen. 'I don't care if you're a Mini, or a Ford Fiesta, or even a Rolls – you just keep out of my kitchen! It's a funny thing to think that a fine car like a Rolls can steal a bun out of my tin – it ought to be ashamed of itself!'

'Well, if I can't get petrol, I've got to get *something* to run on, haven't I?' demanded Tinker. 'Look at Mischief – *he's* helping himself to apples in the larder, but you don't say anything to him!'

'Oh, lands sakes, is that creature in the larder again?' cried poor Joanna, rushing across the kitchen. 'Who left it open, I'd like to know?'

'Timmy did,' said Tinker.

'You little liar!' said Joanna as she shooed Mischief out of the larder. 'Timmy would never do a thing like that. He's as honest as the day, not like that little thief of a monkey of yours!'

'Don't you like him?' said Tinker, sorrowfully. 'He likes *you*.'

Joanna glanced across at the tiny monkey. He sat huddled in a corner, his arms over his face, looking very small and sad. One small brown eye peeped out at Joanna.

'You're a humbug, you are!' said Joanna. 'Looking as if you're the unhappiest monkey in the world, when all the time you're thinking what mischief to do next. Here – come and get this biscuit, you rascal – and don't you dare to go near Timmy this morning. He's very very angry with you.'

'What did Mischief do to Timmy?' asked Tinker, surprised.

'He went to Timmy's dish and stole one of the bones there,' said Joanna. 'Timmy growled like a roll of thunder! I really thought he would bite off the monkey's tail. My word, you should have seen Mischief skedaddle!'

Mischief had now crept up cautiously to Joanna, eyeing the biscuit she held. He had had one or two slaps from her for stealing, and he was rather wary of her quick right hand.

'Here you are – take the biscuit, for goodness' sake,' said Joanna. 'And don't look such a little misery, or I might suddenly find myself giving you another biscuit. Hallo – where's he gone?'

The monkey had snatched the biscuit with one of his tiny paws, and had scampered away to the door. It was shut, so Tinker opened it for him. At once Timmy came in. He had been lying outside the door, sniffing the good smell of soup cooking on the stove.

Mischief leapt to the top of a chair back and made a strange little whinnying sound – rather apologetic and sad. Timmy stood still and pricked up his ears. He understood animal language very well!

Mischief still held the biscuit. He leapt down to the seat of the chair – and then, to Joanna's enormous surprise, he held out the biscuit to Timmy! He chattered in a very small voice, and Timmy listened gravely. Then the big dog took the biscuit gently, threw it into the air, chewed it once, and swallowed it!

'Well, did you ever see anything like *that* before!' said Joanna, marvelling. 'For all the world as if Mischief was apologising to Timmy for stealing his bone – and offering him his biscuit to make up! Well, whatever will George say when she hears!'

Timmy licked his lips to see if any biscuit crumbs were left, and then put his big head forward, and gave the monkey a sudden lick on the tip of his funny little nose.

'Timmy's saying thank you!' cried Tinker, in delight. 'Now they'll be friends – you see if they won't!'

Joanna was astonished and pleased. Well, well – to think of that monkey being clever enough to present Timmy with a biscuit that he very much wanted to eat himself! He wasn't a bad little thing! She went upstairs to find George and tell her.

But George didn't believe her. 'Timmy would never take a biscuit from that silly little monkey!' she said. 'Never! You made all that up, Joanna, just because you're getting fond of Mischief. You wait till he runs off with your toasting-fork again!'

All the same, George went down with Joanna, curious to see if the two animals *were* becoming friendly – and she saw a very strange sight indeed!

Mischief was on Timmy's back, and Timmy was solemnly trotting round the kitchen, giving him a ride! The monkey was chattering in delight, and Tinker was shouting in glee.

'Go faster, Tim, go faster! You're a very fine horse! You'd easily win the Derby! Go on, gallop!'

'I don't want Timmy to give rides to the monkey,' said George. 'Stop it, Timmy! You look silly.'

The monkey suddenly leaned forward and hugged Timmy round the neck. Then he slid off and looked at George as if to say, 'All right! I won't make your dog look silly!'

Timmy knew that George was cross and he went to lie down on the rug. At once Mischief came sidling across to him, and settled himself between Timmy's big front paws, cuddling there without fear. Timmy bent his big head and licked him very gently.

Tears came suddenly to Joanna's eyes. That Timmy! He was just about the nicest dog in the whole world. 'See that!' she said to George. 'Big-hearted and kind that dog of yours is! Don't you scold him now for being great enough to make friends with a little creature who stole his bone!'

'I'm not *going* to scold him!' said George, astonished and proud. 'He's a marvel – the best dog in the world! Aren't you, Timmy darling?'

And she went over to Timmy and stroked his big soft head. He whined lovingly and licked her, looking up as if to say, 'Well, everything's all right now – we're *all* friends!'

Tinker had been watching from a corner of the kitchen, saying nothing. He was rather afraid of George and her quick temper. He was delighted when he saw her go over and pat Timmy, without even disturbing the monkey. In his joy he began to honk like a lorry, and startled everyone so much that they yelled at him:

'Stop it, Tinker!'

'Be quiet, you little nuisance!'

'Woof!' That was from Timmy.

'You'll have Mr Kirrin in here if you honk like that,' said Joanna. 'Can't you be something quiet for a change – a bicycle, for instance?'

Tinker thought that was quite a good idea. He ran round the kitchen and out into the hall, making a hissing noise like the sound of a bicycle's wheels on the road. Then he decided to make a noise like a bicycle bell, and produced a very loud ringing noise indeed! It was so like the ringing of a bell that Aunt Fanny ran out of the living room, thinking there was someone at the front door!

Then the study door flew open and out came Uncle Quentin and Tinker's father. Poor Tinker was caught, and his father shook him so hard that two pencils shot out of his pocket and rolled over the floor.

Tinker began to yell – and *how* he could yell! George came out of the kitchen to see what was happening, and Dick, Julian and Anne raced down the stairs. Joanna rushed out into the hall, too, and almost sent Uncle Quentin flying.

Then George did a very silly thing. She began to laugh – and when George laughed properly, her laugh was wonderful to hear! But neither Uncle Quentin nor Professor Hayling thought it wonderful – they merely thought it rude! George was laughing at *them* – and that wouldn't do at all!

'This is absolutely the last straw!' shouted Uncle Quentin, his face red with rage. 'First this boy ringing bells all over the place – and George encouraging him by laughing! I won't have it! Don't you know that very very important work is going on here, in Kirrin Cottage – work that may bring great benefits to the world! Fanny, send these children away somewhere. I won't have them in the house, disturbing us when we are doing such important work. Do you hear? SEND THEM AWAY! And that's my LAST word!'

And he and the professor stalked back to the study and banged the door. WELL! Now what was to be done?

CHAPTER FOUR

Tinker has a wonderful idea

AUNT FANNY had appeared during the row, and sighed when she heard her husband shouting. Oh, dear, dear – these scientists who liked to do wonderful things for the world – and yet often made their own families unhappy! She smiled at George's angry face, and took her arm.

'Come into the living room, dear, and bring the others with you. We'll have to decide what can be done. Your father really *is* doing wonderful work, you know – and I must say that Tinker and Mischief and Timmy don't help very much! All right, all right, George – I know it isn't Timmy's fault – but he does have a very loud bark, you know!'

She took the five children and Timmy into the living room. The monkey, scared at the shouting, had gone into hiding and was nowhere to be seen. Aunt Fanny called to Joanna.

'Joanna – come and help us to discuss what's to be done. This kind of thing can't go on.'

They all sat down, looking rather solemn. Timmy flopped down under the table, and put his nose on his paws. Where was that little monkey who had given him his biscuit?

The discussion began. George spoke first, most indignantly.

'Mother, this is our *home*. Why do we have to go away just because Father wants this scientist friend to stay with him? I have to do holiday homework, and I don't make a

193

row every time Father bangs a door when I'm studying. But if I so much as . . .'

'That will do, George,' said her mother. 'You ought to understand your father better than you seem to. You are both exactly the same – impatient, short-tempered, bangers-of-doors, and yet both so kind, too! Now – let's see if we can find a way out.'

'I only wish we could stay at *my* home,' said Julian, feeling awkward. 'But it's all shut up, now that my parents have gone away.'

'Can't we take tents over to Kirrin Island?' said George. 'Yes, Mother, yes – I know what you're going to say – it's only the beginning of April, and it's far too cold and all the rest of it, and . . .'

'The forecast for the weather is very bad,' said her mother. 'Rain, rain, nothing but rain. You can't possibly go and camp in the pouring rain – and row to and fro, getting drenched each day – I'd have you all in bed with bronchitis before three days had gone – and *then* what should we do!'

'All right, Mother – have *you* any good suggestions?' said George, still cross.

'Hey – what's that monkey doing?' said Dick, suddenly. 'Stop him!'

'He's only poking the fire,' said Tinker. 'He thinks it's cold in here.'

'Well, what next!' said Joanna and took the poker firmly from the monkey's little paw. 'Do you want to set the house on fire, you – you little . . .'

'Monkey!' finished Dick, with a grin. 'I must say that Mischief is always up to mischief! Can't keep your eye off him for a moment!'

'Well, now – if we can't go to Kirrin Island, or back home, or stay here – where *can* we go?' said Julian, looking serious. 'Hotels are too expensive – and which of our friends would like to have five of us to stay, plus a wicked little monkey and a big dog with an enormous appetite?'

There was a silence. What a problem! Then suddenly Tinker spoke up.

'*I* know where we could go – and we'd jolly well have some fun, too!' he said.

'Oh – and where is this wonderful place?' asked George disbelievingly.

'Well – I was thinking of my lighthouse,' said Tinker, most surprisingly. And then, as no one said anything, but merely stared at him in astonishment, he nodded at them. 'I said my *lighthouse* – don't you know what a lighthouse is?'

'Don't be silly, please,' said Dick. 'This is no time for jokes.'

'It's *not* a joke,' said Tinker, indignantly. 'It's perfectly true. You ask my father.'

'But, Tinker dear – you can't possibly *own* a lighthouse,' said Aunt Fanny, smiling.

'Well, I do,' said Tinker, quite fiercely. 'You see, my father had some very special work to do, that couldn't be done on land – so he bought an old empty lighthouse, and did his work there. I went to stay with him – my, it was grand there, with the wind and the waves crashing about all the time.'

'But – surely he didn't *give* it to you, did he?' said Julian, disbelievingly.

'Yes, he did. Why shouldn't he, if I wanted it badly?'

demanded Tinker. '*He* didn't want it any more, and
nobody would buy it – and I wanted it terribly, so he
gave it to me on my last birthday. And it's mine, I tell
you.'

'Well, I'm blessed!' said Julian. 'Here's old George
owning an island given to her by her mother – and Tinker
owning a lighthouse given to him by his father! I wish my
parents would present me with a volcano, or something
really thrilling!'

George's eyes shone as she looked at the surprising
Tinker. 'A lighthouse – of your very own! Where is it?'

'About twenty miles along this coast to the west,' said
Tinker. 'It's not an awfully *big* one, you know – but it's
smashing! The old lamp is still there, but it's not used
now.'

'Why not?' asked Dick.

'Well, because a big new lighthouse was built farther
along the coast, in a better position for warning ships,'
explained Tinker. 'That's how it was this old one was put
up for sale. It was fine for my father to work in. Nobody
ever disturbed him there – though he did get very angry
with the seagulls sometimes. He said they mewed like
great cats all the time, and made him feel he ought to put
out milk for them.'

This made everyone burst into loud laughter, and
Tinker sat beaming round proudly. How clever he must
be to make these children laugh like that – yes, and even
Joanna and Aunt Fanny too! He broke into their laughter by banging on the table.

'You do believe me now, don't you?' he said. 'It's quite
true that the lighthouse is mine. You ask my father. Do
let's all go and stay in it till our two fathers have finished

their work. We could take Timmy and Mischief too –
there's plenty of room.'

This proposal was so astonishing that no one answered
for a few moments. Then George gave him a friendly dig
in the chest.

'*I'll* come! Fancy living in a *lighthouse*! I bet the girls at
school won't believe *that*!'

'Aunt Fanny! May we go?' said Anne, her eyes shining
too.

'Well – I don't know,' said her aunt. 'It really is a most
extraordinary idea. I shall have to discuss it with your
uncle, and with Tinker's father too.'

'My father will say yes, I know he will!' said Tinker.
'We left some stores there – and some blankets – I *say*,
wouldn't it be grand to run a lighthouse ourselves!'

The idea certainly appealed to all the Five – even Timmy thumped his tail on the floor as if he had understood every word. He probably had – he never missed anything that was going on!

'I've a map that shows where my lighthouse is,' said Tinker, scrabbling in one of his pockets. 'It's rather crumpled and dirty because I've looked at it so often. Look – here's a map of the coastline – and just there, built on rocks – is my lighthouse. It's marked by a round dot, look!'

Everyone pored over the grubby map. Nobody had the least doubt but that this was the answer to all their problems! Dick stared at the excited Tinker. How lucky he was to own a *lighthouse*! Dick had never before met a lighthouse owner – and to think it should be this funny little Tinker!

'The rocks that the lighthouse is built on used to wreck many ships,' said Tinker. 'Wreckers used to work along that coast, you know – they would shine a light as if to guide ships along the coast, and make them go on the rocks. Crash! They'd be broken to pieces, and everyone drowned – and the wreckers would wait till the ship was washed up on the shore, and then take everything they could from her.'

'The wicked wretches!' said Dick, horrified.

'There's a Wreckers' Cave there, too, where the wreckers stored the things they stole from the wrecked ships,' said Tinker. 'I haven't been very far into it – I'm too scared to. They do say there's an old wrecker or two there still.'

'Oh, nonsense!' said Aunt Fanny, laughing. 'That's probably just a tale to keep children away from dangerous caves and rocks. Well, dears – I really don't see any reason why you shouldn't go to Tinker's lighthouse, if his father agrees.'

'Mother! THANK YOU!' cried George, and gave her mother a hug that made her gasp. 'I *say* – living in an old *lighthouse* – it's too good to be true! I shall take my binoculars and keep watch for ships!'

'Well, Julian had better take his record-player as well,' said Mrs Kirrin. 'If it's stormy weather, it may be a bit duller than you think, cooped up in a lonely lighthouse!'

'It will be MARVELLOUS!' cried Tinker, and he suddenly became a racing car, tearing round the room at top speed, making a most extraordinary noise. Timmy barked and Mischief began to chatter loudly.

'Shush!' said Aunt Fanny. 'You'll make your father cross, Tinker, and that will be the end of your fine idea. Switch your engine off, please, and sit down quietly! I'll talk to your father as soon as I can!'

CHAPTER FIVE

Tinker's lighthouse

MRS KIRRIN thought that she might as well go immediately to the study, and see if her husband and Professor Hayling could talk about the children going away to this lighthouse of Tinker's. Could it really be true? She knocked discreetly at the closed door.

She could hear voices inside the room, but nobody called 'come in'. She knocked again.

'What is it NOW!' shouted Uncle Quentin. 'If it's you, George, go away and keep away. And if it's Tinker, tell him to go to the garage and park himself there. I suppose it's he who has been making all that row this morning!'

Aunt Fanny smiled to herself. Well, well – if all scientists were like her husband and Professor Hayling, it was a wonder they were ever calm enough to get any work done!

She went away. Perhaps she could bring up the subject of the lighthouse at dinner-time. What a relief it would be to have a peaceful house for a few days!

She went into the kitchen to find Joanna. The monkey was there, helping her! He had slipped away from Tinker and gone to see if there were any titbits about. Joanna was talking away to him as she rolled out pastry.

'See, I roll it like this – and like that – and I pick off a tiny bit for you!' And she gave Mischief a snippet for himself. He was very pleased, and leapt on Joanna's shoulder. He lifted a piece of her hair and whispered in her ear. Joanna pretended to understand.

'Yes, Mischief. If you're good I'll give you another titbit in a minute. Now get off my shoulder, and stop whispering. It tickles!'

'Well, Joanna – I never thought to see you rolling pastry with a monkey on your shoulder!' said Aunt Fanny. 'Joanna, what do you think about this lighthouse idea? I haven't been able to get into the study yet! My husband thought I was Tinker, and told me to go and park myself in the garage!'

'And a very good idea too,' said Joanna, rolling her pastry vigorously. 'Isn't that Tinker out in the hall now – sounds like a car of some sort! Well, I'd say that if the lighthouse is habitable, why shouldn't the Five go there, with Tinker and the monkey? They'd enjoy themselves all right, and Timmy would look after them. Sort of thing that they love – rushing off to a lighthouse! Ugh! Nasty lonely place, with waves crashing round and a wind fit to blow your head off!'

'Yes, but do you think they'd be all right all alone there, Joanna?' said Aunt Fanny.

'Well, Julian and Dick are old enough to look after the others – though I must say I wouldn't like the job of being in charge of that Tinker,' said Joanna. 'All I hope is that he doesn't imagine he's an aeroplane all of a sudden, and take off from the top of the lighthouse!'

Aunt Fanny laughed. 'Don't say that to *him*!' she said. 'His idea of being a car is bad enough. Well, Joanna, I feel very mean sending George and the others away immediately they come here – but with two excitable scientists in the house, I don't see that there's anything else to do. Look out for that monkey – he's found your bag of raisins!'

'Oh, you little mischief!' said Joanna, and made a grab at the monkey. He shot off to the top of a cupboard with the bag of raisins firmly held in one paw. He made a tiny chattering noise, as if he were scolding Joanna.

'You come down with those raisins!' said Joanna, advancing to the cupboard. 'Else I'll tie you to a chair with that long tail of yours. You little monkey!'

Mischief said something in his funny little voice that sounded rather cheeky. Then he put his paw into the bag and took out a raisin. But he didn't eat it – he threw it straight at Joanna! It hit her on the cheek, and she stared at Mischief in astonishment.

'What! You'd pelt me with my own raisins! Well, that I will NOT have!' She went to the sink and filled a cup with water, while Mischief pelted both her and Aunt Fanny with raisin after raisin! He danced about on the top of the cupboard, screeching loudly in glee!

A bowl on the top of the cupboard fell off as the monkey danced about, and crashed to the ground. The noise scared him, and, with a flying leap, he shot off the cupboard and landed on the top of the half-open door. He pelted the two women from there, making the most extraordinary noises.

The study door was flung open, and out came Uncle Quentin, followed by the professor. 'What was that crash? What's happening here? How *can* we w . . .'

It was most unfortunate that Joanna should have thrown the cup of water at Mischief at that moment. He sat there on the top of the door – and the water fell all over him, splashed over the top of the door – and down on to Uncle Quentin's head as he pushed the door open!

Joanna was horrified. She disappeared into the scullery at once, not knowing whether to laugh or to make her apologies.

Uncle Quentin was astounded to find himself dripping wet. He stared angrily up at Mischief, absolutely certain that it was the monkey who had emptied the water over him.

By this time the Five had come out of the living room, wondering what the noise was. 'It's old Mischief,' said Tinker. 'Throwing water, I should think!'

'Well, actually, *I* threw the water,' began Joanna apologetically, peeping out of the scullery, 'because . . .'

'YOU threw it?' said Uncle Quentin, amazed. 'What *is* happening in this house? Things have come to a pretty pass if *you* start flinging water at people, Joanna. You ought to be ashamed of yourself! Are you mad?'

'Listen, Quentin,' said his wife. 'Nobody's mad at present, but pretty soon we all shall be, if this sort of thing goes on! Quentin, are you LISTENING? I've something important to say to you – and to you too, Professor.'

The professor remembered his manners. 'Please go on,' he said politely, and then flinched as a raisin hit him squarely on the head. Mischief had found one on the floor, and had taken a pot shot at the professor. Dick looked at the monkey admiringly – he really was a very good shot!

'What's that little idiot of a monkey throwing!' said Uncle Quentin, fiercely, and knew at once when a raisin hit him smartly on the nose. 'Get rid of him! Put him in the dustbin! Why have I to put up with monkeys that throw things and boys that chug about the house like cars gone mad? I tell you Fanny, I will NOT have it!'

Aunt Fanny looked at him very sternly. 'Listen Quentin, I have something to say. LISTEN! Tinker says his father gave him a lighthouse for his own, and he suggests that he and all the others should leave here and go and stay in the lighthouse. Quentin, are you listening?'

'A lighthouse! Are you mad? What, that little monkey of a boy says he owns a *lighthouse*? And you believed him?' said Uncle Quentin amazed.

'Tinker's quite right, as it happens,' said Professor Hayling. 'I bought a lighthouse to work in when I wanted to get right away from everywhere and concentrate – and when I'd finished, I couldn't sell it – so as Tinker pestered me for it, I gave it to him. But not to *live* in!'

'A *lighthouse* to work in!' said Uncle Quentin, thinking what a truly marvellous idea this was. 'I'll buy it from you! I'll . . .'

'No, Quentin, you won't do anything of the sort,' said his wife, firmly. 'Will you PLEASE listen to me, both of you. Professor Hayling, is the lighthouse fit for these five to stay in – and if so, they want to know if they can go there until you two have finished your work here. They're a nuisance to you – and to be quite honest, you're a nuisance to *them*!'

'Fanny!' said her husband, astonished and angry.

'Father, listen. We'll all get out of your way as soon as possible, if you'll say we can go to Tinker's lighthouse,' said George, planting herself firmly in front of her father. 'Say one word – 'YES' – that's all we want.'

'YES!' shouted Uncle Quentin, suddenly tired of all the argument, and longing to get back to his papers with the professor. 'YES! Go to the lighthouse – go to the Tower of London – go and live at the Zoo, if you like! The monkeys will welcome that mischievous little creature, sitting grinning up there on the cupboard! But go SOME-WHERE!'

'Oh, thank you, Father!' said George, joyfully. 'We'll go off to the lighthouse as soon as we can. HURRAY! THREE CH . . .'

But before she could continue, the study door shut with a bang behind the two exasperated men. George bent down, took Timmy's two front legs, and proceeded to dance all round the living room with him, shouting 'HURRAY! THREE CHEERS!' over and over again.

Aunt Fanny sat down suddenly in a chair, and began to laugh. Joanna laughed too. 'If we don't laugh, we shall cry!' she said. 'What a hullabaloo! Well, it's a good thing they'll soon be off. That loft is much too draughty for the boys, you know. Look at poor Julian – he's got such a stiff neck he can hardly turn it this morning.'

'Who cares?' said Julian. 'We'll soon be off again together, all the Five – and two more to keep us company. It will be quite an adventure!'

'An adventure?' said Tinker, surprised. 'But you can't have adventures in a lighthouse – it's out on the rocks, all by itself, as lonely as can be! There aren't any adventures to be found *there*!'

Ah – you wait and see, Tinker! You don't know the Five! If there's any adventure about, they're bound to be right in the middle of it!

CHAPTER SIX

Making plans

IT WAS very exciting making plans to go to the lighthouse. Tinker told them all about it, time and time again. 'It's very tall, and there's an iron stairway – a spiral one – going from the bottom up to the top. And at the top is a little room for the lamp that used to flash to warn ships away.'

'It sounds smashing,' said George. 'What about Timmy, though? Can he climb up a spiral stairway?'

'Well, he can live down at the bottom, can't he, if it's too difficult for him to climb up?' said Tinker. 'Mischief can climb it easily – he simply *races* up!'

'If Timmy has to live at the bottom, I shall live there with him,' said George.

'Why not wait and see the lighthouse before you arrange the sleeping places?' said Julian, giving her a friendly punch. 'Now first we must find out exactly where it is – and the way to get there. It's a pity Tinker can't turn into a *real* car – he could run us there in no time!'

Tinker at once imagined himself to be a large van, taking the Five and all their luggage along the road. He raced round the room, making his usual car noise, and hooting so loudly that he made everyone jump. Julian caught him as he raced round the table and sat him down firmly.

'Any more of that and we leave you behind,' he said.

207

'Now – where's that map of yours – let's have a look at it – and then we'll get Aunt Fanny's big map of the coast, and track down the road to your lighthouse.'

Soon Tinker and the Five were studying a large-scale map of the coast, Mischief sitting on Dick's shoulder and tickling his neck.

'See – that's the way to go,' said Julian. 'It really wouldn't be far by sea – look, round the coast here, cut across this bay, round the headland – and just there are the rocks on which the old lighthouse stands. But by road it's a very long way.'

'Better go by car, though,' said Dick. 'We've a good bit of luggage to take – not only our clothes, but crockery and things like that. And food.'

'There are still some stores there,' said Tinker, eagerly. 'Dad left some when we went away from the lighthouse.'

'They'll probably have gone bad,' said Julian.

'Well – don't take too much,' said Tinker. 'It's a pretty rough way over the rocks to the lighthouse – there isn't a road that runs right up to it, you know. We shall have to carry everything ourselves, once we get to the place. We can always get fresh food if we want it – the village isn't all that far away – but there are some days when you can't even leave the lighthouse! You see the waves splash house-high over the rocks when there's a rough wind. We'd have to get across by boat if the tide's in – the rocks are covered then!'

'This sounds too exciting for words!' said Dick, his eyes shining. 'What do *you* think about it, Anne? You haven't said a word!'

'Well – I do feel just a *bit* scared!' said Anne. 'It sounds

208

so lonely. I do hope no ships will be wrecked on those
awful rocks while *we're* there!'

'Tinker said there was a fine new lighthouse farther
along the coast,' said Julian. 'Its light will keep every ship
away from that wicked stretch of rocks. Look, Anne, you
would like to come, wouldn't you? If not, Aunt Fanny
wouldn't mind just *you* staying here – you're a little
mouse, you wouldn't bother Uncle Quentin or the professor at all!'

'I shouldn't DREAM of not coming with you,' said
Anne, indignantly. 'Julian – you don't think there are
still wreckers about do you? I should hate that.'

'They belong to years gone by,' said Julian. 'Cheer up,
Anne – this is just a little visit we're going to pay to
Tinker's seaside house! He is kindly taking in visitors this
spring!'

'Well, let's get on with our plans,' said Dick. 'We go
there by car – er, *what* was that you just said, Tinker?'

'I said I'll drive you, if you like,' said Tinker. 'I could
dr . . .'

'You haven't a driving licence, so don't talk nonsense,'
said George, crossly.

'I know I haven't – but all the same I *can* drive!' said
Tinker. 'I've driven my father's car round and round our
garden, see? And . . .'

'Oh, do shut up,' said Dick. 'You and your pretend
cars! Julian, when shall we go to his lighthouse?'

'Well, why not tomorrow morning?' said Julian. 'I'm
sure everyone would be glad if we left as soon as possible!
It's hard on Aunt Fanny and Joanna to have so many
here. We'll see about a car and someone to drive us, and
then we'll pack and make our getaway!'

'Hurray,' said George in delight, and pounded on the table, making Mischief leap up to the top of a bookcase in fright. 'Oh, sorry, Mischief – did I scare you? Timmy tell him I'm sorry, I didn't mean it. He probably understands your doggy language.'

Timmy looked up at Mischief, gave two little whines and a comforting wuff. Mischief listened with his head on one side, and then leapt down, landing neatly on Timmy's back.

'Thanks for giving him my message, Tim,' said George, and everyone laughed. Good old Timmy! He wagged his long tail and put his head on George's knee, looking up at her beseechingly.

'All right old thing – I understand your language, whether you talk with your voice or your eyes,' said George, patting him. 'You want a walk, don't you?'

'Woof!' said Timmy joyfully, and tore to the door.

'Let's walk down to the garage and see if they have a car or a van to hire out to us,' said Julian. 'We'll have to have a driver too, because someone has to take back the car. Come on, Timmy-dog!'

They all set off to the garage in the village. The rain held off for a while, and the sun came out, making Kirrin Bay sparkle and shine.

'I wish we could have gone to stay on my island,' said George. 'But it really is too damp to camp out. Anyway, a lighthouse will be nice for a change!'

The man at the garage listened to Julian's tale of wanting a car to go to the lighthouse. 'It's the old lighthouse at Demon's Rocks, not the new one at High Cliffs,' he said. 'We're going to stay there.'

'Stay at a *lighthouse*!' said the man. 'This isn't a joke is it?'

'No. It happens to belong to one of us,' said Julian.
'We have a few things to take there, of course, and we
hoped you'd have a taxi tomorrow for us. We'd let you
know somehow when we are ready to come back from
the lighthouse, and you can send the same car for us
then.'

'Right,' said the man. 'And you're staying at Kirrin
Cottage now, you say? Oh – your uncle is Mr Kirrin?
Well, I know Master George here, of course – but I
wasn't certain who *you* were. Some funny people order
cars, you know!'

George was pleased to be called *Master* George. It was
nice to be thought a boy. She dug her hands deep down in
the pockets of her jeans.

'We'd better take a few rugs and cushions,' said Julian.
'And some sweaters and wind-cheaters. I can't imagine
it's very warm in the lighthouse.'

'There's an oil-heater there,' said Tinker. 'I think it
was for the lighthouse lamp when it was in use. We can
use that for warmth, if we're cold.'

'What sort of stores did you and your father leave
there?' asked Dick. 'We'd better order some foodstuffs at
the grocer's – and some ginger beer or something – and
take it all in the car.'

'Well – there's plenty of tinned food, I think,' said
Tinker, trying to remember. 'We left it there in case my
father wanted to come back at any time and work again
in peace and quiet.'

'Hm. It's a pity he didn't fix up with Uncle Quentin to
have him there with him,' said Julian. 'Then everyone
would have been happy!'

They went to the grocer's and Anne tried her best to

order what she thought they would need, outside of tinned food. 'Sugar – butter – eggs – oh dear – help me, George. How much shall I order?'

'Don't forget we *can* go shopping in Demon's Rocks village,' said Tinker. 'Only it's a bit of a nuisance if there's windy weather – the path over the rocks isn't very safe then. We might have to stay in the lighthouse for a day or two without leaving it. Even a boat might be too risky.'

'It sounds thrilling!' said George, picturing them all marooned by fierce storms, waiting to be rescued from peril and starvation! 'Get some biscuits, Anne. And bars of chocolate. And lots of ginger beer. And a big bottle of lemonade. And a . . .'

'Wait a minute – do you know who's paying for all this?' said Julian. '*I* am. So don't ruin me completely!' He took out his wallet. 'Here's five pounds,' he said. 'That's all I can spare at present! Dick can buy the next lot of food we want!'

'Well, I've plenty of money too,' said Tinker, taking out a handful from his pocket.

'You would have!' said George. 'I suppose your father just hands out money whenever you ask him. He's so vague he wouldn't know if he paid you three times a day!'

'Well, *yours* seems pretty vague too,' said Tinker, smartly. 'He poured the coffee over his porridge this morning, instead of the milk. I saw him. And what's more, he ate it without even *noticing* it was coffee!'

'That's enough,' said Julian. 'We don't tell tales about our parents in public. Tinker, don't you want to take anything for Mischief to eat while we're in the lighthouse? George has bought biscuits for Timmy, and we're going to lay in a supply of bones, too.'

'I'll buy Mischief's food myself, thank you,' said Tinker, not very pleased at being ticked off by Julian. He gave an order for a packet of raisins, a packet of currants, a pound of apple rings and some oranges. Mischief eyed all these with very great *pleasure*.

'Paws off!' said George, sharply, as the little monkey slyly slid his paw into the bag of biscuits put ready for Timmy. Mischief jumped on to Tinker's shoulder and hid his face in his tiny paws, as if he were ashamed!

'We'll just buy some more fruit,' said Julian, 'and then I think we'll have enough. We'll take it all round to the garage, and put it in the car ready to take away tomorrow.'

'Tomorrow!' said George, her eyes shining. 'Oh, I hope it comes soon. I can't *wait* for it!'

CHAPTER SEVEN

Off at last!

IT WAS very exciting that evening to talk about the next day – the taxi coming to fetch them – the drive round the coast to Demon's Rocks – exploring the lighthouse – looking out over the endless sea, and watching the great waves coming in to pound on the rocks!

'What *I'm* looking forward to is our first night there,' said George. 'All alone, high up in that old lighthouse! Nothing but wind and waves around! Snuggling down in our rugs, and waking up to hear the wind and waves again.'

'And the gulls,' put in Tinker. 'They cry all the time. You can watch them from the lighthouse top. I wish I had wings like a gull – spread out wide – sitting on the wind as they glide!'

'Sitting on the wind – yes, that's exactly what they do!' said Anne. 'I just wish their cry didn't sound so mournful though.'

Aunt Fanny was half-inclined not to let the children go after all! The weather forecast was bad, and she pictured them sitting half-frozen, and perhaps very scared, in the old deserted lighthouse. But no sooner did she begin to wonder out loud if she ought to let them go than the children raised their voices in indignant chorus!

'But we've ordered the TAXI!'

'And heaps of food! And Joanna has packed up a big tin of all kinds of things. She even baked a special cake for us!'

OFF AT LAST!

'*Mother*! How *could* you think of saying no when you've already said yes!'

'All right, all right, dears!' said Aunt Fanny. 'I wouldn't really stop you going. But do send me a card or two, will you? That's if there's anywhere to post one!'

'Oh, there's a tiny post office in the village,' said Tinker. 'We'll send a card every day. Then you'll know we're all right.'

'Very well – but if a card doesn't come I'll be very worried,' said Aunt Fanny. 'So please do keep your word! You won't forget your anoraks will you – and your rubber boots, and . . .?'

'Mother! I feel as if you're going to mention *umbrellas* next!' said George. 'But honestly, we'd be blown out to sea if we put an umbrella up on Demon's Rocks. Tinker says there's always a gale blowing round the coast there.'

'You can think of us playing snap with our packs of cards, and having a fine time in the lighthouse while storms rage round and howl like demons!' said Dick. 'We'll be sitting snug in our rugs, with ginger beer beside us, and chocolate biscuits all round . . .'

'Woof,' said Timmy, at once, pricking his ears up at words he knew so well.

'Ha – you think you're going to feed on chocolate biscuits, do you, Tim?' said Dick, ruffling the dog's hairy head. 'And please don't interrupt the conversation. It's not good manners.'

'Woof,' said Timmy apologetically, and licked Dick's nose.

'I think you'd all better go to bed early tonight,' said Aunt Fanny. 'You've still some packing to do tomorrow – and you say you've ordered the taxi for half past nine.'

'We'll be down to breakfast at eight o'clock sharp,' said Julian. 'I bet the professor won't be down till about eleven, and forget all about his bacon and eggs! Tinker, does your father *ever* have a really hot meal? I mean – it seems to me he either forgets them altogether, or wanders in hours late, and then doesn't know if he's having breakfast, dinner, or supper!'

'Well, I can always eat up everything that's there, if I think he's forgotten to come,' said Tinker, sensibly. 'Mischief helps too. You'd be surprised how fond Mischief is of fat bacon.'

'I'm not a *bit* surprised at anything Mischief does,' said Julian. 'I'm just wondering how we are going to put up with his tricks when we're all cooped up in the lighthouse together! We can't send him out into the garden then, to work off some of his high spirits. Aunt Fanny, do you know he took my pencil this morning and scribbled monkey words all over my wallpaper? It's a good thing I can't read monkey language for I'm sure he wasn't scribbling anything polite!'

'You're not to say things like that about Mischief,' said Tinker, offended. 'He's very good-mannered for a monkey. You should see *some* monkeys I know!'

'I'd rather not, thanks,' said Julian.

Tinker was cross. He picked up Mischief and went out of the room. Soon there was the noise of a car out in the hall – one that needed repairing by the sound of it!

'R-r-r-r-RRRRRR-r-r-r-r, OOOOOOPH, Rrrrrrr, PARP!' Aunt Fanny rushed to the door. 'You *know* you've been told not to be a car out in the hall. Come back before your father hears you, Tinker. My goodness me, this house will be an entirely different place, once it is

216

rid of all the cars that have driven about in it since you came!'

'I was only being a tractor,' said Tinker, surprised. 'I always feel as if I *must* go and be a car when people are horrid to me or Mischief.'

'Oh, be your age!' said George.

'I shall go up to bed,' said Tinker, offended again.

'Well, that's not a bad idea, seeing that you have to be punctual tomorrow morning,' said Aunt Fanny. 'Good night, then, Tinker dear. Good night, Mischief.'

Tinker found himself gently propelled to the door. He went up the stairs, grumbling, Mischief on his shoulder. But he soon stopped frowning as he undressed and thought of the next day. Off to the lighthouse – HIS lighthouse! Ha, that would make George and the others sit up. He snuggled down in bed with Mischief nestling beside him, one little paw down the front of Tinker's pyjama jacket.

Next morning George awoke first. She sat up, afraid that the weather forecast might be right, and that it would be pouring with rain. No – it was wrong for once – the sun shone down and she could not hear the sound of the sea – that meant that there was not much wind to blow up big waves that pounded on the shore.

She awoke Anne. 'Lighthouse day!' she said. 'Buck up – it's half past seven.'

They were all down very punctually to breakfast – except Professor Hayling! As usual he did not appear until breakfast was over, and then he sauntered in at the front door!

'Oh – you *are* up then,' said Aunt Fanny, 'I thought you were still asleep in bed.'

'No – Tinker woke me up at some very early hour,' complained the professor. 'Or else it was the monkey – I really don't know. They both look alike to me in the early morning.'

Uncle Quentin was already down, but hadn't come into breakfast. He was in his study as usual. 'George – go and fetch your father,' said Aunt Fanny. 'His breakfast will soon be inedible.'

George went to the study door and knocked. 'Father! Don't you want your breakfast?'

'I've had it!' said a surprised voice. 'Very nice – couple of boiled eggs.'

'Father! That was your *yesterday's* breakfast!' said George, impatiently. 'It's bacon and *fried* eggs today. You've forgotten as usual. Do come. We're leaving for the lighthouse soon.'

'Lighthouse – what lighthouse?' said Uncle Quentin, in tones of great astonishment. But he had no answer, George had gone back to the dining room, not knowing whether to laugh or frown. Really! Father was so forgetful that he would forget where he lived next!

There was great excitement after breakfast. Rugs – coats – night clothes, the warmest that could be found – tins of cakes and mince-pies packed by Joanna – sandwiches to eat on the way – books – games – as George said, anyone would think they were going away for a month!

'The car's late!' said Dick, impatiently. 'Or else my watch is fast.'

'Here it comes!' said Anne, excited. 'Oh, Aunt Fanny, I wish you were coming too! We're going to have such fun!

Where's Mischief – oh, there he is! And Timmy – Timmy, we're going to live in a lighthouse! You don't even know what that is, do you?'

The car came up to the front gate of Kirrin Cottage, and the driver blew his horn, making Uncle Quentin almost jump out of his skin. He turned on poor Tinker at once. 'Was that *you* up to your silly tricks of pretending to be a car, and hooting again? Own up, now!'

'No, it wasn't, on my honour it wasn't,' said Tinker indignantly, hopping out of the way of what looked as if it might be a very powerful slap. 'See – it's that car!'

'I'll just ask the driver what he means by driving up here and hooting fit to scare us all!' said Uncle Quentin indignantly. 'What's he come here for, anyway?'

'FATHER! It's the TAXI that's come to take us to the LIGHTHOUSE!' said George, not knowing whether to laugh or be cross.

'Ah yes,' said Uncle Quentin. 'Why didn't you tell me before? Well, goodbye, goodbye! Have a good time, and don't forget to dry yourselves well after a bathe.'

They piled into the car, and the man put their luggage into the big boot. He stared as Timmy and Mischief leapt in. 'Sure you've all got enough room?' he said. 'What a carful!'

Then to the accompaniment of a loud R-r-r-r-r-RRR from the car's engine, and an equally loud one from the delighted Tinker, the car turned and drove away down the sandy lane.

'We're off,' said George, in a happy voice. 'Off all by ourselves again. It's the thing I like best of all. Do you like it too, Tim?'

'WOOF!' said Timmy, agreeing heartily, and lay down with his head on George's foot. Ah – now for a lovely holiday with George. Timmy didn't mind where he went – even to the end of the world – so long as he was with George!

CHAPTER EIGHT

There's the lighthouse!

ONCE THEY were out on the main road, Tinker began to
talk to the driver, asking him questions about all kinds of
cars. The others listened, amused.

'Well, I don't think much of the new cars,' said Tinker.
'All gadgets!'

'Some of the new gadgets are very good,' said the
driver, amused with the cocky little boy, and he touched
a little lever beside him. At once the window next to
Tinker went down smoothly, with a curious low moan.
Tinker was extremely startled.

'Oh, don't open that window,' said Anne, as a rough
wind swooped in. 'For goodness sake shut it, Tinker.'

Tinker shut it and began to talk about cars again. Once
more the driver touched the lever beside him, and once
more Tinker's window slid mournfully down, and a cold
draught came in.

'TINKER! Don't mess about with the windows,' ordered
Julian.

'I never touched the thing,' said Tinker, eyeing the
window with suspicion. It suddenly shut itself, sliding
upwards very smoothly. Tinker began to feel uncomfortable. He watched the window closely, afraid that it might
play tricks again. The others, knowing perfectly well that
the driver could open and shut any of the windows auto-
matically from his own seat, nudged one another, and
giggled. 'That shut up poor old Tinker!' murmured Dick.

It had. Not another word about new cars or old came from Tinker during the whole drive! It was a very pleasant one, mostly round the coast, and very little inland. The views were magnificent.

'That dog of yours seems to like the views,' said the driver. 'His head has been out of the window all the time.'

'Well – I always thought it was because he liked the fresh air,' said George. 'Timmy, is it because you enjoy the views?'

'Woof,' said Timmy, and withdrew his head to give George a lick. He also gave the little monkey a lick. Poor Mischief didn't much like the motion of the car. He sat very still indeed, afraid that he might be sick. The car purred along, sounding just like Tinker's usual imitation!

They stopped for an early lunch, and ate their sandwiches hungrily, sitting on a cliff. The driver had brought his own, and once Mischief had discovered that half the man's sandwiches were made of tomato, he sat on his knee in a very friendly manner, sharing his sandwiches in delight.

'We'll be there in about ten minutes,' said the man. 'Where are you staying at Demon's Rocks? The garage didn't tell me.'

'At the lighthouse,' said Julian. 'Do you know it?'

'Yes – but people don't *stay* there!' said the driver, thinking that Julian was pulling his leg. 'What hotel are you going to – or are you staying with friends?'

'No. We really *are* going to the lighthouse,' said Tinker. 'It's mine. My very own.'

'Well – you're certainly got a place with a fine view!' said the driver. 'I was born at Demon's Rocks. My old great-grandad is still in the same cottage where I was born. My word – the stories he used to tell me of that old lighthouse – and how the wreckers got into it one night and grabbed the keeper there, and doused the light, so that a great ship might go on the rocks.'

'How horrible – and *did* it get wrecked?' asked Dick.

'Yes. Smashed to bits,' said the driver. 'Ab-so-lutely – smashed – to bits! And then they waited for the tide to wash up the wreckage. You ought to look up my old great-grandad, and get him to tell you his tales. He might even show you the Wreckers' Cave . . .'

'Oh – we heard about that,' said George. 'Is it really true – *can* we see it? And is there someone in there still?'

'No – no, all the old wreckers are gone long ago,' said the driver. 'As soon as the new lighthouse was built, the wreckers' day was done. It's so powerful, you see. Its beams can be seen even in the fiercest storm. The beam from the lighthouse you're going to wasn't very good – but it saved a good many ships, all the same!'

'What's your great-grandad's name?' asked George, making up her mind to look him up as soon as she could. 'Where does he live?'

'Ask for Jeremiah Boogle,' said the driver, carefully skirting a herd of cows. 'You'll find him sitting somewhere on the quay, smoking a long pipe, and scowling at anyone that comes near him. But he likes children, so don't you be afraid of his scowl. He'll tell you a few tales, will my old great-grandad! Well, bless us all, if there isn't *another* herd of cows coming round the corner.'

'Hoot at them,' said Tinker.

'Ever heard the rhyme about the cow that jumped over the moon, boy?' said the driver. 'Well, someone hooted when it came by, see? And that's what it did – jumped over the moon! No good driver hoots at cows. It scares them silly, and they jump like hares. Look – see that cliff round the curve of the coast there? Well, that's the first bit of Demon's Rocks. We'll soon be there now.'

THERE'S THE LIGHTHOUSE!

'Why is it called that?' asked George.

'Well, the rocks there are so wicked that it was reckoned they could only have been put there by some kind of savage demon,' said the driver. 'Some are just below the water so that they catch the keel of a boat and rip it. Others stick up sharp as sharks' teeth – and there's a great ledge of rocks where a boat can be pounded to bits by the waves. Ah, they're Demon's Rocks all right!'

'When shall we see the lighthouse?' asked Tinker. 'We ought to see it soon.'

'Wait till another bit of the coast comes in sight as soon as we get to the top of this hill,' said the driver. 'And just tell that monkey of yours to take his paw out of my coat pocket. I've no more tomatoes there!'

'Behave yourself, Mischief,' said Tinker, so sternly that the little creature hid its face in its paws and whimpered.

'Little humbug!' said George. 'There's not a *tear* in his eye! Oh look – is *that* the lighthouse?'

'Yes. That's it,' said the driver. 'You get a good view of it now, from this hill. Fine one isn't it, for an old one? Ah, they could build well in those days. That one's made of stone. It's wave-swept so it has to be fairly tall, or the shining of the lamp would have been hidden by the spray falling on the windows.'

'Where did the lighthouse keeper live?' asked Dick.

'Oh, there's a cosy enough room just under the lamp room,' said the driver. 'My grandad took me up there once. I never saw such a view of a stormy sea in my life!'

'My father lived there all one summer,' boasted Tinker. 'I was with him most of the time. It was grand.'

'Why did your father want to live in a lighthouse?'

asked the driver, curiously. 'Was he hiding, or something?'

'Of course not. He's a scientist, and he said he wanted peace and quiet, with no telephones ringing, and no one coming to see him,' said Tinker.

'And do you mean to say he had peace and quiet with *you* there?' said the driver teasingly. 'Well, well!'

'It's not so quiet there really,' said Tinker. 'The waves make such a noise, and so does the wind. But my father didn't really notice those. He only notices things like bells ringing, or people talking, or somebody knocking at the door. Things like that drive him mad. He loved the lighthouse.'

'Well – I hope you enjoy yourselves there,' said the driver. 'It's not my cup of tea – hearing nothing but waves and gulls crying. Better you than me!'

They descended the other side of the hill and the lighthouse was no longer to be seen. 'Soon be there now,' said Tinker. 'Mischief, will you like to be at the lighthouse again? How quickly you could go up the spiral staircase and down – do you remember?'

The car swept down almost to the edge of the sea. The lighthouse was now plainly to be seen, a good way out from the shore. A small boat bobbed at a stone jetty, and Tinker pointed it out with a scream of joy. 'That's the boat we had – the one that took us to and from the lighthouse when the tide was in! It's called *Bob-About*, and it does bob about too.'

'Is it yours?' asked George, rather jealously.

'Well, it was sold with the lighthouse, so I suppose it is,' said Tinker. 'Anyway, it's the one we'll use when we can't wade over the rocks.'

'Well, see you don't get storm-bound in the light-house,' said the driver, bringing the car to a stop. 'The sea between Demon's Rocks and the jetty will be too rough for that little boat, in stormy weather.'

'I can manage boats all right,' said George. 'I've had one since I was small.'

'Yes. You're pretty good with them, that I do know,' said the driver. 'Well – here we are. Are you going to go straight to the lighthouse – in that boat? Shall I help you carry your things to it?'

'Well, thanks,' said Julian, and between them they carried everything to the little boat. An old man sat nearby, and he touched his cap to them. 'Message came through from Kirrin to say I was to get the old boat out for you,' he said. 'Which of you's Master Hayling?'

'I am,' said Tinker. 'And that's *my* boat, and *that's* my lighthouse! Come on, everyone – let's row to the light-house – come on! I can hardly wait to get there!'

CHAPTER NINE

Inside the lighthouse!

THE FIVE children jumped down into the boat, which was certainly acting up to its name of *Bob-About*! Timmy leapt in after George, but Mischief the monkey cried in terror when Tinker took him into the bobbing boat and sat down, holding him firmly.

'It's all right, Mischief,' said Tinker. 'Don't you remember this little boat of mine? You never did like going in a boat, though, did you?'

There were two pairs of oars. Julian took one pair, and George was going to take the other, when Dick quietly took them himself, grinning at George's angry face.

'Sorry – there's a good old swell on the sea, and we've to row through some pretty good waves. I'm just a *bit* stronger than you, George!'

'I row *just* as well as you do,' said George. The boat gave a great roll to one side just then, and she just managed to save one of their suitcases from toppling overboard.

'Well saved!' said Julian. 'And only just in time too! What a swell there is just here!'

'Are you going to row right over the rocks?' asked Anne peering down into the water. 'They are covered by the water now – we shan't scrape the bottom of the boat at all.'

'These are the rocks that we can walk over when the tide's out,' said Tinker. 'Lovely pools there are in them,

228

too! I used to wallow in a nice warm one that was so well-heated by the sun that I wished I had a cold tap to turn on when the water felt too hot!'

Anne chuckled. 'I wish it was warm enough to bathe now,' she said. 'My word – look down and see what horrible rocks there are, just beneath the boat!'

'Yes – I bet they ripped up many a poor ship in the old days,' said Julian. 'No wonder they called them Demon's Rocks! It's a bit of a pull over them, isn't it, Dick?'

'Let *me* have a turn,' said George, grabbing at one of Dick's oars.

'Nothing doing,' said Dick, with a grin. 'You just look after those bags, old thing!'

'Is it a very *old* lighthouse?' asked Anne, as they swung over the hidden rocks, and the lighthouse came nearer and nearer. 'It *looks* old!'

'Yes, it is,' said Tinker. 'It's an odd little lighthouse, really – built by a rich man years and years ago. His daughter was drowned in a ship that was wrecked on these rocks – so he built a lighthouse, partly as a memorial to the girl, and partly to prevent other shipwrecks.'

Anne gazed at it. It was sturdily built and seemed very tall to her. Its base was firmly embedded in the rocks below it. Dick thought that the foundations must go very deep down into the rocks, to hold the lighthouse firmly in the great gales that must blow in bad weather. A gallery, rather like a verandah, ran round the top, just below the windows through which the lighthouse lamp once shone. What a view there would be from that gallery, thought Anne.

They came near to the lighthouse, which had stone steps running from the rocks up to a doorway built some way above the crashing waves.

'Will the door be locked?' asked Dick, suddenly. 'I wouldn't want to row all this way and then find we can't get into the place!'

'Of course the door will be locked,' said Tinker. 'Anyone got the key?'

'Oh, don't be a donkey!' said Julian, resting his oars, and glaring at Tinker. 'Do you mean to say we can't get in, after all this?'

'It's all right!' said Tinker, grinning at Julian's dismayed face. 'I just wanted to pull your leg. Here's the key! It's *my* lighthouse, you see, so Dad gave me the key, and I always carry it about with me. It's very precious.'

It was an extremely large key, and George marvelled that Tinker could keep it in his pocket. He flourished it at them, grinning again. 'I'm looking forward to unlocking *my* lighthouse with *my* key!' he said. 'I bet *you* wish you had a lighthouse of your own, George.'

'Well, yes, I do,' said George, gazing up at the towering lighthouse, now so near to them.

'You'd better be a bit careful now,' said Tinker to the boys. 'Wait till a big waves swells up, then ride over it, and make for that rock over there – the one standing out of the water. There's a calm bit beyond it, for some reason, and you can row up to the steps quite safely. Look out for a stone post there, and chuck the rope round it, George. You're in a better position than I am for that.'

It was all done much more easily than the Five hoped. The boat swung into a stretch of fairly calm water, and the two boys rowed hard for the steps. George neatly threw the loop of rope over the post – and there they were, at the foot of the lighthouse, with only a few rocks to climb over to reach the steps. These rocks were not under water, and one by one the children and Timmy jumped out, and stared up at the lighthouse. It seemed much bigger now that they were just at the bottom!

'I'll unlock the door,' said Tinker, proudly, and climbed up the steep stone steps. 'Look at the enormous great stones that my lighthouse is made of. No wonder it has stood so long!'

He thrust the great key into the lock of the stout wooden door, and tried to turn it. He struggled for a minute, and then turned to the others with a scared face. 'I can't open the door!' he said. '*Now* what do we do?'

'I'll have a try,' said Julian. 'It's probably stuck.' He took hold of the key, gave it a strong twist – and opened the door! Everyone was most relieved. Julian pushed the others in out of the wind and the spray, and shut the door firmly.

'Well – here we are!' he said. 'Isn't it dark! Good thing I brought a torch!'

He shone the torch round, but all that was to be seen was a steep iron staircase spiralling up the middle of the lighthouse!

'The staircase goes right up to the top, to the lamp-room,' explained Tinker. 'It passes through a few rooms on the way. I'll show you. Hang on to the railing of the staircase, you may feel giddy going up round and round so steeply.'

Tinker proudly led the way up the steep little staircase, that went round and round and round! They came to a hole through which the stairway passed into a little dark room. 'One of the storerooms,' said Tinker, and flashed his torch round. 'See – there are tins of food that I told you my father and I left here. Now we go on up to the oil-room – that's not very big.'

'What's the oil-room?' asked Anne.

'Oh it was just where tins of paraffin oil used to be kept – the oil they used for the light at the top of the light-house. The old lamp had to burn oil, you see – there wasn't electricity in those days. Look – here's the oil-room.'

The oil-room had a very low ceiling, no window, and was packed with old tins. It had a nasty smell, and Anne held her nose with her fingers.

'I don't like this room,' she said. 'It has a horrid smell and a horrid *feel* about it! Let's go on up the staircase.'

The next room had one of the few little windows in the lighthouse, and as the sun came through it, it was much lighter and more cheerful.

'This was where my father and I slept,' said Tinker. 'Look, we forgot to take that old mattress away with us. What a bit of luck! We can use it!'

Up the spiral staircase they went once more, and this
time they came to a room with a higher ceiling than the
others, and a good window, though small. The sun came
through this one too, and it looked quite homely! It had a
table, and three chairs, and a box. It also had an old desk,
and a little paraffin stove for boiling water or frying
food.

'There's my old frying-pan!' said Tinker. 'We'll find
that jolly useful. And a kettle – and a saucepan. And we
left spoons and forks and knives behind, though not
enough for all five of us, I'm afraid. And there's crockery
too – though not as much as there ought to be. I broke
rather a lot. But there are some tin cups and plates – I
used just to wipe them clean with a cloth. Water's
precious in a lighthouse you know.'

'Where is the water tank?' asked George. 'We'll have
to have some water.'

'My father arranged a catch-tank on the west side of the
lighthouse,' said Tinker, proudly. 'It catches rainwater,
and runs into a pipe that goes through one of the windows
and fills a little tank over a sink. I forgot to show you that.
There's a tap to turn the water on and off. My father's very
clever you know – and a thing like that is as simple as
ABC. He didn't want to have to fetch water every day for
washing in! Gosh, we did have fun here!'

'Well, it looks as if you'll have some *more* fun!' said
Dick. 'You've plenty of company this time! You must
have been jolly lonely before.'

'Oh, well – I had Mischief,' said Tinker, and when he
heard his name, the little monkey came scampering over
to him, and leapt into the boy's arms, cuddling into him
lovingly.

INSIDE THE LIGHTHOUSE!

'And what's the next room in this marvellous little lighthouse?' asked Julian.

'There's only one more – and that's the lamp-room. I'll show you that – it used to be the most important room in the place – but now it's lonely – never used – quite forgotten! Come and see!' And up the last spiral of the stairway went Tinker. How very, very proud he was of his lighthouse!

CHAPTER TEN

Settling in

ONCE MORE they all climbed up the spiral stairway, Timmy
rather slowly, for he found the winding stairs difficult.
Mischief shot up in front of them, almost as if *he* were the
owner of the lighthouse, and was showing off his home!

The lamp-room was a high room with big windows all
round it. It was very bright, for the sun shone steadily
into it. The view was magnificent!

Anne gave a shout of wonder. The lighthouse was so
high that the children could see for miles and miles over
the heaving dark blue sea. They went all round the lamp-
room, looking in every direction.

'Look! There's a door here!' cried Dick. 'Does it open
on to that little balcony, or gallery, or whatever it is that
runs all round this room?'

'Yes. The gallery goes completely round the lamp
room,' said Tinker. 'You should see it sometimes when
the weather's rough, and the gulls go seeking somewhere
out of the storm. They perch on that gallery by the dozen!
But you can't go out there except in calm weather – you
might be blown right off! You've no idea what it's like
when there's a storm. Honestly, one night when my
father and I were here I thought I felt the lighthouse
rocking!'

'This is about the most exciting place I've ever stayed
in,' said Anne, her eyes shining. 'Tinker, I think you are
the luckiest boy in the world!'

'Do you really?' said Tinker, pleased. He gave Anne a little pat. 'I hoped you'd like it. Mischief loves it – don't you, Mischief?'

Mischief was up on top of the great lamp. He chattered down to Timmy as if he were telling him all about it. Timmy listened, his ears cocked, his head on one side.

'He looks just as if he understood that monkey-gabble!' said George. 'Tinker – this lamp is never lit now, is it?'

'No, never,' said Tinker. 'I told you there is a fine new lighthouse a bit farther down the coast. It has a terrific lamp – run by electricity. We shall see its beams sweeping the sea at night.'

'Why don't people build lighthouses and live in them?' wondered George, as she gazed out over the wide blue sea.

'Anyone feeling hungry?' asked Tinker, rubbing his tummy. 'I feel jolly empty. Oh gosh – we haven't taken the things out of my boat! Come on – let's carry them all indoors, and have a meal. What's the time? Past four o'clock! No wonder I feel empty. Come on, Mischief – to work! You can carry some of the things in too.'

They ran down the spiral stairway, through room after room, and came to the great door. 'I suppose it had to be built as thickly and strongly as possible, because of the sea dashing against it in storms,' said Julian, pulling it open. The wind rushed in and almost knocked him over! They pushed their way out, and climbed back over the rocks to where they had left the boat. It was bobbing gently up and down in the little stretch of calm water.

'Hallo, *Bob-About*!' said Tinker. 'Did you think we were never coming? Got all our goods safely? Good little boat!'

'Idiot!' said Dick, grinning. 'Come on, Ju – I'll take half the heavy things, you take the rest. The girls and Tinker can manage the smaller things. Hey, Mischief, what do you think you're doing?'

Mischief had picked up a parcel or two, and was

bounding off with them. 'It's all right! He's used to helping!' shouted Tinker. 'He often goes shopping with me, and carries bags and things. Let him help, he likes it.'

The monkey certainly was very useful. He scampered to and fro with all kinds of little things, and chattered happily. Timmy stood staring at him, his tail down, wishing he could use his paws as nimbly as Mischief could. George gave him a loving pat.

'It's all right, Timmy, darling. Here – take this basket.'

Timmy took the basket in his mouth by the handle and leapt happily up the steps of the lighthouse. He might not be able to pick up the little things that Mischief so easily managed – but at least he could carry baskets!

'We'll leave the boat bobbing up and down,' said Tinker. 'It will be quite all right there, tied to the post, unless the sea gets terribly rough – then we'll have to pull it halfway up the steps.'

'Let's have our meal and unpack before we arrange our things,' said Anne. 'I really do feel very hungry now. What sort of a meal shall we have? I feel as if I want something more than a tea-time meal!'

'That's the worst of living in a lighthouse,' said Tinker, quite seriously. 'You're awfully hungry nearly all the time. I used to have five or six meals a day when I stayed here with my father.'

'Sounds all right to *me*,' said Dick, with a grin. 'Let's have a "tea-sup" meal, shall we? A mixture of tea and supper! Tea-sup!'

Some of the things were put into the bedroom and some into the living room. Soon Tinker popped a saucepan of water on the stove to boil. Because of the rainy weather, the little rain catch-tank had provided plenty of water for the small inside tank set over the sink, which was most conveniently put in the living room. When Tinker turned on the tap, out came clear rainwater!

'Magic!' said Anne, delighted. 'I feel as if I'm in a dream!'

Eggs were put into the saucepan, and were soon boiled. 'Exactly three minutes and a half,' said Anne, ladling out each one with a spoon. 'TWO eggs each! At this rate we shall have to go shopping every day! George, you cut some bread-and-butter. The bread's in that bag – but goodness knows where the butter is. I know we bought some.'

'What about having a few of Joanna's famous mince pies too?' said Dick, taking the lid off a big square tin. 'Whew! Dozens! And cherry buns as well! And home-made macaroons – Joanna's speciality! I *say* what a meal!'

'What shall we have to drink?' said Julian. 'Ginger beer? Lemonade? Or shall we make some tea?'

Everyone voted for ginger beer. It was a very pleasant and cheery meal that the Five had in the old lighthouse, with Mischief and Tinker. The gulls called outside, the wind gave the lighthouse an occasional buffet, and the sound of the sea was mixed with all the other noises – lovely! Anne hugged her knees as she waited for her ginger beer. To think they were going to stay here for days and days. All by themselves.

When the meal was over, Anne and George washed up in the little sink. 'Oh don't wash up – just give the things a quick wipe-over!' said Tinker. 'Like this!'

'Oh *no*!' said Anne. 'That's just like a boy! You'd better leave this side of things to me. I *like* doing jobs like this, see?'

'Just like a girl!' said Tinker, with a grin.

'No, it isn't,' said George. 'I hate doing them, and *I'm* a girl – though I wish I wasn't!'

'Never mind – you *look* like a boy, and you're often as *rude* as a boy, and you haven't an awful lot of manners,' said Tinker, quite thinking that he was comforting George.

'I've more manners than *you*,' said George, and stalked off in a huff to look out of the windows. But nobody could be in a huff for long, with that wonderful view – sea for miles and miles, tipped here and there with white breakers. George gave a sigh of pleasure. She forgot that she was annoyed with Tinker, and turned to him with a smile.

'If I could own this view, I'd feel I was the richest person in all the world!' she said. 'You're very lucky, Tinker.'

'Am I?' said Tinker, thinking it over. 'Well, you can have half the view, if you like. I don't want it all.'

Julian laughed, and clapped the boy on the back. 'We'll all share it, while we're here!' he said. 'Come on – let's unpack and arrange everything. Girls, you had better sleep here in this living room – and we three boys will sleep down in the bedroom. That all right by you, Tinker?'

'Fine – so long as you don't mind Mischief sleeping with us,' said Tinker. 'Anyway I expect Timmy will sleep with the girls.'

'Woof,' said Timmy, agreeing. He was certainly not going to sleep anywhere without George!

They all had fun unpacking, and putting the things in the different places. 'Storeroom for that,' Julian said, 'and living room for this and this – and bedroom for these rugs – though these two had better go to the living room, because the girls will sleep there.'

'Cards for the living room,' said Dick, handing them to Anne. 'And books. And papers. Gosh, we mustn't forget to send a card each day to Aunt Fanny. We promised we would.'

'Well, she'll know we arrived safely today because the taxi driver will be sure to send a message to her,' said George. 'But tomorrow we'll go down to the village and buy a stock of postcards – and we'll send one every single day. I know Mother will worry if we don't.'

'All mothers are worriers,' said Dick. 'It's a nuisance – but on the other hand it's one of the nice things about them. Now then – what about a game of cards?'

And there they all are in the lighthouse, playing cards with shouts and laughter, Timmy and Mischief watching. You do have fun together, Five, don't you?

CHAPTER ELEVEN

Jeremiah Boogle

WHEN IT began to get dark, Tinker left the card table, and fetched an old-fashioned oil-lamp. He shook it.

'It's still got some oil in,' he said. 'Good. I'll light it, then we can see properly.'

'What a pity we can't light the great oil-lamp at the top of the lighthouse,' said George. 'That must have been the lighthouse keeper's great moment – lighting up the lamp to warn ships away. I wonder who first thought of a lighthouse – someone whose folk sailed, and might be wrecked on rocks, I suppose?'

'One of the first great lighthouses was built ages ago on an island called Pharos at the mouth of the Nile, not far from the great port of Alexandria,' said Julian.

'What was it built of – stone, like this one?' asked Tinker.

'No. It was built of white marble,' said Julian. 'I thought of it today when we went up the spiral staircase here – because the Pharos lighthouse had one too – much, much bigger than ours.'

'What was their lamp like?' asked Tinker.

'I don't know if it had a *lamp*,' said Julian. 'It's said that an enormous fire was built each night on the top of the lighthouse, whose flames could be seen by ships a hundred miles away!'

'Goodness – it must have been a pretty high light-house, then, this Pharos!' said Dick.

'Well, it was supposed to be about 180 metres high!'
said Julian.

'Whew! I wonder the wind didn't blow it down!' said
Dick. 'Let's go and see it one day – if it's still there.'

'Idiot!' said Julian. 'It's gone long since. After all, it
was built over twenty-two hundred years ago! An earthquake came along one day and the magnificent lighthouse was shaken to bits – completely destroyed!'

There was a shocked silence. Everyone looked round
at the walls of the lighthouse they were in. An earthquake! What a catastrophe that would be for even a *little*
lighthouse!

'Cheer up, Anne!' said Julian, with a laugh. '*We're*
not likely to be visited by an earthquake tonight! That
old lighthouse on Pharos Island was one of the Seven

Wonders of the Ancient World. No – *don't* ask me the others – I'm getting too sleepy to remember!'

'I wish we could light the lamp in *this* lighthouse,' said Anne. 'It can't like being a *blind* lighthouse, after shining brightly for so many years. *Could* the lamp be lit, Tinker, or is it broken now?'

'Anne – if you think we're going to scramble round that lamp-room and light the lamp just because you feel sorry about it, you're mistaken,' said Dick, firmly. 'Anyway, it's sure to be out of order after all these years.'

'I don't see why it should be,' objected Tinker. 'The lamp's never been interfered with.'

'Look – are we going to go on with our game, or are we not?' said Julian. 'I may as well remind you that I have won practically every game so far! Unless someone else wins a game soon I shall consider that I'm playing with a bunch of nitwits!'

That was quite enough to make everyone pick up their cards, and see if they couldn't possibly beat Julian!

'We'll jolly well play till you're well and truly beaten!' said Dick.

But no – nobody could beat Julian that night. Luck went his way all the time. At the end of the fifth game Anne yawned loudly.

'Oh, sorry!' she said. 'Don't think I'm bored. That yawn came too suddenly for me to stop it!'

'Well, I feel decidedly yawny too,' said Dick. 'What about a snack of something – and then we'll go to bed. We had such an enormous tea-sup that I feel I can't manage another *meal* – but a chocolate biscuit or two would be quite welcome.'

'Woof!' said Timmy at once, agreeing heartily, and

Mischief said something in his little chattering voice, and tugged at Tinker's sleeve.

'I'll bring you a snack or two,' said Anne, getting up. She soon came back with a tray on which she had put lemonade, large slices of Joanna's new cake, and a chocolate biscuit for everyone, including Timmy and Mischief.

They ate with enjoyment, feeling lazy and comfortable. 'And now to bed!' said Julian. 'Girls, do you want any help with your mattress or rugs or anything?'

'No, thanks,' said Anne. 'Do you boys want to wash, and clean your teeth at the sink here? Because if so, do it now.'

Before a quarter of an hour had gone, everyone was bedded down comfortably. The three boys curled up in rugs in the bedroom below, with Mischief cuddled into Tinker's neck. The two girls and Timmy lay on a mattress, with a blanket over them, Timmy lay beside George, occasionally licking her ear with his big tongue.

'*Dear* Timmy!' said George, sleepily. 'I love you – but do please keep your tongue to yourself!'

And soon they were all asleep, boys, girls, and animals too. Outside, the sea sighed and splashed and swirled, and the wind cried like the daytime gulls. But all was peace and quiet inside the old lighthouse. Not even Mischief the monkey stirred in his sleep.

It was fun to wake up in the morning, and hear the gulls screaming round; fun to have breakfast of eggs and bread and butter, and apples to crunch afterwards – fun to plan what to do that day.

'I vote we do a bit of shopping and buy some more eggs, and fresh bread, and a bottle or two of creamy milk,' said Anne.

'And we might try and find the taxi driver's great-grandad, and ask him a few things about the light-house, and the wreckers that came in the old days,' said Dick.

'Yes – and he might show us the Wreckers' Cave!' said Julian. 'I'd like to see that! Let's buck up with whatever jobs there are to do, and we'll go over the rocks to the jetty. The tide should be out, so we ought to be able to walk over.'

'Well, we *must* be back before the tide comes in, then,' said Tinker. 'Because if we leave the boat tied up here by the lighthouse, we shan't be able to get back once the sea sweeps over the rocks and cuts us off!'

'Right,' said Julian. 'Be ready as soon as you can.'

Everyone was ready very quickly, and the little party set off over the rocks that at low tide lay between the lighthouse and the shore. Wicked rocks they were too –

with sharp edges and points that would hole a ship at once!

Soon the children were on the little stone jetty. 'What was the name of old Great-Grandad?' said Dick frowning.

'Jeremiah Boogle,' said Anne. 'And he smokes a long pipe, and scowls at people.'

'Well – he *should* be easy to find!' said Julian. 'Come along. He's probably somewhere on the quay.'

'There he is!' said George, spotting an old man with a long pipe in his mouth. 'That's Jeremiah, I'm sure!'

Yes, there he was, sitting with his legs stretched out in front of him, an old, old man, smoking a very long pipe! He had a fine beard, a yachting cap askew on his head, and such enormous shaggy eyebrows that it was difficult to see his eyes beneath them!

The Five went up to him, with Timmy trotting behind, and Mischief on Tinker's shoulder. The old man spotted Mischief at once.

'Well, well – a monkey!' he said. 'Many's the little monkey I've brought home from my voyages.' He snapped his fingers and made a curious noise in his throat. Mischief stared at him, listening. Then he leapt from Tinker's shoulder on to the old man's, and rubbed his head against the old sailor's hairy ear.

'Mischief!' said Tinker, amazed. 'Look at that, George. He never goes to a stranger!'

'Well, maybe I knew his great-grandfather!' said the old sailor, laughing, and scratching Mischief's neck.

'All monkeys like me – and I like them!'

'Er – are you Mr Jeremiah Boogle?' asked Julian.

'Jeremiah Boogle, that's me,' said the old fellow, and touched his cap. 'How do you know my name?'

'Well, Jackson, the taxi driver, told us he was your great-grandson,' said Julian. 'You see we're staying at the old lighthouse – and Jackson said you could tell us a few things about it – its history, you know. And about the wreckers that lived here before the lighthouse was built.'

'Oh, I can tell you tales all right!' said Jeremiah, puffing out a cloud of smoke, and making Mischief cough. 'That's more than that silly young great-grandson of mine can! He don't know nothing, nothing at all – except about cars. Well, who wants cars, nasty, smelly noisy things? Pah! That young George Jackson is a ninny!'

'He's not. He's the cleverest mechanic in the place!' said George, at once. 'There's not a thing he doesn't know about cars!'

'CARS! There now, what did I say – nasty, noisy, smelly things!' said Jackson's great-grandad, with a snort.

'Well, look – we don't want to talk about cars,' said Julian. 'You tell us about the old days – the wreckers and all that!'

'Ah – the old days!' said Great-Grandad. 'Well, I knew some wreckers myself, once – there was One-Ear Bill, now . . .' And then old Jeremiah told a story that the Five could hardly believe!

CHAPTER TWELVE

Jeremiah's tale

'Now when I was a boy,' began the old man, 'a boy not much older than this here youngster,' and he poked Tinker with his horny forefinger, 'there wasn't a lighthouse out there – but there were always those wicked rocks! And many's the time in a stormy season when ships have been caught by their teeth, a-glittering there, waiting. You know what they're called, don't you?'

'Yes. Demon's Rocks,' said Tinker.

'Well, up on that high cliff there, lived a wicked old man,' said Jeremiah. 'And he had a son as bad as himself, and a nephew too. The Three Wreckers, they was called, and I'll tell you how they came by their name.'

'Did you know them?' asked Dick.

'That I did! And if I was hidden behind a bush when they came marching by, I'd send a stone skedaddling after them!' said the old man. 'Mean and cruel and wicked they were. And everyone was scared of them, right down afraid! There was One-Ear, the old man. They say his left ear was chewed off by a monkey, but do I blame that monkey? No, I do not, not more than I'd blame *your* monkey for chewing off the ear of somebody else I know – but I won't mention no names, he might hear me.'

The old fellow looked over his shoulder as if the man he was thinking of might be about.

'Well – there was One-Ear, the old man – and there

was Nosey, the son – and Bart, his nephew – and not a
pin to choose between them for meanness. There was
only one thing they was after – and that was money! And
a mighty wicked way they chose to get it.' The old man
stopped and spat in disgust on the pavement.

'Pah! I'll tell you how they got rich, oh yes, I'll tell you.
And I'll tell you what happened to them in the end too.
Be a lesson to you and to everyone! Well now, you see

that high cliff away down the coast there – the one with the flag-post and the flag a-waving in the wind?'

'Yes,' said everyone, looking at the waving flag.

'Now ships mustn't hug the coast beyond that point!' said Great-Grandad. 'If they do, they'll be forced inland by the current, and thrown on those rocks down there – Demon's Rocks. And that's the end of them. No ship has ever been able to escape the sharp teeth of those wicked rocks, once she's caught in that current. Well now, to stop the ships going near to the cliff in those days, they flew a flag in the daytime – and lit a lamp up there at night. And both said as plain as could be "BEWARE! KEEP OUT! DANGER".

'Of course, all sailors knew the flag and the lamp too, and many a one blessed them, and took their ships out to sea, away from Demon's Rocks. But that didn't suit old One-Ear Bill. *He* didn't mind a wreck or two! He'd be down on the beach picking up what he could, if a ship came smashing down on the rocks. And would he save a single soul – not he! There were some people who said he was the Demon of Demon's Rocks himself!'

'What a wicked old man!' said Anne horrified.

'Aye, you're right, missie,' said the old fellow. 'Well, the wrecks didn't come often enough for him and Nosey and Bart. So they put their ugly heads together and thought up as wicked a plan as any man could think of!'

'What was it?' said Tinker, his eyes almost falling out of his head.

'Well, on a stormy night he put out the lamp shining brightly on the far cliff, and he and Nosey carried it to that bit of cliff over there, see?' and the old man pointed to a jutting-out piece nearby. 'And you know what's just below *that* cliff, don't you – all round the lighthouse!'

'Rocks! Sharp, horrible rocks – the Demon's Rocks!' said George, horrified.

'Do you mean to say that One-Ear Bill and the others deliberately shone the lamp there on stormy nights, to guide ships straight on to the rocks?' said Julian.

'Aye, that's exactly what I mean,' said Jeremiah Boogle. 'And what's more I met old One-Ear Bill myself one dark night when the storms were on – and what was he carrying between himself and Nosey – the lamp! They'd doused the light, of course, but I'd my own little lantern with me, and I saw the lamp plain enough. Aye, that I did! And when they saw me, they set Bart on to me, to push me over the cliff, so I wouldn't tell on them. But I got away, and I DID tell on 'em! Ho, yes, I told all right. And One-Ear Bill went to prison, and serve him right, the wicked man. But he didn't care – and why should he? He was rich! RICH!'

'But how was he rich?' asked Dick.

'Well, young man, the ships that came sailing round this coast in those days, came from far-off countries, and many of them carried treasure,' said Jeremiah. 'And One-Ear Bill stole so much gold and silver and pearls and other things from the wrecks, that he knew he wouldn't need to do another day's work when he came out of prison. A rich man he would be – he wouldn't even need to wreck a ship again!'

'But why weren't the stolen goods taken from him?' said Julian.

'He'd hidden them!' said the old man. 'Ah he'd hidden them well, too. Not even Nosey his son, nor Bart his nephew, knew where he'd put them. They were sure he'd got everything hidden in one of the caves in the cliff – but search as they might, they never found the treasure! They went to prison too, but they came out long before old One-Ear Bill was due out – and how they hunted for the gold and silver, and all that One-Ear had hidden away!'

'Did One-Ear Bill get it when he came out of prison?' asked Dick, thinking this was a much more exciting story than he had ever read in a book – and a true one too!

'No. No, he didn't get it,' said Jeremiah, puffing out a cloud of smoke. 'And glad I am to say that. He died in prison, the wicked old man.'

'Well then – what happened to the treasure from the wrecked ships?' asked George. 'Who found it?'

'No one,' said the old man. 'No one at all! It's still there, hidden wherever that old rascal put it. His secret went with him. Bart looked for it, and Nosey too – ho, I've seen 'em in those caves day after day, and with a lamp night after night. But they never found even a pearl necklace. Ho – that was a good joke, that was! They're dead and gone now – but there're relatives of theirs still living in Demon's Rocks, who could do with a bit of that treasure – poor as church mice they are, with two children as skinny as ever you'd see!'

'Doesn't anyone even have an *idea* where the loot from the wrecked ships is?' asked Julian. 'What about the cave we've been hearing about – the Wreckers' Cave?'

'Oh aye – we've a Wreckers' Cave, all right,' said the old man, knocking out his pipe. 'And I reckon about five thousand people have been in it, scouting round, looking into holes and corners hoping to find what Bart and Nosey never did find! Or maybe ten thousand, who knows? I don't mind telling you, I've been there meself

– but not a smell of a little gold coin did I ever see! I'll take you there myself some day if you like. But mind – don't you hope to find anything. It's my belief that One-Ear Bill never did hide his treasure there – he just said it was there to fool Nosey and Bart!'

'We'd love to go and see the cave,' said Dick, and George nodded her head in delight. 'Not to hunt for treasure, of course – it's pretty obvious it's not there now – maybe somebody *did* find it, and took it away secretly!'

'Maybe,' said Jeremiah. 'All right, young man – you come and tell me when you're ready. I'm sitting here most days. And if you've any nice sweets you don't have any use for, think of me, see?'

'We'll go and buy you some straightaway,' said Julian. He couldn't help laughing. 'What kind do you like?'

'Oh, you tell Tom the sweetshop owner it's for old Jeremiah Boogle – he'll give you what I like,' said the old man. 'And mind now – don't you go snooping round them old caves by yourselves – you might get lost. It's a proper laby – laby . . .'

'Labyrinth,' said Julian, smiling. 'Right – we'll be careful.'

The Five went off, Timmy glad to be on the move again. He couldn't understand the old man's story of course, and he wondered why George hadn't taken him for his usual after-breakfast walk. He gave a little whine, and she patted his big head.

'Sorry, Timmy!' she said. 'That old man told such an interesting story that I quite forgot you were longing for a walk. We'll go for one now.'

'Let's call in at the sweetshop first, shall we?' said Julian. 'That old chap deserves an extra something for

255

his tale. Goodness knows how much was true – but he certainly told it well!'

'Of *course* it was true!' said George. 'Why ever should he tell lies?'

'Well – he might have, to get some sweets, you know!' said Julian, smiling. 'I don't blame him! It's a jolly good story – but please don't think there's any treasure still hidden somewhere, George. It's no use believing that.'

'Well, I do believe it!' said George, defiantly. 'I think he was telling the truth, sweets or no sweets. Don't you, Tinker?'

'Oh *yes*,' said Tinker. 'You wait till you see the caves round about here! Hoo – there might be any *amount* of treasure there, and no one would ever know! I did hunt round a bit myself – but those caves are scary, and when I coughed once, my cough came echoing back to me a hundred times and I was so scared I ran for my life – and fell splash into a pool!'

Everyone laughed. 'Let's buck up and do our shopping,' said Dick. 'And then what about going for a good long walk?'

'Well, *I* don't want to carry eggs and bread and milk for miles,' said George. 'I say a walk first – and then we'll come back, have ice-creams, do our shopping – and go back to the lighthouse.'

'Right!' said Julian. 'Come on, Timmy. We're off for a WALK – a WALK! Ha, that's the word to set your tail wagging, isn't it? Look at it, Mischief. Don't you wish you could wag *your* tail like that!'

CHAPTER THIRTEEN

A pleasant morning – and a shock!

'WHERE SHALL we go for our walk?' said George, as they wandered through the village. 'Oh look – there's a tiny little shop with Tom's Sweetshop written over the door. Let's get the sweets while we remember.'

So in went Julian, and rapped on the counter. A very small man, like a hobgoblin, appeared out of a dark corner.

'I want some sweets for Jeremiah Boogle, please,' said Julian. 'I think you know the kind he wants.'

'I do that!' said Tom, scrabbling about on a shelf. 'The amount that old Jeremiah has eaten since I've been here would keep an army going for years. There you are, young man!'

'He tells a fine story,' said Julian, putting down the money for the sweets.

Tom laughed. 'He's been going on about Bart and Nosey and all them old folks, I suppose,' he said. 'He's a funny one, is old Jeremiah. Never forgets a thing, even if it happened eighty or more years ago! Never forgives, either. There're two folk in this village that he spits at when he passes by them. Naughty old man, he is.'

'What have they done to earn his spite?' asked Dick, in surprise.

'Well, they're some kin of his old enemy, One-Ear Bill,' said Tom. 'I reckon he told you about him all right, didn't he?'

'Yes, he did,' said Julian. 'But all that business about the wrecking happened years and years ago! Surely Jeremiah doesn't vent his anger on any descendants of the wicked One-Ear Bill!'

'Oh, but he *does*!' said Tom. 'You see, these two

fellows he spits at have the job of showing people round
the caves here – especially the Wreckers' Cave – and I
reckon old Jeremiah still broods about One-Ear's hidden
treasure, and is scared in case these two chaps ever find it.
Find it! It's nearly seventy years since all that happened.
Why, that lighthouse over there was built over sixty years
ago – after that wrecking business went on. No one will
come across any treasure now!'

'But surely they *might*,' said George. 'It depends where
it was hidden. If it was in some dry, watertight place, it
should still be all right. After all, gold and silver don't
decay, do they? Wherever it was hidden, it must still be
there!'

'That's what all you visitors say!' said Tom. 'And
that's what Ebenezer and Jacob say – they're the two
chaps who show people round the caves. But they only
say that to make a bit of a thrill for the visitors, you
know. Same as old Jeremiah does. Takes them in properly! Well – you believe what you like, youngsters – but
you won't find any treasure! I reckon the sea took that
years ago! Good day to you! I'll give Jeremiah the sweets
when he calls in.'

'Well,' said Dick, as soon as they were outside the
shop, 'this is all very interesting! I think probably old
Tom's right. The reason why the treasure was never
found is because it was probably hidden where the sea
managed to get at it – in some water-hole, or somewhere
like that.'

'I still believe it's somewhere safe,' said George. 'So
does Tinker.'

'Oh well . . . I should think probably Timmy believes it
as well,' said Dick. 'He has a childlike mind too!'

Dick at once received a hard punch on the back from George. He laughed. 'All right! We'll give you a chance to hunt for the treasure, won't we, Ju? We'll visit the Wreckers' Cave as soon as we can. Let's go up on the cliffs for our walk, and see if we can spot where the first old lamp used to be, that warned ships to swing out to sea, and avoid Demon's Rocks.'

It was a lovely walk along the cliffs. The celandines and tiny dog violets were out, and clumps of pale yellow primroses were everywhere. The breeze blew strongly, and Mischief held tightly to Tinker's right ear, afraid of being blown off his shoulder. Timmy enjoyed himself thoroughly, bounding along, tail flourishing happily, sniffing at everything.

They came to the flag-post set high on the cliff, its great red flag waving vigorously in the breeze. A notice-board was beside it. George read it.

'This flag warns ships off Demon's Rocks by day. By night the great lighthouse at High Cliffs, farther along the coast, gives warning. In the old days a lamp shone from this spot to give the ships warning, and later a small lighthouse was built out on Demon's Rocks. It is still in existence, but is no longer in use.'

'Ha – they're wrong there!' said Tinker, pointing to the last sentence. '*We're* using it! I'll alter the notice!' and Tinker actually took a pencil to scratch out the last six words!

Julian took it from him. 'Don't be silly. You can't mess about with public notices. Don't say you're one of the idiots who like to scribble all over the place!'

Tinker held out his hand for the pencil. 'All right. It was just that I thought it wanted correcting. I'm *not* the

260

kind of idiot who scribbles on walls or public notices.'

'Right,' said Julian. 'Tinker, can we see Demon's Rocks – the rocks themselves, I mean, with our lighthouse – from these cliffs?'

'No,' said Tinker. 'The cliff swings away to the left, look, and the Demon's Rocks are away right round the corner, if you see what I mean – so no ship should follow the coastline here, but should keep well out at sea, or it'd be on the rocks. You can see quite well that if the wreckers took the lamp from its warning place here, and put it much farther back, along the way we've come, the ships would swing too far inland, and find themselves wrecked!'

'I think *I* should have hated old One-Ear Bill as much as old Jeremiah does,' said George, imagining the beautiful ships being ground to pieces all those years ago – just because of a greedy man who liked the pickings from wrecks!

'Well, we'd better go back,' said Julian, looking at his watch. 'We've some shopping to do, remember! Better buck up too – it looks like rain all of a sudden!'

He was right. It was pouring by the time they reached the village! They crowded into a little shop that said 'Morning Coffee' and ordered a cup each, and buns. The buns were so nice that they bought some to take back to the lighthouse with them. Then Anne remembered postcards.

'We *must* buy some,' she said, 'and send one off today. Better get some now, and write one and post it while we're here.'

Dick slipped out of the coffee shop and returned with a packet of very gaudily coloured cards. 'Some of them

show the lighthouse,' he said. 'We'll send one of those –
and you choose a card to send to your father too,
Tinker.'

'It would be a waste,' said Tinker. 'He wouldn't even
bother to read it.'

'Well, send one to your mother,' said Anne.

'I haven't one,' said Tinker. 'She's dead. She died when
I was born. That's why my father and I always go about
together.'

'I'm very, very sorry, Tinker,' said Anne, shocked. The
others were sorry too. No wonder Tinker was so wild. No
mother to teach him anything! Poor Tinker! Anne felt as
if she wanted to buy him every bun in the shop!

'Have another bun, Tinker,' she said. 'Or an ice-cream.
I'll pay. Mischief can have one too.'

'We're *all* going to have another bun each, *and* an ice-
cream,' said Julian. 'Timmy and Mischief too. Then we'll
do our shopping and go home – home to the lighthouse.
That sounds grand, doesn't it!'

They wrote three cards – one to Uncle Quentin and
Aunt Fanny – one to Joanna – and one to the professor.
'Now they'll know we are safe and happy!' said Anne,
sticking on the stamps.

The rain had stopped, so they went to do their shopping – fresh bread, more butter and eggs, two bottles of
milk, some fruit and a few other things. Then off they
went down to the little jetty.

'Tide will soon turn,' said Julian, as they jumped down
from the jetty to the rocky little beach. 'Come on – we'll
just have time to walk over the rocks to the lighthouse.
PLEASE don't drop the eggs, Tinker!'

They made their way over the rocks, jumping over

little pools here and there and avoiding the slimy strands of seaweed that in places covered the rocks. The lighthouse seemed very tall as they came up to it.

'It's *tiny* compared to the great new one away at High Cliffs,' said Tinker. 'You ought to go over that! The revolving lamp at the top is magnificent! Its light is so powerful that ships can see it for miles!'

'Well, this little lighthouse looks nice enough to me at the moment,' said Dick, climbing up the stone steps to the strong wooden door. 'Hallo! Look – two bottles of milk on the top step! Don't tell me the milkman's been!'

'He used to call when my father and I were here,' said Tinker. 'Only when the tide was out in the morning though, because he hasn't a boat. I suppose he heard *we* were all staying here, and came to see if we wanted milk – and left two bottles when he found we were out. He probably yelled through the letter-box and when we didn't answer he just left the milk, on chance.'

'Sensible fellow!' said Dick. 'Get out your key, Tinker, and unlock the door.'

'I don't remember locking it behind us when we went out this morning,' said Tinker, frantically feeling in all his pockets. 'I must have left it in the lock on the inside of the door. Let's see now – we locked the door last night, and left the key in the lock. So I *must* have unlocked it this morning for us all to get out.'

'That's right – but after you unlocked it you ran straight down the steps with George, and the rest of us followed,' said Julian. 'Anne was last. Did *you* lock the door after you, Anne?'

'No. I never thought of it!' said Anne. 'I just shut the

door with a bang and raced after you all! So the key must still be on the other side of the door!'

'Well, if we push the door, it should open!' said Julian, with a grin. 'And the key will be on the inside, waiting for us! Let's go in!'

He pushed hard, for the door shut very tightly – and sure enough, it swung open. Julian put his hand round to the inside lock to feel for the key.

It wasn't there! Julian looked at the others, frowning. '*Someone's been here* – and found the door unlocked – taken the key – and probably plenty of other things as well!' he said. 'We'd better go and look. Come on!'

'Wait – there's something on the doormat,' said Dick, picking up a letter. 'The postman has visited the light-house too – here's a letter forwarded from Kirrin – so at least *two* people came while we were out! But surely neither of them would take the key – or anything else either!'

'Well – we'll soon see!' said Julian, grimly, and up the first bend of the spiral stairway he went, at top speed!

CHAPTER FOURTEEN

The old, old map

JULIAN AND Dick went into each room of the lighthouse, racing up the spiral stairway from one to the other. Why, oh why, hadn't they watched to see that Tinker locked the door and took the key!

Yes – a few things *had* been taken!

'My rug!' said George. 'That's gone!'

'And my purse,' said Anne. 'I left it here on the table. That's been taken, too!'

'So has my little travelling clock,' groaned Julian. 'Why did I bring it? I could have used my watch!'

There were a few other things gone, all small. 'Horrible fellow, whoever he is, to creep into the lighthouse while we were out and take our things!' said Anne, almost crying. 'Who would come here – they would surely be seen from the quay, wouldn't they?'

'Yes – you're right there,' said Julian. 'Though probably the thief slipped in when it was pouring with rain, and the quay was deserted! I think we'll have to tell the police, you know. Let's have our dinner, and then I'll take the boat and slip across to the village. The tide will be in then, and I shan't be able to walk over the rocks. Blow that thief! I was looking forward to a nice quiet read this afternoon!'

After their meal, Julian took the boat and rowed across to the jetty. He went straight to the police station, where a stolid-looking policeman listened to him, and wrote slowly in a book.

'Have you any idea who the thief might be?' asked the policeman. 'Or if anyone came to the lighthouse while you were out?'

'Well, two people seem to have come,' said Julian. 'The milkman, because we were surprised to find milk bottles on the step. And the postman. There was a letter for us on the mat inside the door. I don't know of anyone else.'

'Well, as far as I can tell you, both Willy the Milkman, and Postie are as honest as the day,' said the policeman, scratching his chin with his pencil. 'There may have been a third visitor – one who didn't leave milk or a letter! I'll see if anyone was on the quay this morning, who saw the thief going over the Demon's Rocks. Er – do you suspect anyone?'

'Good gracious, no!' said Julian. 'I don't know anyone here – unless you can count Jeremiah Boogle, or Tom the sweetshop owner!'

'No. No, I think we can rule both of them out,' said the policeman, smiling. 'Well, I'll do what I can, and let you know if I hear of anything. Good afternoon, and by the way, as you can't lock that lighthouse door now, and it's plain there are thieves about, I shouldn't leave the light-house empty, see?'

'Yes. Yes, I'd already thought of that,' said Julian. 'I can jam the door all right with something when we're *in* the lighthouse – but I can't do that when we're out.'

'Well – it looks as if we're in for a wet spell,' said the policeman. 'So maybe it won't be much hardship to keep indoors. I hope you're comfortable in the lighthouse – seems a funny place to stay, really.'

'Oh we're *very* comfortable, Constable,' said Julian, smiling. 'Why not pay us a call sometime, and see us?'

'Thanks,' said the policeman, and took Julian to the door.

The constable was right in forecasting a wet spell. It poured all that afternoon, and the little company in the lighthouse whiled away the time playing cards. Julian and Dick had managed to find a heavy piece of wood in the storeroom to jam the door from the inside. They all felt much safer when they knew that had been done! Now no one could get in without making a terrific noise!

'I'm stiff,' said George, at last. 'I want to stretch my legs. I've a good mind to run up and down the stairway half a dozen times.'

'Well, go on, then,' said Dick. 'Nobody's stopping you!'

'How far down does the lighthouse go, Tinker?' asked George. 'We always scoot up the first bit of the spiral stairway and never think about the lighthouse foundations deep down in the rock. *Are* they deep down?'

'Oh, they are,' said Tinker, looking up from his book. 'My father told me that when the lighthouse was built, they drilled right down into the rock for a long way – made a kind of shaft. And he said that under these rocks there are all kinds of queer holes and tunnels – the drill kept shooting downwards when it came to a sudden space.'

'*Really?*' said Dick interested. 'I hadn't thought of what would have to be done to make a high lighthouse safe from the gales and storms. It would *have* to have deep foundations, of course!'

'My father found an old map somewhere,' said Tinker. 'A sort of plan made when the lighthouse was first built.'

'Like architects draw when they plan how to build a house?' said Anne.

'Something like that,' said Tinker. 'I can't remember much about it. I know it showed all the rooms in the lighthouse, connected by the spiral stairway – and it showed the big lamp-room at the top – and at the bottom of the map the foundation shaft was drawn.'

'Can you go down the shaft?' asked Dick. 'Is there a ladder, or anything?'

'I don't know,' said Tinker. 'I've never been down there. I never thought about it!'

'Do you know where the old map is – the one made by the architect who drew up plans for the lighthouse builder to follow?' said Julian. 'Where did your father put it?'

'Oh, I expect he threw it away,' said Tinker. 'Wait a minute though – it may be in the lamp-room! I remember him taking it up there, because it had a drawing of how the lamp worked.'

'Well, I'd rather like to go and see if I can find it,' said Julian, interested. 'Come up with me, Tinker. Thank goodness you don't keep turning into some sort of car now – you must be growing up!'

So the two of them went up the spiral stairway to the lamp-room at the very top of the tower. Again Julian marvelled at the magnificent views all around. The rain had stopped for a time, and the sea, swept by strong winds, was a swirling tumult of angry waters.

Tinker scrabbled about in a little dark space under the lamp. He at last brought up a roll of something white and waved it at Julian. 'Here's the map. I thought it would be in the lamp-room.'

Julian took it down to the others, and they spread it out. It showed the plan of the lighthouse, and was very clearly and beautifully drawn.

'How is it that architects draw so marvellously?' said George. 'Are they architects because they can do this kind of thing so well – or do they draw beautifully because they are architects?'

'A bit of both, probably,' said Julian, bending over the finely drawn plan. 'Ah – here are the foundations, look – my goodness, they do go down a long way into the rock!'

'Great tall buildings like this *always* have deep, strong foundations,' said Dick. 'Last term at school we studied how . . .'

'Let's not talk of school,' said Anne. 'It's already looming in the distance! Tinker – can anyone get down into this foundation place?'

'I told you – I don't know,' said Tinker. 'Anyway I should think it would be a horrible place down there – dark and smelly, and narrow, and . . .'

'Let's go and see,' said George, getting up. 'I'm so bored at the moment that if I don't do something, I'll fall asleep for a hundred years.'

'Idiot,' said Dick. 'Still – quite a good idea of yours. We'd have a bit of peace and quiet while you were sleeping! Oooooch – don't jab me like that, George!'

'Come on,' said George. 'Let's trot down and find out what's down the shaft.'

Anne didn't want to go down the shaft, but the others ran down the stairway, Timmy too, and soon came to the bottom, opposite the entrance door of the lighthouse.

Tinker showed them a large, round trap-door in the floor there. 'If we open that, we'll be looking down into the foundation shaft,' he said.

So they pulled up the large, round, wooden trap-door, and gazed downwards. They could see nothing at all except darkness! 'Where's my torch?' said Julian. 'I'll fetch it!'

Soon his torch was lighting up the round shaft, and they saw an iron ladder going down it on one side. Julian climbed down a few steps and examined the walls of the shaft.

'They're cement!' he called. 'And they must be enormously thick, I should think. I'm going on down.'

So down he went, and down, marvelling at the sturdy cement lining of the enormous shaft. He wondered why it had not been filled in. Perhaps a hollow cement-lined shaft was stronger than a filled-in one? He didn't know.

He came almost to the bottom – but he didn't go down the last steps of the iron ladder. A peculiar noise came from below him! A gurgling, choking noise! What in the world could it be?

He shone his torch down to see – and then stared in amazement! There was water at the bottom of the shaft, water that swirled and moved around, making a strange, hollow, gurgling noise. Where did it come from?

As he watched it, it disappeared – then it came back again! He shone his torch here and there to find out how the water made its way into the shaft.

There must be a tunnel or a passage of some sort down there, that the sea can enter, he thought. It's high tide now – so the water is swirling in. I wonder – now I *wonder* – if it's free of water when the tide is out! And if so where does that tunnel, or whatever it is, lead to? Or is it always under water? I'll go back and tell the others – and have another look at that old map!

He climbed back, glad to be out of the smelly darkness of the old shaft. The others were at the top, looking down rather anxiously.

'Here he is!' said George. 'See anything interesting, Julian?'

'I did, rather,' said Julian, climbing out of the shaft. 'Got that old map with you? I want to look at something, if so.'

'Come upstairs, then,' said Dick. 'We can see better there. What was down there, Ju?'

'Wait till we're up in the living room,' said Julian. He

took the map from Tinker as soon as he arrived there, and sat down to look at it. He ran his finger down the shaft to the bottom, and then jabbed at a round mark drawn there.

'See that? That's a hole at the bottom of the shaft, through which sea-water comes in. It's high tide now, so the water is seeping into the shaft – but it's not very deep. At low tide there wouldn't be a single drop coming in. Wouldn't I love to know where that water-tunnel went to – up to the surface of the rocks? Through them to somewhere a good way off? Or what?'

'An undersea tunnel!' said George, her eyes bright. 'Why don't we explore it sometime when the tide is out?'

'Well – we'd have to be pretty certain we wouldn't suddenly be drowned!' said Julian, rolling up the map. 'Very interesting, isn't it? I suppose the hole was left in case the constant push of water there, when the tide was in, might undermine the foundations. Better to have the shaft half-full of water than eaten away by constant tides!'

'Well,' began Anne, and then suddenly stopped in fright. A very loud voice came up the stairway, and made everyone jump violently.

'ANYONE AT HOME? HEY, ANYONE AT HOME?'

CHAPTER FIFTEEN

Jacob is in trouble

'Who's that shouting like that?' said Anne, fearfully. 'It can't be the robber, can it?'

'Of course not,' said Julian, and went to the door of the living room. He yelled down the stairway:

'Who is it? What do you want?'

'It's the police!' shouted back the enormous voice.

'Oh. Come on up, then,' said Julian, relieved. Footsteps could be heard coming up the iron stairway, accompanied by loud puffs and pants. Then a policeman's helmet appeared, followed by his shoulders and the rest of him. Soon he was standing in the living room, beaming round at the surprised company, panting with the effort of climbing so many stairs.

'How did you get in?' asked George. 'We jammed the door shut from the inside.'

'Well, I managed to unjam it, miss,' said the policeman, mopping his forehead, and smiling. He was the same policeman that Julian had seen that afternoon. 'Not much protection that, really. You ought to get a new key made.'

'How did you get over here – the tide's in,' said Julian. 'You couldn't have walked over Demon's Rocks.'

'No. I got Jem Hardy's boat,' said the policeman. 'By the way, my name's Sharp – Police Constable Sharp.'

'A very good name for a policeman,' said Julian, with a cheerful grin. 'Well, have you caught the thief who took our key, and the other things?'

'No. But I've a pretty good idea who it is,' said Sharp. 'I couldn't find anyone who'd been sitting on the quay during the time you were away from the lighthouse, but I did by chance find a lady whose windows look down on the jetty, and she happened to see someone standing about there. She said he went over the rocks to the lighthouse.'

'Who was it? The milkman, the postman?' asked Dick.

'Oh no, I told your friend they were good fellows,' said the constable, looking quite shocked. 'It was er – well, a man who's a bit of a bad lot.'

'Who's that?' asked Julian, suddenly afraid it might be old Jeremiah. *Could* he be a bad lot – he had sounded such a good fellow!

'Well, it's no one you know,' said Sharp. 'It's one of a family with rather a bad name – a man called Jacob – Jacob Loomer. He comes of a family that used to do a bit of wrecking, and . . .'

'Wrecking! Old Jeremiah was telling us of long-ago wreckers!' said Dick. 'One was called Nosey – and another was called Bart – relations of a well-known wrecker called One-Ear – er, One-Ear . . .'

'Bill,' said Sharp. 'Ah, yes – One-Ear Bill. He lived a long time ago, when old Jeremiah was a young man. This here Jacob, the one that was seen going into your light-house today, would be his great-great-great grandson, I reckon – something like that. Living image of old One-Ear Bill, according to Jeremiah. There's a bad strain in that family – can't seem to get it out!'

'Well – you say it was Jacob who came into the lighthouse? Why can't we have him arrested then?' said Julian. 'And make him give up the key he took – and the other things?'

'Well, if you'll come along with me and identify your things, maybe I can do something about it,' said the constable. 'But he may have hidden them all by now – though he's that free-handed I wouldn't be surprised if he hasn't *given* them all away. A bit of a fool, Jacob is, as well as a rogue. Ah – he'd have liked the job of wrecking ships, he would – right up his street.'

'I'll come with you now,' said Julian. 'The others don't need to, do they?'

'Oh no – you'll do,' said the policeman, and he and Julian went down the spiral stairway to the entrance. The others heard the door bang, and looked at one another.

'Well! To think that a great-great-great grandson of that horrid old One-Ear Bill is still living in the same place that the old wrecker himself did!' said Dick. '*And* he's a rogue too. History repeating itself?'

'We *must* go and see the Wreckers' Cave tomorrow, if we can,' said George. 'Jeremiah Boogle said he would show it to us.'

'So long as there isn't an old, old wrecker hiding there!' said Anne. 'Older than Jeremiah Boogle – with a beard down to his feet – a sort of Old Man of the Sea – with a horrid gurgling voice, and eyes like a fish!'

'*Really*, Anne!' said George astonished. 'I'll be scared to go into caves if you say things like that!'

'I wonder how Julian's getting on,' said Tinker. 'Mischief, stop jigging up and down – you make me feel out of breath!'

Julian was at Jacob's house, and there, sure enough, were the things he had stolen – the rug, the clock and Anne's purse – empty now!'

'And what about the key?' demanded the constable. 'Come on now, you took the key out of the door of the lighthouse, we know you did. Give it here, Jacob.'

'I didn't take it,' said Jacob, sullenly.

'I'll have to take you in, you know, Jacob,' said the constable. 'You'll be searched at the police station. Better give up the key now.'

'Search me all you like!' said Jacob. 'You won't find that key on me. I tell you. I didn't take it. What would I want that key for?'

'For the same reason that you usually want keys for,' said the constable. 'For breaking in and stealing. All right, Jacob. If you won't let this young gentleman have his key, I'll have you searched at the police station. Come along with me.'

But alas, no key was found on the surly Jacob, and the

constable shrugged his shoulders and raised his eyebrows at Julian.

'If you take my advice, I'd get a different lock put on your door. Jacob's got your key somewhere. He'll be at the lighthouse again as soon as he sees you all go out.'

'Bah!' said Jacob, rudely. 'You and your keys. I tell you I didn't take it. There wasn't a key there . . .'

'Come along with me, Jacob,' said the constable. He turned to Julian. 'Well, that's all. We'll have his house searched. The odds are that he's hidden the key somewhere. He's an artful dodger, this one!'

Julian went back to the lighthouse, rather worried. It might take a few days, in a little place like this, to have a new lock put in. In the meantime they would either have to keep themselves prisoners in the lighthouse – or leave a front door that anyone could open!

The others listened excitedly to his tale, when he went back. They were glad to have the rug, the clock and the purse again – though Anne was sad that all her money was gone.

'We'll have to get a new lock and key,' said Julian. 'After all, this lighthouse has only been *lent* to us, and it's our responsibility to look after it and all it contains. It's a good thing it was only *our* things that were taken – not Professor Hayling's!'

'It's getting rather late,' said Anne, jumping up. 'We haven't had our tea yet! I'll get it. Anyone feel like buns with butter and jam?'

Everyone did, and soon Anne produced a large plate of delicious-looking buns. They talked as they drank their tea, and ate the buns.

'I vote we go and find Jeremiah Boogle tomorrow, and

see if he's heard of the robbery, and if he has anything interesting to say about it,' said George.

'And also we really must get him to show us the Wreckers' Cave,' said Julian. 'By the way, what were the names of the two men who have the job of showing the visitors round the caves? I'm pretty sure one was Jacob!'

'You're right – it was – and the other man was called Ebenezer!' said Dick. 'Well – let's hope Jacob is locked up, or out of the way somewhere when we go to see the caves. We shall get some black looks from him, if not!'

'Well, we can give him some back!' said George, putting on a terrific scowl, and making Timmy give a sudden whine. She patted him. 'It's all right, Timmy – that scowl wasn't for you!'

'We'd better go to the caves tomorrow morning when the tide will be more or less out,' said Julian. 'And I'd better see if I can find a locksmith here who can give us a new lock and key quickly!'

'Why not slip out now?' said Dick. 'I'll come with you for a bit of fresh air. Want to come, girls?'

'No, I'd like to finish my book,' said Anne, and George said the same. Tinker was playing with Mischief, and he didn't want to come either.

'Well, you and the lighthouse will be safe with Timmy and Mischief to look after you!' said Julian, and down the stairway he went, with Dick close behind him.

The locksmith promised to come and look at the door in the next day or two. 'Can't leave my shop just now,' he said. 'Nobody to see to it! It'll take me a few days to do the job for you, I'm afraid.'

'Oh, blow!' said Julian. 'We've already had a thief in

the lighthouse! We don't like to go out and leave it empty now!'

They rowed back to the lighthouse, shut and jammed the door as best they could, and went up to the girls. Timmy gave them an uproarious welcome, and Mischief took a flying leap from a chair back on to Dick's shoulder.

'No lock or key for a few days,' said Dick, sitting down and tickling the delighted little monkey. 'I did want to go and see the caves tomorrow – especially the famous Wreckers' one – but we can't possibly leave the lighthouse empty.'

'Woof,' said Timmy at once.

'He says, why not leave *him* behind, and let him guard it,' said George, solemnly, and Timmy at once said, 'Woof', again.

They all laughed. Dick patted Timmy, and ruffled the fur behind his ears. 'Dear old Tim – all right, *you* guard the lighthouse – you shall have a Very Special Bone for a reward!'

'That's settled then. We leave Timmy here on guard, and we all go off to the caves,' said Julian. 'Well, one of the brothers who show visitors round will be missing tomorrow, I fear – Jacob will *not* be there!'

'I bet we'll get some scowls from the other brother – what's his name now – Ebenezer?' said Anne. 'We'll have to be careful that we don't get pushed into a deep pool of water!'

'Dear me, yes,' said Julian. 'One never knows! We'll certainly be on our guard!'

CHAPTER SIXTEEN

Down in the caves

NEXT MORNING George awoke with a jump. Timmy was pushing her gently with his nose. 'What is it, Tim?' said George. Timmy gave a bark, and ran to where the spiral stairway led downwards.

'Go down and tell the boys what it is you want,' said George, sleepily. So down the stairway went Timmy, and into the room where the boys were sleeping. He trotted in and nudged Julian with his nose, but Julian was so fast asleep that he didn't stir.

Timmy pawed at him, and Julian awoke with a jump. He sat up. 'Oh, it's you, Tim – what on earth do you want? Is anything wrong with the girls?'

'Woof,' said Timmy, and ran to the spiral stairway. He disappeared down it, barking.

'Blow! He's heard someone!' said Julian, yawning. 'Well, if it's Ebenezer or Jacob – no, it can't be Jacob, of course – I'll tell him what I think of people who steal!'

He unjammed the door of the lighthouse and opened it. On the step stood two milk bottles! 'Well, really, Timmy, fancy waking me because the milkman came!' said Julian, taking in the bottles. 'Good old milkman – I wonder if he had to come by boat – the sea's pretty high this morning – but I suppose he *could* just about have waded over the rocks!'

At breakfast the Five remembered that they meant to see the caves that morning. They had a very fine meal of fried bacon, bought the day before, and eggs, with buttered toast and marmalade to follow. Anne had made some good hot coffee, and they all enjoyed themselves immensely. Mischief made himself a real nuisance by putting a paw deep in the marmalade jar and then, when smacked, running all over the place leaving sticky marmaladey marks everywhere!

'We'd better all take a wet rag with us as we go about the room,' said Anne, in disgust. 'He's run over the table and desk and everything. BAD Mischief! I do so hate feeling sticky.'

Mischief was sad to feel himself in disgrace, and leapt on to Tinker's shoulder, putting his sticky paws lovingly round the boy's neck. 'That's right!' said Tinker, 'rub all your stickiness off on *me*, you little monkey!'

'We'll wash up in the sink, and you boys can tidy up the rooms,' said Anne. 'Then we'll all go out. It's a lovely day.'

'Looks a bit stormy to me,' said Dick. 'What do *you* say, Tim?'

Tim agreed. He thumped his tail vigorously on the floor, making Mischief pounce on it in joy. Anne gathered up the crockery and took it to the sink.

In an hour or so they were ready to go out. 'Let's write a card to Aunt Fanny before we leave,' said Anne. 'Then *that* will be done. We won't say a word about the things that were stolen, though. She might feel upset, and tell us to go back! And *then* what would Uncle Quentin and Professor Hayling say?'

'I bet they're having a wonderful time, arguing all day long, working out figures, and studying papers!' said Julian. 'And I'm pretty certain that Aunt Fanny will have to call them to a meal at least twenty times before they arrive at the table!'

Anne wrote the postcard and put on a stamp. 'Now I'm ready,' she said, standing up. Timmy ran to the top of the stairs, glad that everyone seemed to be on the move at last. He did so love a walk.

'Darling Timmy,' said George, 'I'm afraid you'll have to be left behind to guard the lighthouse! You see, we haven't a key – and we can't jam the door from outside. So please, Timmy dear, stay behind – on guard. You know what *that* means, don't you? ON GUARD!'

Timmy's tail went right down. He gave a small whine. He did so hate being left out of anything – especially a walk. He pawed gently at George as if to say, 'Do please change your mind.'

'On guard, Timmy, now,' said George. 'The lighthouse is in your charge. Don't let ANYONE *in*. You'd better lie on the mat just inside the entrance.'

Timmy ran slowly down behind Julian and the others, looking very mournful indeed. 'Now lie there,' said George, and gave him a pat on the head. 'We'll take you out again soon, and then one of *us* will stay to guard the lighthouse – but this time we *all* want to go out. ON GUARD!'

Timmy lay down on the mat, and put his head on his paws, his brown eyes looking up at George. 'Dear old faithful,' she said ruffling the hair on his head. 'We won't be very long!'

They slammed the door and went down the lighthouse steps. The tide was still out far enough for them to be able to wade over the rocks to the jetty. 'We must be back before it's well in,' said Julian. 'Or we'll have to stay ashore till it's out again. Our boat is tied to the lighthouse post, remember!'

They went for a stroll along the quay and who should be there, sitting on a stone seat, but old Jeremiah Boogle, smoking his long pipe, staring solemnly out to sea.

'Good morning, Jeremiah,' said Dick, politely. 'I hope we bought the right kind of sweets for you from Tom.'

'Oh aye,' said Jeremiah, puffing out very strong-smelling smoke. 'Hallo, little monkey – so you've come to my shoulder again, have you? Well, what's the news from Monkey Lane?'

The others laughed as Mischief at once poured out a stream of monkey chatter into the old man's ear. 'We thought we would go and see the caves today,' said Julian. 'Especially the old Wreckers' Cave.'

'Now don't you let that Ebenezer take you round!' said the old man, at once. 'You won't find Jacob there – oho –

I know what's happened to *him*. And serve him right. Never could keep his fingers to himself, that one! Ebenezer's as bad. He could steal the buttons off your coat, and you'd never know! Now look – what about *me* showing you the caves? I know them inside out, and I can show you things that that rat of an Ebenezer doesn't even know of.'

'Well – we'd certainly much rather *you* took us, and not Ebenezer,' said Julian. 'Ebenezer may be feeling rather angry because we told the police about his brother stealing things. We'll give you some more sweets if *you'll* guide us round.'

'Well, let's go now,' said Jeremiah, getting up very spryly. 'This way!'

And off they went, Mischief too – the little monkey did Jeremiah the honour of sitting on his shoulder all the way down the village street. The old man was delighted to see how everyone stared and laughed.

He took them round the foot of some very high cliffs. They came to a rocky beach farther along, and walked over it. 'There's the entrance,' said the old man, pointing to a large hole in the cliff nearby. 'That's the way to the caves. Got a torch?'

'Yes – we brought one each,' said Julian, patting his pocket. 'Do we have to pay to go in?'

'No. People give Ebenezer a tip – fifty pence or so – if he shows them round – or Jacob, when he's there,' said Jeremiah. '*I'll* deal with Ebby, though. Don't you waste your money on that scoundrel!'

The hole in the cliff led to the first cave, which was a big one. Lighted lanterns hung here and there, but gave very little light.

'Mind your step, now,' warned Jeremiah. 'It's really slippery in places. This way – through this old arch.'

It was cold and damp in the cave, and the children had to go carefully, and avoid the puddles left by the sea. Then suddenly Jeremiah turned a corner and went in a completely different direction! Down and down and down they went!

'Hey – we're going towards the *sea* now surely?' said Julian, in surprise. 'Do the caves go *under* the sea, then? Not away back into the cliff?'

'That's right,' said Jeremiah. 'This is a real rocky coast – and the way we're taking leads down a tunnel under the rocks, and then into the caves deep underground. See the rocky roof over our heads – well, if you listen, you can hear the sea now, mumbling and grumbling over it – that roof is the bed of the sea!'

That was a very strange thought indeed, and rather alarming! Anne gazed fearfully up at the rocky roof overhead, and shone her torch on it, half-expecting to see a few cracks leaking salt water from the sea rolling over the rocky roof! But no – there was a little moisture shining on it, and that was all.

'Are we soon coming to the Wreckers' Cave?' asked George. 'Mischief, stop making those noises. There's nothing to be scared of!'

Mischief didn't like this cold, dark, strange walk underground, and had begun to make harsh, frightened noises, and then suddenly gave a loud scared screech.

'Don't! You made me jump!' said Anne. 'Goodness – listen to the monkey's screech echoing all along the tunnel and back! Sounds like a hundred monkeys chattering at once! *Our* voices echo too!'

Mischief was most alarmed to hear the enormous amount of screeches and chattering noises that now filled the tunnel. He began to cry almost like a baby, and clung to Tinker as if he would never let him go.

'I expect he thinks this place is absolutely full of screeching monkeys,' said Anne, sorry for the terrified little creature. 'It's only the echo, Mischief.'

'He'll soon get used to it,' said Tinker, hugging the monkey close to him.

'You want to hear the echo just round the next bend of the tunnel!' said Jeremiah, stroking the little monkey, and very foolishly gave an enormous yell just as they got there!

The yell came back ten times as loud, and the tunnel seemed suddenly full of shouts tumbling over one another. Everyone jumped violently, and Mischief leapt high in the air in terror. He sprang to the ground, and scampered away at top speed, wailing in his little monkey voice. He tore down the tunnel, tail in air, and disappeared round the corner. Tinker was very upset.

'Mischief! Come back!' he yelled. 'You'll get lost!'

And along came the echo at once. 'Get lost, get lost, get lost – lost – lost!'

'Don't you worry about your monkey,' said Jeremiah, comfortingly. 'I've had a score of monkeys in my time – and they always come back!'

'Well, I'll jolly well stay down here till Mischief *does* come back!' said Tinker, in rather a shaky voice.

They came out into a cave. This too was lit by lanterns, though very poorly. They had all heard the murmur of voices as they came to it, and wondered who was there.

Three other visitors were in the cave, sightseeing, like

the children. A big burly fellow was with them, with jet-black hair, deep-set dark eyes, and a surly mouth – so like Jacob that Julian guessed at once that he was the brother, Ebenezer.

As soon as Ebenezer set eyes on Jeremiah, he roared in fury.

'You get out! This is *my* job – you get out. *I'll* show the caves to those youngsters!'

And with that such a battle of words followed that the Five were almost deafened, especially as the echo repeated everything very loudly indeed! The three visitors fled away up the tunnel, fearing a fight. Anne was very frightened, and clung to Julian.

Ebenezer came shouting up to old Jeremiah, his hand raised. 'Haven't I told you more than a hundred times to keep out of these caves? Haven't I told you I'm the one to show folks around – and Jacob too?'

'Don't listen to him!' said Jeremiah, turning his back on the angry man. 'He's nothing but a big-mouth, same as his brother Jacob!'

'Look out!' yelled Julian, as the angry Ebenezer rushed at Jeremiah, his fist raised to strike him. 'LOOK OUT!'

CHAPTER SEVENTEEN

Mischief again – and a surprise!

JEREMIAH SAW the angry man coming at him, and very neatly side-stepped. Ebenezer couldn't stop, stepped heavily on a strand of very slippery seaweed – and went sprawling into a corner!

'Ho!' said Jeremiah, delighted. 'Very nice, Ebenezer! Get up, and run at me again!'

'He'd better not,' said Julian, in his most grown-up voice. 'I shall report him to the police if he does – and that will make a pair of them in two days. Jacob got into trouble yesterday – and now it will be Ebenezer.'

Ebenezer got up, scowling, and glared at Jeremiah, who grinned back in delight. 'Coming at me again, Ebby?' he said. 'It's grand fun to hit an old man, isn't it?'

But Ebenezer was very much afraid that Julian would do what he had threatened, and report him to the police. He rubbed his shoulder where it had struck a piece of rock, and debated what to do.

'Come along,' said Jeremiah, to the five watching children. 'I'll take you down to the Wreckers' Cave. Ebby can come too, if he can behave himself. But maybe he'd like to run away home, and get his shoulder looked to!'

That was enough for Ebby! He was determined to follow the little company, and made rude remarks all the time. So he tailed them, and shouted at them from a safe distance. How they wished they had Timmy with them! He would have made short work of the rude Ebenezer!

'Don't take any notice of him,' said Julian. 'Lead on, Jeremiah. My word, isn't it dark in this tunnel! Good thing we all brought good torches!'

The tunnel came to an end at last and opened out into an extraordinary cave. The roof was unexpectedly high, and the irregular sides were ridged with shelves of rocks. On the shelves were dirty old boxes, a crate or two and some sacks.

'What in the world are those?' asked Dick, shining his torch on them.

'Well young sir, they're just what they look like – ordinary boxes and sacks,' said Jeremiah. 'Put there by Ebenezer and Jacob to fool people! They tells everybody they're what the old wreckers got out of ships they wrecked, years ago! Hoo-hoo-hoo! Anybody that be-

lieves those lies *deserves* to be fooled. They're all from
Ebby's backyard. Seen them lying there myself! Hoo-
hoo-hoo!'

His hoo-hooing laugh echoed round the cave, and
Ebenezer made an angry growling noise rather like a dog.

'*I'm* not going to fool these kids,' said Jeremiah. 'You
and your sacks and boxes! I know where the old things
are, the real old things – oh yes I do!'

'They're no better than the sacks and boxes there,
wherever they are!' said Ebby, in a growling voice.
'You're lying, old Jeremiah – you don't know nothing!'

'Take us on farther,' said Dick. 'There must be more
caves. I think this is exciting. Is this really where the old
wreckers hid the things they salvaged from the wrecks
they caused – or just a tale?'

'Oh, this is their cave, that's true enough. Dressed up a
bit by Ebby there!' said Jeremiah. 'But *I* know the caves
farther on. Ebby doesn't! He's too scared to go farther
under the sea. Aren't you, Ebby?'

Ebby said something that sounded rude. Julian turned
to Jeremiah eagerly. 'Oh, do take us farther – if it isn't
dangerous!'

'Well, *I'm* going farther on, anyway,' said Tinker
suddenly. 'Mischief hasn't come back – so he must be
lost – and *I'm* going to find him!'

Julian saw that Tinker was quite determined. 'Right,'
he said. 'We'll come with you. Jeremiah, lead the way!
But it's not *really* dangerous, is it? I mean – we don't
want to find the sea sweeping through these caves, right
up to where we are!'

'Tide's not on the turn yet,' said Jeremiah. 'We're all
right for a while. When it comes in, it swirls up this

passage here – but it stops at the Wreckers' Cave – that's just too high for it, see? The tunnel runs downwards fast now. It goes right under your lighthouse, have you seen it down at the bottom of the shaft?'

'Good gracious, yes!' said Julian, remembering. 'I went down it – and the sea was swirling in and out at openings in the bottom of the shaft. Do you mean to say that the sea that rises in the shaft at high tide comes racing up into these tunnels too?'

'Aye, that it does,' said Jeremiah. 'You can get from here to the lighthouse under the rocky seabed right to that foundation shaft. But nobody dares! Tide comes in so quickly, you might get caught and drowned!'

Ebby at once shouted something rude again – it sounded as if he was telling Jeremiah to go and get drowned too!

'Do let's go on farther,' said Dick. 'Come on, Jeremiah.'

So Jeremiah led them farther on under the rocky bed of the sea. It was strange and rather frightening to hear the constant noise of the water racing over the roof of the winding tunnel. Their torches lit up slimy walls, and rocky shelves and hollows.

'You know – this would have been a very good place to hide treasure,' said Julian, glancing up at a dark hollow in the roof of the tunnel. 'Though I don't know how anyone would set about looking for it – there are hundreds of nooks and crannies – and isn't it *cold* in this tunnel!'

'Well, the sun's rays never penetrate down *here*,' said Dick. 'My word, the sea sounds pretty loud now!'

'I wish we could find Mischief,' said Anne to George.

'Look at poor Tinker. He's crying. He's pretending not to, but I could see the tears rolling down his cheeks last time I flashed my torch on him.'

They stopped to look at something – a strange jelly-like thing, like an enormous sea anemone. Ebby caught them up, and bumped into Dick. He rounded on Ebby at once.

'Keep off! Follow us if you like, but don't come so near. We don't like you!'

Ebby took no notice but kept as close behind everyone as he possibly could, and Dick realised that he was probably feeling very scared! Then, as they rounded another corner of the tunnel, and saw yet another cave, Tinker gave a yell that echoed everywhere.

'MISCHIEF! LOOK! THERE HE IS! MISCHIEF!'

And sure enough, there was the little monkey, crouched under a small shelf of rock, shivering in fright. He wouldn't even go running to Tinker. Tinker had to pick him up and hug him.

'Mischief! Poor Mischief – were you very frightened?' he said. 'You're trembling all over! You shouldn't have run away! You might have been lost for ever!'

Mischief had something clutched in his tiny paw. He chattered to Tinker, and put his furry little arms round his neck. As he did so, he opened one paw – and something fell out and rolled over the rocky floor.

'What have you dropped, Mischief?' said Dick, and shone his torch down on to the floor of the cave. Something was glittering there – something round and yellow! Everyone stared, and a shock of excitement went through Julian, who was nearest. 'A gold coin!' he cried, and picked it up. 'As bright as when it was minted.

Mischief, where did you get it from? Look, Dick, look
George – it's gold all right!'

Immediately everyone was full of the greatest excitement, one thought only in their heads.

The treasure! Mischief must have found the treasure! It

was an old coin – very old. Where *could* Mischief have found it?

'Oh, let's go farther on and see!' cried Dick. 'Jeremiah, it *must* be the treasure! Mischief will lead us to it!'

But Mischief would do nothing of the sort. He was NOT going to lose himself again. He was going to sit on Tinker's shoulders, with an arm safely round the boy's neck! He hadn't liked being lost, all by himself in the dark.

Jeremiah would not go any farther, either. He shook his head. 'No – not today. Tide will soon be sweeping up these tunnels – faster than we can walk. Better turn back now, in case we're caught. Many's the visitor that's had to run for his life, when the tide came up all of a sudden!'

George's sharp ears caught the sound of a 'swooshs-woosh'! Somewhere the tide had crept in! 'Come on!' she said. 'We'd better do what Jeremiah says. The sea's coming up the tunnel now as well as over it – and soon it will be sweeping up the beach too, and in at the cliff passages. We'll be caught in the middle, and have to stay here for ages!'

'No need for alarm, missy,' said old Jeremiah. 'There's a bit of time yet. Halloo – where's Ebenezer gone?'

'Blow – he must have heard us talking about Mischief's gold piece,' said George. 'I forgot all about him! Now he knows that Mischief has found a gold coin, he'll feel sure that the treasure *may* be somewhere down here – and he'll look for it as soon as ever he can! WHY didn't we keep quiet about it?'

'I forgot he was standing near us,' groaned Dick. 'Well I suppose the whole of Demon's Rocks village will know by now that a monkey has found the treasure – and hordes of sightseers will swarm down here, hoping to find it. It must have been put in a pretty dry place, surely, for that coin to be so bright and untarnished.'

'Buck up – we'd better go back as quickly as possible,' said Julian. 'Look at old Jeremiah – he's too thrilled for words! He's planning to find the treasure himself at the earliest possible moment!'

'Well, I vote we have a shot at it ourselves tomorrow,' said Dick, excitement welling up in him at the thought. 'Good old Mischief! You're better than any detective!'

Then away up the tunnels they went, making all kinds of plans. WHAT an excitement!

CHAPTER EIGHTEEN

Back in the lighthouse – and an exciting talk!

OLD JEREMIAH was as excited as the others, but he said very little. He was angry to think that Ebenezer should have been there to see the find. He didn't trust that Ebby – nor that Jacob either! They'd be ferreting after that treasure as sure as nuts were nuts, and monkeys were monkeys! Ha – wouldn't they like to know where it was! He stumped on, up the old tunnels, thinking hard, and at last they came out into the welcome daylight again!

'Here, Jeremiah – buy yourself some more sweets,' said Julian, putting some money into the old man's hand. 'And don't count too much on that treasure! I expect it's just an odd coin that Mischief found in a dry corner somewhere!'

'Thank you!' said the old man. 'I don't want the treasure myself – I'm just hoping that Ebby and Jacob don't find it. They'll be hunting all the time for it now!'

They were glad to be out in the open again. The sun had gone now, and the wind had whipped up. It was raining hard.

'I say – we'd better buck up, else we shan't be able to walk back to the lighthouse over the rocks!' said Julian, worried. But fortunately the wind was against the tide and they just had time to wade over to the lighthouse steps.

'There's our little boat bobbing about,' said Tinker. 'And listen – I can hear old Timmy barking! He's heard us coming!'

So he had. He had been lying on the doormat, his ears glued to the crack under the door, listening. Nobody had come near the lighthouse and not a sound did old Timmy hear but the wind and the sea, and a few gulls gliding by.

'We're back, Timmy!' yelled George, and she pushed at the door. It opened, and Timmy leapt out, almost knocking her over. Mischief sprang on to the dog's back, and chattered at him without stopping.

'He's telling him about the gold coin he found,' said Tinker, with a laugh. 'Oh, I WISH you'd been with us, Timmy. It was grand!'

'It feels as if we've been away for ages,' said George. 'But it wasn't very late after all – unless my watch is slow! I'm hungry. Let's have something to eat and talk about everything – and what we're going to do!'

So, over biscuits and sandwiches and coffee, they talked and talked. 'We must get down to the caves again as soon as possible!' said George. 'I'm absolutely certain that Jacob and Ebby will be down there, hunting for coins, as soon as the tide's out again.'

'Well, we can't do anything today, that's certain,' said Dick. 'For one thing the tide's in now – and for another thing it's blowing up for a storm. Just *listen* to the wind!'

Timmy was sitting as close to George as he possibly could. He hadn't liked her going out without him. She sat with her arm round him, eating her biscuits, occasionally giving him half of one. Tinker was doing the same with Mischief!

The children talked and talked. Where could Mischief have found that coin? Was it one on its own, that the sea had swept into the tunnel? Or was it part of a whole lot of coins? Had it come from an iron-bound box whose wooden sides had rotted away? They talked endlessly, their eyes bright, the round gold coin on the table in front of them.

'I suppose it would be treasure trove if we found it?' said Dick. 'I mean – it would be so old that it would belong to the Crown, and not to anyone in particular.'

'I expect we'd be allowed to keep a few coins ourselves,' said George. 'If only we could go straight away now and hunt in that tunnel! I feel as if I can't wait!'

'Woof,' said Timmy, agreeing though he really hadn't much idea of what they were talking about!

'I say – LISTEN to the sea crashing over the rocks between us and the jetty!' said Julian, startled at the sudden booming. 'The wind must be working up to a gale!'

'Well, bad weather's been forecast for some time,' said Dick gloomily. 'Blow! It'll be jolly difficult rowing to and fro in that little *Bob-About* boat. I doubt if we'd be able to walk across the rocks, even at low tide, with a big sea running before the wind.'

'Oh, don't be so gloomy!' said Anne.

'Well, do you want us to be prisoners here in the lighthouse?' demanded Dick.

'It wouldn't matter – there's plenty of food,' said Anne.

'No there isn't! Remember there are five of us – and Timmy and Mischief as well,' said Dick.

'Shut up, Dick,' said Julian. 'You're scaring Anne and Tinker. This storm will soon blow over – we'll be able to pop out and do some shopping tomorrow.'

But the storm grew fiercer, and the sky became so dark that Anne lit the lamps. Rain slashed against the lighthouse, and the wind made a loud howling noise that made Timmy growl deep down in his throat.

Anne went to look out of the window. She felt frightened when she saw the great waves that came surging over the rocks below. Some of them broke on the rocks, and the spray flew so high that it spattered the window out of which she was looking! She drew back in alarm.

'Do you know what hit the window then? It was spray from a great wave!'

'Whew!' said Julian, and went to the window himself. What a wonderful sight! The sea was grey now, not blue, and it raced along towards the shore, great waves curling over into white manes, spray flying. Out to sea there were angry waves too, topped with white, which turned into spray as the strong wind caught them. Only a few gulls were out, screaming in excitement, allowing the wind to take them along on their great white wings.

'Well, I certainly wouldn't mind being a gull today,' said Dick. 'It must be a wonderful feeling to ride on a storm – no wonder they are screaming in joy!'

'Ee-oo, Ee-oo, EE-OOO, ee-ooooo! cried the gulls, sounding like cats mewing in hunger.

'I'm sorry for the ships out in this,' said Julian. 'Goodness – think of the sailing ships in the olden days, caught on this rocky coast in a wind like this – it's almost a hurricane!'

'And think of that wicked old One-Ear Bill, gloating when he saw a ship sailing nearer and nearer the rocks!' said George. 'And even taking the warning lamp out of its place on the cliff, and bringing it near here to make sure that any ship out that night would make straight for the rocks – CRASH!'

'Don't,' said Anne. 'I hate to think of things like that.'

'Let's have a game,' said Julian. 'Where are the cards? Move that lamp a bit closer to the table, Dick. It's getting so jolly dark. Now no more talk of wrecks! Think of something cheerful – tea-sup, for instance – the treasure – and . . .'

'You know, I think it would be quite easy to find the treasure,' said Dick, bringing the lamp close to the table. 'Mischief is a very clever little thing. I'm sure he would remember where he found that coin, and lead us straight to the place.'

'It might have been just an odd coin, dropped by the man who hid the hoard,' said Anne.

'It might – but wherever it was found I think we can safely say that the main hoard wouldn't be very far away,' said Dick.

'Well, if we do go hunting we'll have to go when the

tide is well out,' said Julian. 'I don't really fancy scrabbling about in those caves and tunnels under the rocky seabed, when I know that somehow or other when the tide is coming in the water gets *under* the seabed, as well as on it.'

Dick sat frowning, thinking out something. 'Ju,' he said at last, 'you remember the direction we went in, as soon as we were underground this morning? We went leftish all the way, didn't we?'

'Yes, we did,' said Tinker, at once. 'I had my little compass with me – look – it clips to my wristwatch – and we went sharp west all the time.'

'Towards the lighthouse, that would be,' said Julian, and drew a quick plan. 'See – here's the lighthouse, say – and just here is the entrance into the cliff, where we first went – here's the path we took, curving right back to the sea again, under the rocky beach here it goes – and that's a cave, see, then more tunnel, and caves – the way always curving sharply to the left . . .'

'A bit farther on and we'd have been almost under the lighthouse!' said Dick, in amazement.

'That's right,' said Julian. 'And maybe in the old days, before this lighthouse was built, and ships were sent crashing on the rocks on which it now stands, there was a tunnel down from those lighthouse rocks that joined up with the tunnel we were in this morning – so that the wreckers would find it very easy to stow away anything valuable they found in a wrecked ship, without being seen!'

'Whew! You mean they waited till the ship smashed up, then waded over the rocks, as we do, took what they could find, and disappeared down a tunnel there to hide it!'

'And came out the other end!' said Anne.

George stared at Julian, and her eyes were bright.

'Maybe the tunnel is *still* somewhere in these rocks!' she said. 'Somewhere down at the edge of them, because we know the sea gets into the tunnel. Julian, let's look for it tomorrow. I think you're right. There *may* be a hole in the rocks here somewhere, that drops down into the tunnel we were in.'

Nobody wanted to play a game after that! They felt much too excited. They studied Julian's plan again and again, glad that Tinker's little compass had shown him so clearly that morning that the undersea passages had led due west to the lighthouse rocks.

'Do you suppose that everyone has forgotten the old hole?' said Dick. 'Nobody has told us anything about it, not even Jeremiah. Do you think it may have been blocked up?'

Julian frowned, thinking hard.

'Well, yes – it may have been,' he said. 'It *is* odd that Jeremiah didn't say anything about it. Anyway we'll have a good hunt tomorrow.'

'And if we find it, we'll drop down and hunt for the treasure!' said Tinker, his eyes shining. 'WHAT a shock for Ebenezer and Jacob if we find it first!'

CHAPTER NINETEEN

A nasty shock!

THE STORM blew itself out that evening, and next day was much calmer. The sky still looked angry, and rain fell now and again, but it was possible to get out of the lighthouse door in the morning, and go down the steps on to the rocks.

'Shall we go shopping first – or look for the hole?' said Julian.

'Look for the hole,' said Dick, promptly. 'The wind is still pretty strong, and the storm might blow up again – just look at that angry sky! We wouldn't be able to mess about round the edge of the rocks if the sea gets any rougher.'

They spread out and went cautiously over the great rocks on which the lighthouse was built. At low tide the rocks stood well up, out of the sea. The lighthouse was built on the highest part, and seemed to tower over the searchers as they clambered here and there, seeking for any hole that looked as if it might lead down into some tunnel below.

'Here's a hole!' called Anne, suddenly, and they all clambered over to her in excitement, Timmy too. Julian looked down to where Anne was pointing. 'Yes – it does look a likely one,' he said. 'Big enough to take a man, too. I'll climb down and see.'

He slid down the hole, holding on to projecting pieces of rock as he went. The others watched, thrilled. Timmy

305

barked. He didn't like to see Julian disappearing like this!

But before Julian quite disappeared, he shouted again; 'I'm afraid it's no good! It's come to a sudden end! I'm standing on firm rock, and though I've felt all round with my feet, there's no opening anywhere. It's a dead end!'

What a disappointment! 'Blow!' said Dick, lying down on the rocks and putting his arm down the hole to help Julian to climb up again. 'I had high hopes then! Julian – here's my hand. Do you want any help?'

'Thanks – it is a bit difficult!' said Julian. He climbed up with difficulty, and squeezed out of the hole thankfully. 'I wouldn't like to get *wedged* in here!' he said. 'Especially with the tide coming in!'

'It's beginning to pour with rain again!' said Anne. 'Shall we go shopping now – or wait a bit?'

'Oh, let's wait,' said George. 'I'm cold and wet now. Let's go into the lighthouse and make some hot coffee. WHAT a disappointment! Never mind – we can always go down the tunnels we were in yesterday and search around – maybe Mischief will show us where he found the gold coin!'

They all went into the lighthouse, and once more Julian jammed the door. 'I wish that locksmith would come,' he said. 'If we go down into the caves, we'll have to leave old Timmy behind on guard – and it is such a shame!'

'Woof,' said Timmy, heartily agreeing. They all went upstairs and Anne began to make the coffee. As they were sitting drinking it, Timmy suddenly sprang to his feet with a most blood-curdling growl. Everyone jumped, and Anne spilt her coffee.

'Timmy! What's up?' said George, in alarm. Timmy

was standing with his nose towards the closed door of the room, his hackles rising up on his neck. He looked truly fierce!

'What on *earth* is the matter, Tim?' said Julian, going to the door. 'There can't be anyone on the stairway – the entrance door's jammed!'

Timmy raced out of the door as soon as Julian opened it and tore down the spiral stairway at such a speed that he fell, and rolled to the bottom. George gave a terrified scream. 'Timmy! Have you hurt yourself?'

But Timmy leapt to his feet at once, and ran to the entrance door, growling so ferociously that Anne felt really frightened. Julian ran down and went to the door. It was still well and truly jammed.

'Timmy! Maybe it's just the poor milkman, come with some milk again,' he said, and unjammed the door. He took hold of the handle to open it.

It wouldn't open! Julian pulled and tugged, but it was of no use. The door simply would NOT open!

By this time everyone was down beside him. 'Let *me* try,' said Dick. 'The door must just have stuck.'

No – he couldn't open it either! Julian looked gravely round at everyone. 'I'm afraid – very much afraid – that SOMEBODY has locked us in!' he said.

There was a horrified silence. Then George cried out in anger. 'Locked us in! How dare they! Who's done this!'

'Well – I think we can guess,' said Julian. 'It was whoever came and stole our key the other day!'

'Ebenezer – no, Jacob!' cried Dick. 'One of the two, anyway. How DARE they? What are we going to do? We can't get out. Why have they done this – this – silly – *wicked* thing?'

'I'm afraid it's because they think we might go looking for the treasure – and find it,' said Julian, his face
grave, 'We felt sure that Mischief might remember
where he had found the gold coin – and lead us there
– and I'm pretty sure they think the same. So this is
their way of making sure *they* have time to find the
treasure, before we do!'

'They're wicked, they're wicked!' cried George, taking
hold of the handle of the door, and pulling it violently.
'We're prisoners!'

'Don't pull the handle off, old thing,' said Julian. 'That
wouldn't help at all. Let's go upstairs and talk about it.
We'll have to think of some way out of this unexpected
difficulty.'

They went soberly upstairs again, and sat down in the
living room. Yes – they were certainly prisoners!

'What are we going to do?' said Dick. 'We are in a real
fix, Julian.'

'Yes. You're right,' said Julian, looking worried. 'We
can't get out of the lighthouse, that's certain. On the
other hand – how can we get help? No telephone.
Shouting would never be heard. Can't use our boat.
No one would ever know we are prisoners – they've
seen us going in and out of the lighthouse, and if we
suddenly don't appear any more they'll simply think we
have gone home, and that the lighthouse is empty again!'

'We shall die of starvation!' said Anne, scared.

'Oh no – I expect we shall think of something,' said
Dick, seeing that Anne was really frightened. 'All the
same, it's a puzzle. We can't get *out* – and no one can get
in! Whoever locked that door has certainly taken the key
away with him.'

They talked and they talked, and finally they felt hungry, so they had a meal – though they felt that they ought to eat sparingly, in case their food ran short too quickly.

'And I feel so hungry,' complained George. 'I *keep* feeling hungry here.'

'That's what I told you. Living in a lighthouse somehow makes you feel hungry all the time!' said Tinker.

'We'll try and catch the milkman tomorrow morning,' said Julian, suddenly. 'Let's see, now – we could write a note, and push it under the door, so that he would see it tomorrow when he comes. We could put HELP – WE ARE LOCKED IN.'

'It would blow away,' said George. 'You know it would.'

'We could pin it down our side – and then it wouldn't,' said Anne. 'Half of it would still stick out under the door.'

'Well, it's worth trying,' said Dick, and immediately wrote out the note on a large sheet of paper. He shot downstairs to pin it to the mat – and shoved half the paper underneath so that it stuck out on the other side of the door.

He ran back upstairs. 'I don't for a moment think that the milkman will come across the rocks in this weather,' he said. 'They'll be almost impassable. Still we'll hope for the best.'

There didn't seem anything else to do. The evening came early, for the sky was dark again, and the wind once more got up, and howled dismally. Even the gulls decided that it was no longer a good idea to glide to and fro.

They played games that evening, and tried to laugh and make jokes. But secretly everyone was worried. Suppose that the stormy weather went on and on, and nobody guessed they were locked in the lighthouse, and the milkman didn't bring any milk, and didn't see the note – and they ate all their food and . . .

'Cheer up, everyone,' said Julian, seeing the dismal looks around the table. 'We've been in worse fixes than this.'

'Well, *I* don't think we have!' said Anne. 'I just can't see ANY way out of this one!'

There was rather a long silence during which Timmy sighed heavily, as if he too was worrying! Only the monkey seemed cheerful, and went head-over-heels at top speed round the room, sitting up for laughs at the end. But nobody laughed. Nobody even seemed to notice him. Mischief felt very sad, and crept over to Timmy for comfort.

'There is one idea that *might* be a good one,' said Julian, at last. 'It's been running round in my head for a while – and I'm not sure whether it's possible or not. Anyway, it's one we might try tomorrow, if help doesn't come.'

'What?' asked everyone at once, and Timmy lifted his head and whined, as if he too quite understood.

'Well, do you remember that I went down that foundation shaft?' said Julian, 'and saw the water swirling at the bottom? Now – do you suppose it's at all possible that that shaft was bored down through a *natural* hole – and the lighthouse builders chose to put the foundation shaft there because there was a ready-made shaft they could use? – a fine hole going right down through the rock! And they made the hole into a cement-lined shaft, strong and everlasting, so that the lighthouse would never be at the mercy of the waves and wind – but would stand firm, whatever happened?'

This was a new idea to everyone, and it took a little while to sink in. Then Dick smacked the table top and made them all jump.

'Julian! You've got it! Yes – that strong cement-lined shaft runs down a *natural* hole – and that hole must be the one we've been looking for! The one that connects up with the tunnels we were in yesterday! No wonder we couldn't find it when we hunted all over the rocks! The shaft-makers used it!'

There was silence again. Everyone was taking this in, even Tinker. Julian looked round the table and smiled. 'Have you all jumped to it?' he said. 'If that *is* the hole we were looking for – what about one of us going down that iron ladder again to the bottom – and finding out if it *does* lead into the tunnel we were in yesterday?'

'And walking through it, and up the passage and coming out through the cliff entrance we used yesterday!' said George. 'Julian! What an absolutely wonderful idea! We could escape that way! What a shock for Ebby and Jacob! We'll do it somehow – we'll DO it!'

CHAPTER TWENTY

Down the shaft and into the tunnel

IT WAS a most exciting idea to think that the iron ladder in the great cement-lined shaft might possibly lead to the tunnel they had been into yesterday. Julian had seen water swirling at the bottom, when the tide was in – possibly if they went down it when the tide was going out, there would be no danger of being trapped!

The storm was very fitful now – sometimes it came back again, and then the wind blew so hard that it seemed as if the buffeted lighthouse must fall! Rain fell in torrents that night, and during the dark early hours of the morning, when the tide was in, great waves pounded over the rocks, sending spray almost over the top of the lighthouse. Julian awoke and looked out of the bedroom window in awe.

'I hope there's no ship out anywhere near here to-night,' he said, and then gave a sudden exclamation. 'What's that – something swept right across the sky!'

'It's the beam from the new lighthouse at High Cliffs, said Dick. 'I saw it last night. It must have a very powerful beam, mustn't it, to show even on a night like this?'

They watched for a little while, and then Julian yawned.

'Let's try to go to sleep,' he said. 'We thought we were going away for a nice little holiday – and BANG – we're in the middle of something again!'

'Well, let's hope that we come out of it all right,' said Dick, settling down in his rugs once more. 'I must say that I feel a bit cut off from civilisation at the moment. 'Night, Julian.'

In the morning the storm was still about, and the wind was terrific. Julian ran down to the entrance door to see if the milkman could possibly have come – and had seen their message for help.

But no – the paper was still half on their side, flapping on the mat. Obviously the milkman hadn't dared to cross the rocks that morning, either on foot or by boat!

Dick had looked out of the window to make sure that their boat was still safely moored to the post – and to his surprise and distress, it was no longer there! Tinker was very upset.

'Where's my little boat gone? Has somebody stolen it?'

'Maybe – or possibly the storm broke the mooring rope, and the boat was smashed to pieces on the rocks,' said Julian. 'Anyway, it's gone. Poor old Tinker. What a shame!'

Tinker was very sad, and Mischief tried to comfort him, doing all sorts of silly tricks to make him laugh. But Tinker wouldn't laugh. He really was right down in the dumps.

They had rather a sparse breakfast, and were very silent. Anne cleared away and washed up, and then Julian called them all together.

'Well, now we must decide about this descent down the shaft to what we hope will be the tunnel we were in,' he said. 'I am going down myself.'

'Toss for it!' said Dick, at once. 'There's no reason why *I* shouldn't go, is there? Or what about us both going, in case one gets into trouble, and needs help?'

'Not a bad idea,' said Julian. 'Except that there won't be anyone to look after the girls and Tinker.'

'WOOF!' said Timmy, indignantly, standing up at once. Julian laughed and patted him.

'It's all right, Timmy. I just wanted to see if you thought *you* could guard them well. All right – Dick and I will go down the shaft. The sooner the better. We simply must go while the tide is out. What about now, Dick?'

Solemnly they all went down the spiral stairway to the entrance door, where the trap was that opened on to the great shaft. Julian pulled up the lid and gazed down into blackness. He shone his torch down, but he could not see the bottom. 'Well – here goes,' he said, and lowered himself down into the shaft, his feet seeking the rungs of the iron ladder. 'Keep cheerful, girls. We'll get through the tunnels and passages, and to the entrance in the cliff – and fetch help for you in no time at all!'

'Julian, please take care,' said Anne, in a shaky voice. 'Please, please do take care!'

Down went Julian, his torch now held between his teeth. After him went Dick. The girls shone their own torches down the shaft, but soon the boys were so far down that they could not be seen. Only their voices came up now and again, sounding very hollow and peculiar.

'We're at the bottom!' shouted Julian, at last. 'It's rock, and there's no water at present! We've a clear way to follow! I crawled out of the hole at the bottom, and there's some kind of tunnel there all right. We're off now – crawling out, and into the tunnel. Cheer up, all of you! See you soon!' And then the peculiar hollow voice stopped, and the girls and Tinker heard nothing more.

Timmy began to whine. He couldn't understand these strange goings-on at all!

Julian and Dick were feeling pleased with themselves. It hadn't been very difficult to squeeze out of the arches at the bottom of the shaft. Now they were in a dark narrow tunnel, whose roof sometimes came down so low that they had to bend double. It smelt damp and sea-weedy, but there seemed to be plenty of air. In fact at times quite a little breeze seemed to flow round them.

'I shall be glad when we come into a tunnel we recognise!' said Julian, at last. 'We surely must be near where we were yesterday. Hallo, what's this? Dick – look, Dick!'

Dick looked to where Julian's torch was shining and gave a shout. 'A gold coin – another one! We must be near where old Mischief ran off to. Look – there's another – and another. Where on earth did they come from?'

The boys shone their torches all around, and saw at last where the coins had fallen from. Above their heads was a dark hole, running up into the rock. As they shone their torches on it, a gold coin slid out and dropped down to join the others.

'*This* is where Mischief found the coin!' cried Dick. 'Julian there must be a box or something up there which is rotting away, and letting out the money it contains bit by bit.'

'Whoever would have guessed at such a hiding place!' said Julian, marvelling as he shone his torch above his head. 'There's absolutely nothing to be seen except that dark hole – no box, nothing. It must have been pushed right into a recess at the side of the hole, by someone who knew a good hiding place was there.'

'Give me a leg-up so that I can put in my hand and feel,' said Dick. 'Buck up – this is too exciting for words!'

Julian gave him a leg-up, and Dick put his head and shoulders into the hole. He felt to one side – nothing – felt to the other side, and his hand came across something hard and cold – an iron band perhaps? He ran his hand over it and touched something soft and crumbly – old, old wood rotting away, maybe – possibly a wooden chest – only held together by the iron bands. He scrabbled about and Julian gave a sudden shout.

'Hey – you've showered me with money! Whew – I never saw so many gold coins in my life!'

'Julian – I think there's more than one box or chest up there,' said Dick, jumping down, and looking at the big heap of shining coins at his feet. 'There may be a fortune there! Talk about treasure trove! Look – let's not disturb anything else up that hole. No one knows about it except ourselves. Better gather up these coins though, just in *case* that awful Ebby takes it into his head to come down this way!'

So they filled their pockets with the coins and then made their way onwards again. To their joy they soon recognised one of the tunnels they had been in before. 'Plain sailing now,' said Dick joyfully. 'We'll soon be out, and then we'll get the locksmith to pick the lock of the lighthouse, so that we can get in.'

'Sh!' said Julian, suddenly. 'I think I can hear something.' They listened, but went on again, thinking that Julian was mistaken.

But he wasn't! As they turned a dark corner that led into a cave, someone leapt at them! Julian went down to the ground at once, and Dick followed. He just had time to see that Ebenezer was there with someone else – Jacob perhaps?

As Dick fell, gold coins spilled out of his pocket. Ebenezer gave a cry and bent down to them at once. Julian tried to take his chance and slip by him – but the other man caught him and sent him spinning backwards. 'Where did you find that money? You tell us or you'll be sorry!' shouted Ebenezer, and the echo came back at once, 'Sorry – sorry – sorry!'

'Run, Dick!' panted Julian. 'It's our only chance!' He gave Ebenezer a terrific shove, which sent him into the other man – yes, it *was* Jacob, who must somehow have escaped from police custody – and then he and Dick were off at once, running as fast as they could, back along the way they had come. 'You come here!' yelled Ebenezer, and they heard him pounding after them.

'Hurry!' panted Dick. 'If only we can get to the shaft, we're all right.'

But alas, they took the wrong turning, and soon found themselves in a cave they had never seen before. Ebenezer and Jacob blundered past without seeing them. 'Better stay here a while,' said Julian. 'Let them get a good way off.'

So they stayed still and quiet, and then at last ventured out of their hiding place and tried to find their way back to the right path.

'You know – if we get lost down here, we're done for!' said Julian. 'And once the tide flows in, we shall be in a pretty poor way! Somehow we've got to get out through the cliff way or back to the shaft. Hang on to me, Dick. We mustn't get separated, whatever happens!'

They stumbled on, not really knowing whether they were going in the right direction or not. They seemed to go through endless tunnels and caves – what a labyrinth there was in that great stratum of rocks! Then they heard voices!

'That's Ebby's voice – and Jacob's too,' whispered Julian. 'They're coming this way. Hide here, and keep still!'

So they hid quietly, and listened to Ebby and Jacob. 'Those boys have *got* to come back here,' said Ebby. 'We'll wait. Don't make a sound!'

'We'll have to make a dash for it, and hope for the best!' whispered Julian. 'Come on! We'll be caught by the tide soon if we're not quick!'

They both made a sudden rush, and passed the surprised Ebby and Jacob at a run. Then down the tunnel beyond them they went as fast they could, bumping their arms and legs and heads against the rocky walls, but holding their torches steadily in front of them. On they went and on – and behind them, breathing heavily, came Ebby and Jacob.

'I think this must be a bad dream!' panted Dick. 'JULIAN! JULIAN! look – there's water coming along this tunnel! The tide's coming in!'

'Come *on*,' said Julian. 'I feel as if the shaft isn't far away now. I seem to know this tunnel – and this cave. Come *on*, Dick, we haven't a minute to spare! We've GOT to get to the ladder!'

'Look! There's the shaft!' yelled Dick at last. 'Come on – we shall just about be able to squeeze under the arch at the bottom! Hurry, Julian – the water's up to our ankles now!'

They reached the shaft and squeezed under the small archway that let the water run through from side to side over the rocky bottom of the shaft. They began to mount the ladder, and then stopped to hear if there were any sounds from Ebby or Jacob.

They heard yells. 'EBBY! COME BACK! Tide's flowing in!' and then they heard Ebby's angry voice.

'I'm coming! They've gone farther down – and they won't like it! They'll be drowned before they get much farther!'

Dick grinned. 'Come on, Ju, – up we go! I can see the light through the trap-door at the top. The girls have left it open, bless them.'

And soon the two boys were clambering out of the trap-door, with Timmy barking madly and licking their necks, the girls and Tinker too excited for words!

'What happened? Didn't you get out of the tunnel to find help for us? Were those men there? What *happened*?'

'Plenty!' said Julian. 'But unfortunately we didn't get past Ebby and Jacob, who were lying in wait for us. So we're *still* stuck in this lighthouse, with nobody to help us. BUT . . .'

'But what?' asked George, shaking his arm. 'Julian, you look excited. What's happened?'

'We found the treasure!' said Julian. 'Come on – we'll tell you all about it!' And he led the way up the spiral stairway, with Tinker and the excited girls close behind.

Soon the boys were telling their story, and George and Anne and Tinker listened and exclaimed and danced about, and were altogether marvellous listeners to a marvellous tale.

'It MUST have been the treasure – in an iron-bound chest – oh, Ju, weren't you excited when the coins poured out?'

'Yes. It was certainly a very fine moment,' said Julian. 'Mischief, stop pulling my hair. Wow! It's been an exciting morning! What about a drink of lemonade – and by the way, what's the weather been like? We couldn't see a thing down below!'

'Oh, it's *awful* again, Julian!' said Anne. 'There's another storm coming – look at those scurrying black clouds.'

'It does look bad,' said Julian, his excitement leaving him, as he saw clearly that another big storm was blowing up. 'We certainly shouldn't be able to get out of here today, even if we could get out of the door!'

'Julian, Tinker found his father's old pocket radio in a cupboard,' said Anne. 'And it still works. We listened to the weather report, and it gave an important warning to all ships at sea or by the coast. It said they must run to safety as soon as they could.'

'Well, I'm blessed if I know what to do for the best,' said Julian, looking out of the window. 'How in the world are we to let people know we're here, marooned in the lighthouse? We'll simply *have* to think of something!'

But that was easier said than done! How did one get help when there was no way to get help? How did one escape out of a locked lighthouse when there was no key?

CHAPTER TWENTY-ONE

A wonderful idea

'I'M THIRSTY,' said Tinker. 'I'll get some lemonade.'

'Well, go slow with it, then,' said Dick. 'You don't know how long we may be locked up here – and we haven't endless food and drink!'

Tinker looked alarmed. 'Might we be locked up here for weeks and weeks?' he said.

'If people thought we had left the lighthouse and gone back home because of the bad weather, we might easily be here for some time,' said Julian, soberly. 'Nobody would bother about us – they'd think we were safe at home.'

'But Mother would soon feel worried if she didn't hear from us,' said George. 'We said we'd send her a card each day, you know – and if she doesn't have one for a day or two, she would be sure to get worried, and send someone over here.'

'Hurrah for mothers!' said Dick, relieved. 'All the same – I don't fancy a week or so here with hardly anything to eat. We'll have plenty of one thing though – and that's rainwater!'

'There must be *some* way out of this,' said Julian who had been sitting silent, frowning at his thoughts. 'Can't we get a message out *somehow*? Are there any flags here, Tinker, that we could wave out of the window?'

'No,' said Tinker. 'I've never seen any. What about a white tablecloth? We've one of those.'

'Yes. That would do,' said Julian. 'Fetch it, Tinker.'

Tinker pulled it off the table and gave it to Julian. Julian went to the window and looked through the glass, which was misted with spray. 'I don't expect anyone will notice a tablecloth being shaken out of this window,' he said. 'But I'll try it. My word – the window's hard to open. It seems to have stuck.'

He opened it at last, and immediately an enormous gust of wind came in, and everything went flying – papers, books, carpets – chairs fell over, and poor Mischief was blown from one side of the lighthouse room to the other. Timmy barked in fright and tried to catch the flying papers as they went by his nose. The tablecloth disappeared at once!

Julian managed to close the window again after a terrific effort, and once more the room became peaceful. 'Whew!' said Julian. 'I didn't guess there was such a gale outside. I should think that tablecloth is about five miles away by now! The gulls will get a surprise when it comes flapping along in the sky.'

George couldn't help laughing at that, frightened though she was. 'Oh, Julian – it was a jolly good thing you didn't fly off with the tablecloth! My WORD, what a gale! I wonder the lighthouse stands it.'

'Well, we do feel a buffet now and again,' said Dick. 'There – did you feel that? It was either a wave bumping into the rocks or spray forced against us – I distinctly felt the lighthouse shake a little.'

'Rubbish!' said Julian, seeing Anne's scared face. 'Don't make silly jokes like that.'

'You're quite *sure* that the lighthouse can't be blown down?' said Anne, in a small voice.

'Dear Anne, use your commonsense,' said Julian. 'Would it have stood for all these years if it hadn't been strong enough to stand against storms far worse than this?'

'Mischief is feeling frightened too,' said Tinker. 'He's gone and hidden, look.'

'Well, long may he stay there,' said Julian. 'At least, he's not trying to open the biscuit tin, or delve into the bag of sweets! I should just like to know how many of our sweets he has eaten up to now!'

WHOOOOOOOOOSH!

That was an extra big gale of wind that buffeted the lighthouse, and made Timmy stand up and growl. Rain pattered against the window, sounding as if someone was throwing pebbles.

Julian was very worried. It really did look as if the stormy weather was going on and on. It might quite well continue for a few days, and their food certainly would not last long. There were still some tins left, and they had plenty of water, of course – the rain saw to that – but somehow they were all always so *hungry*!

'Cheer up, Julian,' said George. 'You do look grim.'

'I feel it,' said Julian. 'I cannot for the life of me think of any way to escape from here, or even to get help. We've no way of signalling . . .'

'Pity the lighthouse lamp is no longer going,' said Tinker. 'That would have been a fine signal.'

To Tinker's enormous surprise Julian suddenly gave a shout, leapt up, came over to Tinker, and gave him such a clap on the back that the surprised boy almost fell off his chair!

'W-w-what's the matter?' stammered Tinker, rubbing his shoulder.

'Don't you *see* – perhaps we can set the old lamp going, and make it shine out as it used to do – not to warn ships, of course – but to make people realise that we are prisoners in the lighthouse!' said Julian, jubilantly. 'Tinker – do you know if it's *possible* to light the lamp?'

'I think so,' said Tinker. 'My father showed me how it

worked, and I think I remember. Oh – and there's a bell that can be struck, too!'

'Better and better!' said Julian. 'Where is the bell?'

'It was dismantled and put away,' said Tinker. 'It used to hang in that sort of verandah place that runs outside, round the lamp-room – there's a big hook for it there.'

'Oh – it hung in that outside gallery, did it?' said Julian. 'Well – that means that one of us would have to go out there in the wind and hang it up – not too good! There must be a ninety-mile-an-hour gale up there. Anyway, let's get the bell and have a look at it.'

The great bell was down in the storeroom, covered up. It was made of brass, and once had had a hammer that struck it at intervals, worked by some simple machinery. But the machinery was in pieces – no good at all!

'We'll take the bell upstairs,' said Julian. 'Gosh, it's heavy as lead. Dick, I'll want your help.'

Between them the two boys carried the heavy bell up to the living room, and Tinker brought up the old hammer that used to strike it. Julian and Dick held up the bell by its loop of iron. 'Hit it with the hammer, Tinker,' said Julian. 'See if it still sounds loudly.'

Tinker struck it hard with the hammer – and at once a great deep clang filled the room from side to side, making Timmy jump almost out of his skin. He and Mischief left the room at top speed and fell down the spiral stairway together. All the others jumped too, and stared at one another in awe. The sound of the bell went booming round and round the room, filling their ears so that they had to shake their heads to try and get rid of the sound. Julian at last clasped the rim of the bell with both his hands and the sound died away.

'What a WONDERFUL bell!' he said, in awe. 'Look how old it is, too – see, it says, "Cast in 1896"! If only we could get it hung up in its place on the gallery, the sound of it would go right to the village and beyond! I wonder how many ships heard it in the old days, booming out every now and again as the hammer struck it.'

Tinker raised the hammer again, but Dick stopped him. 'No – you saw how scared Timmy and Mischief were. They'll probably jump through a window, glass and all, if we sound the bell again!'

'We'll wait till we think the wind has died down a bit, and then try to hang the bell,' said Julian. 'Now let's look at the lamp. Will it want oil, Tinker?'

'It may do – though I think there's some still in it, left when the lighthouse was closed down,' said Tinker. 'But there is plenty down in the storeroom.'

'Good,' said Julian, feeling decidedly more cheerful.

'Now – if the gale dies down at all, we'll try to hang the bell. We can strike that as soon as it's hung, and not wait till we light the lamp.'

But the gale seemed to get worse, and Julian really did wonder if the old lighthouse would stand up to it! Should he take everyone down to the storeroom? Just in case? I will if the gale gets worse, he thought. 'Though if the lighthouse should fall, there wouldn't be much chance for us, whatever part of it we're in!'

They went up to the lamp-room in the afternoon and looked at the great old lamp. Tinker explained how it worked. 'It used to go round and round mechanically,' he said, 'and there were screens here – and here – that shut out the light in places as it went round – so that the light seemed to go on and off, if any ship was watching it – it seemed to *flash*, you see, instead of to shine steadily. Ships noticed it more quickly then.'

The screens were broken in pieces. There was still some oil in the lamp, but Julian added more. The wick seemed perfectly good. Now, if only they could light the lamp, and keep it going, someone would be sure to see it, and wonder about it!

Julian felt in his pocket for matches. As the lamp-room was enclosed in glass, it was easy to keep the match alight. He touched the oily wick with it – and, hey-presto, the lamp was lit!

It was a very big lamp, and, close to, the light was quite blinding. Dick crowed with delight. 'We've done it! Old lighthouse, you're going to shine once more tonight! You're alive again!'

'Now to hang the bell,' said Julian, and he cautiously opened the door leading on to the gallery outside, having waited until the wind died down for a moment. He and Dick lifted the bell up to the hook there and slipped the iron loop over it. It hung there, swinging, and Julian lifted the hammer – but at that moment a great gust took him and he staggered, almost falling over the railing!

Dick caught him just in time, and, with George's help, dragged him into the lamp-room. They were all very white-faced! 'That was a narrow escape,' said George, her hands shaking and her body trembling. 'We'll have to be careful if we go out on the gallery again! Perhaps we had better rely only on the lamp.'

'I vote we all go down and have some hot tea,' said Julian, thankful for his escape. His legs felt shaky as he went down the stairs. He was not surprised! Julian was seldom scared, and it was peculiar to have legs that suddenly gave at the knees!

However, everyone soon recovered when they were drinking hot tea and eating ginger biscuits. 'I wish it was dark so that we could see how bright the light is from the lamp when it shines,' said Dick. 'It will be dark very quickly today.'

It was! So dark that the light streaming from the old lamp at the top of the lighthouse was brilliant! It cut a shining path through the night, gleaming yellow.

And through the roar of the sea went a great clanging, as Julian, with Dick holding on to him, struck the old bell hanging in the gallery.

'Listen!' said George, her hand on Timmy's collar. 'Listen! BOOM! BOO-OOO-OOM! BOOOOM! Tim, that bell must feel happy tonight – it's found its voice again!'

BOOOOOOOOOM! Has anyone heard that old bell on this stormy night? Has anyone seen the light from the old, old lamp?

BOOOOOOOOOM!!!

CHAPTER TWENTY-TWO

The end of the adventure

DOWN IN the village of Demon's Rocks that night, people drew their curtains, made up their fires, and sat down in their armchairs. They were thankful not to be out in the wind and the rain.

Old Jeremiah Boogle was lighting his pipe, sitting by his own roaring fire, when he heard a sound that made him drop the flaring match, and listen in amazement.

BOOOOOOM! BOOOOOOM!

'A bell! A bell I've not heard for nearly forty years!' said old Jeremiah, standing up, hardly able to believe his ears. 'No – it *can't* be the lighthouse bell. That's been gone for many a day!'

BOOOOOOM!

Jeremiah went to his window and pulled aside the old curtain. He stared out – and could not believe his eyes! He gave a yell. 'MILLIE! Where's that grand-daughter of mine? MILLIE!'

'What is it, Grandad, now?' said a plump little woman, bustling in.

'Look, Millie – am I seeing right – isn't that the lighthouse lamp shining there?' said Jeremiah.

'Well – there's a bright light shining out there high above Demon's Rocks,' said Millie. 'But I never in *my* life saw the lighthouse lamp shining out before! And what's that booming noise, Grandfather – like a wonderful great bell?'

334

'That's the old bell in the lighthouse!' said Jeremiah. 'I couldn't mistake that! Many's the time I heard it booming out to warn ships off Demon's Rocks in the old days. Millie, it can't be! It doesn't hang there any more. And the light doesn't shine any more. What's happening?'

'I don't know, Grandad,' said Millie, scared. 'There isn't anyone in the lighthouse, far as *I* know!'

Old Jeremiah smacked his hand down on the window-sill, knocking over a plant pot. '*There are* folk there – three boys and two girls, and a monkey too – and a dog as well!'

'Well, there now!' said Millie. 'And what would they be there for? Did *they* set the lamp going and sound that bell? booom – there it goes again – enough to wake all the babies in Demon's Rocks village!'

Millie was right. It did wake all the babies, and the children – and amazed every man and woman in the place, including Ebenezer and Jacob. They had leapt to their feet when they had heard the bell, and were astounded to see the great light shining out steadily in the night.

They heard people hurrying by their cottage, on their way to Demon's Rocks jetty. They heard Jeremiah's big voice booming out too. 'It's those children up there in the lighthouse, banging that bell, and setting that light shining. Something's wrong! It's help they're needing, folks! Something's wrong!'

Ebenezer and Jacob knew quite well what was wrong! The children were locked in the lighthouse and couldn't get out! They might be ill or hurt – or starving – but they couldn't get out to fetch help. And now the whole village was aroused, and when the morning came, a boat would bob out on the great waves and find out what had happened!

Ebby and Jacob disappeared that night! It wasn't Constable Sharp they feared – it was the people of the village! They slipped away in the dark and the rain, and were gone. But you'll be caught, Ebby, you'll be caught, Jacob! And no one will be sorry for you. No one at all!

When daylight came, there were many people on the jetty, ready to go across to the lighthouse. The wind was so rough that great waves still rolled over the rocks on which the lighthouse stood. Soon a boat was launched, and Jeremiah, Constable Sharp and the village doctor went across, the boat careering from side to side like a mad thing, as the waves caught it.

They went up the steps to the lighthouse and banged at the door – and from the other side came Julian's glad voice, 'You'll have to break down the door. Ebby and Jacob locked us in and took the key. We can't get out, and we're running short of food!'

'Right. Stand back,' shouted Jeremiah. 'Constable and I are going to break in!'

Jeremiah was old but he was still hefty, and Constable Sharp was heftier still. The lock suddenly splintered under their enormous shoves, and the door flew wide open! Jeremiah and the policeman shot inside and bumped into Julian and the rest, sending them flying. Timmy barked in astonishment and Mischief fled up the stairway!

Soon they were all in the living room, and Julian was pouring out his story. Anne made tea and handed round steaming cups. Jeremiah listened open-mouthed, and the policeman busily took notes. The doctor, glad that no one was ill or hurt, sipped his tea and listened, too.

'We didn't know *how* to get out when we were locked in,' said Julian, coming to the end of his long story. 'So in the end we lit the old lamp, and hung up the old bell, and struck it with the hammer. I could hardly stand in the gallery, though, there was such a wind! I struck it for half an hour, and then my brother here went on till he felt too

337

cold. The lamp didn't burn all night – it went out early this morning.'

'But both bell and light did their job well, son,' said Jeremiah, looking twenty years younger, he was so excited. 'Ah, to think that old lamp shone again, and that old bell sounded – I thought I must be dreaming!'

'We'll be after that Ebenezer and Jacob,' said the policeman, shutting his notebook. 'And it seems to me you'd all better go home. This weather's going on for a bit – and there's nothing to keep you here, is there?'

'Well,' said Julian, 'actually there *is* something to keep us here. You know the old wreckers' lost treasure you told us about, Jeremiah? Well – we've found it!'

Jeremiah was so astounded that he couldn't say a word! He goggled at Julian, and opened and shut his mouth like a fish. Julian took some golden coins out of his pocket and showed them to the policeman and the doctor, and to Jeremiah.

'There you are!' he said. 'We know where there are thousands of these – they are in iron-bound boxes and chests down in one of the tunnels in the rock. What do you think of that? We can't leave here till we've given the treasure into the hands of the police! It belongs to the Crown, doesn't it?'

'Yes, it does,' said Constable Sharp, gazing at the bright gold coins. 'But you'll get a fine reward – all of you will! Where's this treasure? I'd better get it straight-away.'

'Well – you have to go down the foundation shaft of the lighthouse,' said Julian, gravely, but with a twinkle in his eye, 'and crawl under the archway at the bottom, and then make your way down the tunnel – but be careful the sea doesn't catch you – and then when you come to . . .'

The policeman stopped scribbling down what Julian was saying, and looked startled. Julian laughed.

'It's all right – Dick and I will fetch it ourselves today, and give it to you, complete with every single gold coin,' he said. 'We don't *need* to go down the shaft – there's another way in – the way *you* took us, Jeremiah. We'll go this morning, for a last excitement. And then – home! Perhaps you would kindly telephone Kirrin Garage for a car to fetch us at twelve o'clock, Constable?'

'Oh *good*!' said Anne. 'An adventure is always exciting but I've really had enough at the moment! This was such a bad-weather one! Oh, Constable, look out – that monkey has pulled out your whistle!'

So he had – and what is more he blew it – PHEEEEEEEEEE! Jeremiah almost jumped out of his skin, and Mischief received a slap that almost made *him* jump out of his skin too!

'Goodbye, Jeremiah,' said Julian. 'It's been fine meeting you – and thanks for coming to rescue us. We'll see you again some day. Come along, Constable – we'll go and find the treasure with you now.'

'I don't think I'll come,' said Anne, who really didn't like dark, smelly tunnels and caves. 'I'll do the packing.'

'Timmy and I will help you,' said George, who knew that Anne wouldn't like to be left alone in the lighthouse.

The boys went off with Jeremiah, the doctor and Constable Sharp, rowing over the rocks to the jetty. The doctor and Jeremiah said goodbye at the jetty, and the three boys and Mischief took Constable Sharp to find the treasure. They had to push their way through quite a crowd of people who had collected on the quay, anxious to know why the light had shone out from the lighthouse in the night, and why the bell had sounded.

'Make way, please,' said the policeman, politely. 'Everything is all right. These children were locked in the lighthouse and couldn't get out. Make way, please. There is no need for any excitement!'

'No – that's all over now – isn't it, Ju?' said Dick. 'Whew – it was just a bit *too* exciting at times! I shall be quite glad to be at Kirrin Cottage again, with peace and quiet all around us.'

'You've forgotten that Uncle Quentin and his friend will still be there,' said Julian, with a grin. 'There'll be plenty going on while they're around! I'm afraid they won't be at all pleased to see us back!'

Oh yes, they will, Julian – especially when they hear the exciting story you have to tell! You'll have some fun showing round a gold coin or two. Timmy is to have one hung on his collar, as a reward for guarding you so well – how proud he will be!

Well, goodbye to you all! Goodbye, Julian and Dick, and a good journey home! Goodbye, Anne and George – and Tinker too, and Mischief, you funny little monkey!

And goodbye, dear old Timmy, best of friends. How we wish we had a dog like you! See you all again some day!

FIVE HAVE A MYSTERY TO SOLVE

CONTENTS

Special note from Enid Blyton

My readers will want to know if Whispering Island is
real, set in the great blue harbour in the story – and if the
little cottage on the hills is there still – and the golf course
in the story – and Lucas, who tells the children about the
island. Yes, the island is real, and lies in the great
harbour, still full of whispering trees. The little cottage
on the hills is still there, with its magnificent view and its
old well – and Lucas can be found on the golf course,
nut-brown and bright-eyed, telling stories of the animals
and birds he loves so much. I have taken them all and put
them into this book for you – as well as the friends you
know so well – The Famous Five.

CHAPTER ONE

Easter holidays

'THE NICEST word in the English language is holidays!' said Dick, helping himself to a large spoonful of marmalade. 'Pass the toast, Anne. Mother, do you feel downhearted to have us all tearing about the place again?'

'Of course not,' said his mother. 'The only thing that *really* worries me when holidays come, is Food – Food with a capital F. We never seem to have enough in the house when all three of you are back. And by the way – does anyone know what has happened to the sausages that were in the larder?'

'Sausages – sausages – let me think!' said Julian, frowning. Anne gave a sudden giggle. She knew quite well what had happened.

'Well, Mother – you said we could get our own meal last night, as you were out,' said Julian. 'So we poked about and decided on sausages.'

'Yes, but Julian – two *whole* packets of sausages!' said his mother. 'I know Georgina came over to spend the evening – but even so . . .!'

'She brought *Timmy*,' said Anne. '*He* rather likes sausages too, Mother.'

'Well, that's the last time I leave the larder door unlocked, when I go out!' said her mother. 'Fancy cooking those lovely pork sausages for a *dog* – especially Timmy, with his enormous appetite! Really, Anne! I meant to have them for our lunch today.'

347

'Well – we rather thought we'd go and spend the day at Kirrin, with George and Timmy,' said Dick. 'That's if you don't want us for anything, Mother.'

'I *do* want you,' said his mother. 'Mrs Layman is coming to tea, and she said she wants to see you about something.'

The three groaned, and Dick protested at once. 'Oh *Mother* – the first day of the holidays – and we have to be in for tea! It's too bad – a glorious spring day like this, too!'

'Oh – we'll be in for tea all right,' said Julian, giving Dick a sharp little kick under the table, as he saw his mother's disappointed face. 'Mrs Layman's a nice old thing – she's been so kind since we moved near to Kirrin.'

'And she gave me a present last birthday,' said Anne. 'Do you think we could ask George over too – with Timmy? George will be awfully disappointed if we aren't with her the first day of the hols.'

'Yes, of course you can,' said her mother. 'Go and ring her up now, and arrange it. And don't forget to put our old Tibby-cat in the shed, with a saucer of milk. She's scared stiff of Timmy – he's so enormous. And please, all of you, TRY to look clean at teatime.'

'*I'll* see to Dick and Anne,' said Julian, with a grin. 'I must remember to find their overalls!'

'I'm going to phone George now, this very minute,' said Anne, getting up from the table. 'Do you mind, Mother? I've finished – and I'd like to catch George before she takes Tim for a walk, or does some shopping for Aunt Fanny.'

'Uncle Quentin will be glad to be rid of George, even for a meal,' said Dick. 'He fell over her lacrosse stick yesterday, and wanted to know why she left her *fishing* net about! George didn't know what he was talking about!'

'Poor old Georgina,' said his mother. 'It's a pity that both she and her father have exactly the same hot tempers. Her mother must find it difficult to keep the peace! Ah – here's Anne back again. Did you get George on the phone, dear?'

'Yes. She's thrilled,' said Anne. 'She says it's just as well we're not going to spend the day with her, because Uncle Quentin has lost some papers he was working on, and he's turning the house upside-down. George said she will probably be mad as a hatter by the time she arrives this afternoon! Uncle Quentin even made Aunt Fanny turn out her knitting bag to see if the papers were there!'

'Dear old Quentin,' said her mother. 'Such a truly brilliant scientist – remembers every book he's ever read – every paper he's ever written – and has the finest brain I know – and yet loses some valuable paper or other almost every week!'

'He loses something else every day of the week too,' said Dick, with a grin. 'His temper! Poor old George – she's always in some sort of trouble!'

'Well, anyway, she's jolly glad to be coming over here!' said Anne. 'She's biking over, with Timmy. She'll be here for lunch. Is that all right, Mother?'

'Of course!' said her mother. 'Now – seeing that you had today's dinner for last night's supper, you'd better do a little shopping for me. What shall we have?'

'SAUSAGES!' said everyone, at once.

'I should have thought you were quite literally *fed up* with sausages, after last night's feast,' said their mother, laughing. 'All right – sausages. But Timmy can have a bone – a nice meaty bone. I am NOT going to buy any more sausages for him, that's quite certain.'

'And shall we get some nice cakes for tea as Mrs Layman is coming?' said Anne. 'Or are you going to make some, Mother?'

'I'll make a few buns,' said her mother. 'And you can choose whatever else you like – so long as you don't buy up the shop!'

The three went off shopping, cycling along the lane to the village. It was truly a lovely spring day. The celandines were golden in the ditches, and daisies were scattered everywhere. Dick burst into song as they went, and the cows in the nearby fields lifted their heads in surprise as Dick's loud voice swept round them.

Anne laughed. It was good to be with her brothers again. She missed them very much when she was at school. And now they would have almost a whole month together with their cousin George too. She was suddenly overwhelmed with joy, and lifted up her voice and joined Dick in his singing. Her brothers looked at her with affection and amusement.

'Good old Anne,' said Dick. 'You're such a quiet little mouse, it's nice to hear you singing so loudly.'

'I am NOT a quiet little mouse!' said Anne, surprised and rather hurt. 'Whatever makes you say that? You just wait – you may get a surprise one day!'

'Yes – we may!' said Julian. 'But I doubt it. A mouse can't suddenly turn into a tiger! Anyway, one tiger's enough. *George* is the tiger of our family – my word, she can put out her claws all right – and roar – and rant and rave!'

Everyone laughed at the picture of George as a tiger. Dick wobbled as he laughed and his front wheel touched Anne's back wheel. She turned round fiercely.

'LOOK OUT, IDIOT! You nearly had me over! Can't you see where you're going? Be sensible, can't you?'

'Hey, Anne – whatever's the matter?' said Julian, amazed to hear his gentle little sister lashing out so suddenly.

Anne laughed. 'It's all right. I was just being a tiger for a moment – putting out my claws! I thought Dick and you might like to see them!'

'Well, well!' said Dick, riding beside her, 'I've never heard you yell like that before. Surprising – but quite pleasing! What about you showing old George your claws sometime when she gets out of hand?'

351

'Stop teasing,' said Anne. 'Here's the butcher's. For goodness' sake go and get the sausages, and be sensible. I'll go and buy the cakes.'

The baker's shop was full of new-made buns and cakes, and smelt deliciously of home-made bread. Anne enjoyed herself choosing a vast selection. After all, she thought, there will be eight of us – counting Timmy – and if we're all hungry, cakes soon disappear.

The boys were very pleased to see all the paper bags.

'Looks like a good tea today,' said Dick. 'I hope the old lady – what's her name now? – Layman – who's coming to tea today, has a good appetite. I wonder what she's going to tell us about.'

'Did you buy a nice meaty bone for Timmy?' asked Anne. 'He'll like that for his tea.'

'We bought such a beauty that I'm pretty sure Mother will say it's good enough to make soup from,' said Dick, with a grin. 'So I'll keep it in my saddle-bag till he comes. Dear old Tim. He deserves a jolly good bone. Best dog I ever knew!'

'He's been on a lot of adventures with us,' said Anne, bicycling beside the boys, as the road was empty. 'And he seemed to enjoy them all.'

'Yes. So did we!' said Dick. 'Well – who knows? An adventure may be lying in wait for us these hols too! I seem to smell one in the air!'

'You don't!' said Anne. 'You're just making that up. *I'd* like a bit of peace after a hectic term at school. I worked really hard this last term.'

'Well – you were top of your form, and captain of games – so you deserve to have the kind of holiday you like,' said Julian, proud of his young sister. 'And so you shall! Adventures are OUT! Do you hear that, Dick? We keep absolutely clear of them. So that's that!'

'Is it, Ju?' said Anne, laughing. 'Well – we'll see!'

CHAPTER TWO

A visitor to tea

GEORGE AND Timmy were waiting for Julian, Dick and Anne when they arrived home. Timmy was standing in the road, ears pricked, long tail waving. He went quite mad when he saw their bicycles rounding the corner, and galloped towards them at top speed, barking madly, much to the horror of a baker's boy with a large basket.

The boy disappeared into the nearest garden at top speed, yelling 'Mad dog, mad dog!' Timmy tore past, and forced the three to dismount, for they were afraid of knocking him over.

'*Dear* Timmy!' said Anne, patting the excited dog. 'Do put your tongue in – I'm sure it will fall out some day!'

Timmy ran to each of them in turn, woofing in delight, licking everyone, and altogether behaving as if he hadn't seen them for a year!

'Now that's enough, old boy,' said Dick, pushing him away, and trying to mount his bicycle once more. 'After all, we did see you yesterday. Where's George?'

George had heard Timmy barking, and had now run out into the road too. The three cycled up to her, and she grinned happily at them.

'Hallo! You've been shopping, I see. Shut up barking, Timmy, you talk too much. Sorry you couldn't come over to Kirrin Cottage – but I'm jolly glad you asked me to come to *you* – my father still hasn't found the papers he's lost, and honestly, our place is like a madhouse – cupboards being turned out, even the kitchen store-cupboard – and I left poor Mother up in the loft, looking there – though *why* Father should think they might be there, I don't know!'

'Poor old George – I can see your father tearing his hair, and shouting, and all the time he's probably put the papers into the waste-paper basket by mistake!' said Dick, with a chuckle.

'Gracious – we never *thought* of that!' said George. 'I'd better phone Mother at once, and tell her to look. Bright idea of yours, Dick.'

'Well, you go and phone, and we'll put our bikes away,' said Julian. 'Take your nose away from that bag of sausages, Timmy. You're in disgrace over sausages, let me tell you. You're suspected of eating too many last night!'

'He did eat rather a lot,' said George. 'I took my eye off him, and he wolfed quite a few. Hey, who's this

Mrs Layman who's coming to tea? Have we *got* to stay in and have tea with her? I hoped we might be going off for a picnic this afternoon.'

''Fraid not,' said Dick, 'Mrs Layman is apparently coming to talk to *us* about something. So we have to be in – with clean hands, nice manners, and everything. So behave yourself, George!'

George gave him a friendly punch. 'That's unfair,' said Dick. 'You know I can't punch you back. My word, you should have seen Anne this morning, George – yelled at me like a tiger howling, and showed her teeth, and . . .'

'Don't be an idiot, Dick,' said Anne. 'He called me a mouse, George – he said we had *one* tiger – you – and that was enough in the family. So I went for him – put out my claws for a moment, and gave him such a surprise. I rather liked it!'

'Good old Anne!' said George, amused. 'But you're not really cut out to be a tiger, and rage and roar, you know.'

'I could be, if I had to,' said Anne, obstinately. 'One of these days I'll surprise you all. You just wait!'

'All right. We will,' said Julian, putting his arm round his sister. 'Come on, now – we'd better get indoors before Timmy gets some of the cakes out of the bags. Stop licking that bag, Tim – you'll make a hole in it.'

'He can smell the cherry buns inside,' said Anne. 'Shall I give him one?'

'NO!' said Julian. 'Cherry buns are wasted on him, you know that. Don't you remember how he chews the bun apart and spits out the cherries?'

'Woof,' said Timmy, exactly as if he agreed. He went to sniff at the bag with his bone inside.

'That's your dinner, Tim,' said Anne. 'Plenty of meat on it, too. Look, there's Mother at the window, beckoning. I expect she wants the sausages. NO, Timmy – the sausages are NOT for you. Get down! Good gracious, I never in my life knew such a hungry dog. Anybody would think you starved him, George.'

'Well, they'd think wrong, then,' said George. 'Timmy, come to heel.'

Timmy came, still looking round longingly at the various bags that the others were now taking from their saddle-bags.

They all went indoors, and deposited the goods on the kitchen table. Doris, the lady who helped their mother in the holidays, opened the bags and looked inside, keeping a sharp eye on Timmy.

'Better take that dog of yours out of my kitchen,' she said. 'Funny how sausages always disappear when he's around. Get down, now – take your paws off my clean table!'

Timmy trotted out of the kitchen. He thought it was a pity that cooks didn't like him. He liked *them* very much indeed – they always smelt so deliciously of cooking, and there were always so many titbits around which he longed for, but was seldom offered. Ah well – he'd trot into the kitchen again when Doris had gone upstairs for something! He might perhaps find a few bits and pieces on the floor then!

'Hallo, Georgina dear!' said her aunt, coming into the kitchen, Timmy following her in delight. 'Timmy, go out of the kitchen. I don't trust you within a mile of sausages. Go on – shoo!'

Timmy 'shooed'. He liked Anne's mother, but knew

357

that when she said 'Shoo!' she meant it. He lay down on a rug in the living room, with a heavy sigh, wondering how long it would be before he had that lovely meaty bone. He put his head on his paws, and kept his ears pricked for George. He thought it most unfair that George shouldn't be shooed out of the kitchen too.

'Now, for goodness' sake keep out of my way while I cook the lunch,' said Doris to the children milling round her kitchen. 'And shut the door, please. I don't want that great hungry dog sniffing round me all the time, making out he's starving, when he's as fat as butter!'

'He's NOT!' said George, indignantly. 'Timmy has never been fat in his life. He's not that kind of dog. He's *never* greedy!'

'Well, he must be the first dog ever born that wasn't greedy,' said Doris. 'Can't trust any of them! There was that pug-dog of Mrs Lane's – crunched up lumps of sugar whenever it could reach a sugar bowl – and that fat poodle next door – came and knocked over the cream that the milkman left outside the back door – *deliberately* knocked it over, mark you – and then licked up every drop. Ha – his mistress tried to make out he didn't like cream – but you should have seen his nose – covered in cream up to his eyes!'

Timmy looked in at the kitchen door, his nose in the air, for all the world as if he were deeply offended at Doris's remarks. Julian laughed. 'You've wounded his pride, Doris!' he said.

'I'll wound him somewhere else, too, if he comes sniffing round me when I'm cooking,' said Doris. That made George give one of her scowls, but the others couldn't help laughing!

A VISITOR TO TEA

The morning went very pleasantly. The Five went down to the beach and walked round the high cliffs, enjoying the stiff breeze that blew in their faces. Timmy raced after every seagull that dared to sit on the smooth sand, annoyed that each one rose up lazily on great wings as soon as he almost reached it.

They were all hungry for their dinner, and not one single morsel was left when they had finished! Doris had made a tremendous steamed pudding, with lashings of treacle, which was, as usual, a huge success.

'Wish I had a tongue like Timmy's and could lick up the lovely treacle left on the bottom of the dish,' said George. 'Such a waste!'

'You certainly won't be able to eat any tea, I'm sure of that!' said her aunt. But, of course, she was wrong. When teatime came they all felt quite ready for it, and were most impatient when Mrs Layman was late!

The tea looked lovely, laid on a big table covered with a white lace cloth. The children sat and looked at it longingly. When would Mrs Layman arrive?

'I begin to feel I'm not going to like Mrs Layman,' said George, at last. 'I can't *bear* looking at those cream cakes when I'm hungry.'

The front door bell rang. Hurrah! Then in came a cheerful, smiling old lady nodding to everyone, very pleased to see such a nice little party waiting for her.

'Here's Mrs Layman, children,' said Julian's mother. 'Sit down, Mrs Layman. We're delighted to have you.'

'Well, I've come to ask the children something,' said Mrs Layman. 'But we'll have tea first, and then I'll say what I've come to say. My, my – what a wonderful tea! I'm glad I feel hungry!'

Everyone else was hungry too, and soon the bread and
butter, the sandwiches, the buns, the cakes and everything else disappeared. Timmy sat quietly by George,
who slipped him a titbit now and again when no one was
looking. Mrs Layman chatted away. She was a most
interesting person, and the children liked her very much.

'Well now,' she said, when tea was finished, 'I'm sure
you must be wanting to know why I asked to come to tea

today. I wanted to ask your mother, Julian, if there was any chance of you three . . . and this other boy here, what's his name – George! . . . would you like to help me out of a difficulty?'

Nobody pointed out that George was a girl, not a boy, and that George was short for Georgina. George, as usual, was pleased to be taken for a boy. They all looked at Mrs Layman, listening to her with interest.

'It's like this,' she said. 'I've a dear little house up on the hills, overlooking the harbour – and I've a grandson staying with me there – Wilfrid. Well, I have to go to look after a cousin of mine, who's ill – and Wilfrid can't bear to be left alone. I just wondered if your mother would allow you children to share the little house with Wilfrid, and, well keep him company. He feels a bit scared being on his own. There's a nice woman there, who comes in to cook and clean – but poor Wilfrid's really scared of being in such a lonely place, high up on the hill.'

'You mean that lovely little house with the wonderful view?' said Julian's mother.

'Yes. It's rather *primitive* in some ways – no water laid on, only just a well to use – and no electricity or gas – just candles, or an oil-lamp. Maybe it sounds too old-fashioned for words – but honestly the view makes up for it! Perhaps the children would like to come over and see it, before they decide?' Mrs Layman looked earnestly round at everyone, and nobody knew quite what to say.

'Well – we'll *certainly* come and see it,' said Julian's mother. 'And if the children feel like it, well, they can stay there. They do like being on their own, of course.'

'Yes,' said Julian. 'We'll come and see it, Mrs Layman. Mother's going to be busy with a bazaar soon – she'll be glad to get us out of the way – and, of course, we *do* like being on our own!'

Mrs Layman looked extremely pleased. 'Tomorrow, then?' she said. 'About ten o'clock. You'll love the view. Wonderful, wonderful! You can see right over the great harbour, and for miles around. Well – I must be going now. I'll tell Wilfrid you children may be keeping him company. He's *such* a nice lad – so helpful. You'll love him.'

Julian had his doubts about the nice, helpful Wilfrid. He even wondered if Mrs Layman wanted to get away from Wilfrid, and leave him to himself! No – that was too silly. Anyway, they'd soon see what the place was like, tomorrow.

'It *would* be fun to be on our own again,' said George, when Mrs Layman had gone. 'I don't expect this Wilfrid would be any bother. He's probably just a silly kid, scared of being left alone – though apparently there *is* a woman there! Well – we'll go tomorrow! Maybe the view will make up for dear Wilfrid!'

CHAPTER THREE

The cottage on the hill – and Wilfrid

NEXT DAY the children prepared to go and see the cottage belonging to Mrs Layman. 'You coming too, Mother?' asked Julian. 'We'd like your advice!'

'Well no, dear,' said his mother. 'I've rather a lot to do – there's a meeting on at the village hall, and I promised to go to it.'

'You're full of good works, Mother,' said Julian, giving her a hug. 'All right, we'll go by ourselves. I daresay we shall know at once whether we'd like to stay in the cottage – or not. Also, we MUST know what this Wilfrid is like! It's a quarter to ten, and George is already here, with Timmy. I'll call the others and we'll get our bikes.'

Soon the four were on their bicycles, with Timmy, as usual, running alongside, his long tongue out, his eyes bright and happy. This was Timmy's idea of perfect happiness – to be with the four children all day long!

They went along a road that ran on the top of a hill. They swung round a corner – and there, spread far below them, was a great sea vista that included a wonderful harbour, filled with big and little ships. The sea was as blue as the Mediterranean, quite breath-taking. Anne jumped off her bicycle at once.

'I must just feast my eyes on all this before I go any further!' she said. 'What a panorama! What miles of sea and sky!'

She put her bicycle against a gate and then climbed over and stood by herself, gazing down at the view. Dick joined her.

Then suddenly a voice shouted loudly 'FORE! FORE!' A small white thing came whizzing through the air and landed just by Anne's foot. She jumped in surprise.

'It's a golf ball,' said Dick. 'No, don't pick it up. Whoever's playing with it has to come and hit it from exactly where it fell. Good thing you weren't hit, Anne. I didn't realise that this gate led on to a golf course!'

'We ought to have a walk over it,' said Anne. 'Just look at those gorsebushes over there, absolutely flaming with yellow blossom – and all the tiny flowers springing up everywhere – speedwell and coltsfoot and daisies and celandines – beautiful. And what a view!'

'Yes – and if Mrs Layman's cottage has a view anything like this, I'd certainly like to stay there!' said Dick. 'Think of getting out of bed in the morning and seeing this enormous view out of the window – the harbour – the sea beyond – the hills all round – the great spread of sky . . .'

'You ought to be a poet, Dick!' said Anne, in surprise. The golfers came up at that moment, and the children stood aside and watched one of them address the ball, and then strike it easily and strongly. The ball soared through the air, and landed far away on a smooth green fairway.

'Good shot!' said the man's partner, and the two sauntered off together.

'Funny game, really,' said Anne. 'Just hitting a ball all round the course.'

'Wish I had some clubs!' said Dick. 'I'm sure I could hit some smashing shots!'

'Well, if that cottage is anywhere near the golf course perhaps you could pay to have a lesson,' said Anne. 'I bet you could hit a ball as far as that man!'

The others were now yelling for them to come back, so they went to fetch their bicycles. Soon they were all riding along the road again. 'We have to look for a small white gate, with "Hill Cottage" painted on it,' said George. 'On the hillside facing the sea.'

'There it is!' cried Anne. 'We'll pile our bicycles together against the hedge, and go in at the gate.'

They left their bicycles in a heap and went through the gate. Not far to their left stood a funny old cottage, its back to them, its front looking down the steep hill that ran towards the great harbour and the sea beyond.

'It's like a cottage out of an old fairy-tale,' said Anne. 'Funny little chimneys, rather crooked walls, a thatched roof, all uneven – and what tiny windows!'

They walked down a little winding path that led to the cottage. They soon came to a well, and leaned over it to see the water deep down. 'So that's the water we'd have to drink!' said Anne, wrinkling up her nose. 'And we'd have to let down the bucket by winding this handle – and down it would go on the rope! Do you suppose the water is pure?'

'Well, seeing that people must have drunk it for years on end – the ones living in that cottage, anyway – I should imagine it's all right!' said Julian. 'Come on – let's find the front door of the cottage – if it has one!'

It had a wooden door, hung rather crooked, with an old brass knocker. It faced down the hill, and was flanked on each side by small windows. Two other small windows were above. Julian looked at them. The bedrooms would be very small, he thought – would there *really* be room for them all?

He knocked at the door. Nobody came to open it. He knocked again, and then looked for a bell, but there wasn't one.

'See if the door is unlocked,' said Anne. So Julian turned the handle – and at once the door gave under his hand! It opened straight into a room that looked like a kitchen-living room.

Julian gave a shout. 'Anyone at home?'

There was no answer. 'Well – as this is obviously the cottage we were meant to see, we'd better go in,' said Julian and they all went.

It was old, very old. The carved wooden furniture was

old too. Ancient oil-lamps stood on two tables in the room, and in a recess there was an oil-stove with a saucepan on top. A narrow, crooked stairway made of wood curved up to the floor above. Julian went up, and found himself in a long, darkish room, its roof thatched with reed and held up by black beams.

'This place must be hundreds of years old!' he called down to the others. 'I don't think it's big enough for us four and the others too – Wilfrid and the helper.'

Just as he finished calling down the stairs, the front door was flung open and someone came in.

'What are you doing here?' he shouted. 'This is *my* cottage!'

Julian went quickly down the stairs, and there, facing them all, stood a boy of about ten, a scowl on his brown face.

'Er – are you Wilfrid, by any chance?' asked Dick, politely.

'Yes, I am. And who are you? And where's my grandmother? She'll soon chuck you out!' said the boy.

'Is your grandmother Mrs Layman?' asked Julian. 'If so, she asked us to come and see her cottage, and decide if we'd like to keep you company. She said she had to go away and look after a sick relative.'

'Well, I don't want you!' said the boy. 'So clear off. I'm all right here alone. My grandmother's a nuisance, always fussing around.'

'I thought there was a lady who looks after you too,' said Julian. 'Where is she?'

'She only comes in the morning, and I sent her off,' said Wilfrid. 'She left me some food. I want to be alone. I don't want *you*. So clear off.'

'Don't be an idiot, Wilfrid,' said Julian. 'You can't live all alone here. You're just a kid.'

'I shan't be living all alone. I've plenty of friends,' said Wilfrid, defiantly.

'You CAN'T have plenty of friends here in this lonely place, with only the hills and sky around you,' said Dick.

'Well, I *have*!' said Wilfrid. 'And here's one – so look out!' And, to the horror of the two girls, he put his hand into his pocket, and brought out a snake!

Anne screamed, and tried to hide behind Julian. Wilfrid saw her fright and came towards her, holding the snake by its middle, so that it swayed to and fro, its bright little eyes gleaming.

'Don't be scared, Anne,' said Julian. 'It's only a harmless grass-snake. Put the creature back into your pocket, Wilfrid, and don't play the fool. If that snake is the only friend you have, you'll be pretty lonely here by yourself!'

'I've *plenty* of friends, I tell you!' shouted Wilfrid, stuffing the snake back into his pocket. 'I'll hit you if you don't believe me.'

'Oh no, you won't,' said Dick. 'Just show us your other friends. If they're kids like you, it's just too bad!'

'Kids? I don't make friends with *kids*!' said Wilfrid, scornfully. '*I'll* show you I'm speaking the truth. Come out here on the hillside, and see some of my other friends.'

They all trooped out of the little cottage, on to the hillside, amazed at this fierce, strange boy. When they were in the open, they saw that he had eyes as bright blue as the speedwell in the grass, and hair almost as yellow as the celandines.

'Sit down and keep quiet,' he ordered. 'Over there, by that bush. And don't move a finger. I'll soon make you believe in my friends! How dare you come here, doubting my word!'

They all sat down obediently beside the gorsebush, puzzled and rather amused. The boy sat down too, and drew something out of his pocket. What was it? George tried to see, but it was half-hidden in his right hand.

He put it to his mouth, and began to whistle. It was a

soft, weird whistle that grew loud and then died away again. There was no tune, no melody, just a kind of beautiful dirge that pulled at the heart. Sad, thought Anne, such a sad little tune – if you could *call* it a tune!

Something stirred a little way down the hill – and then to everyone's astonishment, an animal appeared – a hare! Its great ears stood upright, its big eyes stared straight at the boy with the curious little pipe. Then the hare lolloped right up to Wilfrid – and began to dance! Soon another came, but this one only watched. The first one then seemed to go mad, and leapt about wildly, utterly unafraid.

The tune changed a little – and a rabbit appeared. Then another and another. One came to Wilfrid's feet and sniffed at them, its whiskers quivering. Then it lay down against the boy's foot.

A bird flew down – a beautiful magpie! It stood nearby, watching the hare, fascinated. It took no notice of the children at all. They all held their breath, amazed and delighted.

And then Timmy gave a little growl, deep down in his throat. He didn't really mean to, but he just couldn't help it! At once the hares, the rabbits and the magpie fled, the magpie squawking in fright.

Wilfrid faced round at once, his eyes blazing. He lifted his hand to strike Timmy – but George caught his fist at once.

'Let go!' yelled Wilfrid. 'That dog scared my friends! I'll get a stick and whip him. He's the worst dog in the world, he's . . .'

And then something strange happened. Timmy came gently over to Wilfrid, lay down, and put his head on the angry boy's knee, looking up at him lovingly. The boy, his hand still raised to strike, lowered it, and fondled Timmy's head, making a curious crooning noise.

'Timmy! Come here!' ordered George, amazed and angry. To think that *her* dog, her very *own* dog, should go to a boy who had been about to strike him! Timmy stood up, gave Wilfrid a lick, and went to George.

The boy watched him, and then spoke to them all. 'You *can* come and stay in my cottage,' he said, 'if you'll bring that dog too. There aren't many dogs like him – he's a *wonderful* dog. I'd like him for one of my friends.'

Then, without another word, Wilfrid sprang up and

ran away down the hill, leaving four most astonished people – and a dog who whined dismally because the boy had gone. Well, well, Timmy – there must indeed be something about that boy, if you stand looking after him as if you had lost one of your very best friends!

CHAPTER FOUR

Settling in

THE FIVE stared after Wilfrid in silence. Timmy wagged his tail and whined. He wanted the boy to come back.

'Well, thank you, Timmy, old thing,' said Anne, patting the big dog on the head. 'We certainly wouldn't have had this lovely little cottage, with its incredible view, if you hadn't made friends with Wilfrid. What a funny boy he is!'

'Rather peculiar, *I* think!' said George, still amazed at the way that Timmy had gone to Wilfrid, when the boy had been about to strike him. 'I'm not sure that I like him!'

'Don't be silly, George,' said Dick, who had been very much impressed by the boy's handling of the hares, the rabbits and the magpie. 'That boy must have a wonderful love for animals. They would never come to him as they did, if they didn't trust him absolutely. Anyone who loves animals as he does must be all right.'

'I bet I could make them come to *me* if I had that pipe,' said George, making up her mind to borrow it if she could.

Anne went back into the cottage. She was delighted with it. It must be very, very old, she thought. It stands dreaming here all day long, full of memories of the people who have lived here and loved it. And how they must all have loved this view – miles and miles of heather, great stretches of sea – and the biggest, highest widest sky

373

I've ever seen. It's a happy place. Even the clouds seem happy – they're scurrying along, so white against the blue!

She explored the cottage thoroughly. She decided that the room above, under the thatch, should be for the three boys. There were two mattresses – one small, one larger. The little one for Wilfrid – the big one for Dick and Julian, she thought. And George and I can sleep down in the living room, with Tim on guard. I wonder if there are any rugs we could sleep on. Ah – wait a bit – this couch is a pull-out bed – just right for us two girls! Good!

Anne enjoyed herself thoroughly. This was the kind of problem she liked – fixing up this and that for the others! She found a little larder, facing north. It had a few tins in it, and a jug of milk, slightly sour. It also had two loaves of extremely stale bread, and a tin of rather hard cakes.

Mrs Layman doesn't seem to be a very good house-keeper for herself and Wilfrid, thought Anne, seriously. We'll have to go down to the village and put in a stock of decent food. I might get a small ham – the boys would like that. Goodness – this *is* going to be fun!

Julian came to the door to see what she was doing. When he saw her happy, serious face, he chuckled. 'Acting "mother" to us, as usual?' he said. 'Deciding who's going to sleep where, and which of us is to do the shopping, and which the washing-up? Dear old Anne – what should we do without you when we go off on our own?'

'I love it,' said Anne, happily. 'Julian, we need another rug or two, and a pillow, and some food. And . . .'

'Well, we'll have to go back home and collect a few

clothes and other things,' said Julian. 'We can shop on the way back, and get whatever we want. I wonder if that woman that Mrs Layman spoke about will be coming in to help?'

'Well – Wilfrid said he sent her off,' said Anne. 'And I think perhaps as the cottage is so small, it might be better if we managed it ourselves. I think I could do a bit of cooking on that oil-stove in the corner – and anyway we can pretty well live on cold stuff, you know – ham and salad and cheese and fruit. It would be easy enough for any of us to pop down to the village on our bikes, to fetch anything we needed.'

'Listen!' said Julian, cocking his head to one side. 'Is that somebody calling us?'

Yes – it was. When Julian went outside, he saw Mrs Layman at the gate that led on to the hillside where the cottage stood. He went over to her.

'We LOVE the cottage!' he said. 'And if it's all right, we'd like to move in today. We can easily pop home and bring back anything we want. It's a glorious old place, isn't it – and the view must be the finest anywhere!'

'Well, that harbour is the second biggest stretch of water in the whole world,' said Mrs Layman. 'The only stretch that is any bigger is Sydney harbour – so you have something to feast your eyes on, Julian!'

'You bet!' said Julian. 'It's amazing – and so *very* blue! I only wish I could paint – but I can't. At least, not very well!'

'What about Wilfrid?' said Mrs Layman, anxiously. 'Is he behaving himself? He's – well – he's rather a *difficult* boy at times. And he can be very rude. He hasn't any brothers to rub off his awkward corners, you see.'

'Oh, don't you worry about Wilfrid!' said Julian, cheerfully. 'He'll have to toe the line, and do as he's told. We all do our bit when we're away together. He's a wonder with animals, isn't he?'

'Well – yes, I suppose he *is*!' said Mrs Layman. 'Though I can't say I like pet snakes, or pet beetles, and owls that come and hoot down the chimney at night to find out if Wilfrid will go out and hoot back at them!'

Julian laughed. 'We shan't mind that,' he said. 'And he's managed to get over what might have been our biggest difficulty – he has made friends with our dog, Timmy. In fact, he informed us that if Timmy stayed, we could *all* stay – but *only* if Timmy stayed!'

Mrs Layman laughed. 'That's so like Wilfrid,' she said. 'He's an odd boy. Don't stand any nonsense from him!'

'We shan't,' said Julian, cheerfully. 'I'm surprised he

wants to stay on with us, actually. I should have thought
he would rather go home than be with a lot of strangers.'

'He can't go home,' said Mrs Layman. 'His sister has
measles, and his mother doesn't want Wilfrid to catch it.
So you'll have to put up with him, I fear.'

'And he'll have to put up with us!' said Julian. 'Thanks
very much for letting us have the cottage, Mrs Layman.
We'll take great care of everything.'

'I know you will,' said the old lady. 'Well, goodbye,
Julian. Have a good time. I'll get back to my car now.
Give Wilfrid my love. I hope he doesn't fill the cottage
with animals of all kinds!'

'We shan't mind if he does!' said Julian, and waited
politely until Mrs Layman had disappeared and he could
hear the noise of a car starting up.

He went back to the cottage and stood outside, looking down at the amazing view. The harbour was full of
boats, big and little. A steamer went busily along, making for a great seaside town far away on the other side.

Anne came to join Julian. 'Glorious, isn't it?' she said.
'We're so very high up here that it seems as if we can see
half the world at our feet. Is that an island in the middle
of the harbour, Ju?'

'Yes – and a well-wooded one too!' said Julian. 'I
wonder what it's called – and who lives there. I can't see a
single house there, can you?'

Dick called to Anne. 'Anne! George and I are going to
fetch our bikes and ride down to the village. Give us your
shopping list, will you? Julian, is there anything special
you want us to pack for you at home, and bring back,
besides your night things and a change of clothes?'

'Yes – don't go off yet!' called Julian, hurrying into the

cottage. 'I've made a list somewhere. I think I'd better go with you. There will be food and other things to bring back – unless Mother would bring everything up by car this afternoon.'

'Yes – that's a good idea,' said Dick. 'We'll go to Kirrin Cottage first and get George's things – and then home to get ours. I'll leave all the shopping with Mother, and all our luggage, so that she can pop up here in the car with it. She'll love the view!'

'I'll stay behind and tidy up the cottage, and find out how the stove works,' said Anne, happily. 'I'll have everything neat and tidy by the time Mother comes this afternoon, Dick. Oh, here's Julian with the list. Why don't you go off on your bike with George and Dick, Julian? I'll be quite happy here messing about.'

'Yes, I'm going to,' said Julian, putting his list into his pocket. 'Look after yourself, Anne! We'll take Timmy with us, to give him a run.'

Off went the three, Timmy loping behind, very glad of the run. Anne waited till they were out of sight, then went happily back to the cottage. She was almost there when she heard someone calling her. She turned and saw a fresh-faced woman waving.

'I'm Sally!' she called. 'Do you want any help with the cooking and cleaning? Wilfrid told me not to come any more, but if you want me, I will.'

'Oh, I think we can manage, Sally,' said Anne. 'There's so many of us now, we can all do the jobs. Did you sleep here?'

'Oh no!' said Sally, coming up. 'I just came in to help, and then went back home. You tell me if you want me any time, and I'll gladly come. Where's that monkey of a

Wilfrid? He spoke to me very rudely this morning the little devil! I'll tell his grandmother of him – not that that's much good! He just laughs at her! Don't you stand any nonsense from him!'

'I won't,' said Anne, smiling. 'Where do you live, in case we *do* want you?'

'Just the other side of the road, in the small wood there,' said Sally. 'You'll see my tiny cottage when you go by the wood on your bikes.'

She disappeared up the hill and across the road there. Anne went back happily to her household tasks. She cleaned out the little larder, and then found a pail and went to the well. She hung the pail on the hook at the end of the rope, and then worked the old handle that let the pail down to the water, swinging on the rope. Splash! It was soon full, and Anne wound it up again. The water looked crystal clear, and was as cold as ice – but all the same Anne wondered if she ought to boil it.

Someone came quietly behind her – and jumped at her with a loud howl! Anne dropped the pail of water, and gave a scream. Then she saw it was Wilfrid, dancing round her, grinning.

'Idiot!' she said. 'Now you just go and get me some more water.'

'Where's that big dog?' demanded Wilfrid, looking all round. 'I can't see him. You can't any of you stay here unless you have that dog. I like him. He's a wonderful dog.'

'He's gone down to the village with the others,' said Anne. 'Now will you please pick up that pail and get more water?'

'No, I won't,' said Wilfrid. 'I'm not your servant! Get it yourself!'

'Very well, I will. But I'll tell George, who owns Timmy, how rude you are – and you may be *quite* sure that Timmy won't be friends with you,' said Anne, picking up the pail.

'I'll get the water, I'll get the water!' shouted Wilfrid, and snatched the pail. 'Don't you dare to tell George or Timmy tales of me. Don't you dare!'

And off he went to the well and filled the pail. Well! What a time they were all going to have with such a very peculiar boy! Anne didn't like him at all!

CHAPTER FIVE

Wilfrid is most annoying – and Anne is most surprising!

WILFRED BROUGHT back the pail to Anne, and dumped it down. 'Like to see my pet beetles?' he said.

'No thank you,' said Anne. 'I don't like beetles very much.'

'Well, you ought to!' said Wilfrid. 'I've two very beautiful ones. You can hold them if you like. The tiny feet feel very funny when they walk all over your hand.'

'I don't *mind* beetles, but I don't want them walking over my hand,' said poor Anne, who really was a bit afraid of what she called 'creepy-crawly' things. 'Do get out of my way, Wilfrid. If you had any manners, you'd carry that pail indoors for me.'

'I *haven't* any manners,' said Wilfrid. 'Everybody tells me that. Anyway, I don't want to carry your pail if you don't want to see my beetles.'

'Oh, go away!' said Anne, exasperated, picking up the pail herself. Wilfrid went to a little thick bush and sat down by it. He put his face almost on the grass, and looked under the bush. Anne felt uncomfortable. Was he going to call his beetles out? She couldn't help putting down her pail, and standing still to watch.

No beetles came out from under the bush – but something else did. A very large, awkward-looking toad came crawling out, and sat there, looking up at Wilfrid with the greatest friendliness. Anne was amazed. How did Wilfrid know the toad was there? And why in the world should it come out to see *him*? She stood and stared – and shivered, because she really did *not* like toads. I know they have beautiful eyes, and are intelligent, and eat all kinds of harmful insects, but I just can't go near one! she thought. Oh goodness – Wilfrid's tickling its back – and it's scratching where he's tickled – just like *we* would!

'Come and say how-do-you-do to my pet toad,' called Wilfrid. 'I'll carry your pail for you then.'

Anne picked up her pail in a hurry, afraid that Wilfrid might whistle up a few snakes next. What a boy! How she wished the others would come back! Why, Wilfrid might own a boa constrictor – or have a small crocodile somewhere – or . . . but no, she was being silly! If *only* the others would come back!

To her horror the toad crawled right on to Wilfrid's hands, and looked up at him out of its really beautiful eyes. That was too much for Anne. She fled into the cottage, spilling half the water as she went.

I wish I was like George, she thought. She wouldn't really mind that toad. I'm silly. I ought to try and like *all* creatures. Oh my goodness, look at that enormous spider in the corner of the sink! It's sitting there, looking at me out of its eight eyes! 'Wilfrid, Wilfrid – PLEASE come and get this spider out of the sink for me!'

Wilfrid sauntered in, fortunately without the toad. He held his hand out to the spider and made a curious clicking, ticking noise. The spider perked up at once, waved two curious little antennae about, and crawled across the sink to Wilfrid's hand. Anne shuddered. She simply couldn't help it! She shut her eyes and when she opened them, the spider had gone and so had Wilfrid.

I suppose he's now teaching it to dance, or something, she thought, trying to make herself smile. I can't *think* how insects and animals and birds like him. I simply can't *bear* him. If *I* were a rabbit or a bird or beetle, I'd run miles away from him. What's this curious attraction he has for creatures of all kinds?

Wilfrid had completely disappeared, and Anne thankfully went on with her little jobs. I'll tidy up the loft where the boys will sleep, she thought. I'll wash this living room floor. I'll make a list of the things in the larder. I'll clean that dirty window over there. I'll . . . good gracious, what's that noise?

It was the sound of magpies chattering noisily – a harsh but pleasant noise. Anne peered out of the little cottage window. Well, what a sight! There stood Wilfrid in front of the window, a magpie on each outstretched hand – and one on the top of his head! It stood there, chattering loudly, and then turned round and round, getting its feet mixed up in the boy's thick hair.

'Come out here and I'll tell one of my magpies to sit on your head too!' shouted Wilfrid. 'It's such a nice feeling. Or would you like a young rabbit to cuddle? I can call one for you with my little pipe!'

'I don't *want* a magpie on my head,' said Anne, desperately. 'For goodness sake get a nice little baby rabbit. I'd like that.'

Wilfrid jerked the magpies off his hands and shook his head violently so that the third one flew up, squawking cheerfully. He then sat down and pulled out his funny little whistle-pipe, as Anne called it. She watched, fascinated, as the strange little dirge-like tune came to her

384

ears. She found her feet walking to the door. Good gracious – could there be some peculiar kind of magic in that pipe that made *her* go to Wilfrid, just as the other creatures did?

She stopped at the door, just as a baby rabbit came lolloping round a tall clump of grass. It was the funniest, roundest, dearest little thing, with a tiny bobtail and big ears.

It went straight to Wilfrid and nestled against him. The boy stroked it and murmured to it. Then he called to Anne softly.

'Well – here's the baby rabbit you asked for. Like to come and stroke it?'

Anne went softly over the grass, expecting the rabbit to bolt at once. Wilfrid continued to fondle it, and the little thing looked at him with big, unwinking eyes. Anne bent down to stroke it – but immediately it leapt in fright and fled into the grass.

'Oh *dear* – why did it do that?' said Anne, disappointed. 'It was quite all right with *you*! Wilfrid, how do you get all these creatures to come to you?'

'Shan't tell you,' said Wilfrid, getting up. 'Is there anything to eat in the cottage? I'm hungry.'

He pushed Anne aside and went into the cottage. He opened the larder door, and took down a tin. There was a cake inside and he cut off a huge piece. He didn't offer Anne any.

'Couldn't you have cut *me* a piece too?' said Anne. 'You really are a rude boy!'

'I *like* being rude,' said Wilfrid, munching his cake. 'Especially to people who come to my cottage when I don't want them.'

'Oh, don't be so *silly*!' said Anne, exasperated. 'It *isn't* your cottage – it belongs to your grandmother. She told us so. Anyway, you said we could stay if Timmy stayed too.'

'I'll soon make Timmy *my* dog,' said Wilfrid, taking another bite. 'You'll see! Soon he won't want that girl George any more – and he'll follow at my heels all day and night. *You'll* see!'

Anne laughed scornfully. Timmy following at this boy's heels? That could never happen! Timmy loved George with all his doggy heart. He would never desert her for Wilfrid, no matter how much he whistled on pipes, or put on his special croony voice. Anne was absolutely certain of that!

'If you laugh at me, I'll call up my grass-snake *and* my adder!' said Wilfrid, fiercely. 'Then you'll run for miles!'

'Oh no I won't!' said Anne, hurrying into the cottage. 'Just watch *yourself* run!' She picked up the pail of water, went out with it, and threw it all over the astonished Wilfrid! Somebody else was *most* astonished too – and that was Julian, who had arrived back before the others, anxious not to leave Anne alone in the cottage for too long.

He came just in time to see Anne drenching Wilfrid, and stared in the utmost amazement. *Anne* behaving like that? Anne looking really *fierce* – quiet, peaceful Anne! What in the world had happened?

'Anne!' he called. 'What's the matter? What's Wilfrid been doing?'

'Oh – *Julian*!' said Anne, glad to see him, but horrified that he had come just then. Wilfrid was drenched from head to foot. He stood there, gasping, taken aback, bewildered. Why, Anne had seemed such a *quiet*, frightened little thing – scared even of a spider!

'That girl!' said Wilfrid, half-choking, shaking the water off himself. 'That bad, wicked girl! She's like a tiger! She sprang at me, and threw the water all over me! I won't let her stay in my cottage!'

The boy was so angry, so wet, so taken aback, that Julian had to laugh! He roared in delight, and clapped Anne on the back. 'The mouse has turned into a tiger! Well, you said you might one day, Anne – and you haven't lost much time! Let me see if you've grown claws!'

He took Anne's hands and pretended to examine her nails. Anne was half-laughing, half-crying now, and pulled her hand away. 'Oh Julian, I shouldn't have soaked Wilfrid – but he was so IRRITATING I lost my temper, and . . .'

'All right, all right – it's quite a good thing to do sometimes,' said Julian. 'And I bet young Wilfrid deserved all he got. I only hope the water was icy cold! Have you a change of clothes here, Wilfrid? Go and get into them, then.'

The boy stood there, dripping wet, and made no effort to obey. Julian spoke again. 'You heard what I said, Wilfrid. Jump to it! Go and change!'

The boy looked so wet and miserable that Anne felt suddenly sorry for what she had done. She ran to him and felt his wet shoulders. 'Oh, I'm *sorry*!' she said. 'Truly I am. I don't know *why* I turned into a tiger so suddenly!'

Wilfrid gave a little half-laugh, half-sob. 'I'm sorry too,' he mumbled. 'You're nice – and your nose is like that baby rabbit's – it's – it's a bit woffly!'

He ran into the cottage and slammed the door. 'Let him be for a while,' said Julian, seeing that Anne made a move to go after him. 'This will do him good. Nothing like having a pail of cold water flung over you to make you see things as they really are! He was really touched when you said you were sorry. *He's* probably never apologised to anyone in his life!'

'*Is* my nose like a rabbit's?' said Anne, worried.

'Well, yes – just a bit,' said Julian, giving his sister an affectionate pat. 'But a rabbit's nose is very nice, you know – very nice indeed. I don't think you'll have much trouble with Wilfrid after this little episode. He didn't know that you had the heart of a tiger, as well as a nose like a rabbit's!'

Wilfrid came out of the cottage in about ten minutes, dressed in dry clothes, carrying his wet ones in a bundle. 'I'll hang those out on the bushes for you, to dry in the sun,' said Anne, and took them from him, smiling. He suddenly smiled back.

'Thanks,' he said. 'I don't know how they got so wet! Must have been *pouring* with rain!'

Julian chuckled and smacked him gently on the back. 'Rain can do an awful lot of good at times!' he said. 'Well, Anne, we've brought you back a whole lot of goods for your larder. Here come the others. We'll carry everything in for you – with Wilfrid's help too!'

CHAPTER SIX

Lucas – and his tale

IT WAS fun storing all the shopping away. Anne enjoyed it more than anyone, for she really was a most domesticated little person.

'A real home-maker!' said Dick, appreciatively, when he saw how neat and comfortable she had made the loft, where the three boys were to sleep. 'Just about room for the three of us, plus all the baggage in the corner! And how good the larder looks!'

Anne looked at her well-stocked larder, and smiled. Now she could give her little 'family' really nice meals. All those tins! She read the names on them. Fruit salad. Tinned pears. Tinned peaches. Sardines. Ham. Tuna. A new cake in that round tin, big enough to last for at least three days. Biscuits. Chocolate wafers – good old Julian – he knew how much she loved those – and George did, too!

Anne felt very happy as she arranged all her goods. She no longer felt guilty at drenching poor Wilfrid. Indeed she couldn't help feeling a little thrill when she remembered how she had suddenly turned into a tiger for a minute or two! It was fun to be a tiger for once. I might even be one again, if the chance arose, thought Anne. HOW surprised Wilfrid was – and Julian too. Oh dear – poor Wilfrid. Still, he's much nicer now.

And indeed he was! He was most polite to both the girls, and, as Dick said, he didn't 'throw his weight about' nearly so much. They all settled down very well together in the little cottage.

They had most of their meals out of doors, sitting on the warm grass. It was rather a squeeze indoors, for the cottage really was very small. Anne enjoyed herself preparing the meals, with sometimes a little help from George – and the boys carried everything out. Wilfrid did his share, and was pleased when he had a clap on the back from Julian.

It was glorious sitting out in the sun, high up on their hill. They could look down on the harbour, watch the yachts and the busy little boats, and enjoy the wonderful views all around.

George was very curious about the island that lay in the middle of the harbour. 'What's it called?' she asked Wilfrid. But he didn't know. He did know, however, that there was a strange story about it. 'It belonged to a lonely old man,' he said. 'He lived in a big house in the very middle of the wood. The island was given to his family by a king – James the Second, I think. This old man was the very, very last one of his family. People kept wanting to buy his island, and he had some kind of watchmen to keep people from landing on it. These watchmen were pretty fierce – they had guns.'

'Gosh – did they shoot people who tried to land, then?' asked Dick.

'Well – they just shot to frighten them off, not to hurt them, I suppose,' said Wilfrid. 'Anyway, a lot of sightseers had an awful fright when they tried to land. BANG-BANG! Shooting all round them! My granny told me that someone she knew, who had a lot of money, wanted to buy part of the island – and *he* had his hat shot right off when his boat tried to land!'

'Is there anyone there now?' asked Julian. 'I suppose the old fellow is dead? Has he a son or anyone to follow him?'

'I don't think so,' said Wilfrid. 'But I don't know an awful lot about it. I tell you who does, though – one of the groundsmen on the golf course, called Lucas. He was once one of the watchmen who kept visitors away from the island.'

'It might be rather interesting to talk to him,' said Dick. 'I'd rather like to walk over the golf course, too. My father plays a good game of golf, and I know something about it.'

'Well, let's go now,' said George. 'Timmy is longing for a good long walk, even though he ran all the way down to the village and back yesterday! Walk, Timmy? Walk?'

'Woof-woof,' said Timmy, and leapt up at once. Walk? Of *course* he was ready for a walk! He leapt all round George, pretending to pounce at her feet. Wilfrid tried to catch hold of him, but couldn't. 'I wish you were *my* dog,' he told Timmy. 'I'd never let you out of my sight.'

Timmy ran up to him then, and gave him a loving lick. It was astonishing how he seemed to like Wilfrid. Nobody could understand it. As George said, 'Timmy is usually so particular about making friends! Still, Wilfrid *is* nicer than he was!'

The Five, with Wilfrid too, went up the hill, crossed over the road that ran along the top, and climbed over a stile. They found themselves on one of the fairways of the golf course not far from a green, in which stood a pole with a bright red flag waving at the top.

Wilfrid knew very little about the game of golf, but the

others had watched their parents play many a time. 'Look out – someone's going to pitch his ball on this green,' said Julian, and they stood by the hedge to watch the man play his ball. He struck it beautifully with his club, and the ball rose, and fell right on to the green. It rolled very close to the hole in which the flag-pole stood.

Timmy ran forward a few steps, as he always did when a ball rolled near him. Then he remembered that this was golf, and he must never, never touch a ball on the fairway or on the green.

The players passed, and went on with their game. Then they disappeared, to play off another tee.

'Well, let's see if we can find Lucas now,' said Wilfrid, crossing the fairway to where he could get a good look over the course. 'You'll like him. There's not much he doesn't know about the animals and birds here. *I* think he's a wonderful man!'

Wilfrid stood on the slope of a hill and looked all round. 'There he is!' he said, pointing to where a man was trimming up a ditch. 'See? Down there. He's using his billhook to make things tidy.'

They went down the hill towards the ditch at the bottom. 'I bet there's an awful lot of balls in that ditch,' said Wilfrid. 'Hey, Lucas! How are you?'

'Morning, young man,' said the groundsman, turning towards them. His face was as brown as a well-ripened nut, and his arms and shoulders were even browner. He wore no shirt or vest, and his dark, deep-set eyes twinkled as they took in the five children and the dog.

He held out a brown hand to Timmy, who licked it gravely, wagging his tail. Then Timmy smelt Lucas all over and finally lay down with his head on the man's feet.

'Ha!' said Lucas to Timmy, and gave a loud, hearty laugh. 'Think I'm going to stand here all morning, do you? Well, I'm not. I've got work to do, old dog, so get up! You're a right good-un, you are, lying on my foot so I can't move a step! Want me to stop and have a rest don't you?'

'Lucas, we came to ask you something,' said Wilfrid. 'About the island in the harbour. What's its name – and does anyone live there now?'

'We can see it from that little cottage almost at the top of the hill on the other side of the road,' said Dick. 'It looks awfully quiet and lonely.'

'And so it is,' said Lucas, sitting down on the bank of the ditch. Timmy at once sat up beside him, sniffing him with pleasure. He put his arm round the dog, and began to talk, his bright eyes going from one to another of the children. He was so friendly, and so completely natural, that the children felt he was an old, old friend. They sat down too, sniffing the smell of the gorsebushes nearby. They smell like coconut, thought Anne. Yes – just like coconut!

'Well, now,' said Lucas, 'that island's always been a mystery place. It's called Wailing Island by some folks because the wind makes a right strange wailing noise round some of its high cliffs. And others call it Whispering Island because it's full of trees that whisper in the strong winds that always blow across it. But most of us call it Keep-Away Island – and that's the best name of all, for there's never been any welcome there, what with the dark cliffs, the cruel rocks, and the dense woods.'

Lucas paused, and looked at the listening faces around him. He was a born storyteller, and knew it. How often

Wilfrid had listened to his tales of the birds and animals he met during his work on the course! Lucas was one of the few people that the boy admired and loved.

'Do go on, Lucas!' said Wilfrid, touching the man's bare, warm arm. 'Tell us about the rich old man who hated everyone, and bought the island years ago.'

'I'm telling the story my own way,' said Lucas, with great dignity. 'Be patient now, or I'll start my ditching again. Sit like this dog, see – he doesn't even twitch a muscle, good dog that he is. Well now, about this rich old man. He was so afraid of being robbed that he bought that lonely island. He built himself a great castle right in the middle of the thick woods. Cut down about a hundred trees to make room for it, so the story goes, and brought every single stick and stone from the mainland. Did you see the old quarry on this here golf course, as you came along to me?'

'Yes, we did,' said Julian, remembering. 'I felt sorry for anyone who sent a golf ball there!'

'Well, out of that quarry came the great stones that the old man used for his castle,' said Lucas. ''Tis said that big, flat-bottomed boats had to be made to ferry the stones across to the island – and to this day the road through this golf course is the one made by horses dragging the great stones down to the water's edge.'

'Were you alive then?' said Wilfrid.

'Bless you, boy, no, of course not,' said Lucas, with a great chuckle of a laugh. 'Long before my time, that was. Well, the stone house – or castle, whatever you like to call it – was built. And the old man brought to it all kinds of treasures – beautiful statues, some of gold, it was said, but I don't believe that. There are many strange tales I've heard of what that rich old man took over to Whispering Island – a great bed made of pure gold, and set with precious stones – a necklace of rubies as big as pigeons' eggs – a wonderful sword with a jewelled handle, worth a king's fortune – and other things I can't remember.'

He paused and looked round. Julian asked him a quick question. 'What happened to all these things?'

'Well now, he fell foul of the king of the land, and one

morning, what did he see landing on the shores of his island but ships of all kinds,' said Lucas, enjoying the rapt attention of his audience. 'A lot of them were sunk by the wicked rocks but enough men were left to storm the strange stone castle in the wood, and they killed the old man and all his servants.'

'Did they find the treasures the old fellow had collected?' asked Dick.

'Not one thing!' said Lucas. 'Not one thing. Some say it was all a tale – the old man never did bring any wonders there, and some say they're still there, on Whispering Island. I think it's all a yarn – but a good yarn at that!'

'Who owns the island now?' asked Dick.

'Well, an old fellow and his wife went to live there – maybe they paid rent to the Crown for it, maybe they bought it – but they didn't care for anything except for the birds and the animals there,' said Lucas, picking up his curved billhook again, and hacking lightly at some briars. 'They wouldn't allow anybody there, and it was they who kept the gamekeepers with guns to frighten away sightseers. They wanted peace and quiet for themselves, and for all the wildlife on the island – and a fine idea too. Many a time when I was there with the other keepers – three of us there were – many a time I've had rabbits gambolling over my feet, and snakes gliding by me – and the birds as tame as canaries.'

'I'd *love* to go there,' said Wilfrid, his eyes shining. 'I'd have a good time with all the wild creatures! Can anyone go there now?'

'No,' said Lucas, getting up. 'Not a soul has lived in the old stone castle since the old man and his wife fell ill and died. The place is empty. The island belongs to a great-nephew of the old couple now, but he never goes there. Just keeps a couple of men on the island to frighten off visitors – pretty fierce they are, so I've been told. Well, there you are, that's the story of Whispering Island – not very pleasant – a bit grim and ugly. It belongs to the birds and the beasts now, and good luck to them!'

'Thank you for telling us the story,' said Anne, and the old countryman smiled down at her, his eyes wrinkling, and his brown hand patting her cheek.

'I'll be off to my hedging and ditching again,' he said, 'and I'll feel the sun warm on my bare back, and hear the birds singing to me from the bushes. That's happiness enough for anyone – and it's a pity that more folks don't know it!'

CHAPTER SEVEN

Up on the golf course

THE CHILDREN walked round the golf course together, after talking to old Lucas. 'We must keep out of the way of anyone playing,' said Dick, 'or we might get hit on the head with a ball! Hey, Timmy, what are you doing in the bracken?'

Timmy came out with something in his mouth. He dropped it at George's feet. It was a golf ball, fairly new. George picked it up. 'What do we do with this?' she said. 'There's no golfer near us. It must be a lost ball.'

'Well, all balls lost on golf courses should be taken in to the pro,' said Julian. 'By right they belong to him if found on the course.'

'What's a pro?' asked Anne.

'A professional golfer – a man who's very, very good at the game, and is in charge of a golf course,' explained Julian. 'Hey look! Here comes old Tim again with *another* ball. Timmy, we ought to hire you out to golfers who keep losing their balls – you'd save them no end of trouble!'

Timmy was pleased to be patted and praised. He set off into the rough again at once, sniffing here and there.

'Anyone would think that golf balls smelt like rabbits or something, the way Timmy sniffs them out!' said Anne, as Timmy ran up with yet another ball. 'Golfers must be jolly careless, losing so many balls!'

They went on round the course, which was set with

400

great stretches of gorse, full of brilliant blossom. A baby rabbit fled from the bracken as Timmy nosed there for balls. Timmy chased it, and the frightened little creature dodged this way and that, trying to escape. 'Let it go, Tim, let it go!' yelled George, but Timmy was much too excited to pay any attention.

Wilfrid suddenly bent down as the rabbit raced near him, and gave a curious low whistle. The rabbit swerved, came straight towards him, and leapt into his arms, lying there trembling. Timmy jumped up to it at once, but George dragged him away.

'NO, Timmy. Sorry, but NO, you can't have the little thing. Down! DOWN, I say!'

Timmy gave George a disgusted look, and pattered off into the bracken, nosing for balls again. He was very cross with George. Rabbits were meant to be chased, weren't they? Why did George have to spoil his fun?

George stared at Wilfrid. The rabbit was still nestling

in his arms, and he was making a curious noise to it. The tiny thing was trembling from head to tail. Everyone watched it, glad that it was safe. They were all silent, astonished at the way that Wilfrid had rescued the little creature. How had the rabbit known that Wilfrid's arms were ready to save it?

He took it to the bracken, dropped it gently, and watched it race like lightning to the nearest burrow. Then he turned and patted Timmy, who stood silently by, watching.

'Sorry, Tim,' he said. 'It's so little, and you're so big!'

'Woof,' said Tim, exactly as if he understood, and he gave Wilfrid's hand a quick lick. Then he pranced round the boy, barking, as if he wanted a game, and Wilfrid raced off with him at top speed.

The others followed, impressed once again by Wilfrid's uncanny way with animals. He was such a horrid little boy in some ways – so rude, so mannerless, so selfish – then how was it that animals liked him so much? George frowned. She thought it was all wrong that animals should love Wilfrid and go to him – why, even Timmy was all over him! If she wasn't careful he would spend more time with Wilfrid than with her! That would never do!

Timmy found five more balls, and soon Julian's pockets were heavy with them. They made their way to the small clubhouse in the distance, meaning to give in the balls. It was set in a little dip, and looked friendly and welcoming. They all went in at the door, and Julian walked over to the pro, who was checking some scorecards. He emptied his pockets of balls and grinned. 'A present from our dog!' he said.

'My word – did he find all those?' said the pro, pleased. 'Not bad ones, either. I'll stand you all some lemonade or orangeade – which will you have?'

They all had orangeade, and the pro sent a packet of biscuits to Timmy, who was waiting patiently outside. He was delighted!

'We're staying in that little cottage up on the hillside,' said Dick. 'Do you know it?'

"Course I do!' said the pro. 'My grandmother lived there once upon a time. You've a wonderful view there, haven't you? One of the finest in the world, I reckon! You can see Whispering Island from there, too. Ought to be called Mystery Island! It's said that folks have gone there and never come back!'

'What happened to them?' asked Anne.

'Oh well – maybe it's all a tale!' said the pro. 'There's supposed to be priceless things there, packed away some-where – and collectors from all over the world have come here, and tried to get over to that island – not to steal, you understand, but just to see if they could find any-thing worthwhile and buy it for museums – or maybe for their own collections. It's said there are statues in the wood, white as snow – but that I never did believe!'

'And didn't the collectors ever come back?' asked Julian.

'It's said that a lot of them didn't,' said the pro, 'but that may all be silly tales. But I do know that two men came down here from some museum in London, and hired a boat to go across. They took a white flag with them so that the two keepers wouldn't shoot them – and after that nobody heard a word about them. They just disappeared!'

403

'Well – what could have happened to them?' asked
Julian.

'Nobody knows,' said the pro. 'Their boat was found
miles out to sea, drifting – and empty. So the police
reckoned a mist came down, they lost direction, and
ended by drifting way out to sea.'

'But did they jump out of their boat, and try to swim
back – and get drowned?' asked Dick. 'Or did a passing
steamer or yacht save them?'

'They weren't picked up, that's certain,' said the pro.
'Else they'd have arrived safely back at their homes,
sometime or other. But they didn't. No – I reckon the
poor fellows were drowned. Of course, maybe they were
shot by the keepers, when they tried to land, and their
boat was set adrift!'

'Didn't the police do anything?' asked Julian, puzzled.

'Oh, yes – they went across to the island in the coast-
guard patrol boat,' said the pro. 'But the keepers swore
they'd seen nobody arriving, and that they were the only
people on the place. The police landed and searched
everywhere, and they found nothing except the great
white castle-like house in the woods and hundreds of
wild animals, so tame that they'd sit and watch you as
you walked by.'

'All very mysterious,' said Julian, getting up. 'Well,
thanks for the welcome orangeade, and for your infor-
mation! We'd already heard a bit from a groundsman of
yours – Lucas – a real old countryman, and a born
storyteller!'

'Ah, Lucas – yes, he knows that island well,' said the
pro. 'He was once one of the keepers, I believe! Well –
come and see me again some time – thanks for the balls.

It isn't everyone who's honest enough to come and give them in when they find them!'

They all said goodbye and went out. Timmy pranced along in joy. Sitting down outside the club-house didn't suit him at all!

'Did you enjoy your biscuits, Tim?' asked George, and he ran up and gave her hand a quick lick. What a question! He *always* enjoyed biscuits! He ran off into the bracken and began to nose about there again, hunting for balls.

The others went to walk up the hill, talking about the island. 'I wonder what really *did* happen to those two collector men who were never heard of again,' said Anne. 'Funny that their boat was found adrift and empty.'

'They must have been drowned, of course,' said Dick. 'I wonder if anything *is* left of the old treasures that were once taken there. No – there wouldn't be – the police would have made a very thorough search!'

'I wish *we* could go to the island!' said George. 'I don't expect the keepers would shoot at *us*, would they? They might even let us on, to make change for them – they must be so bored with only themselves to talk to.'

'That's *very* wishful thinking, George,' said Julian. 'We are CERTAINLY not going near the island, so put that right out of your head.'

'Well – I knew it was impossible, really,' said George. 'But wouldn't it be a *grand* adventure if we managed to get on the mysterious Whispering Island and explore it without the keepers knowing!'

'Not such a grand adventure if we were all peppered with shot from the keepers' guns!' said Dick. 'Anyway, we wouldn't find anything of interest – the treasures must have been removed long ago. The only possible things of interest would be the very tame wild creatures there! Wilfrid would go mad with joy – wouldn't you Wilfrid?'

'I'd like it very much,' said the boy, his eyes shining. 'What's more, I might hire a boat myself and row round the island to see if I could spot any animals there.'

'You'll do nothing of the sort!' said Julian, at once. 'So don't try any silly tricks, see?'

'I shan't promise! said Wilfrid, irritatingly. 'You just never know!'

'Oh yes, I do know! You're just trying to sound big!' said Julian. 'Come along quickly, everyone – it's past our dinner-time, and I'm ravenous! What's for lunch, Anne?'

'We'll open a tin of tuna,' said Anne, 'and there's plenty of bread left, and lettuce, which I left in water. And tomatoes. And heaps of fruit.'

'Sounds good!' said George. 'Dinner, Timmy, dinner!'

And, hearing that welcome word, Timmy shot up the steep hill at top speed, his tail waving joyously.

'Wish I was a dog and could tear up a hill like that!' said Anne, panting. 'Give me a push, Julian! I'll *never* get to the top!'

CHAPTER EIGHT

Mostly about Wilfrid

TIMMY WAS waiting for the children at the top of the hill, his tail waving, his mouth open as he panted. He picked something up, as the children came, threw it into the air, and caught it.

'Another golf ball, Timmy?' said Dick, as Timmy threw the ball into the air again with a toss of his big head.

'No – it's too big for that,' said George. 'Drop it, Timmy. What have you found?'

Timmy dropped the ball at George's feet. It was bigger than a golf ball, and had a hole right through it. 'Oh, it's one of those balls that children throw up and try to catch on a stick,' said George. 'Somebody must have dropped it. All right, Tim, you can have it.'

'He won't swallow it, will he?' said Wilfrid, anxiously. 'It's not *awfully* big – and I once saw a dog swallow something by mistake, that he threw into the air to catch.'

'Timmy's *much* too sensible to swallow *any* ball,' said George. 'You needn't worry about *him*. Anyway, *I* can do any worrying necessary. He's *my* dog.'

'All right, all right, all right!' said Wilfrid. 'Miss High-and-Mighty can look after her own dog. Fine!'

George looked round at him furiously and he made a face at her. Then he whistled to Timmy – yes, he actually dared to whistle to him!

'Nobody whistles for my dog except me,' said George. 'And anyway, he won't come to *you*.'

But, to her surprise and horror, Timmy *did* go to Wilfrid, and pranced all round him, expecting a game. George called him sternly, and he looked at her in surprise. He began to trot over to her when Wilfrid whistled again, and obediently Timmy turned as if to go to him.

George caught hold of the dog's collar, and aimed a punch at the whistling boy. It missed him, and he danced round, laughing.

'Stop it now, you two,' said Julian, seeing George's look of fury. 'I said STOP IT! Wilfrid, go on ahead, and *keep* going. George, don't be an ass. He's only teasing you to make you lose your temper. Don't please him by losing it!'

George said nothing more, but her eyes blazed. Oh dear! thought Anne, now we shan't have any peace! She won't forgive Wilfrid for making Timmy go to him! Blow Wilfrid – he really is a little pest at times.

They were all very hungry for their lunch and very pleased with everything that Anne provided. Dick went into the little cottage to help her, because George insisted on keeping her hand on Timmy's collar all the time, in case Wilfrid should entice him to his side.

'He's making some of his peculiar noises now,' said Dick to Anne. 'Noises that animals can't seem to resist! I don't wonder that George has got Timmy tightly by the collar! I'm not a dog, but I find those little whiny noises Wilfrid is making very curious indeed, and I'd love to go nearer!'

'Well, I hope we're not going to have black looks from

George from now on,' said Anne. 'Wilfrid's an awful little idiot at times, and MOST irritating – but he's not bad underneath, if you know what I mean.'

'Well, I don't really,' said Dick, cutting some tomatoes in half. 'I think he's a badly brought-up little pest – and if I were a dog, I'd bite him, not fawn on him! Have I cut up enough tomatoes, Anne?'

'Good gracious, yes!' said Anne. 'How ever many do you think we're going to eat – forty or fifty? Look, you open this tin for me, Dick. I hate opening tins. I nearly always cut myself.'

'Don't you ever open one again, then,' said Dick. 'I'm the official tin-opener from now on! Dear old Anne, whatever should we do without you? You take everything on your shoulders, and we just *let* you! We all ought to help you more.'

'No, don't,' said Anne, in alarm. 'I *like* doing things on my own. You lot would only break things or upset them. You're all so ham-handed when it comes to washing-up or setting out crockery, though I know you *mean* well.'

'So we are all ham-handed, are we?' said Dick, pretending to be offended. 'When have *I* ever broken anything, I'd like to know? I'm just as careful as you when I handle crockery!'

Alas for Dick! The glass he was holding suddenly slipped from his hand, fell to the floor, and broke! Anne looked at him and gave a sudden delighted giggle. 'Old ham-hand!' she said. 'Can't pick up a glass without dropping it! Look, take out this tray for me, and for goodness' sake don't drop *that*!'

They all had a delicious lunch, and ate practically everything. Wilfrid sat a little away from everyone, scattering crumbs around as he ate. Birds of all kinds were soon round him, even hopping on to his hands. A magpie flew down to his left shoulder. Wilfrid greeted it like an old friend. 'Hallo, Maggie Pie! How's the family? I hope Polly Pie has recovered from her cold. And is Peter Pie's bad leg better? And what about old Grandpa Pie – does he still chase you young ones?'

The magpie put its glossy head on one side and chattered back to him in bird language, which Wilfrid appeared to understand. He stroked the bird's gleaming breast, and fondled it lovingly. George deliberately

410

didn't watch. She turned her back on Wilfrid and the magpie, and talked to Timmy. The others couldn't help being amused.

The magpie put an end to Wilfrid's conversation very suddenly. The boy was about to put half a tomato into his mouth when the bird bent down its head and snatched away the tomato with its powerful beak. Then it rose quickly into the air on its big wings, making a noise exactly as if it were laughing!

Everyone roared with laughter except the surprised Wilfrid. 'He's gone to take your tomato to Polly Pie, I should think,' said Anne, and that made everyone laugh again.

'I'll have another tomato now, please,' said Wilfrid.

'Sorry. You're unlucky. They're all gone,' said Dick.

It was lovely sitting up on the hillside, watching the boats in the harbour, and seeing the beautiful, white-sailed yachts bending to and fro in the strong wind that blew there. They could all see Whispering Island quite clearly, and noticed that no boats went anywhere near it. Clearly everyone knew that men might be there, watching for intruders.

'There might be badgers there,' said Wilfrid, suddenly. 'I've never been really *close* to a badger.'

'I shouldn't think anyone but you would *want* to be!' said George. 'Smelly things! There's one thing – you can't call one with your whistle-pipe – there aren't any here!'

'Wilfrid – get out your pipe and make the little rabbits come again,' said Anne, suddenly. 'While we're all sitting here quietly. Would they come?'

'Yes, I think so,' said Wilfrid, and felt in his pocket. He felt in another pocket, and looked worried. Then he stood up and patted himself all over, looking really distressed. He stared round at the others, anguish on his face.

'It's gone,' he said. 'I must have lost it! It's gone. I'll never have another one like it, never.'

'Oh, it *must* be in one of your pockets,' said Dick, touched by the look on the boy's face. 'Here, let *me* feel.'

But no – the pipe wasn't there. Wilfrid looked as if he were about to burst into tears. He began to hunt all round, and everyone helped him. No – not quite everyone. George didn't. Dick glanced at her, and frowned. George was *pleased* that the precious pipe was lost. How she must dislike poor Wilfrid! Well, he *was* dislikeable at

412

times, no doubt about it – but he was so distressed now that surely nobody could help feeling sorry for him!

George got up and began to clear away the remains of the meal. She carried plates and glasses to the cottage, and after a while Anne followed her.

'I'm sorry for poor old Wilfrid, aren't you?' she said.

'No, I'm not,' said George, shortly. 'Serves him right! I hope he never finds his silly pipe. That will teach him not to try and get Timmy away from me!'

'Oh, don't be silly! He only does it for fun!' said Anne, shocked. 'Why do you take things so seriously, George? You know Timmy loves you better than anyone in the world and always will. He's your dog and nobody, nobody else's! Wilfrid's only teasing you when he tries to get Timmy to go to him.'

'Timmy goes, though,' said George, desperately. 'And he shouldn't. He *shouldn't*.'

'He can't help it, I think,' said Anne. 'Wilfrid has some peculiar attraction for animals – and that little whistle-pipe of his is like a magic call to them.'

'I'm *glad* it's gone!' said George. 'Glad, glad, glad!'

'Then I think you're silly and unkind,' said Anne, and walked off, knowing that she could do nothing with George in this mood. She worried a little as she went. Did George *know* where the pipe was? Had *she* found it – and hidden it – or destroyed it? No – no! George could be difficult and unkind at times, but she wasn't *mean*. And *what* a mean thing it would be, to destroy the beautiful little pipe with its magic trills!

Anne went back to the others, meaning to try and comfort Wilfrid – but he wasn't there. 'Where's he gone?' asked Anne.

'To look for his precious whistle-pipe,' said Dick. 'He's really heartbroken about it, I think. He says he's going to walk back the way we came from the golf course, and then he's going to walk everywhere there that we walked this morning, and hunt and hunt. He's even going down to the clubhouse to see if he dropped it there. He'll never find it!'

'Poor old Wilfrid!' said Anne, tender-hearted as ever. 'I wish he'd waited for me. I'd have gone with him. He's awfully upset, isn't he? Won't he be able to call the wild animals to him any more?'

'I've no idea,' said Dick. 'Er – I suppose old George doesn't know anything about it? Perhaps that's a mean thing to say – but George might have found it and kept it just for a joke.'

'No. No, I don't think she'd do that,' said Anne. 'It would be a *very* poor joke. Well – we'll just have to hope Wilfrid finds it. What are you going to do this afternoon? Sleep, by the look of you!'

'Yes – sleep out in the warm sun here, till three o'clock,' said Julian. 'Then I'm going for a walk – down to the harbour. I might even have a bathe.'

'We'll all go,' said Dick, sleepily. 'Oh how lovely it is to feel lazy – and warm – and well-fed – and sleeeeeeepy! So long, everyone! I'm asleep!'

CHAPTER NINE

Off to Whispering Island

THE TWO boys, and Anne and George, slept soundly in the sum until just past three o'clock. Then a large fly buzzed around Anne's head and awoke her. She sat up and looked at her watch.

'Gracious! It's ten past three!' she said, in surprise. 'Wake up, Julian! Dick, stir yourself! Don't you want to go and bathe?'

Yawning loudly the two boys sat up, and looked all round. George was still asleep. Wilfrid hadn't yet come back.

'Still hunting for his precious pipe, I suppose,' said Anne. 'Get up, you two boys. Dick, you're *not* to lie down, you'll only go to sleep again. Where are your bathing things? I'll get them. And does anyone know where our bathing towels are? We'll probably have to dress and undress with them round us!'

'They're up in our room, chucked into a corner,' said Dick, sleepily. 'Gosh, I *was* sound asleep. I really thought I was in my bed when I awoke!'

Anne went to fetch the bathing towels and the bathing things. She called back to the boys. 'I've got everything. Buck up, Julian, *don't* go to sleep again!'

'Right!' said Julian, sitting up and stretching himself. 'Oh, this sun – it's GLORIOUS!'

He poked Dick with his toe. 'Get up! We'll leave you behind if you snore again. George, goodbye – we're going!'

George sat up, yawning, and Timmy stood over her and licked her cheek. She patted him. 'All right, Timmy, I'm ready. It's so warm that I'm LONGING for a dip – and you'll love it too, Tim!'

Carrying their bathing things they made their way down the hill, and across a stretch of moorland to the edge of the sea, Timmy running joyously behind them. Beyond lay Whispering Island, a great tree-clad mass, and all around and about little boats plied, and yachts sailed in the wind, enjoying themselves in the great harbour which stretched far beyond the island to a big seaside town on the opposite coast.

The four went behind some rocks, and stripped off their clothes, emerging three minutes later in their scanty bathing things. Anne raced to the edge of the water, and let it lap over her toes. 'Lovely!' she said. 'It's not a bit cold! I *shall* enjoy my swim!'

'Woof!' said Timmy and plunged into the water. He loved the sea too, and was a fine swimmer! He waited for George to come in and then swam to her. She put her arms round his neck and let him drag her along with him. Dear Timmy! How strong he was, thought George.

They had a wonderful time in the water. Further out the waves were big and curled over like miniature water- falls, sweeping the children along with them. They yelled in joy, and choked when the water splashed into their mouths. It was an ideal day for bathing.

When they came out, they lay on the sand in the sun, Timmy beside George, keeping guard as usual. It was really warm. George sat up and looked longingly out to sea, where the wind was whipping up the waves tremen- dously.

'Wish we had a boat!' she said. 'If we were back home, I could get out my own boat, and we could go out in the cool breeze and get dry.'

Julian pointed lazily to a big notice not far off. It said 'BOATS FOR HIRE. ENQUIRE AT HUT.'

'Oh good!' said George. 'I'll go and enquire. I'd *love* a good row!'

She slipped on her sandals, and went to the hut to which the sign pointed. A boy of about fifteen sat there, staring out to sea. He looked round as George came along.

'Want a boat?' he said.

'Yes, please. How much?' asked George. 'For four of us – and a dog.'

'Three pounds an hour,' said the boy. 'Or six pounds a day. Or fifteen pounds a week. Better to take it by the week if you're staying here. It works out very cheap then.'

George went back to the boys and Anne. 'Shall we take the boat by the week?' she said. 'It'll cost fifteen pounds. We could do lots of rowing about, and it would be fun.'

'Right,' said Dick. 'Anyone got any money?'

'There's some in my pocket, but not enough, I'm afraid,' said Julian. 'I'll go and fix up the boat for us to have tomorrow – we'll take it for a whole week. I can easily bring the money with me in the morning.'

The boat boy was very obliging. 'You can have the boat today and onwards, if you like, you needn't wait till tomorrow,' he said. '*I* know you'll bring me the money all right! So, if you'd like to have it this after-noon, it's up to you. Choose which boat you like.

417

They're all the same. If you want to take it out at night too and do some fishing, you can – but tie it up safe, won't you?'

'Of course,' said Julian, going to look at the boats. He beckoned to the others, and they all came over.

'Any boat we like, day *or* night!' said Julian. 'Which do you fancy? *Starfish – Splasho – Adventure – Seagull – Rock-a-bye*? They all look good, sound little boats to me!'

'I'd like *Adventure*, I think,' said George, thinking that that particular little boat looked sturdy, clean and sound. 'Nice name – and nice little boat!'

So *Adventure* it was! 'And a jolly good name for any boat of ours!' said Dick, pushing it down to the sea with Julian. 'Whooooosh! There she goes! Steady, my beauty – we want to get in! Chuck in all clothes, George! We can dress when we feel cold.'

Soon they were all in the boat, bobbing about on the waves. Julian took the oars and pulled out to sea. Now they were in the full breeze – and a strong one it was too! 'I'm certainly not hot any more!' said George, pulling her bathing towel round her shoulders.

The tide was running out, and pulled the boat strongly out to sea. Whispering Island suddenly seemed very much nearer! 'Better look out!' said George, suddenly. 'We don't know if a keeper's on guard somewhere on the shore of the island. We're getting pretty near.'

But the outgoing tide swept the boat on and on towards the island, so that very soon they could see a sandy shore. Dick then took one oar, and Julian the other, and they tried to row against the tide and take the boat back into calm water.

It was no good. The tide was far too strong. Very soon the boat was quite near the shore of the island, and then an enormous wave flung them right up the sand and left the boat grounded as it went back again. It slid over to one side, and they all promptly fell out!

'Whew!' said Julian. 'What a tide! I'd no idea it ran so strongly, or I'd never have brought the boat out so far.'

'What shall we do!' said Anne, rather scared. She kept looking all round for a keeper with a gun. Suppose they got into real trouble through coming right on to the island?

'I think we'll have to stay on the island till the tide turns, and we can row back on it,' said Julian. 'I can't think why that boat boy didn't warn us about the tide. I suppose he thought we knew.'

They pulled the boat a little further up on the firm sand, took out their bundles of clothes and hid them under a bush. They walked up the beach towards a wood, thick with great trees. As they neared them, they heard a strange, mysterious sound.

'Whispering!' said George, stopping. 'The trees are *really* whispering. Listen! It's just as if they were talking to one another under their breath! No wonder it's called Whispering Island!'

'I don't like it much,' said Anne. 'It almost sounds as if they're saying nasty things about us!'

'Shooey, shooey, shooey, shooey!' said the trees, nodding towards one another as the wind shook them. 'Shooey, shooey!'

'JUST the noise of whispering!' said George. 'Well – what do we do now? We'll have to wait an hour or two till the tide turns again!'

'Shall we explore?' said Dick. 'After all, we've got Timmy with us. No one is likely to attack us if they see *him*!'

'They can shoot him, can't they, if they have guns?' said George. 'If he growled one of his terrifying growls, and ran at them showing his teeth, they'd be scared to bits and fire at him.'

'I think you're right,' said Julian, angry with himself for landing them all into what might be serious trouble. 'Keep your hand on Timmy's collar, George.'

'You know what I think?' said Dick suddenly. 'I think we ought to try and find the guards, and tell them the tide swept us on to the island quite by accident – we couldn't stop the boat surging on! We're not grown-ups, come to snoop around, so they're sure to believe us – and we'd be safe from any chasing or shooting then.'

They all looked at Julian. He nodded. 'Yes – good idea. Give ourselves up, and ask for help! After all, we hadn't any real intention of actually *landing* – the tide simply *threw* the boat into that sandy cove!'

So they walked up to the back of the cove and into the wood, whose whispering was very loud indeed, once they were actually among the trees. No one was to be seen. The wood was so thick that it was in parts quite difficult to clamber through. After about ten minutes very hard walking and clambering, Julian came to a stop. He had seen something through the trees.

The others pressed behind him. Julian pointed in front, and the others saw what looked liked a great grey wall, made of stone.

'The old castle, I imagine!' Julian whispered, and at once the trees themselves seemed to whisper even more loudly! They all made their way to the wall, and walked alongside it. It was a very high wall indeed, and they could hardly *see* the top! They came to a corner and peeped round. A great courtyard lay there – quite empty.

'Better shout, I think,' said Dick, beginning to feel rather creepy, but before they could do that two enormous men suddenly came down a flight of great stone steps. They looked so fierce that Timmy couldn't help giving a blood-curdling growl. They stopped short at once and looked all round, startled.

'The noise came from over there,' said one of the men, pointing to his left – and, to the children's great relief, both swung off in the wrong direction!

'We'd better get back to the cove,' whispered Julian. 'I don't like the look of those men at all – they look proper thugs. Quiet as you can, now. George, don't let Timmy bark.'

They made their way back beside the stone wall, through the whispering trees, and there they were at the cove.

'We'd better row back as quickly as we can,' said Julian. 'I think something's wrong here. Those men looked like foreigners. They certainly weren't game-keepers. I wish we hadn't come.'

'Ju – where's our boat?' said Dick in a shocked voice. 'It's gone. This can't be the right cove!'

The others stared round. Certainly there was no boat! They *must* have come to the wrong cove.

'It looks the same cove to *me*,' said George. 'Except that the sea has come in a bit more. Do you think it took our boat away – gosh, look at that big wave sweeping right in – and sucking back!'

'My word, yes! Our boat could easily have been dragged out on a wave like that!' said Julian, very worried. 'Look out – here comes another!'

'It *is* the same cove!' said Anne, looking under a bush at the back. 'Here are our clothes, look! We hid them here!'

'Take them out quickly!' called Julian, as another big

wave swept right in. 'What an idiot I am! We should have pulled our boat as far up as we could.'

'I'm cold now,' said Anne. 'I'm going to dress. It will be easier to carry a bathing-suit than a heap of clothes!'

'Good idea!' said Dick, and they all promptly dressed, feeling warmer at once.

'We might as well leave our bathing things under the bush where we left our clothes,' said George. 'At least we'll know it's the same cove if we find them there!'

'The thing is – what are we going to do *now*?' said Julian, worried. 'No boat to get back in – and why on earth did we choose one called *Adventure*! We might have *known* something would happen!'

CHAPTER TEN

The Five are in a fix

JULIAN WENT to the mouth of the cove and looked out over the waves, hoping that he might see their boat bobbing somewhere. I could swim out to it if so, he thought, and bring it in. No – there's not a sign of a boat! I could kick myself for being so careless!

Dick came up, looking worried. 'I suppose it's too far to swim back to the mainland, isn't it?' he said. 'I could have a shot – and get another boat and come back for everyone.'

'No. Too far,' said Julian. 'The tide's too strong for any swimmer at the moment. We're certainly in a fix!'

'We can't signal, I suppose?' said Dick.

'What with?' asked Julian. 'You could wave a shirt for an hour and it wouldn't be seen from the mainland!'

'Well – we must think of *something*!' said Dick, exasperated. 'What about trying to find a boat *here*? Surely those men must have one to get to and fro.'

'Of course!' said Julian, clapping Dick on the back. 'Where are my brains? They seem to be going soft or something! We could snoop round and about tonight, to see if there's a boat anywhere. They may have two or three. They'd have to get food from the mainland at times.'

The two girls and Timmy came up then, and Timmy whined. 'He doesn't seem to like this island,' said George. 'I think he smells danger!'

'I bet he does!' said Dick, putting his hand on Timmy's firm head. 'I'm jolly glad he's with us. Can you girls think of any good ideas? We can't!'

'We could signal,' said George.

'No good. A signal from here couldn't be seen,' said Dick. 'We've already thought of that.'

'Well – if we lit a fire here on the beach tonight, when the tide's out, surely *that* would be seen?' said Anne.

Dick and Julian looked at one another. 'Yes!' said Julian. 'If we lit it on a hilly bit it would be better still–on that cliff up there, for instance.'

'Wouldn't the guards see it?' asked Dick.

'We'd have to chance that,' said Julian. 'Yes – we could do that. Good idea, Anne. But we're going to get jolly hungry, aren't we? Anyone got anything to eat?'

'I've two bars of chocolate – a bit soft now though,' said George, digging into the pocket of her shorts.

'And I've some peppermints,' said Anne. 'What about you boys? You always take barley-sugars about with you, Dick – don't say you haven't any just when we could all do with them!'

'I've a new packet!' said Dick. 'Let's all have one now!' He pulled the packet from his pocket and handed it round. Soon they were all sucking barley-sugars. Timmy was given one too, but his was gone in a flash!

'Wasted on you, Tim, absolutely *wasted*!' said Anne. 'Crick, crack, swallow – that's all a barley-sugar means to you! Why can't dogs suck a sweet as we do! They never seem to suck *anything*. No, Timmy, don't go sniffing into Dick's pocket for another!'

Timmy was disappointed. He went snuffling round the cove, and then, scenting a rabbit smell, he followed it

425

with his nose to the ground. The children didn't notice that he had disappeared but went on talking, trying to solve their very real difficulty.

No boat. No food. No way of getting help except by signalling in some way. *Not* very funny, thought Dick.

And then, very suddenly, a loud sound broke the silence – CRACK!

Everyone jumped up at once. 'That was a gunshot,' said Dick. 'The keepers! But what are they shooting at?'

'Where's Timmy?' cried George, looking all round. 'Tim, Tim, where are you TIM!'

Everyone's heart went cold. Timmy! No, the shot couldn't have been meant for old Timmy! Surely the keepers wouldn't shoot a *dog*!

George was nearly mad with dread. She clutched at Dick, tears streaming down her cheeks. 'Dick! It couldn't be Timmy, could it? Oh Timmy, where are you? TIMMY! Come to me!'

'Listen! Listen a minute, George!' said Dick, as shouts came from the distance. 'I thought I heard Tim whine then. Isn't that him coming through the bushes?'

There was the noise of rustling as some creature pressed through the last year's bracken fronds – and then Timmy's head appeared, his bright eyes looking for them.

'Oh Timmy, darling Timmy, I thought you'd been shot!' cried George, hugging the big dog. '*Did* they shoot at you? Are you hurt anywhere?'

'I bet I know why he was shot at,' said Dick. 'Look what he's got in his mouth – half a ham! Drop it, you robber, you!'

Timmy stood there, the ham in his mouth, wagging his
tail joyously. He had felt hungry, and was sure the others
did too – so he had gone hunting!

'Where did you get that, you bad dog?' said Julian.
Timmy wished he could tell him. He would have said,
'Well, I went sniffing after a rabbit – and I came to a shed

stored with tins of food – and one was open with this piece of ham inside, waiting for me. And here it is!'

He dropped the ham at George's feet. It smelt extremely good. 'Well, thanks, old fellow,' said Julian. 'We could do with some of that – though we'll have to pay for it when we meet the owner, whoever he is!'

'Julian – he *has* been shot at!' said George, in a trembling voice. 'Look – his tail's bleeding, and some fur is gone.'

'Oh, yes!' said Julian, examining Timmy's tail. 'Good gracious – those fellows mean business. I really think I'd better find them and tell them we're here, in case they take a pot-shot at us too!'

'Well, let's go *now* – all of us,' said Dick. 'They probably thought Timmy was a wolf or a fox or something, slinking through the trees. Poor old fellow!'

Timmy was not at all disturbed. He was so proud of finding and bringing back the ham that he even wagged his wounded tail!

'It's quite certain that no animals or birds will be tame and friendly on this island now,' said Anne. 'They'll have been scared stiff by the gamekeepers potting at this and that.'

'You're right,' said Julian. 'It rather makes me think that the fellows on the island are no longer merely gamekeepers, put in to preserve the wildlife, and to frighten sightseers away – but real, fierce guards of some kind. Like those two horrible men we saw in the court-yard!'

'Well, what *are* they guarding then?' said George.

'That's what I'd very much like to find out,' said Julian. 'And I think perhaps I'll snoop round a bit and see what I can discover. When it's getting dark, though, not now.'

'I wish we hadn't come,' said Anne. 'I wish we were safe in our cottage with Wilfrid. I wonder if he's found his whistle-pipe. Goodness, it seems *ages* since we hired that boat!'

'Can't we go quietly through the woods and explore a bit?' asked George. 'Or walk round the shore to see if there's a boat anywhere?' I'm getting bored, sitting here, talking.'

'Well – I suppose old Tim would give us warning at once if he heard anyone near,' said Julian, who was also longing to stretch his legs. 'We'll go in single file and make as little noise as we can. Timmy can go ahead. He'll give us instant warning if we come near any of the keepers.'

They all stood up, and Timmy looked at them, wagging his nicked tail. 'I'll look after you,' said his two bright eyes. 'Don't be afraid!'

They made their way carefully and quietly through the whispering trees. 'Sh, sh, sh, shoo, shooey,' said the leaves above their heads, as if warning everyone to go as quietly as possible. And then suddenly Timmy stopped and gave a low, warning growl. They all stood still at once, listening.

They could hear nothing. They were in a dense part of the wood, and it was dark and sunless. What was Timmy growling at? He took a step forward, and growled softly again.

Julian went forward too, as silently as he could. He stopped suddenly and stared. What in the world was that strange figure, gleaming out of the shadows? His heart began to beat loudly. The figure stood there, silently, an arm outstretched as if pointing at something!

He thought it moved and he took a step backwards in fear. Was it a ghost or something? It was so very, very white and shone so strangely. The others, coming up behind, suddenly saw it too and stopped in fright. Timmy growled again, and all the hackles on his neck rose up. What was THIS?

Everyone stood absolutely still, and Anne gave a gulp. She took hold of Dick's arm, and he held it tightly against him. And then George gave a very small laugh. To everyone's horror she went forward, and touched the hand of the gleaming figure.

'How do you do?' she said. 'It is so nice to meet a well-mannered statue!'

Well! A statue! Only a *statue*! It had looked so real standing there, and yet so ghostly. Everyone heaved a sigh of relief, and Timmy ran forward and sniffed at the statue's flowing robes.

'Look around you,' said Julian. 'The wood's full of statues just here – and aren't they BEAUTIFUL! I hope they don't suddenly come alive – they really look as if they might!'

CHAPTER ELEVEN

A strange discovery

THE CHILDREN were astonished to see so many gleaming statues standing in the darkness of the wood. They wandered round them, and then came to a large shed. They peeped inside.

'Look here!' said Dick, excited. 'Long, deep boxes, strong as iron! And see what's in these two!'

They all came to look. In the first, packed in what looked like sawdust, was a beautifully carved statue of a boy. The next box seemed to be entirely full of sawdust, and Anne had to scrape quite a lot away to see if anything was packed there too.

'It's a little stone angel!' she said, scraping sawdust from a quaint little face, a small crown and the tips of small wings. 'Lovely! Why are these statues being pack away like this?'

'Use your brain!' said Dick. 'It's obvious that they're works of art – and are probably very old. They're being packed to send away in some boat or ship – to be transported somewhere where they'll fetch a lot of money – America, probably!'

'Did they come from the old castle, do you think?' asked George. 'It's quite near. I expect this shed belongs to it. But how was it that the police didn't find them in the castle when they searched? They must have gone there, and looked into every corner! And what about the statues in the wood outside – why haven't *they* been packed away?'

'Too big, probably,' said Julian. 'And too heavy. A small boat wouldn't be strong enough to take great things like that. But those little statues are quite perfect for transporting – they don't weigh as much as the big ones – and they aren't marked by the weather, through standing in rain, sun and snow! Not a mark on them!'

'You're right,' said Anne. 'I noticed that those big ones outside were green here and there, and some had bits knocked off them. I wish we could get inside the castle and see the things there!'

'The man at the golf club, the one we took those lost balls to – *he* said something about statues as white as snow, standing in this wood – do you remember?' said Dick.

'Yes. They must have stood there for some time,' said Julian. 'I don't feel they can be very valuable, else they

432

would be put carefully indoors, under cover. But these little beauties – I guess they're worth a lot of money!'

'Who do you suppose packed them in here?' said Anne.

'Maybe those big men we saw,' said Julian. 'Even small statues like these need someone very strong indeed to carry them here to this shed, and pack them like this. Then, of course, they would have to be carried to some boat – or ship – probably to a boat first and then rowed out to a waiting ship. But I don't think those guards are the men behind all this – someone with a great knowledge of old things must be the ringleader. He probably heard the old legend of the island, came to have a look round, and made quite a lot of interesting discoveries!'

'*Where?*' asked George. 'In the castle?'

'Probably – though carefully hidden away!' said Julian. 'For all we know there may be scores of really valuable old treasures hidden there still. That sword with a jewelled handle, for instance! And the bed made of gold, and . . .'

'To think they might all be quite near us, somewhere on Whispering Island!' said Anne. 'Wouldn't I love to be able to say I'd slept on a bed of pure gold!'

'Well, I think you'd find it jolly hard,' said Dick.

Timmy suddenly gave a small whine, and licked George's hand. 'What is it?' she said. 'What do you want, Timmy?'

'Perhaps he's hungry,' said Anne.

'Thirsty, more likely!' said Julian. 'Look at his tongue hanging out!'

'Oh, *poor* Tim – you haven't had a drink for hours!' said George. 'Well – where on earth can we get you one?

We'll have to look for a puddle, I'm afraid. Come on!'

They left the shed where the beautiful little statues were lying in their sawdust, and went out into the sunshine. Everywhere was dry, Julian felt worried.

'We shall *all* be thirsty soon!' he said. 'I wonder where we can get some water?'

'Would it be too dangerous to go near the castle and see if there's a tap anywhere?' asked George, ready to face almost anything to get her dog a drink!

'Yes, it would,' said Julian, in a very decided voice. 'We're not going near any of those men with guns. They might have been told to shoot on sight, and that wouldn't be very pleasant. We'd be peppered all over with shot!'

'Look – what's that round thing over there – like a little circular wall?' said Dick, pointing to something behind the shed where the statues lay in their boxes.

They all went over to it – and Anne guessed what it was at once! 'A well! An old well!' she said. 'Look, it has an old wooden beam over the top, with a pulley to wind and unwind a bucket. *Is* there a bucket – let's hope so! We can let it down to the water and fill it for Timmy then.'

Timmy put his paws on the rim of the wall and sniffed. Water! That was what he wanted more than anything. He began to whine.

'All right, Timmy – we'll send the bucket down,' said George. 'It's still on the hook! Julian, this handle's awfully stiff – can you turn it to let down the bucket?'

Julian tried with all his strength – and quite suddenly the rope loosened, and the bucket gave a sudden jerk and jump. Alas – it jumped right off the hook, and with a weird echoing, jangling sound, fell from the top to the bottom of the well – landing in the water with a terrific splash!

'Blow, blow, blow!' said Julian, and Timmy gave an anguished howl. He peered town at the lost bucket, now on its side in the water at the bottom of the well gradually filling itself.

'It'll probably sink below the water now,' said Julian with a groan. 'Is there a ladder down the well? – if so I could shin down and get the bucket.'

But there wasn't, though it looked as if there had been at some time, for here and there were staples in the brick side of the well wall.

'What can we do?' asked Anne. 'Can we possibly pull up the bucket?'

'No – I'm afraid we can't,' said Dick. 'But wait a minute – I could shin down the rope, couldn't I, and pick the bucket out of the water? And easily get up again, because George and Julian could turn the well handle, and pull me up that way!'

'Righto. Down you go then,' said Julian. 'The rope's good and strong, not frayed or rotten. We'll wind you and the bucket up all right!'

The boy sat on the side of the well wall, and reached out for the rope. He swung himself on to it, and swayed there a moment or two, looking down the long, dark hole below him, with the water at the bottom. Then down he went, hand-over-hand, just as he often did at school in the gym.

He came to the bottom, reached down, took hold of the bucket handle, and filled the bucket full. The water felt as cold as ice to his hand. 'All right. Pull me up!' he shouted, his voice sounding very hollow and strange as it rose up through the well walls.

Dick was heavy to pull up. Julian and George turned

the handle valiantly, but it was slow work. Gradually Dick came up nearer and and nearer to the top. When he was halfway they heard him give an exclamation, and call out something; but they couldn't make out what it was and went on winding the groaning rope, slowly but surely.

They reached down and took the bucket from Dick as soon as his head appeared at the top. Timmy fell on it with excited barks, and began to lap vigorously.

'Didn't you hear me yelling to you to stop when I was halfway up?' demanded Dick, still swinging on the rope. 'Don't let go that handle. Hang on to it for a minute.'

'What's the excitement?' asked Julian, in surprise. '*Why* did you yell to us? We couldn't make out what you said.'

Dick swung himself to one side, caught hold of the well top and hauled himself up, so that he could sit on the well wall. 'I shouted because I suddenly saw something quite peculiar as I came up the well,' he said. 'And I wanted to stop and see what it was!'

'Well – what *was* it?' asked Julian.

'I don't quite know. It looked awfully like a little door! An iron door,' said Dick. 'Hey, don't let Timmy drink all that water – he'll be ill. We'll let the pail down again in a minute and get some more for ourselves.'

'Go on about what you saw,' said George. 'How *could* there be a door in the side of a well going deep down into the earth?'

'Well, I tell you, there *was* one,' said Dick. 'Look, Timmy's gone and upset the pail now! Let's send it down on the pulley to be filled again, and I'll go down on the rope again too. But when I come up and you hear me shout "Stop" just stop winding, see?'

'Here's the bucket for the hook,' said Julian. 'I'll be careful not to jerk it off this time. Ready?'

Down went Dick and the bucket again – splash went the bucket and filled with water once more. Then up came Dick again, wound up by Julian and George as before. As soon as they heard him shout 'Stop', they stopped their winding and peered down.

They saw Dick peering hard at the side of the well wall,

and pulling at it with his fingers. Then he shouted again. 'All right. Up we go!'

They hauled him up to the top, and he clambered off the rope, swung himself on to the well wall and sat there.

'Yes. It *is* some kind of opening in the well wall – it *is* a door – and it has a bolt this side to undo, but it was too stiff for my fingers. I'd have to go down and jiggle it about with my knife before I could loosen it.'

'A door in a well! But where on earth would it lead to?' said Julian, astonished.

'That's what we're going to find out!' grinned Dick, rather pleased with himself. 'Who would ever think of putting a door in the side of a well? *Some*body did – but WHY? Very cunning – and mysterious – and unguessable. I rather think I'll go straight down again and see if I can't open that door – and discover what it leads to!'

'Oh DO, Dick do!' said George. 'If you don't, *I* will!'

'Hang on to the rope. Down I go again!' said Dick. And down he went, much to Timmy's surprise. The others looked down anxiously. Could Dick open the well door? What would he find behind it? Quick, Dick, quick – everybody's waiting for you!

CHAPTER TWELVE

A great surprise – and a shock for George

As soon as Dick shouted 'Stop', Julian and George hung on to the rope to stop it going down any further. Dick was swinging just opposite the strange door. He began to feel round it, and to jiggle it. It had no lock, apparently, but there was a bolt on his side. He tried to push back the bolt – and suddenly it came away from the door, and dropped down into the well. It had rusted so much that it could not even hold to the door, once it was handled!

The door felt loose, now the bolt was gone. Dick ran his hands round it, trying to loosen it further and banged it with his fist. Rust fell off it, and Dick's hands were soon brown with the old, old rust.

He saw a little knob at the top of the door and gave it a tug. Ah – the door felt looser now. He ran his knife all round the edges, scraping away all the rust he could find. Then he managed to get his strongest knife-blade in between the door edge and the well wall, and used it as a lever to force the door open.

It opened slowly and painfully, with creaks and groans. It was about fifty centimetres high and not quite so much wide. Dick pulled it back with difficulty and then peered through the hole.

He could see nothing at all but black darkness – how very disappointing! He fumbled in his pocket to see if he had a torch. Yes – good! He shone it through the little door, his hand trembling with excitement. What would he see?

His torch was small and not very powerful. The light fell first of all on a face with gleaming eyes, and Dick had such a shock that he almost fell down the well. The eyes seemed to glare up at him in a very threatening manner! He switched his torch to the right – and yet another face gleamed up to him. An odd face, thought Dick. Yellow as can be! YELLOW! YELLOW! I believe that face is made of gold!

His hand was trembling even more, he shone his torch here and there through the opening, catching first one yellow face in its light, and then another. The faces had yellow bodies too, and their eyes glinted very strangely.

I believe – yes, I really do believe – that I've found the hiding place of the golden statues, thought Dick. And those gleaming eyes must be precious jewels. I did have a shock when I saw them all looking at me! Whatever is this place they're in?

'DICK! What can you see? Do tell us!' yelled Julian, and poor Dick almost fell off the rope when the shouts echoed round him. 'Pull me up!' he shouted. 'It's too extraordinary for words. Pull me up and I'll tell you!'

And before a minute had passed he was standing by the others, his eyes gleaming almost as brightly as the eyes of the golden statues, his words tumbling over one another.

'That door leads into the place where all the treasures are hidden. The first thing I saw was a golden statue staring at me – brilliant eyes in a yellow face – a golden face, real gold! There are dozens of them. I don't think they liked me very much – they glared so! Thank goodness they didn't say a word – though I half expected them to. What a hiding place – right down under the earth!'

'There must be another entrance to it,' said Julian, thrilled to hear such extraordinary news. 'The well door must be a secret one. Statues couldn't be pushed through it. My word, what a find, Dick.'

'Let's all go down in turn and look through the door!' said George. 'I can't believe it. I think I must be dreaming it. Quick, let me go down!'

One by one they all went down on the rope and looked through the door. Anne came back rather scared. She had felt very strange when she had seen the silent statues looking at her. 'I know they're not *really* looking, it's only that their eyes gleam,' she said. 'But I kept expecting one or other to take a step forward and speak to me!'

'Well – the next thing to do is to climb through the

door, and see exactly where the statues are underground,'
said Julian. 'And find out the opening *they* were brought
in by. There must be a door the other end of their room,
through which they were brought. What a hiding place,
though! No wonder the police could find nothing in the
way of statues or other treasures.'

'We might find the golden sword there, with the
jewelled handle!' said Anne. 'And the golden bed.'

She had hardly finished speaking when there came a
loud noise from behind them. Timmy was barking his
head off! Whatever was the matter?

'Sh!' said George, fiercely. 'You'll bring the guards
here, you idiot! Stop it!'

Timmy stopped barking and whined instead. Then he
ran off towards the wood, his tail waving happily. 'Who
in the world is he going to meet?' said George, amazed.
'Someone he knows, by the look of his tail!'

The others all followed Timmy, who raced along
towards the cove where they had landed – and lost their
boat. And there, in the cove, was another boat! A small
one, to be sure, but still a boat – and by it, fondling
Timmy, was Wilfrid! Wilfrid! What an amazing thing!

'WILFRID! How did you get here – did you hire that
boat? Did you come all by yourself? Did you . . .'

Wilfrid grinned round in delight, thrilled at the surprise he was giving everyone. Timmy licked him without
stopping, and George didn't even seem to notice!

'Well,' he said, 'you didn't come back, so I guessed
something was wrong – and when the boat boy told me
you'd taken one of his boats and it had been reported
tossing about, empty, on the water near the island, I
guessed what had happened – I said, "Aha! they didn't

make the boat fast when they got to the island – and now they're marooned there!" You were pretty mean to go without me – but I guessed you'd be pleased to see me if I borrowed a boat and came over!'

Anne was so pleased that she gave the boy a hug. 'Now we can go back whenever we want to,' she said.

'But we *don't* want to, at the moment,' said Dick. 'We've made some startling discoveries, Wilfrid – and I'm jolly pleased you'll be able to share in them! Er – what have you got in your pocket? Something keeps poking its head out at me.'

'Oh, that's only a baby hedgehog,' said Wilfrid, taking it out gently. 'It got trodden on – by a horse, I think – so I'm just caring for it for a day or two.' He put it back into his pocket. 'But go on – tell me what you've found. Not the lost treasures, surely?'

'Yes!' said Anne. 'We saw them when we went down a well near the castle.'

'Gracious – did somebody throw them into the water there?' said Wilfrid, amazed.

'No,' said Dick, and told him about the curious door in the side of the well wall. Wilfrid's eyes nearly fell out of his head.

'I *am* glad I came!' he said. 'I nearly didn't. I thought you wouldn't really want me – and I knew George wouldn't be pleased, because of Timmy. I can't help him coming round me – and anyway he'd feel hurt if I pushed him off.'

Timmy came nosing round him at that moment, with his ball. He wanted Wilfrid to throw it for him. But Wilfrid didn't notice the ball. He just patted the soft head, and went on talking.

'The boat boy wasn't very pleased when he heard that the boat you hired was loose on the sea. He said you'd hired it for a week, and there it was, back the same day, wet and empty! His cousin brought it in. No damage done.'

'I'll make it up to him when I see him,' said Julian. 'I haven't paid him for the hire of it either, but he knows I will, when I get back. I had no idea that the sea would throw up waves here whose backwash would drag out an unmoored boat.'

'You ought to have taken me with you,' said Wilfrid, grinning. Timmy tired of trying to make him throw his ball, went off to George, who was only too pleased to. She threw it into the air, and Timmy leapt up and caught it.

Then, very suddenly, he made a horrible noise and rolled over, kicking as if he were in great pain. 'What's the matter, Timmy?' cried George, and rushed to him. Wilfrid ran too. The dog was choking, and his eye were almost starting out of his head.

'That ball's stuck in his throat!' cried Wilfrid. 'I knew it was dangerous! I told you it was! Cough it up, Timmy, cough it up. Oh, you poor, choking thing! Oh Timmy, Timmy!'

The boy was beside himself with fear that the dog would choke, as he had once seen another dog do, and as for George, she was wild with terror. Poor Timmy's eyes looked terrible as he choked and choked, trying to get the ball out of his throat.

'He'll choke to death,' cried Wilfrid. 'Julian, force his mouth open, and hold it. I must try to get out the ball. Quick!'

444

Timmy was growing weaker, and it was not too difficult to force his mouth wide open. Wilfrid could see the ball down the dog's throat – the ball with the hole in the middle. He put his small hand into the dog's big mouth, and forced his forefinger into the hole in the ball. His finger joint stuck there – Wilfrid gently drew back his hand – and the ball came too, on his finger! There it was, with his finger still stuck in the hole! Timmy began to breathe again, great panting breaths, while George stroked his head and cried for joy that he was all right.

'I shouldn't have given you that ball, I shouldn't!' she said. 'It was too small for a big dog like you – and you *will* throw them up in the air and catch them. Oh Timmy, Timmy, I'm very very sorry. Timmy, are you all right?'

Wilfrid had gone off, but now came back with some water in the pail. He dipped his hand in it and let drops of water drip into the dog's mouth. Timmy swallowed it gratefully. His throat was sore, but the water was cool and soothing. George let Wilfrid do this without a word. She looked rather white and shaken. Why – Timmy might be dead by now if Wilfrid hadn't put his finger into that hole in the ball and drawn it out!

'Thank you, Wilfrid,' she said, in a low voice. 'You were very clever.'

'Thank goodness the ball had a hole through it,' said Wilfrid, and he put his arms round Timmy's neck. The dog licked him gratefully. Then he turned and licked George too.

'He says he belongs to both of us now,' said George. 'I'll share him with you. You saved his life.'

'Thanks,' said Wilfrid. 'I'd love to have just a *bit* of him – he's the nicest dog I know!'

CHAPTER THIRTEEN

A meal – a sleep – and a disappearance

'I FEEL hungry again,' said George, who always had a very good appetite indeed. 'We've finished all that ham, haven't we? I *had* to give old Timmy some. What about a barley-sugar, Dick?'

'Two more left for each of us – just ten,' said Dick, counting. 'Sorry, Timmy, old thing – none for you this time. Have one, everybody. We'll have five left then!'

'Oh, I quite forget to tell you,' said Wilfrid, taking a barley-sugar. 'I brought some food in my boat! I didn't think you'd taken any, and I guessed you'd soon be jolly hungry!'

'You're a marvel, Wilfrid!' said Julian, wondering why he had ever disliked the boy. 'What have you brought?'

'Come and see,' said Wilfrid, and they all went over to the boat, Timmy walking as close to the boy as he could. Higgledy-piggledy in the boat was a pile of tins, a large loaf of bread, and some butter, looking rather soft.

'Oh good!' said Anne, in delight. 'But how in the world did you carry all this from the cottage to your boat? Look, everyone, Wilfrid has even brought some plates and spoons!'

'I put everything into a sack, and carried it over my shoulder,' said Wilfrid, enjoying everyone's delighted surprise. 'I fell over going down the hill to the shore and all the tins rolled out, and *shot* down the slope!'

Everyone laughed at the thought of tins rolling at top

447

speed down the hill. Anne slipped her arm through Wilfrid's and gave it a squeeze.

'You did really well,' she said and Wilfrid beamed at her, astonished and pleased at everyone's warm friendliness. Timmy went up to the boat and began sniffing at the bread. Then he turned and barked as if to say 'Is there anything here for *me*?'

Wilfrid understood at once. 'Oh *yes* Timmy!' he said. 'I brought a special tin of dogmeat for you – here you are – a large tin of Waggomeat!'

Timmy recognised the tin at once, and barked joyfully. He pawed Wilfrid as if to say 'Come on, then – open it! I'm hungry!'

'Anyone got a tin-opener?' said George. 'It would be too dreadful if we couldn't open the tins!'

'Gosh – I never even *thought* about that!' said Wilfrid. 'What an idiot I am!'

'It's all right. I've got a thing on my pocket-knife that's *supposed* to open tins,' said Dick, taking out a very large closed knife. 'I've never bothered to use it – so let's hope it *will* do the trick. Chuck me a tin, Wilfrid.'

Wilfrid threw him the tin of Waggomeat. With everyone watching very anxiously indeed, Dick opened a peculiar-looking tool in his knife, and jabbed the point into the top of the tin. It worked!

'First time I've ever used it,' said Dick, running the gadget round the tin top. 'Three cheers for the man who thought of including it in a knife!'

'Will Timmy be able to swallow yet?' asked George, anxiously. 'His throat must still be hurting him where that wooden ball choked him.'

'Oh, Timmy will be able to judge that for himself,' said

Julian. 'If I know anything about him not even a sore throat will stop him from wolfing half that tin!'

Julian was right. As soon as Dick scraped out a third of the meat with his knife on to a flat stone nearby, Timmy was wolfing it in great gulps!

'Nothing much the matter with your throat now, Tim!' said Anne, patting him. 'Dear old Tim. Don't ever choke again. I simply couldn't bear it!'

'Let's have a meal ourselves now,' said George. 'We'll open more of those tins. We don't need to be stingy about them because we can leave in Wilfrid's boat at any time, and get back to the mainland.'

Soon they had opened a tin of tuna, two tins of fruit and a large tin of baked beans. They cut the big loaf into six pieces (one for Timmy, of course) and then sat down at the back of the cove to feast.

'Best meal I ever had in my life!' said Dick, enjoying himself. 'Tasty food – fresh air – sea nearby – sun on our heads – and friends sitting all round me!'

'Woof!' said Timmy, at once, and gave Dick a very wet lick.

'He says he couldn't agree more,' said Anne with a laugh.

'The sun's going down,' said George. 'What are we going to do? Go back to the mainland in Wilfrid's boat – or stay here for the night?'

'Stay here,' said Julian. 'Nobody knows we're here, and I want to snoop round a bit tonight, when those men can't see me. There's a lot of things that puzzle me. For instance, how on earth do they send away the things from here – such as those packed statues we saw? It must mean that a fairly big vessel comes along to collect them, I suppose. And I'd like to know how many men there are on the island – presumably the guards we saw, with guns – and the men who have found that underground cave, where everything was hidden. Then we'll go back, tell the police, and leave things to them!'

'Couldn't Wilfrid take the two girls back to the mainland then come back with the boat?' said Dick. 'I don't think we ought to let them run any risk.'

Before Julian could reply, George spoke quickly – and crossly. 'We're staying here – though Anne can go back if she wants to. But Timmy and I are staying with you boys, so that's that.'

'All right, all right, no need to shout!' said Dick, pretending to cover his ears. 'What about you, though, Anne? You're the youngest, and . . .'

'I'm staying,' said Anne. 'I'd be worried stiff all night if I left you on the island. And I certainly don't want to miss any excitement!'

'Right,' said Julian. 'We all stay then. Wilfrid, did you know that Timmy has his nose in the pocket where you keep your hedgehog?'

'Yes. They're just making friends,' said Wilfrid. 'Anyway, the hedgehog's only a baby – his quills won't prick Timmy's nose, they're still too soft. He's a dear little thing. I thought I'd call him Spiky.'

'Wuff,' said Timmy, quite agreeing. He was sitting between George and Wilfrid, very happy indeed, for both fondled him and patted him at the same time.

'I think I'll take a walk round the island,' Wilfrid announced suddenly. 'Timmy, like to come with me?'

Timmy got up at once, but George pulled him down. 'Don't be an idiot, Wilfrid,' she said. 'Timmy's been shot at once by the men here – and I'm not going to risk it again – besides, we don't want them to know we're here.'

'I'd be very careful,' persisted Wilfrid. 'I wouldn't let them spot me. They didn't spot me coming over in the boat.'

Julian sat up very suddenly. 'How do we know they didn't?' he said. 'I never thought of that! They might have a telescope – they might keep watch all the time – they might even have seen *us* in *our* boat! After all, they can't risk being spied on!'

'I don't *think* they could have seen us,' said Dick. 'They would have made a search.'

'I'm jolly sure they didn't see *me*,' boasted Wilfrid. 'They'd have been waiting for me on the shore, if they had.' He got up and looked all round. 'I think I'll go for my walk now,' he said.

'NO! You are DEFINITELY not to go for a walk, Wilfrid,' said Julian, and lay back in the sun again. It was sinking now, but still very bright. Dick began to think of the night, and how he and Julian would snoop round and find the way into that strange place underground where those golden statues stood silently in the darkness.

Then he fell asleep, and only awoke when Anne gave him a friendly punch. He sat up and began a long and leisurely conversation with his sister – and then Anne suddenly looked all round.

'Where's Wilfrid?' she said. They *all* sat up then, and looked startled. Wilfrid was nowhere to be seen!

'He must have slipped away without a sound! said Dick, angrily. 'The little idiot. He's been gone quite a long time! He'll get caught, as sure as can be. Good thing Timmy didn't go with him – he might have been caught too – and shot!'

George put her arms round Timmy in fear. 'Timmy would never go with Wilfrid if I wasn't there too,' she said. 'What a little fool he is! Those men will guess there's someone else on the island with Wilfrid, won't they? They might even *make* him tell all he knew – and where the boat is, and everything!'

'What shall we do?' said Anne. 'We'd better go after him.

'Timmy will track him for us,' said George, getting up. 'Come on, Tim. Find Wilfrid. Find that silly disobedient boy Wilfrid!'

Timmy understood at once. He put his nose to the ground, found Wilfrid's scent, and began to walk away. 'Not too fast, Timmy,' said George, and he at once slowed down. George looked round at the little place among the bushes where they had been sitting. 'Had we better take a tin or two with us?' she said.

'Yes. Good idea,' said Julian. 'You just never know!'

He and Dick took a couple of tins each, stuffed uncomfortably into their pockets. Stupid Wilfrid!

'He must have gone in this direction,' said Dick. 'I never spotted him slinking away, the little nuisance! I'm surprised Timmy didn't make a sound! Track him, Tim, track him!'

'Listen!' said Anne, suddenly, and she stopped. 'Listen!' They all listened – and didn't at all like what they heard. It was Wilfrid's voice, yelling in fright.

'Let me go! Let me go!'

And then a stern, loud and threatening voice came. 'Who are you with? Where are they? You're not alone, we're certain of that!'

'Quick – we must hide!' said Julian, angry and worried. 'Dick, look about for a good place and I will too.'

'No good,' said Dick. 'They'll beat everywhere for us. Better climb trees.'

'Good idea!' said Julian. 'Anne, come with me. I'll give you a shove up. Hurry, everybody! Hurry!'

CHAPTER FOURTEEN

Wilfrid has an adventure on his own

'WHAT ABOUT Timmy? He can't climb,' said George, fearfully. 'He might be shot.'

'Put him under a bush and tell him to sit, sit, sit!' said Julian, urgently. 'He knows perfectly well what that means. Go on, George, quick.'

George took Timmy by the collar and led him to a very thick bush. She pushed him under it. He turned himself round, poked his nose out of the leaves, and looked at her in surprise.

'Sit, Timmy! Sit, and keep quiet!' said George. 'Sit, sit, sit – and keep *quiet*. Understand?'

'Woof,' said Timmy, very quietly, and withdrew his nose so that nothing of him could be seen at all. He knew perfectly well what George meant. Clever old Timmy!

Dick was giving Anne a shove up a tree with drooping branches thick with leaves. 'Get as high as you can,' he said, in a low voice. 'And then stay put till you hear me call you. Don't be afraid. Old Timmy's down here to protect you!'

Anne gave him rather a small smile. She was not like George, fearless and always ready to rush into trouble. Anne was all for a peaceful life – but how could she have that if she was one of the Five!

The boys and George were now high up in trees, listening to the shouting going on. Apparently Wilfrid was not going to give away his friends – one up to him!

'How did you get here?' a man was shouting.

'In a boat,' said Wilfrid.

'Who was with you?' shouted another man.

'Nobody. I came alone,' said Wilfrid, perfectly truth-fully. 'I wanted to visit the island. I'm an animal lover and I heard that all the wild creatures here were tame.'

'A likely story that!' sneered a man's voice. 'Huh! Animal lover!'

'All right then – look what I've got here in my pocket,' said Wilfrid, and apparently showed the man his baby hedgehog. 'He was trodden on by a horse – and I've been looking after him.'

'Very well – you can go back to your boat, and row away,' said the man. 'AT ONCE, mind. And don't look so scared. We shan't hurt you. We've business of our own here, and we don't want strangers round – not even silly little kids with hedgehogs in their pockets!'

Wilfrid took to his heels and fled. He felt lost now. He would never find the others – or the cove where his boat was. WHY had he disobeyed Julian? Had the others heard the men shouting at him? Which way should he go?

He had entirely lost his sense of direction and had no idea whether to go to the left or the right. He began to panic. Where could the others be? He *must* find them, he must! He ran through the trees, wishing that Timmy was with him. Then he stopped. Surely this was quite the wrong way? He turned and went in a different direction. No, this couldn't be right either, he didn't recognise a thing!

He thought he heard voices in the distance. He stood and listened. Could it be the others? If only George would tell Timmy to find him! But she wouldn't, in case he was shot at. *Was* that noise voices – or was it just the wind? Perhaps it was the others looking for him. Wilfrid rushed off towards the distant sound. But alas, it died down. It was only the wind!

The trees thinned out in bushes – and then Wilfrid suddenly saw the sea in the distance! Good! If he could get to it, he could walk round the shore till he came to his cove. He would know where he was then. He began to run towards the blue sea.

Through the bushes he went, and came out at last on

to what seemed to be a very high cliff. Yes – there was the sea, below and beyond. If only he could scramble down the cliff he could bear to the right and at last come to his cove. He came to the edge of the cliff and looked down – and then he started back in fear. What was that noise – that awful, dreadful noise? It was like a giant wailing and wailing at the top of his voice, the wailing going up and down in the wind. Wilfrid found his knees were shaking. He simply didn't dare to go on. He sat down and tried to get his breath, putting his hands over his ears to keep out the horrible wailing.

And then he suddenly remembered something and heaved a sigh of heartfelt relief. Of course – these must be the Wailing Cliffs we were told about, he thought thankfully. We heard about the Whispering Wood – and it *does* whisper – and the Wailing Cliffs – and they *do* wail! At least, it's really the wind, of course. But goodness, what a strange sound!

He sat for a while longer, then, feeling much bolder, he went to the edge of the great cliff, and looked over. He stared down in surprise.

There's somebody down there – three or four people! Mustn't let them see me – they must belong to the men on the island! What are they doing down there?

He lay down and peered over. Four men were there – but, as Wilfrid watched, they disappeared. Where had they gone? He craned over the cliff to see. There must be caves in the cliff, I suppose, he said to himself. That's where they've gone! Gosh, I wish this wailing would stop. I shall start wailing myself in a minute!

After some time voices came faintly up to him, as he lay watching, and he saw two men coming out on to the rocks below again. What are they carrying? A long, deep box – why, it looked exactly like one of the boxes in which the others had seen those beautiful little statues, packed in sawdust!

So *that*'s how they get them away from here – take them down through some passage in the cliffs to a waiting boat. Where's the boat, though? I can't see one. Not arrived yet, perhaps.

He watched with intense interest as the men carried out box after box and piled them on a great flat rock that abutted a stretch of fairly calm water.

Big boxes – little ones – those men have been busy lately! thought Wilfrid, wishing and wishing and wishing that the others were with him. I wonder what's in them. Not the bed of gold, that's certain. I bet it would be far too big to put into a boat. Have to be pulled to pieces first! Hallo – here comes another box – a small one this time. Wow, they'll soon need a steamer to take all these!

Almost as he thought it, he saw a small steamer in the far distance! Well! There's the steamer, just as I said! I bet the boat will appear soon, and be loaded – and then chug off to the waiting steamer!

But the steamer came no nearer, and no boats appeared. Waiting for the tide, I expect, thought Wilfrid. What *will* the others say when I tell them all this! They won't believe me! And I bet they won't scold me for going off by myself!

He decided to go back and find the others and tell them what he had seen. He set off, trying to remember the way. Surely he must be near the place where he had left them? And then quite suddenly, someone leapt out from behind a tree and caught hold of him!

'Let me go, let me go!' shouted Wilfrid, in a panic. And then he gave a cry of relief as he suddenly saw Timmy running towards him.

'Timmy! Save me!'

But Timmy didn't coming running to save him. He stood there, looking up at him, rather puzzled, while poor Wilfrid went on struggling, really frightened!

Then Wilfrid heard a giggle. A GIGGLE? Who in the world could be giggling just then? He forced himself to look round – and saw Dick and Anne, doing their best not to laugh, and George holding her sides. His captor let go of him and began to laugh too. It was Julian!

'This is too bad! You gave me an awful fright,' said Wilfrid. 'I've already been captured once this afternoon. Whatever do you think you're doing?'

459

'Where have you been, Wilfrid?' said Julian, rather sternly. 'I forbade you to go for a walk – and you went.'

'I know. I went off by myself – and a man caught me and scared me. Then I ran away and lost myself. I couldn't find any of you,' said poor Wilfrid. 'But I saw something very very interesting on that walk of mine!'

'What?' asked Julian, at once.

'Let's sit down, and I'll tell you,' said Wilfrid. 'I feel quite shaky. You really were beasts to jump on me like that.'

'Never mind, Wilfrid,' said Anne, feeling sorry for the boy, who really did look rather shaken. 'Now go on, tell us everything that happened.'

Wilfrid sat down. He was still trembling a little. Everything seemed to have happened at once. He began to tell the others about the Wailing Cliffs, and all he had seen.

They all listened with intense interest. 'So *that's* the other way to the underground treasure chamber – through a passage in the cliffs!' said Julian. 'I never thought of that! That is something to know! I vote we go and explore the cliffs ourselves, when there's nobody about.'

'Well, it had better be in the evening,' said Wilfrid. 'Just in case we were spotted climbing down the cliffs to find the passage – if there *is* one, and I think there must be! Those men might be on the watch, now they know there's someone on the island. I bet they guess I'm not the only one – even though I told them I came alone.'

'I vote we have something to eat,' said George. 'We can talk over everything then. It's ages since we had a meal. Let's go and open some more tins, and plan what we're going to do tonight. This is getting too exciting for words. Isn't it, Timmy?'

'Woof,' agreed Timmy. *Too* exciting, he thought. Yes – and dangerous, too. He'd keep close to George that evening, as close as ever he could! If she went into danger, Timmy would be close by her side!

CHAPTER FIFTEEN

Julian has an exciting plan

THE FIVE children talked and talked, as they opened more
tins and had a most peculiar meal of ham spread with
fruit salad and beans. They finished up with another
barley-sugar each. George gave hers to Timmy who
disposed of it with a crick-crack, swallow!

'Have we all got torches?' asked Julian. 'I know it will
be bright moonlight tonight, but as we shall presumably
be getting down – or up – dark caves, we shall want
torches.'

Yes – they each had a torch. Wilfrid, for some reason,
had two, rather small but quite efficient.

'What's the plan going to be, Ju?' asked George, and
Timmy gave a little whine, as if to say 'Yes, tell us.' He
sat by George, listening earnestly, with Wilfrid on the
other side of him. At times he sniffed at the baby hedgehog still in the boy's pocket, and apparently quite happy
there. Wilfrid had been busy catching insects for it, much
to Timmy's interest.

'I propose that we go to the cliffs – the Wailing Cliffs –
as soon as it's twilight, and make our way down,' said
Julian. 'There is probably some kind of pathway down, I
should think – even if only a rabbit path. I'll lead the way
down, of course. Anne and Wilfrid are to come between
me and Dick, with George and Timmy behind.'

'Right!' said everyone.

'We are, of course, to make as little noise as possible,'

said Julian. 'And do try not to send stones hurtling down the path or cliff, just in *case* anyone's about! When we get down to the rocks, we'll let Wilfrid go ahead, because he saw where the men went in and out earlier on.'

Wilfrid felt suddenly important – it was like planning an exploration! He suddenly remembered something – the wailing noise.

'I hope the girls won't be scared when they hear the awful wailing noise,' he said. 'It's only the wind scream-ing in and out of the holes and corners of the great cliffs.'

George made a scornful noise. 'Who's scared of the wind!' she said.

'Timmy might be,' said Julian, smiling. 'We *know* what makes the wailing. He doesn't! You may have to hold him when it begins, George. He'll be a bit uneasy.'

'He won't!' said George. 'Timmy's not afraid of any-thing in the world!'

'Oh yes, he is,' said Dick, at once. 'I know something that scares him dreadfully – makes him put his tail down and flop his ears.'

'You do not!' said George, angrily.

'Well, haven't you seen him when you speak sharply to him?' said Dick, with a chuckle. 'He goes all shaky in the legs!'

Everyone laughed except George. 'He does not,' she said. 'Nothing scares Timmy, not even me. So shut up, Dick.'

'It may be that it would be best for only one or two of us to go right into the depths of the caves,' went on Julian. 'If so, the rest must wait in hiding. Just keep on the look-out for any signal from me. I don't expect we shall see a soul down there tonight, but you never know.

If there is a way through the cliffs to that underground chamber where we saw the golden statues, we shall be in real luck. We shall then be absolutely certain how things can be taken in and out.'

'Taken *in*? But I thought they had been there for ages,' said Dick, 'and were probably only taken out to sell. *Smuggled* out.'

'Well, I think it may be more than that, said Julian. 'It might even be a central clearing-ground for a great gang of high-class thieves, who would hide valuable stolen goods there till it was safe to sell them. However, that's only guessing!'

'*I* think somebody's discovered the underground chamber, full of that rich old man's treasures, and is taking them out bit by bit,' said Dick. 'Anyway, whatever it is, it's awfully exciting. To think we know so much!'

'All because we went down the well to get some water!' said Anne.

'Put on your sweaters,' said Julian. 'It may be freezing cold in the wind that rages round those cliffs!'

'I'm longing to start!' said George. 'It's an adventure, this – do you hear that, Timmy? An adventure!'

'Anything more, Julian?' asked Anne. Julian always sounded so very grown-up when he gave them a plan of campaign. She felt very proud of him.

'That's the lot,' said Julian, 'except that we'll have some sort of a meal before we go this evening. Wilfrid will have to lead the way for us, as he's the only one who knows it – but when we come to the cliff, *I'll* lead you down. Can't have anyone missing a footstep and rolling headlong, frightening any robber or smuggler!'

'Do you hear that, Timmy?' said George, and Timmy whined, and put a paw on George's knee as if to say: 'It's a pity you haven't sure feet like mine, with rubber pads beneath, so that *your* footing is always sure!'

George patted his paw. 'Yes – you've fine sure feet, Tim. I wish I could buy some like them!'

The time seemed to go very, very slowly after that. Everyone was eager to start, and kept looking at their watches! The sun left a bright glow in the sky, so they would probably start more or less in daylight, which would, however, soon fade into twilight.

They had another meal, but strangely enough, nobody felt very hungry! 'We're too excited!' said Julian, giving Timmy a biscuit. Timmy was the only one who didn't seem at all excited. As for George, she fidgeted and fidgeted until everyone was quite tired of her!

At last they started off. Wilfrid led them at first, as he knew the way. Actually he found that he didn't really know it – it was the loud wind that guided him, just as it had done before. 'Awfully like far-off voices shouting to one another,' he said, and everyone at once agreed.

When they came near to the cliff, the sound gradually changed into the mournful wailing noise that gave the cliffs their name. 'EEE-ee-OOOOO-oo-EEEEEEEEAH-OOO!'

'Not very nice,' said Anne, shivering a little. 'It sounds as if someone is crying and sobbing and howling!'

'Good name for this place – Wailing Cliffs,' said Dick. 'Wow – what a wind up here! I'm glad my hair's my own! It would certainly be blown off if it weren't! Hang on to old Timmy, George – he's more blowable than we are – not so heavy!'

George put her hand on Timmy's collar at once. How DREADFUL if Timmy were to be blown over the cliff! He gave a grateful lick. He didn't like the wind here very much – it had a truly miserable voice!

They came to the edge of the cliff and looked down cautiously, in case anyone should be on the rocks below. But, except for some big gulls preening their feathers there, there was no sign of life.

'No boats about – no steamer – nothing,' said Dick. 'All clear, Julian!'

Julian had been looking for a good path down the cliff. There didn't seem to be a continuous one. 'We'll have to go so far – then climb down a bit – then walk along that ledgy bit, see – then climb down that slanting rock – the great big one – and get down on to the more level rocks. OK everyone?'

'I'll let Timmy go first,' said George. 'He is so sure-footed and will know the best way. Go on, Timmy – lead us down!'

Timmy understood at once and went in front of Julian. He took the first little path down the cliff, slid down the next bit, walked along the ledge that Julian had pointed out, and then stood and waited for every-one. He gave a little bark as if to say 'Come along. It's easy! Follow me!'

They all followed, some more carefully than others. George and Wilfrid were least careful, and poor Wilfrid lost his footing and slid quite a long way on his behind. He didn't like it at all, and looked quite scared!

'Watch your feet, now, Wilfrid,' said Julian. 'It's getting a bit dark, so don't try any funny tricks. You tried to *jump* over that big stone instead of stepping over

carefully. I really don't want to send Timmy down to the
bottom of the cliff to pick up your pieces!'

At last they were all down the cliff and on the rocks
below. The tide was out, so that waves did not splash up
and soak them. Anne suddenly slipped into a pool and
made her shoes wet, but that didn't matter. They were
only plastic ones.

'Now – exactly where did you see those men, Wilfrid?'
asked Julian, stopping on a big flat rock. Wilfrid jumped
beside him, and pointed.

'See the cliff over there? See that funny rock shaped rather like a bear? Well, that's where I saw the men. They went by that rock, and disappeared.'

'Right,' said Julian. 'Now, no more talking please – though this wailing sound would drown almost anything. Follow me!'

He went over the rocks towards the big bear-like one that Wilfrid had pointed to. The others followed, a little tide of excitement welling up inside them. Anne caught hold of Wilfrid's hand, and squeezed it. 'Exciting, isn't it?' she said, and Wilfrid nodded eagerly. He knew he would have been scared stiff by himself – but with the others it was an adventure – a really exciting adventure!

They came to the bear-like rock. Near it was a dark place in the cliff – a way in? 'That's where the men came out, Julian,' said Wilfrid, keeping his voice low. 'Do we go in there?'

'We do,' said Julian. 'I'm going in first and I'm going to stand quite still and listen, as soon as I get the sound of the wind and sea out of my ears. If I hear nothing I'll whistle, see? Then you can all come in too.'

'Right!' said everyone, thrilled. They watched as Julian went to the dark slit-like opening. He paused and looked inside. It was so dark that he knew they would all need their torches! He switched on his power-ful one and shone it into the passage. He saw a channel that ran slanting upwards for some way, and on either side a rocky ledge, not too rough. Water ran down the rocky channel and bubbled out beside him, to join the sea over the rocks.

'I'm just going into the cliff tunnel a little way, to see if I can hear anything or anyone,' he said. 'Wait here.' He disappeared inside the dark opening and everyone waited in impatient excitement.

A gull suddenly swooped down close to their heads. 'Ee-ooo, ee-ooo, EEE-OOO!' it screeched, and made them all jump violently. Wilfrid almost fell off his rock, and clutched at George. Timmy growled, and looked up angrily at the seagull. Silly bird, frightening everyone like that!

There came a low whistle, and Julian appeared again, his torch switched on. 'All clear,' he said. 'I can't hear a sound inside the opening, and I've been some way along. It's not hard going. There's a funny little stream flowing down, and a ledge either side we can walk on. Very convenient! Now, no talking please – and be careful even of your whispers – every sound seems to be magnified in here. Keep hold of Timmy, George, in the steepest places.'

Timmy gave a little whine of surprise when George took him inside the cliff. At once his whine was magnified all round them, and everyone jumped. Timmy didn't like it at all.

George took firm hold of Timmy's collar. 'You're to keep close by me,' she whispered, 'and you're not to make a sound. This is an adventure, Timmy – a big adventure – and you're in it as much as any of us. Come along!'

And there they go, all of them, climbing up the dark passage into the cliff! What will they find – what will they see? No wonder their hearts beat fast and loudly, no wonder Timmy keeps close to George. An adventure? He must be on guard then – *anything* might happen in an adventure!

CHAPTER SIXTEEN

A journey underground

IT WAS very dark inside the cliff. The children's torches made bright streaks everywhere, and were very useful indeed for seeing the safest places to tread. As Julian had told the others, there was a curious little stream flowing down the middle of the steep passage, with uneven ledges on each side of it. It had worn this little channel for itself during the many, many years it had flowed down inside the cliff.

'It's probably water draining from the surface of the cliffs,' said Julian in a low voice, picking his way carefully. 'Be careful here – the ledges are *very* slippery!'

'Oooh!' said Wilfrid, treading on a slippery bit, and finding one of his feet in ice-cold water.

The echo took up the noise at once, 'OOOOH-OOOOOOH-OOOOOH!' Poor Wilfrid's little 'Oooh' echoed up and down and all round them! It was very weird indeed and nobody liked it. Anne pressed close to Julian, and he squeezed her arm comfortingly.

'Sorry about my "Oooh",' said Wilfrid, in a low voice. 'My oooh, oooh, oooh!' said the echo at once, and George simply couldn't *help* giving a giggle, which at once repeated itself a score of times!

'You really will have to be quiet now,' came Julian's voice, almost in a whisper. 'I have a feeling we're coming to some big opening. There's suddenly a great draught blowing down this steep passage – I can feel it round my head.'

471

The others felt it too, as they climbed higher up the steep passage, trying to avoid the tiny stream that splashed down its worn channel. It made a nice little noise – very cheerful, Anne thought – and gleamed brightly in the light of their torches.

Julian wondered how in the world anyone could take crates or boxes down such a steep dark passage! It's *wide* enough, I suppose, he thought. But only just – and the bends in it must be very awkward for boxes to get round! I do hope we don't meet anyone round a bend, carrying a crate or two! Wow, the draught is quite a wind now! There *must* be an opening somewhere.

'Ju – we've not only gone upwards, we've gone a good way forward too,' whispered Anne. 'Wasn't the old castle somewhere in this direction?'

'Yes – I suppose it would be,' answered Julian, stopping to think. 'Gosh – I wonder if this passage comes up in one of its cellars! An old castle like that would have huge cellars – and probably a dungeon or two for prisoners! Let me think – we must have left the cliff behind now – and yes – I think we *may* be heading for the castle. Why didn't I think of that before!'

'Well, then – the well wall must run down beside the castle foundations!' said Dick, in much too loud a voice. The echo made everyone jump violently, and Julian stopped climbing and hissed at Dick. 'Whisper, can't you, idiot! You nearly made me jump out of my skin!'

'Skin, skin, skin!' said the echo, in a peculiar whisper that made George want to laugh.

'Sorry!' whispered back Dick.

'I think you may be right about the well wall running down beside the foundations of the castle,' Julian said, whispering again. 'I never thought of that. The castle wasn't very far from the well. It would probably have enormous cellars spreading underground.'

'The wall in the well, that that funny little door was in, was terrifically thick,' said Dick. 'I bet I was looking into one of the castle cellars, when I peeped through it!'

This was all very interesting. Julian thought about it as they went on and on through the endless passage. It ran more or less level now, and was easy to walk through, for it was much wider.

'I think this part of the passage was man-made,' said Julian, stopping and facing the others, his face bright in the light of their torches. He went on in a loud whisper, 'Up through the cliff the passage was a natural one, awfully difficult to climb – but here it's quite different – look at these old bricks here – probably put there to strengthen the tunnel.'

'Yes – a secret way from the castle to the sea!' said Dick, almost forgetting to keep his voice down, in his excitement. 'Isn't it thrilling!'

Everyone began to feel even more excited – all except Timmy, who didn't much like dark, secret passages, and couldn't imagine why Julian was taking them for such a gloomy and peculiar walk. He had splashed solemnly through the stream the whole time, finding the stone ledges much too slippery for his paws.

The draught grew stronger and was very cold indeed. 'We're coming near to the opening where the draught comes from,' whispered Julian. 'All quiet, now, please!'

They were as quiet as possible, and Anne began to feel almost sick with excitement. Where were they coming to? Then suddenly Julian gave a low exclamation.

'Here we are! An iron gate!'

They all tried to crowd round Julian to see. The gate was a big strong one, with criss-cross bars of iron. They could easily see between the bars, and they shivered in the draught that swept through the great gate.

Dick shone his torch through the bars, his hand shaking in excitement. The bright ray of light ran all round what looked like a stone room – quite small – with a stout, nail-studded door at the far end. This door was wide open, and it was through this that the steady draught blew.

'This is a cellar – or a dungeon, more likely!' said Julian. 'I wonder if the gate is locked.'

He shook it – and it swung open quite easily, as if it had been well-oiled! Julian stepped into the dungeon, flashing his torch all round the dark and dismal little place.

He shivered. 'It's cold as ice, even on this warm day!' he said. 'I wonder how many poor, miserable prisoners have been kept down here in the cold!'

'Look – here's a staple in the wall,' said Dick, standing beside him, examining the half-hoop of iron deeply embedded in the stone wall. 'I suppose the unhappy prisoner was tied up to this, to make his punishment even worse.'

Anne shivered. 'How could people be so cruel?' she said, her vivid imagination seeing wretched men here, with perhaps only crusts of bread to eat, water to drink, no warmth, no bed, only the stone floor!

'Perhaps some of them escaped out of the gate and went down the cliff passage,' she said, hopefully.

'No – it's much more likely that the passage was used to get *rid* of the prisoners,' said Dick. 'They could be dragged down to the sea and drowned – and nobody would ever know.'

'Don't tell me things like that,' said Anne. 'It makes me feel I shall hear groans and cries. I don't like this place. Let's go.'

'I hate it too,' said George. 'And Timmy's tail is right down. I feel as if this horrid dungeon is full of miserable memories. Julian, do let's go.'

Julian walked over to the nail-studded door and went through the doorway. He looked out on to a stone-paved passage, with stone walls and ceiling. He could see other doors, iron-barred, along a dismal stone passage. He came back to the others.

'Yes – these *are* the castle dungeons,' he said. 'I expect the castle cellars are somewhere near too – where they stored wine and food and other things. Come on – let's explore. I can't hear a sound. I think this place is absolutely empty.'

They all followed Julian down the stone passage, looking in at each miserable dungeon as they passed. Horrible! Dirty, damp, cold, bare – poor, poor prisoners of long ago!

At the end of the passage was another iron-barred door, but that too was wide open. They went through it and came out into an enormous cellar. Old boxes were there, old worm-eaten chests, broken chairs, loose papers that rustled as their feet touched them – the kind of junk that can be found in a thousand cellars! It all smelt rather musty – though, as Julian said, the draught that blew everywhere took away some of the smell.

They came to some stone steps and went up them. At the top was another great door, with an enormous bolt on it. 'Fortunately the bolt is *our* side,' said Julian, and slid it out of its socket. He was surprised that it went so smoothly – he had expected it to be rusted and stiff. 'It's been oiled recently,' he said, shining his torch on it. 'Well, well – other people have been here not long ago, and used this door. We'd better go quietly in case they are *still* here!'

Anne's heart began to beat loudly again. She hoped there was no one waiting round a corner to jump out at them! 'Be careful, Julian,' she said. 'Somebody may have heard us! They may be waiting to ambush us. They . . .'

'All right, Anne – don't worry!' said Julian. 'Old Timmy would give us a warning growl if he heard a single footstep!'

And good gracious – at that VERY moment Timmy *did*

give a growl – an angry, startled growl that made everyone jump, and then stand still, holding their breath.

Dick looked round at Timmy, who was growling again. His head was down and he was looking at something on the floor. What was it? Dick swung down his torch to see. Then he gave a small laugh. 'It's all right. We don't need to be scared yet. Look what Timmy's growling at!'

They all looked down – and saw a great fat toad, its brilliant eyes staring steadily up at them. As they exclaimed at it, it turned aside, and crawled slowly and clumsily to a little damp spot in the corner of the wall.

'I've never seen such a big toad in my life!' said Anne. 'It must be a hundred years old! Goodness, Timmy, you made me jump when you suddenly growled like that!'

The toad squatted down in its corner, facing them. It seemed to glare at poor Timmy. 'Come away, Tim,' said Dick. 'Toads can ooze out a very nasty-smelling, nasty-tasting stuff. Never bite a toad!'

Julian had now gone through the door at the top of the steps. He gave a loud exclamation – so loud that the others rushed to him in alarm, wondering what was exciting him.

'Look!' said Julian, shining his torch into the dark space beyond. 'See where we've come to! Did you ever see such a storehouse of wonders!'

CHAPTER SEVENTEEN

In the treasure chamber

JULIAN'S TORCH shone steadily into the vast room, which seemed to have no end! The others shone their torches too, and Timmy pressed between their legs to see what the excitement was.

What a sight! They were actually in the enormous chamber that the boys had seen through the opening in the well wall! What a place it was – absolutely *vast*, thought Anne, awed at the size, the height and the great silence.

'There are the golden statues!' said Dick, going over to a group of them. 'Wonderful! Strange faces they have, though – not like ours. And look how their slanting eyes gleam when we shine our torches on them. Makes them look as if they're almost alive, and looking at us.'

Anne suddenly gave a cry and rushed over to something. 'The golden bed!' she said. 'I *wished* I could lie on one – and now I shall!' And with that she climbed on to a vast four-poster bed with a great canopy, now rotting to pieces.

The bed gave a mournful creak, and the part that Anne was lying on suddenly subsided. The canopy collapsed and Anne disappeared in a cloud of dust. The bed had, quite literally, fallen to pieces! Poor Anne.

The others helped her up and Timmy looked at the clouds of dust in surprise. What was Anne doing, making such a dust! He sneezed loudly, and then sneezed again.

Anne sneezed too. She scrambled quickly out of the collapsed bed and dusted herself down.

'It has a carved gold headpiece, and gold legs and end-piece,' said Dick, shining his torch on it. 'What a monster of a bed, though – I should think *six* people could sleep in it at once! What a pity it has been lost here so long – all the hangings fell to pieces as soon as Anne climbed on the bed part! *What* a dust!'

479

There was no doubt about it, there were priceless treasures in this vast underground cellar. The children could not find the sword with the jewelled handle, nor the necklace of rubies, which Julian thought were probably locked away in one of the chests. But they found many other wonderful things.

'Look in this chest – this beautiful carved chest!' called Anne. 'Gold cups and plates and dishes. Still bright and clean!'

'And look what's in here!' shouted George. 'Wrapped up in stuff that falls to pieces when I touch it!'

They crowded round a great enamelled box. In it was a set of animals carved out of some lovely green stone. They were absolutely perfect, and, when Anne tried to stand them up, each of them stood as proudly as once they did many years ago when little princes and princesses played with them.

'They're made of green jade,' said Julian. 'Beautiful! Goodness knows how much they're worth! They should be in some museum, not mouldering away in this cellar.'

'Why didn't those collectors take these – and the golden statues – and all the other things?' wondered Anne.

'Well, that's obvious,' said Julian. 'For one thing this is a secret cellar, I should think, and nobody would be able to get into it unless they knew the secret way to it. There's probably a sliding panel or hidden door that leads to it, somewhere in the castle above. It's very cold, and ruined in many parts – and some of the walls have fallen in – so I suppose it was pretty impossible to get to the cellars even if the secret way was known!'

'Yes – but what about the way *we* came up,' said Dick. 'From the sea – up the cliff passage!'

'Well – I don't know exactly why that hasn't been used before,' said Julian, 'though I could make a guess! Did you notice that great heap of fallen rocks near the entrance to the cliff passage? I should think that that part of the cliff fell at one time, and hid the passage completely – blocked it up. Then maybe a storm came, and the sea shifted some of the rocks – and lo and behold, there was the secret passage – open again!'

'And somebody found it – somebody, perhaps, who had heard the old legends about the castle of Whispering Island!' said Anne.

'A collector of old things, do you think?' asked George. 'What about those two men on the island – the ones we saw in the courtyard – do you suppose *they* know of this entrance?'

'Yes, probably,' said Julian. 'And it's likely they were put on guard in case anyone else found it and came to rob the secret chamber. The things here are priceless! Those men are not there to guard the animals on the island, as they were in the old couple's day. They had *genuine* keepers, like that nice old man Lucas who told us about this island this morning.'

'You think these men are in somebody's pay then – somebody who knows about this great chamber under the castle, and wants to get the centuries-old treasures?' said Dick.

'Yes,' said Julian. 'And what's more I don't believe that the real owner of the island – the great-nephew of the old couple who owned it – even *knows* they're here, or that anyone is taking things from the island. For all we know he may live in America or Australia, and not care tuppence about his island!'

481

'How extraordinary!' said Anne. 'If *I* owned an island like this, I'd live here and never leave it. And all the animals and birds would be protected as they once were, and . . .'

'Dear Anne – what a pity it *isn't* yours!' said Julian, ruffling her hair. 'But now, the thing is – what are we going to *do* about this? We'll talk about it when we're back at the cottage. Hey, it's getting late! It will be pitch dark outside, unless the moon is up and the sky is clear of clouds!'

'Well, come on then, let's go,' said Dick, making for the great nail-studded door. Then, as Timmy suddenly gave a blood-curdling growl, he stopped in fright. They had *shut* the door – but now it was opening. Somebody was coming into the great underground chamber! Who *could* it be?

'Quick – hide!' said Julian, and he pushed the two girls behind a great chest. The others were near the golden bed and they crouched behind it at once, Dick's hand on Timmy's collar. He had managed to stop the dog from growling, but was afraid that Timmy would begin again at any moment!

A man came into the room – one of the two big fellows that the children had seen in the courtyard. He didn't seem to have heard Timmy growling, for he sauntered in, whistling lightly. He shone his torch all round, and then called loudly.

'Emilio! Emilio!'

There was no answer at all. The man yelled again, and then an answer came from beyond the door, and hurrying footsteps could be heard. Then in came the other big rough fellow, and looked round, shining his torch. He lighted an oil-lamp on a box, and switched off his torch.

'You're always sleeping, Emilio!' growled the first man. 'You are always late! You know the boat comes tonight to take the next batch of goods – have you got the list? We must wrap them up quickly and take them to the shore. That little statue has to go, I know!'

He went over to the statue of a boy whose eyes gleamed with emeralds. 'Well, boy,' said the man, 'you're going out into the world! How'll you like that after being in the dark so long? Don't glare at me like that, or I'll box your ears!'

Apparently the golden boy went on glaring, for the man gave his head a sharp smack. The other fellow came over and shifted a long, deep box over from the wall to the little golden statue. Then he began to wrap it up

483

carefully, rolling material round and round it from head to foot while the golden boy stood patiently.

'What time is Lanyon coming for it?' asked Emilio. 'Have I time to wrap another?'

'Yes – that one over there,' said the first fellow, pointing. Emilio went whistling over to it, passing the chest behind which the girls were hiding. They crouched right to the floor, afraid of being seen. But Emilio was sharp-eyed, and thought he saw something move as he passed by the chest. He stopped. What was that poking out by the side of the chest – a foot! A FOOT!

Emilio rushed round the chest, his torch switched on again. He gave a loud shout. 'Carlo! There's someone here! Come quickly!'

Carlo, the second man, dropped what he was holding and raced round to Emilio, who had now pulled the girls roughly to their feet.

'What are you doing here? How did you get in?' shouted Emilio.

Julian shot out from his hiding place at once, followed by Dick and Wilfrid. George was doing all she could to hold back Timmy, who was now deafening everyone with his angry barks. He did his best to get away from George, but she was afraid he might fly at Emilio's throat. The two men were full of amazement to see the five children and Timmy!

'Keep that dog back or I'll shoot him,' said Carlo, producing a gun. 'Who are you? What do you mean by coming into this place?'

'We came by boat – but the boat got washed out to sea,' said Julian. 'We've been camping on the island. We just – er – wandered into this place by mistake.'

'By mistake! Well, I can tell you that you've certainly made the biggest mistake in your life!' said Carlo. 'You'll have to stay here for quite a long time – till our job's done, at any rate!'

'What's your job?' asked Julian, bluntly.

'Wouldn't you like to know!' said Carlo. 'Well – one part of it is to guard the island, and keep off strangers! Now, we've jobs to do tonight and tomorrow, and I'm

485

afraid you're going to have a miserable time! You'll stay down here in this old cellar till we come back again – and what will happen to you after that, I don't know, because I'll have to tell my employer you've been spying down here. I wouldn't be surprised if he doesn't hand you over to the police – or lock you up down here for a month, on bread and water!'

Timmy growled very fiercely indeed, and tugged hard to get away from George and fly at this hateful man. She hung on to him for all she was worth, though how she longed to let him leap at the man and get him on the ground!

'Better go, Carlo, or we'll miss that boat out there,' said Emilio, grumpily. 'We'll deal with these kids when we get back!' He shouldered the box into which he had put the wrapped statue, and started for the door. Carlo followed him, backing all the time to make sure that George did not set Timmy on to him. He shut the great door with a loud bang, and shot the bolt.

'Don't say anything for a minute in case they are listening outside the door,' said Julian. So they all stood in silence, Anne's knees trembling a little. Oh dear – how unlucky to be caught like this!

'Relax!' said Julian at last. 'You all look so stiff and tense!'

'Well, I should *think* so!' said Dick. 'I don't particularly want to stay shut up here till those men deign to come back and do a bit more stealing. Suppose they *never* come back! We'd be here for keeps!'

'No, Dick!' said Anne, and to everyone's surprise, she began to laugh. 'We can *easily* escape!'

'What – through that locked and bolted door?' said Dick. 'Not a hope!'

'But we *can* easily escape!' said Anne, and George suddenly brightened up and nodded her head, smiling. 'Oh yes – of course! Don't look so solemn, Dick! Look up there!'

Dick looked up to where Anne was pointing. 'What am I supposed to look at?' he said. 'The old stone wall?'

'No – just there – over the top of that tall chest,' said Anne.

Dick looked – and then a large smile came over his face. 'WHAT an idiot I am! That's the old iron door in the side of the old well wall, isn't it – the opening I looked through! It looks just like an ordinary ventilation hole from down here – and I don't really believe anyone would ever notice it except us, who know what it is. I see what you're getting at, Anne!'

'Good old Anne!' said George, realising what Anne had in mind. 'Of course – we've only got to climb up to that hole in the wall, open the door there, and then go up the well – and we're safe!'

'Yes. But it's easier said than done,' said Julian, soberly. 'We've got to get hold of the rope, and climb right up it to the top – *not* very easy!'

'Suppose the rope's at the top, with the bucket hanging on the hook,' said Anne. 'We'd never reach it then!'

'We'll think of something!' said Julian. 'Anyway, it's our only hope of escape. Now – we'll push that huge, high chest or wardrobe or whatever it is, right over against the wall, under that opening into the well – there's a sturdy little one over there. Come on! We'll be through that opening in no time, and up the well. What a shock for dear Emilio and Carlo, when they come back and find that the birds have flown!'

CHAPTER EIGHTEEN

A most exciting time!

IT WAS quite a job pushing the heavy chest over towards the stone wall of the castle. It took all of them shoving with all their might, to do it.

'We seem to be making an awful noise with the chest scraping over the floor,' panted Dick. 'I hope we're not heard!'

Timmy wished he could help. He kept jumping up and pressing his paws on the side of the chest, but Dick stopped him. 'You're getting in the way,' he said. 'You go and sit near the door and warn us if you hear those men coming.'

So Timmy ran to the door and sat there, his head cocked to one side listening, while the others went on shoving the heavy chest along. At last it was in position. Then came the job of hoisting a stout little wooden table on top. Julian climb up to the top of the chest to take the table from Dick, but just couldn't manage it, it was so heavy and solid. So Wilfrid climbed up beside him, and between the two of them they pulled up the little oblong table, and set it firmly on top of the chest. Julian stood on it – and found he could easily reach the little iron door that led into the old well.

'Good,' he said, and he gave the door a hard shove. It shook a little but didn't budge. He gave it another hard push. 'What's up?' said Dick, climbing up beside Julian. 'It *must* open – the bolt's not there any more – it fell off

488

into the well. I expect it's rusted a little again. We'll both shove it together.'

The girls watched the boys anxiously, dreading every moment to hear the two men returning. Together the boys pushed at the iron door – and it groaned and then gave way, swinging open inside the well wall! To the boys' delight, there was the rope, hanging near them!

'We've done it!' Dick called down softly to the girls. 'We'll come down and help you up to the table here – then we'll try our luck up the well.'

The girls were soon on the chest top. There wasn't room for everyone on the table, and the boys were debating what to do next.

'*You* go up the rope, Julian,' said Dick. 'You can climb up to the top and get out and look around and make sure there's no one about. Then Wilfrid can climb up – do you think you can, Wilfrid?'

'Of course,' said the boy. 'Then I can help Julian to wind up the girls!'

'Right!' said Dick. I'll stay here with the girls, and help each of them on to the rope, first Anne – and you two can wind the rope up, with her on it. Then George can go – and I'll follow last of all and shut the well door.'

'And when the men come they won't know how in the world we got out of the treasure chamber!' said Anne, grinning. 'What a shock for them!'

'When you've all gone up safely, I'll climb in myself and shut the door,' said Dick. 'Ready, Ju? I'll shine my torch for you!'

Julian nodded. He squeezed through the old iron door, reached out for the rope, and swung on it for a moment. Then up he went, hand-over-hand, till he reached the top, a little out of breath, but delighted to be out in the open air and the bright moonlight. It seemed almost as light as day!

He called down the well. 'I'm at the top, Dick, and all's well. Moon's out, and all is quiet.'

'You next, Wilfrid,' said Dick. 'Can you get hold of the rope all right, do you think? For *pity's* sake don't fall into the water. My torch will give you plenty of light.'

'Don't worry about *me*! It's just like being on the ropes at gym in school,' said Wilfrid, scornfully. He swung his legs into the opening, leapt at the rope, hung on, and began to climb up just like a monkey.

Julian's voice came down the well again, echoing hollowly, sounding rather odd. 'Wilfrid's safely up. Now send Anne – we'll wind up the rope for her so that she doesn't need to climb, only to hang on.'

Through the opening went Anne, and sat on its ledge. 'Can you swing the rope a bit, Julian?' she called. 'It's rather far for me to jump.'

'Watch out! For goodness' sake be careful!' called Julian, in alarm. 'Tell Dick to help you.'

But the well wall opening was so small that Dick couldn't even look through it while Anne was sitting there. 'Don't jump till you've got firm hold of the rope, Anne,' he told his sister, anxiously. 'Is Ju swinging it to and fro? Can you see it clearly? It's so dark in the well, and my torch isn't too good now!'

'Yes. I can see it,' said Anne. 'It bumped against my legs then, and I just missed getting it. Here it comes again – I've got it! I'm going to hold on to it tightly and drop off the ledge. Here I go!'

She sounded very much braver than she felt. She let

herself drop off the ledge, and there she swung on the thick rope, with the black water far below! 'Wind me up, Ju!' she called, and held on as the two boys at the top exerted all their strength. Dick saw her disappear up the well, and heaved a sigh of relief. Now for George.

He climbed down from the table and chest and looked for George and Timmy, shining his torch everywhere. To his utmost surprise he couldn't see them! He called softly, 'Timmy!'

A small stifled whine came from somewhere. Dick frowned. 'George – where are you? For goodness' sake buck up and come out from where you're hiding. Those men might come back at any time! Don't play the fool.'

A dark curly head poked out from behind a large box near the door, and George spoke in a very fierce voice. 'You *know* Timmy can't hang on to a rope! He'd fall and be drowned. I think you are all horrid to forget that he can't climb. I'm staying here with him. You go on up the well.'

'Certainly *not*!' said Dick at once. 'I shall stay here with you. I suppose it's no use asking you to let *me* stay with Tim, while you climb up?'

'Not the slightest use. He's *my* dog, and I'm jolly well sticking by him,' said George. 'He'd never desert *me*, I'm sure of that.'

Dick knew George only too well when she was in one of her determined moods. Nothing, absolutely nothing, would make her change her mind!

'All right, George – I expect I'd feel the same if Timmy was mine,' said Dick. 'I'm staying here with you, though!'

'No,' said George. 'We'll be all right, Tim and I.'

Dick ran to the chest and table that he had used to get up to the opening in the well wall, and climbed quickly to the top. He swung himself through, sat on the edge of the opening and called up the well.

'Julian? Are you there? Listen – George won't leave Timmy because he can't climb up the rope. So I'm staying with her!'

No sooner had he said these words than he heard someone unlocking the door of the room they were in! Timmy growled so fiercely that Dick's heart jumped in fear. Suppose Tim leapt at those men – and one of them had a gun!

George heard the noise and the key turning in the door, and quick as lightning she went behind a pile of boxes with Timmy. 'Go for them, Timmy, just as soon as you can!' she said. 'Get them down before they can hurt you.'

'Woof,' said Timmy, understanding every word. He stood beside George, ears cocked, showing his teeth in a snarl. The door opened, and a man came in, carrying a lantern. 'I've brought you a light,' he began – and then Timmy leapt at him!

Crash! Down went the lantern and the light went out. Down went the man too, shouting in fear as the big dog leapt on his chest, his hairy face so close that the man could feel the dog's hot breath. The man's head struck against the edge of a chest, and he was suddenly still and silent.

'Knocked out, I do believe!' said Dick to himself, and very cautiously shone his torch round. Yes – there was the man on the floor, eyes closed, unmoving!

George was at the open door, looking out, Timmy by

her side. 'Dick! I'm taking Timmy down the secret way through the cliffs. I'll be perfectly safe with him.'

'I must tell Julian,' said Dick. 'He's still at the top of the well, expecting you and Timmy. You go as quickly as you can – and be careful. Timmy will look after you.'

George disappeared at top speed, her shoes making no sound. She looked anxious but not afraid. She's so brave! thought Dick, for the hundredth time. Doesn't turn a hair! Now I'd better get back to that opening in the well, and tell Julian that George and Timmy have gone down the secret way. That man is still knocked out, thank goodness!

He was soon on top of the chest and table, and peering through the hole. He could see the light from Julian's torch far away at the top, the light flashing on and off as if signalling. Dick called up 'Julian!'

'Oh, so you're still there,' said Julian, sounding very relieved. 'Anything happened?'

'Yes,' said Dick. 'I'll tell you in a minute. Swing the rope a bit, Ju.'

The rope swung near Dick, and he caught it, and was just about to swing himself into the well when he heard a noise. He looked back into the vast room, which was now in darkness, for he had switched off his torch.

Someone came in hurriedly. 'What's happened? Why didn't you . . .' Then he stopped as the light from the lantern he carried picked out the figure of the man on the floor. He gave an exclamation and knelt down by him. Dick grinned to himself – what about a nice little shock for this fellow? He reached down to the sturdy little table, gave it a shove that sent it hurtling down to the floor, and then swung himself into the well on the rope. He was just

in time to see the table fall with a crash by the man with
the lantern, and to hear him shout in fear – and then
Julian and Wilfrid hauled him up the well, still grinning
to himself. Bit of a shock for those men! he thought.
George and Timmy disappeared – and the rest of us gone
most mysteriously! Pull, Julian, pull! I've a nice little
story to tell you!

And soon he was up on the well wall, telling the others
what had happened. They laughed in delight.

'Good old George! Good old Timmy!'

'George knows the way down the cliff passage all right – and if she didn't Timmy would take her safely,' said Julian. 'We'll go down on the rocks and meet her, I think. She should be all right because the moon's out now, and everything is as light as day!'

And off they all went through the wood, laughing when they thought how puzzled and mystified those men would be!

CHAPTER NINETEEN

Anne is a tiger!

IN THE meantime, George was hurrying down the secret way through the cliffs. Timmy ran first in front and then behind, his ears pricked for any possible pursuer or danger. He could hear no one. Good! Both he and George were glad to hear the babbling of the funny little underground stream as it ran swiftly down towards the sea. 'It's a nice friendly sound, Tim,' said George. 'I like it.'

Once or twice they slipped from the wet ledges into the water, and George felt a bit afraid of falling and breaking her torch. 'It wouldn't be much fun if we had to go down this passage in the pitch dark!' she told Timmy, and he gave a little woof of agreement.

'What's that bright light?' said George, suddenly, stopping in the passage. 'Look, Tim – *aw*fully bright. Is it someone coming with a lantern?'

Timmy gave a loud bark and rushed in front. *He* knew that lantern all right! It was the one that somebody sometimes hung in the sky, and that George called the moon. Didn't she know?

George soon did know, of course, and cried out in delight. 'Oh, it's the *moon*, of course, dear old moon. I'd forgotten it was a moonlight night tonight. I wonder where the others are, Timmy. You'll have to smell them out!'

Timmy already knew where they were! He had caught

their scent on the wind. They weren't very far away! He barked joyously. Soon they would all be together again!

He and George came out of the tunnel in the cliff and found themselves on the rocks. The sea was splashing over them, and the waves gleamed brightly in the bright moonlight.

George saw something moving in the distance. She put her hand on Timmy's collar. 'Careful, Tim,' she said. 'Is that someone coming over there? Stay by me.'

But Timmy disobeyed for once! He leapt away and splashed through the pools, over seaweed, over slippery rocks, barking madly. 'Timmy!' called George, not recognising who was coming. 'TIMMY! COME BACK!'

And then she saw who were coming over the rocks in the bright moonlight, picking their way through the slippery seaweed. She waved and shouted joyfully.

'Here I am! I've escaped all right!'

What a joyful meeting that was! They all sat down on a convenient rock and talked nineteen to the dozen, telling each other what had happened. And then a big wave suddenly came up and splashed all over them!

'Blow!' said Julian. 'Tide's coming in, I suppose. Come on – let's get back to Whispering Wood.'

Anne gave a most enormous yawn. 'I don't know what the time is,' she said. 'And it's so bright everywhere that I'm not sure if it's day or night. All I know is that I'm suddenly most awfully SLEEPY.'

Julian glanced at his watch. 'It's very late,' he said. 'Long past our bedtime. What shall we do – risk sleeping here on the island – or find Wilfrid's boat and row across to the mainland – and have a nice, long, peaceful snooze in that dear little cottage?'

'Oh, don't let's stay on the island!' said Anne. 'I'd never go to sleep! I'd be afraid those men would find us.'

'Don't be silly, Anne,' said George, trying not to yawn. 'They wouldn't have the remotest idea where to look for us! I honestly don't fancy looking for Wilfrid's boat, rowing all the way to the mainland, and then climbing up that steep hill to the cottage!'

'Well – all right,' said Anne. 'But oughtn't somebody to be on guard – oughtn't we each to take a turn?'

'Why so fussy, Anne?' asked George. 'Timmy would hear anyone!'

'I suppose he would,' said Anne, giving way. 'We'll stay here then.'

They were all very tired. The boys pulled up armfuls of old dry bracken and spread it on a sheltered patch of grass, where bushes surrounded them and sheltered them from the wind. It was not far from the cove where Wilfrid's boat lay. They snuggled into the bracken.

'Nice and cosy!' said George, yawning. 'Ohhh! I've never felt so sleepy in my life!' And in three seconds she was sound asleep! Wilfrid dropped off at once too, and Dick and Julian were soon giving little gentle snores.

Anne was still awake. She felt nervous. I'd dearly like to know if those men are safely underground, she thought. I can't imagine that they are very pleased at us getting away – they'll know we'll go to the mainland as soon as we can and tell everyone what we have found! I should have thought they would try to stop us leaving. They must *know* we have a boat!

She lay and worried, keeping her ears open for any strange sound. Timmy heard her tossing and turning and crept over to her very quietly, so as not to wake George. He lay down beside Anne, giving her a loving lick, as if to say 'Now, you go to sleep, and I'll keep watch!'

But still Anne didn't fall asleep. Still she kept her ears wide open for any unusual sound – and then, quite suddenly, she heard something. So did Timmy. He sat up, and gave a very small growl.

Anne strained her ears. Yes – it was certainly voices she could hear – low voices, that didn't want to be heard. It was the men coming to find Wilfrid's boat! Once they had that, the children couldn't get away from Whispering Island!

Timmy ran a little way from the bushes, and looked round at Anne as if to say 'Coming with me?'

Anne got up quietly and went to Timmy. He ran on in front, and she followed. She really *must* see what was happening, then if it was anything important, she could run back and rouse everyone. Timmy was taking her to the cove where Wilfrid had left his boat, hauled high up on the sand for fear of big waves.

They were both as quiet as they could be. Timmy growled a little when he heard the voices again, much nearer this time.

The men had come quietly round the island in their own boat, to set Wilfrid's boat adrift. Anne saw them pushing Wilfrid's boat down the sand towards the sea. Once it was adrift, she and the others would be prisoners on the island! She yelled at the top of her voice.

'You stop that! It's OUR boat!' And Timmy began to bark his head off, prancing round the men, and showing his big white teeth. The barking awoke all the others and they leapt up at once. 'That's Timmy!' shouted Julian. 'That's Timmy barking! Come on, quickly – but be careful!'

They ran at top speed to the cove. Timmy was still barking madly – and someone was yelling. It sounded like Anne. ANNE – no, no, it couldn't be quiet little *Anne*! thought Julian.

But it was! For when the four arrived at the cove, there was Anne yelling to Timmy to bite the men, and dancing about in a rare old temper!

'How DARE you come and take our boat! I'll tell Timmy to bite you! And he will too! Get them, Tim, get them! How DARE you take our boat! *Bite* them, Timmy!'

Timmy had already bitten both the men, who were now rowing away in their own boat at top speed. Anne picked up a stone and sent it whizzing after them. It struck their boat and made them jump.

Anne jumped too when she turned and saw Julian,
George, Wilfrid and Dick. 'I'm so glad you've come!' she
said. 'I *think* Timmy and I have frightened them off. The
beasts!'

'Frightened them off! You've scared them stiff!' said
Julian, hugging his sister. 'You even scared *me*! Good

gracious – the mouse has certainly turned into a fearsome tiger! I can almost see smoke coming out of your nostrils.'

'A tiger? Did I *really* sound like a tiger?' said Anne. 'I'm glad! I hated you all thinking I was a mouse. You'd better be careful now, I *might* turn into a tiger again!'

The men were now out of sight, and Timmy sent a volley of barks after their vanished boat. What chance had any men against a dog and a tiger? WOOF!

'Julian – why can't we row back to the mainland *now*? demanded Anne. 'I'm so hungry and there's nothing to eat here now. And I wasn't really very comfortable in the brackeny bed. I'm longing to sleep in a *proper* bed. I've a good mind to take that boat of Wilfrid's and row myself back, if you don't want to come.'

Julian couldn't help laughing at this new fierce Anne. He put his arm round her.

'I believe it's dangerous to say no to a tiger,' he said. 'So you shall have your way, Anne. *I'm* awfully hungry too – and I bet the others are.'

And, in five minutes' time, the six of them were out on the sea, Julian taking one oar, and Dick the other. 'Swish-swash – swish-swash' went the oars, and the boat rocked as it sped along.

'I bet if those men spot us out on the sea in a boat, going across to the mainland, they will feel pretty uncomfortable!' said Julian. 'They'll know we'll be going to the police first thing tomorrow. This has been quite an adventure, hasn't it! I shall be glad of a little peace now!'

Well – you'll soon have it, Julian! That little cottage is waiting for you all, with its glorious view over the harbour and Whispering Island. You'll have quite a bit of excitement tomorrow, of course, when the police take you back to the island in their boat, and you show them the old well, the vast treasure chamber, the secret passage, and all the rest. You'll be there when all the men are rounded up, you'll watch them chugging off, prisoners, in the police boat, amazed that the Famous Five should have defeated them. What an adventure! And what a relief when all the excitement is over, and you lie peacefully on the hillside, with the little cottage just behind you.

'Now for a real lazy time!' said Anne, when the Five had seen the last of the police. 'Let's all go out on the hill in the sunshine, and have orangeade and biscuits and fruit salad – and Wilfrid shall play his magic pipe and bring his furred and feathered friends to see us.'

'Has he found his pipe then?' said Dick, pleased.

'Yes. He took the well bucket to get some water to drink – and lo and behold, the pipe was in the bottom of the bucket!' said Anne. 'He thinks it must have fallen there the last time he went to fetch water from the well – and nobody noticed it!'

'Oh *good*!' said George, thankfully. 'Wilfrid, what about playing a tune on your little pipe? I'm so glad it's found. I'd like to hear it again.'

Wilfrid was pleased. 'All right,' he said. 'I'll see if my friends here still remember me!'

He sat down on the hillside a little away from the others and began to blow down the pipe – and out came the strange little tune! At once the birds in the trees around turned their heads. In the bushes the lizards raised themselves, put their quaint heads on one side and listened. Rabbits stopped their play. The big hare

503

bounded up the hill, its great ears taking in every note. A magpie flew down to the boy's foot and sat there.

Wilfrid didn't stir. He just went on playing as the creatures came to listen. Timmy listened too, and went to the boy, pressing against him, licking his ear. Then he went back to George.

We'll leave them all there in the sunshine, quiet and peaceful, watching the little creatures that Wilfrid can always bring around him.

Julian is lying back, looking at the April sky, glad that their adventure ended so well. Dick is looking down at Whispering Island, set in the brilliant blue harbour. Anne is half asleep – quiet little Anne who *can* turn into a tiger if she has to!

And George, of course, is close to Timmy, her arm round his neck, very happy indeed. Goodbye, Five – it *was* fun sharing in your grand adventure!